The Notorious Lord Knightly

"Am I Lord K?"

Facing him, she narrowed her eyes to that of a fine-honed blade designed to slice him to ribbons. "How the devil should I know?"

"I lied earlier. I had skimmed through the pages, until I found the garden scene everyone is on about. I once held you in a garden exactly as described."

She released a long, drawn-out sigh. "Which would make me the author. Well, I didn't lie. I've not read the book, so I've no inkling regarding what transpired in the *garden scene*. However, based upon your reputation, I suspect you held a good many ladies in the same manner in a good many gardens. Look to one of them. Now, good night, *my lord*."

With that, she marched to the door and disappeared through it.

But she was wrong. He'd never held any other woman in a garden in the same manner as described. Only her.

By Lorraine Heath

LORD OF TEMPTATION
SHE TEMPTS THE DUKE
WAKING UP WITH THE DUKE
PLEASURES OF A NOTORIOUS GENTLEMAN
PASSIONS OF A WICKED EARL
MIDNIGHT PLEASURES WITH A SCOUNDREL
SURRENDER TO THE DEVIL
BETWEEN THE DEVIL AND DESIRE
IN BED WITH THE DEVIL
JUST WICKED ENOUGH
A DUKE OF HER OWN
PROMISE ME FOREVER
A MATTER OF TEMPTATION
AS AN EARL DESIRES
AN INVITATION TO SEDUCTION
LOVE WITH A SCANDALOUS LORD
TO MARRY AN HEIRESS
THE OUTLAW AND THE LADY
NEVER MARRY A COWBOY
NEVER LOVE A COWBOY
A ROGUE IN TEXAS
TEXAS SPLENDOR
TEXAS GLORY
TEXAS DESTINY
ALWAYS TO REMEMBER
PARTING GIFTS
SWEET LULLABY
GIRLS OF FLIGHT CITY

LORRAINE HEATH

The Notorious Lord Knightly

The Chessmen: Masters of Seduction

AVONBOOKS

An Imprint of HarperCollins Publishers

THE NOTORIOUS LORD KNIGHTLY. Copyright © 2023 by Jan Nowasky. All rights reserved. Printed in the United States of America. No part of this book may be used or reproduced in any manner whatsoever without written permission except in the case of brief quotations embodied in critical articles and reviews. For information, address HarperCollins Publishers, 195 Broadway, New York, NY 10007.

First Avon Books mass market printing: June 2023

Print Edition ISBN: 978-0-06-311467-8
Digital Edition ISBN: 978-0-06-311468-5

Cover design by Amy Halperin
Cover illustration by Victor Gadino
Cover images © Dreamstime.com

Avon, Avon & logo, and Avon Books & logo are registered trademarks of HarperCollins Publishers in the United States of America and other countries.

HarperCollins is a registered trademark of HarperCollins Publishers in the United States of America and other countries.

FIRST EDITION

23 24 25 26 27 BVGM 10 9 8 7 6 5 4 3 2 1

On behalf of Andrea Hamblin this book is
dedicated as follows to:
Jan Patteyn, who moved from the city of love—Paris,
France—to follow his love Laura to Belgium.
May you live happily ever after.
With my love,
Aunt Andrea

The Notorious
Lord Knightly

CHAPTER 1

*I should have been in the ballroom dancing. Instead,
I was standing in the gardens, away from any light,
listening to the approach of the soft footfalls. His familiar,
enticing sandalwood fragrance mixed with his own
unique scent reached me first and revealed his identity.
Therefore, I held still and waited, my breath sawing in
and out with anticipation. Slowly his arms came around
me, folding over my chest in such a way that his large
and powerful hands cradled my breasts and squeezed
gently as he pulled me into the nook of his body, until
my back rested against his broad chest. Then his mouth,
heated as though by the very fires of Hades, pressed
against the nape of my neck, sending delicious shivers
coursing through me. At that moment, I knew I would do
anything Lord K asked of me.*
—Anonymous, *My Secret Desires, A Memoir*

London
June 5, 1875

Arthur Pennington, the Earl of Knightly, rather
wished he'd stayed in his residence that evening instead of venturing out to his favorite club. He was

no stranger to intense gazes from young swells who sought to emulate him, flirtatious smiles from women—married and not, young and old—who wished to entice him into a secluded corner, and murderous glares from men he'd bested, in business and otherwise. He liked winning, loved it in fact.

In his youth, the game might have been as simple as being the first to introduce a debutante to the pleasures of kissing. He'd not been quite so discerning then. A kiss was just a kiss. Over the years, however, the games had become increasingly complicated, his victories not quite so public. He'd discovered it could be quite delicious to be the only one to know he'd won. Anonymity had its rewards.

But recently, the curious looks were far more frequent, lasted longer, and contained a great deal more speculation. They were also accompanied by whispers and nods, low murmurings, and the occasional giggle—the latter usually released by a young chit experiencing her first Season who had yet to be kissed and was bashful as well as easily mortified by any reference at all to what transpired between consenting adults. He'd hoped by now, nearly six weeks in, that all the conjecture would have dissipated, but the *ton* liked nothing better than a good bit of gossip. And of late, he'd very much become the gossipmongers' favorite topic.

"It seems, Knight, you've replaced me as the scoundrel to be avoided at all costs this Season."

Narrowing his eyes, Knight slowly shifted his attention over to David Blackwood, commonly known as Bishop, who sat beside him with a smirk on his ruggedly handsome face. Two months prior, his long-time friend had been dubbed Blackguard Blackwood because of his reputation for leading married ladies to ruin in such a flagrant public fashion that they were soon divorced. Now he was more popularly identified as Besotted Blackwood, thanks to his newly acquired wife, Marguerite. She occupied the chair on the other side of Bishop, their fingers interlocked in their usual scandalous public spectacle of not being able to keep their hands off each other. Although such displays of affection weren't uncommon in the Twin Dragons. The gaming hell's membership had been extended to include women, resulting in an abundance of wooing going on within these walls.

Not that Knight had ever indulged himself here. These days, he preferred as much privacy as possible in all personal matters. All business matters as well. In all matters, truth be told. He had become a closed book. Even to those who thought they knew him better than anyone. His fellow Chessmen.

A glass of fine scotch in hand, they were presently sitting in their favorite corner of the club's library where they often discussed various investment strategies that had resulted in the moniker associated with them.

"I'm not quite certain how you came to such a deduction," he finally responded laconically. A lie. He knew damned well how it had come about—because of a recently published book that was not quite as closed as he. As a matter of fact, it had been opened by so many curiosity seekers that locating a copy had become a bit of a challenge.

"As you're no doubt aware," Rook said pointedly, "speculation is rampant you are Lord K."

"Any number of Lord Ks are about. Could even be King here," Knight said, tipping his head toward the Duke of Kingsland, who'd also brought his wife, Penelope. But then she was as ruthless when it came to investing as they were and had often joined them for their discussions, even before King realized he was madly in love with her and made her his duchess.

"I'm a duke," King stated. "I wouldn't be referred to as Lord anything."

"It's fiction. Perhaps she used the moniker to throw people off the scent."

"Or he," Marguerite offered succinctly. "Simply because it was written from the point of view of a woman doesn't mean it was necessarily written by a woman." As a private detective, she had a tendency to be suspicious and not trust that things or people were exactly as they seemed. Certainly, her husband's duplicitousness had proven that point well enough.

"You've read it?"

"No, but a gentleman recently sought to employ me to uncover the identity of the author, fearing the tome might have been written by his wife and she was detailing an affair in which she was engaged."

That others were interested in discovering the author's identity was disconcerting, especially if his enemies were striving to uncover knowledge to use against him. He'd considered hiring Marguerite himself but refused to fuel the rumors floating about that the tale was biographical in nature and he had, in fact, been assigned the pivotal role. "Did you discover who she was?"

"I didn't take on the case. I couldn't see it as a pressing concern, and business has been quite brisk of late."

"My wife is the finest inquiry agent in London," Bishop said, his voice rife with pride, even though her investigation of him was responsible for bringing them together. Knight was surprised his friend's buttons didn't pop right off his waistcoat, a result of the manner in which he was preening. "She can be selective regarding how she spends her time. She's approached about more important matters than uncovering the identity of an author."

"It might be interesting to know if the writer is someone from your past, Knight," Rook said. "If she's not or is unknown to you, it would give credence to your denials."

He sighed at the absurdity that he cared anything at all about what people thought. "I should think my word that it is not I would be sufficient."

"But without knowing exactly who wrote it, how can you know for sure?"

"Because I don't approach women in gardens, for God's sake." Except once, years before, when he'd been a very different man than he was now. But that woman, born of scandal, would never pen such provocative prose. She understood all too well the value of a pristine reputation. Keeping the one her father had established for her had been foremost on her mind. She'd reflected a purity that should have eventually led to a beneficial marriage among the nobility but during her first Season she'd chosen poorly. She'd chosen him. He suspected the regret would follow her to the end of her days. It certainly haunted his nights.

"You've read it, then?" Rook asked.

"No, but I've heard enough men and women tittering about the blasted garden passage." Not to mention the numerous fathers who had recently warned him if he took one of their daughters on a stroll about a garden, it would be immediately followed by a brisk walk down the aisle he would be unable to escape without suffering dire consequences. He was tempted to take numerous ladies on a promenade about a garden simply to demonstrate how he didn't take well to threats and most certainly couldn't be forced into marriage—or any other result he didn't desire. On the other hand, he could hardly blame the fathers for their concern. They'd forgiven him once for demonstrating unconscionable behavior toward a woman. As a matter of fact, to his chagrin, they'd hailed him as a hero, but then it hadn't been their daughters he'd betrayed.

A movement out of the corner of his eye caught his attention, and he glanced up at the slender gent who'd arrived at his side just as King greeted his younger brother. "Lawrence, would you care to join us?"

"An invitation into the circle of the Chessmen? I'm honored." He quickly grabbed a leather chair from another sitting area, shoved it into place between King and Knight, and dropped into it. He grinned broadly. "As you have most of the pieces represented—king, knight, bishop, rook, *and* two queens—I suppose I am left to be the pawn."

"Never underestimate the importance of the pawn," Knight said.

Lawrence wiggled his eyebrows. "Especially when he has the ability to get his hands on a rare find." Reaching into his coat pocket, he withdrew a leather-bound book and set it carefully on the table as he might fragile glass. Gold lettering was embossed in the leather. *My Secret Desires, A Memoir.*

No one moved. No one reached for it.

"How the devil did you get that?" King asked, his voice a near whisper of astonishment as though a once-lost ancient treasure had suddenly been unearthed and necessitated a moment of reverence.

"Lord Chesney offered it to cover his wager at the card table. Unfortunately for him, and fortunately for me, I held the better hand. I'm quite looking forward to reading it as I'm given to understand it's rather naughty. Chesney nearly wept when he lost. He said rumors are floating about it's going to be banned for indecency."

"Then we should all read it," Penelope said. "People should not be denied the opportunity to enjoy what they wish. And how does one determine what is indecent? I've yet to visit a museum or an art gallery that does not have a nude statue or a painting revealing a good deal of flesh. They are acceptable in those environments. Why not in all?"

"You're quite passionate about this topic," Knight said.

"I simply don't comprehend how writing a description of a person's body or an act is any different than painting it, and I've heard this book is quite detailed. Although I don't know the specifics, I can only surmise what might be considered indecent."

"Perhaps they, whoever *they* are who determine what is acceptable, fear having less control over what one imagines in the mind when reading as opposed to what is presented on canvas. With words alone, a seed can blossom in the imagination and carry one on a journey into realms unexplored. Or not. Depending upon one's imagination."

"Knight should read it first," Bishop stated succinctly, obviously uninterested in getting into a philosophical discussion. "Then he can tell us if it's indecent."

"You're missing my entire point," Penelope said. "Some of us might find it indecent while others might not. Who is to say which of us is correct?"

"I have no interest in it," Knight lied. He was dying to read it, to determine if the imagination of bored ladies of the *ton* had simply run amok, if they were envisioning him as the main character because he'd become distant during the past few years, giving women—especially those whose mothers shoved them into his path—only the attention politeness dictated. At balls he rarely danced. He never took anyone to the theater, despite having a box. He kept to himself as much as possible.

"Of course you have an interest," Bishop said. "You may be striving to give the appearance you aren't bothered by the rumors circulating that the woman's lover strongly resembles you, but you must be curious. A read should give you the ammunition needed to permanently put the speculation to rest."

"If I ignore it, it will all go away."

"Nothing ignored ever goes away," Penelope said. "Eventually it will come to the fore and wreak its havoc, whether for good or ill."

He didn't know why he was left with the impression she spoke from experience. His two married friends were extremely protective of their ladies, and Knight suspected they all held secrets. Certainly, he had his share.

He glared at the book resting innocently on the table as though incapable of causing harm, when he knew it quite possibly possessed the power to destroy. At the very least it was making his life miserable because it and he were dominating conversations. People were growing bolder, asking him to his face if he was Lord K. He yearned to close his fingers around the book and spread open the pages until they revealed all the mysteries within.

"Bloody hell," he finally ground out before snatching it up. "I'll take it if for no other reason than to keep it out of your hands. Now may we discuss something more pleasant? A plague, perhaps?"

The blighters he called friends had the audacity to grin and chuckle. He wished he'd left the book alone because already it felt like it was scalding his fingertips and seeping into his soul, determined not to let him rest until he knew the truth of it.

MISS REGINA LEYLAND liked shadowed corners. Especially at the Twin Dragons. Her preferred table, where she now sat, was located in just such a corner. She wasn't certain how poker, which apparently was very popular in America, had become part of this establishment's repertoire of games offered. However, it had quickly taken its place as her favorite, and she'd developed the ability to calculate the odds in order to determine the likelihood she held a winning hand. She was also quite accomplished when it came to reading her opponents and deducing whether they were bluffing.

Having grown up along the edge of Society, she'd had ample time to unobtrusively scrutinize those who wandered by, make predictions about their behavior, and discover if she was correct. She'd been like a child pressing her nose against the window of a toy shop, longing to step inside and discover something within had been made specifically for her. That she could select the proper doll that would grant her common ground with all the other little girls. That they'd accept her at last.

But they never had and so she'd simply watched. And in watching, she'd learned how to judge people's temperaments and moods, to know when they were angry or sad or in love. She could determine who was kind and who was unpleasant. Who to favor and who to avoid. Only once in her life had she gotten it completely and absolutely wrong. But it had been a lesson learned and a mistake she'd never make again.

From her vantage point at the table with her back to the wall, she had an unobstructed view of those who entered the gaming hell and often observed them until they disappeared into various hallways leading to rooms where other entertainments awaited. Within her fertile mind, she'd weave scenarios about where they were going, whom they were meeting, and in what activities they might become engaged.

And so it was she'd seen the arrival of Lord Knightly, a man she'd once desperately loved with every fiber of her being and now despised from the very depths of her soul. Being jilted at the altar had a way of changing a woman's heart. Not that she'd been a woman five years ago. An innocent girl, more like, in spite of her advanced age at the time of two and twenty. Believing in hopes and dreams and the veracity of love having the power to overcome all obstacles.

Sheltered and protected. A princess, her father had always called her. He'd been her knight in shining armor and searching for someone to replace him. The Earl of Knightly had certainly seemed to fit the bill—until he no longer had.

Waiting to walk up the aisle, she'd been wearing an ivory gown designed by Charles Worth of Paris himself. She'd never known such happiness and believed the joy she was experiencing would only increase through the years.

Knightly had arrived tardily with the news he'd changed his mind, couldn't marry her after all. No specifics, only a generalized admittance he'd decided they wouldn't suit.

She'd not let on exactly how devastating she'd found his abandonment or how badly she'd been hurt. Instead, she'd gone on a three-year-long trek through Europe, journaling her escapades in a series of articles for a lady's magazine. Although often what appeared in print was how she'd imagined the adventure rather than the reality of it. But no one had been able to discern the difference. More importantly, she'd discovered writing filled an emptiness in her soul, a hollow ache, a bottomless abyss into which she'd become lost on that fateful morning when she'd been at St. George's, expecting to marry—only to be discarded at the last minute.

Now, at twenty-seven, she cared for no one's opinion, save her own. She came here where most of the members were of the aristocracy and flaunted her notoriety while taking their coins. She projected a mien of confidence and daring. She would not be looked down upon. In spite of the circumstances of her birth, she was still the daughter of an earl, as well as the daughter of an accomplished actress. She was proud of her heritage. No one could take it away from her.

She studied the two queens she presently held in her hand. The other cards were worthless, but the queens possessed power, just as she did. She possessed the power to destroy, to destroy the one who had betrayed her. And she would. It was only a matter of time.

Glancing up, she noticed Knightly—apparently moving on from wherever he'd gone upon first arriving—now striding through the gambling area. Incredibly confident, downright arrogant really. Obnoxiously so. She wondered at which table he might alight. Certainly not this one as all the chairs were occupied. Then cursed herself for wondering anything about him at all. After all these years, her thoughts should be void of memories of him, but it was as though an artist had painted upon her mind vivid illustrations of each and every moment when they'd been in each other's company. A polite hello, an accidental glancing touch of their fingers, a heated look lasting too long, a walk in a park, a stroll in a garden, whispered words, and broken promises.

Since that morning when he'd shattered her heart, they'd not spoken, had seen each other only in passing—at a great distance. One she very much wished to maintain. It wasn't fair that his actions had tarnished only her reputation and not his, that the *ton* had celebrated his liberation from her, while vilifying her for daring to dream a man such as he could actually love a woman such as she.

Perhaps the entire point of his wooing her had been to make her believe her origins held no significance and then to make sport of her for falling madly in love with him. To humiliate her for imagining she was lovable to someone other than her parents. To humble her for the audacity of judging herself deserving and worthy of the rise from commoner to countess.

"Miss Leyland?"

She jerked her attention to the dealer. He gave her a wan smile. "Time to reveal your hand."

Ah, yes, she'd been the last one to raise the bet amount, and it seemed only two people had called her on it. The other three had folded. With a smooth, practiced movement, she turned over her cards. Lady Warburton gave her a hard stare while revealing her two jacks. The gentleman sitting directly across from Regina groaned and tossed his cards haphazardly toward the dealer. "That's it for me, then."

He shoved back his chair.

"What? No. Wait," she said with far too much

command in her voice, so much so he stopped halfway up at a rather odd right angle, bent partially over
the table in such a way his bottom was sticking out.
But Knightly was still wending his way around the
games, and she could clearly see his intense gaze
homed in on this corner, like that of a predator who
had spotted his prey. Lord, help the prey, she nearly
muttered aloud. "Surely you want an opportunity to
win back some of your losses."

Not that he would. The man was atrocious at the
game, apparently harboring the belief he was skilled
at bluffing, not realizing his eyes fairly bugged when
he had something of note and squinted when he didn't,
as though if he concentrated hard enough, he could
bring forth the power needed to change the cards he'd
been dealt. But once dealt, cards had to be made the
best of—whether in a game or life. She knew that well
enough.

"You've taken all the blunt I set aside for the night.
I never wager on credit."

"Well . . ." She nearly shoved all the tokens in the
table center toward him, but she'd look the fool if she
did. Desperate. People might wonder why. *Just stay a
few minutes longer, just until—*

Too late. The handsome devil had arrived and
placed his large hand on the gentleman's shoulder.
"I'll take your chair if you're leaving, old chap."

The old chap, who couldn't have seen forty years,
swung around and grinned widely. "Knightly, of
course!" He leaned in as if sharing a daring secret.
"But keep a watch out for Miss Leyland. She took all
my blunt."

Knightly's brilliant blue gaze landed on her like a warm caress. No, not like a caress, like the slash of a thousand swords. Did he have to be so deuced gorgeous in his black coat, bright blue waistcoat, and gray cravat? Did those rebellious front locks of his dark hair still have to fall across his brow in invitation? Her fingers itched to comb through the strands and brush them back into place as they had a thousand times. She didn't want to remember how that forelock played over her own brow when he stretched out over her supine figure, lowered his head, and kissed her.

"I always keep a watch out for Miss Leyland."

His voice was still a deep, rich timbre, with the power to send yearning spiraling through her. She remembered a time when she'd enjoyed his teasing and flirtation, had been mesmerized by every word he uttered. Now she wished only for some affliction to render him mute. She angled her chin haughtily. "Because you expect me to stab you in the back? Ridiculous. I'd do it from the front so you'd know exactly who delivered the devastating blow."

Two gasps and a couple of awkward chuckles followed from the other players still seated. The old chap leapt back as though she was, in fact, wielding a knife at that very moment.

"I would expect no less," Knightly said, bowing his head slightly in acquiescence, in acknowledgment, almost in respect—a salute—his penetrating gaze never wavering from hers. Had he been a true knight upon a jousting field, he might have extended his lance toward her for a favor. Not that she'd ever gift him with a ribbon as she had when she'd loved him.

Then the moment passed, and he pulled out the chair before lowering himself onto the tufted seat. The club ensured members were always comfortable, no doubt to dissuade them from leaving the tables prematurely, with coins still jingling in their pockets. He set a book on the table.

"Oh, my word, you've garnered a copy of *My Secret Desires*," Lady Letitia gushed, any drama played out before completely forgotten. The card game as well, it seemed. "Is it available in the club library?"

He trailed one long, slender finger along the spine, and Regina fought not to recall how delicious it had felt when he'd done the same along hers. "Unfortunately not. It was won in a card game earlier."

"I've been dying to get my little hands on it." Those hands were presently fidgeting with the tokens used to make her bets. "The recounting of a daring woman's scandalous adventures—my understanding of the story from what I've heard whispered—makes for a titillating read."

"Some say it's not a memoir at all," Viscount Langdon offered, "but merely fiction, the memoir in the title simply part of the fantasy it seeks to create. Like *Fanny Hill*, a novel touted as being the memoir of a woman pleasured. Certainly, a publication garners more interest if it's believed to be a confession rather than the result of an active imagination. As a matter of fact, wagers are being made at White's as well as in the betting book here, regarding whether it is truth or fiction."

"Even if it is fiction, one can't write about such intimate matters if one hasn't experienced them." Lady

Letitia leaned forward slightly. "I don't suppose you'd be kind enough to read the opening passage aloud so perhaps we could judge for ourselves."

"We're here to play cards," Regina stated pithily since the dealer seemed to have forgotten his role at the table, "not sit through a droll reading."

"Have you read it?" Knightly asked.

"Of course I've not read the book. I don't waste my time with such rubbish." *Or with the likes of you.* She should leave now but didn't want to give him the satisfaction of chasing her off.

"If you've not read it, how do you know it's rubbish? Perhaps it's a work that will last through the ages."

"With a title such as that? It was no doubt penned by a group of bored spinsters." She was proud of her voice for not giving away any of her emotions. Why did he have to plague her now?

"I say we put it to a vote," Lady Letitia bubbled enthusiastically. "Raise your hand if you'd like Lord Knightly to read us the opening passage."

Her hand quickly shot up as did one from each of the other two ladies. Even Lord Langdon, the scapegrace, raised a hand and arched a brow at Regina to indicate she shouldn't be so prudish. The dealer merely patiently shuffled the cards as though he had no other purpose than to rearrange their order.

Regina glared hotly at him. "You're not going to allow this madness to go forward, surely."

He merely shrugged his narrow shoulders. "My instructions are to keep members happy."

"Well, this member is frightfully unhappy. I'll take my winnings elsewhere." She began gathering up her wooden tokens, which she should have done the moment Knightly sat. She was tempted to toss them all in his face. However, she was not one for public displays of uncontrolled emotion. She'd become extremely skilled at burying her feelings, thanks in large part to the blackguard sitting across from her.

"Come now, Reggie, don't be a spoilsport," Knightly said. "Where's the harm in giving the dealer a short respite while I take on the role of entertainer?"

"Don't call me that. We are no longer on intimate terms." She nearly slammed her eyes closed. She did wish she hadn't used that particular word. *Intimate*. It conjured up images of searing kisses, heated touches, and smoldering gazes. Those damned locks of hair falling across his brow as he leaned in—

"My apologies, Miss Leyland. But you must be as curious as everyone else about this book, surely."

"Did you not peruse it already, looking for those passages that are very likely to see its author in court on charges of indecency?"

"If they can ever discover who the author is—but, no, I was visiting with friends earlier and didn't want to be impolite. However, as I've had a request"—he waved his hand in the direction of Lady Letitia—"and enjoy nothing more than satisfying another's curiosity, perhaps you'll indulge me."

He'd once indulged her curiosity—with a touch, a kiss, and more. He'd opened her up to worlds she'd not even dared to imagine. In spite of the wreckage their relationship had become, during their time together, she'd been deliriously happy, had believed she knew what it was to be loved. More importantly, she had

known what it was to love another, fully and unconditionally. Certainly, she'd always loved her parents,
but what she'd felt for him hadn't been tied to blood. It
had been all-encompassing. Like the stars in the sky,
endless.

With a heavy sigh, she rolled her eyes and crossed
her arms beneath her breasts, not missing the quick
dip of his gaze. Ages ago, he'd admired them and peppered them with kisses. "Oh, very well. I suppose I
can suffer through a few minutes of listening to your
dull repetition of written words."

Lady Letitia clapped gleefully and bounced in her
chair. Everyone else eased forward, even the dealer, in
spite of his sitting beside Knightly. Regina maintained
her straight and stiff posture, refusing to give any hint
at all that she had an interest in witnessing how he
would react to what many had deemed quite saucy.

After slipping his spectacles from his pocket and
putting them in place, he opened the book, applied
fingers that had brought her pleasure to turning pages,
until he reached his destination, cleared his throat,
and began. "'Chapter One. The Gentleman. For me, he
shall always be *the* gentleman, the one I could never
forget, the one no man could ever replace. Our first
meeting occurred at a ball. I must have been introduced to a hundred men before he appeared. Yet, when
my eyes met his of dazzling blue, I could no longer
remember any of the others. It was as if they'd all
transformed into smoke and drifted away on a warm
breeze. Only he was real. Only he was of substance.
Only he mattered. When Lord K took my hand, bent
over it, and pressed his lush lips against my knuckles,

though I wore gloves, I felt the heat of his moist mouth seeping into my flesh.'"

She'd forgotten what an incredibly beautiful voice he had, how he could imbue it with passion. How it could make her laugh. And move her to tears. How it could thoroughly ignite her body until she was cursing and crying out for release. The terribly wicked things he would growl that sent her flying into ecstasy. His voice, low, deep, harsh, soft. It was one of the most erotic things about him.

Very slowly, he closed the book, as though it had suddenly become delicate glass. Or perhaps he had. Maybe his voice had the same effect on him—brought everything to life until he could picture that initial meeting of an innocent girl and a very experienced man. Although the sentences weren't tawdry, were in fact quite tame except for the mention of flesh, still, with his delivery, they conjured up the promise of lurid images that would soon have the couple, and perhaps the reader, sweltering with desire.

"You're not stopping, surely," Lady Letitia said, her breath coming in short little pants.

His penetrating cerulean gaze remained focused on Regina as he responded, "We agreed to one passage."

"It can't have been an entire passage, but merely a paragraph."

He shifted his eyes to Lady Letitia and winked. "It's best to always be kept wanting."

Wanting and needing. He'd carried her to the brink countless times, left her to hover there until she thought she would die, and then he'd restored life to her with a cataclysm that never failed to leave her astonished and grateful nature so rewarded wickedness with such astounding pleasure.

Lady Letitia looked on the verge of weeping, before straightening her shoulders and announcing succinctly, with conviction, "I believe it is indeed a woman's memoir—and she loves him still."

"She never claimed to love him," Knightly said.

"A woman can easily forget a man she does not love." Then a knowing gleam was reflected in her eyes. "Do you recognize the meeting, Lord Knightly? Are you, in fact, Lord K?"

He laughed low, darkly, sending a shiver up Regina's spine. "When we met during your coming-out ball, did I make you forget every man you've ever known, Lady Letitia?"

"That's hardly an answer, my lord. Although I suppose in the one bit you read, clues are sadly lacking. It could be any ball. Any lady. Any gent. However, I am more determined than ever to get my hands on a copy."

"Then I shall guard this one with my life."

Their conversation irritated Regina, but she refused to analyze the reasons behind her annoyance. She no longer had any interest at all in Knightly—except to beat him at this game and rid him of his coins. She sighed mightily with impatience. "May we cease with the flirting now and play?" She didn't wait for a response, but simply flipped a token into the center of the table. Thank the Lord, the others quickly followed suit and the dealer was soon distributing the cards.

But all the while, aware of Knightly studying her, she prayed she was not as easy to read as the tome.

IT HAD BEEN a mistake to come to this table. He'd known it would be. It seemed an eternity had passed since he'd been this close to Regina. Not since that morning in the church when he'd broken her heart. He should have kept his distance, honored the vow he'd made not to inflict his presence upon her.

But King and Bishop had departed for home, taking their lovely wives with them, women with whom they were no doubt at this very moment making mad, passionate love. Rook and Lawrence had decided to leave the club in search of a lady's favor elsewhere.

Alone, Knight had begun riffling through the pages of the damned book, his gaze settling on a passage here or there, each bringing forth memories involving Regina he'd tenaciously tamped down.

Then deciding to leave, heading for the door, he'd spotted her at the table in the far corner. Not for the first time. As a matter of fact, knowing she might be there, he'd deliberately glanced in this direction, a punishment, a reminder of what he might have had if the truth of him had remained unknown. In the past, he'd taken a few seconds to bask in the sight of her before carrying on. Tonight, he'd only wanted to be nearer.

Her blond hair was artfully pinned up with a few strands left to dangle along her neck, to tease a man into wanting to replace those soft curls with his warm lips, knowing the silkiness that would greet him. He also knew the scent of gardenia would be waiting just behind her ear. On her wrists. And in the narrow valley between her breasts. Her emerald gown left her alabaster shoulders bared. They were no doubt dusted with some sort of powder because he couldn't detect the three tiny freckles that had taunted him far too often, that he had kissed, envying the sun because it had kissed her there first.

He hadn't forgotten how beautiful she was. To do so would be like forgetting the wonder of a midnight sky, the majesty of the vast blue ocean, or the prettiness of a butterfly. Even when they weren't within one's field of vision, it was easy to bring the images of them forth in one's mind because at some point the sight of them had inhabited the soul.

Regina Leyland had long ago become part of him. Not carrying through on his promise to marry her had been the hardest thing he'd ever done, because he'd known it would ravage her—and she'd not deserved the devastating blow he'd been forced to deliver. He had struggled to find a way to soften the impact, but the destruction of a dream offers no easy solutions. He imagined the severing off of a limb would have brought each of them less pain and torment. He'd tried to replace her hurt with anger, hoping she'd be determined to carry on with her life, to show him that he didn't really matter at all. She would find another to bring her joy and happiness. And she had. Traveling the Continent, scandalously sampling the men of each country if gossip was to be believed. Her father's failing health had finally brought her home.

Oddly, while he'd gone to the front of the church and announced that *she* had come to her senses and realized he wouldn't make a fitting husband—his reputation for enjoying the ladies was no secret—his esteem among the nobility had risen. He'd avoided being shackled to a lass of cloudy blue blood. Someone illegitimate, who would taint his own bloodlines. He'd been slapped on the back, bought drinks he'd not drunk, offered daughters' hands he'd not accepted. Invitations to social gatherings had increased and he'd been sought after with an unbridled yet baffling diligence.

While she'd been left to suffer the brunt of the embarrassment and shame.

He'd thought it would fall to him, that he'd be ostracized for being proven unworthy. Instead, he'd been venerated.

However, he'd recently heard rumors she had an admirer and might soon be taking another trip to the altar, one that wouldn't end in heartbreak, but the happily-ever-after she so deserved.

Selfish bastard that he was, Knight had wanted to be near her one more time. Wanted to defend the indefensible, explain the inexplicable. Hence there he was, sitting across from her while she concentrated on her cards as though they had the power to solve all the problems of the world . . . or perhaps to cause his demise.

"I've heard Viscount Chidding has begun calling upon you," he said, laconically, striving to keep his true interest from inhabiting his tone.

Without taking her eyes from her cards, she set two down in front of the dealer, who promptly issued her replacements before moving on to Lady Letitia. "I imagine you hear a good many things."

"He's in debt."

"So I've been told."

"You're not bothered by his circumstance?"

Slowly she lifted her gaze until it clashed with his. "I've learned, my lord, there are far worse failings to be found in a man."

Her tone had a sharp edge to it, one that was out of place coming from her tempting mouth. He did not look away, or argue the point, but took the cut as his due. Perhaps he'd been wrong to steer clear of her, to deny her opportunities to put him in his place and enjoy her small victories.

"My lord?" the dealer prodded.

Forcing himself to break the hold of her gaze, Knight glanced over the table, noting two of the players had folded. His hand was atrocious, and he should follow suit, but he wasn't yet ready to admit defeat. He cast off three cards, hoping for a miracle. Although years earlier he'd learned hope was not a strategy, and it proved true this time.

Regina was the first to bet. A quid. Could she have that good of a hand? The remaining two players folded, leaving only him against her. What were the odds she was bluffing? Her implacable facade was impossible to read. That hadn't been the case when he'd first known her. Everything she'd felt was revealed in her sweet smile and dark brown eyes. Eyes that had been so innocent then, trusting.

Now they stated succinctly that she knew fairy

tales were a lie. He'd done that to her. The pain that knowledge confirmed nearly doubled him over.

He met her quid and raised her two. Without hesitation, she tossed in two quid and followed it with three more. Her gaze landed on his with an almost audible thud. Only now he could read the challenge in those icy eyes. If he didn't match her amount, she wouldn't have to show her cards; he wouldn't know what she'd been holding.

It wasn't as though he couldn't afford to lose three more pounds. His coffers were flush. It was the principle of the matter. He didn't want to be taken for a fool if she was bluffing. On the other hand, perhaps winning would give her a reason to smile. He was suddenly desperate for her smile. He slid three tokens, valued at a quid each, across the baize tabletop to the center pile. "I'll call."

With no alteration in her expression at all, she set down her cards, faceup. A pair of aces.

With a slow grin, he revealed his hand—an assortment of numbers and suits that failed to come together in any meaningful way. "I was hoping you were bluffing."

"Unlike you, my lord, I never bluff or render a falsehood." She began gathering her winnings and depositing them into a black pouch. "I'll be calling it a night now."

She stood, and he did the same, stuffing his few remaining tokens into a pocket to be used on another night, and grabbed his book. After she walked past him, he followed. "I'll provide you with a ride in my carriage."

"I have a carriage waiting."

"Then join me in the library for a drink."

Coming to an abrupt halt, she whirled around. "Are you jealous? You hear someone might favor me, and suddenly you're giving me attention. Do not for a single moment believe I am fool enough to trust all the flattering words you are so skilled at delivering with such utter conviction."

"I'm not . . . I just . . . I simply want the opportunity to apologize again, to seek forgiveness."

She waved a hand dismissively. "'Tis given. Now leave me be."

She spun on her heel—

"Am I Lord K?"

Facing him, she narrowed her eyes to that of a fine-honed blade designed to slice him to ribbons. "How the devil should I know?"

"I lied earlier. I had skimmed through the pages, until I found the garden scene everyone is on about. I once held you in a garden exactly as described."

She released a long, drawn-out sigh. "Which would make me the author. Well, I didn't lie. I've not read the book, so I've no inkling regarding what transpired in the *garden scene*. However, based upon your reputation, I suspect you held a good many ladies in the same manner in a good many gardens. Look to one of them. Now, good night, *my lord*."

With that, she marched to the door and disappeared through it.

But she was wrong. He'd never held any other woman in a garden in the same manner as described. Only her.

She hadn't been bluffing at the table, but was she bluffing now? Could she possibly be Anonymous? But knowing how she valued her privacy, he couldn't imagine her putting the personal details of her life to paper and then publishing them. No, what he'd read of the book thus far and the memories of their time together that the words and descriptions conjured were simply coincidence. Introductions happened all the time. As did assignations in gardens.

Yet like the lady in the tome regarding her gentleman, the night they'd met was one he'd never forget.

CHAPTER 2

April 1870

"*N*o flirting this evening, Knight," King grumbled as his coach journeyed over the rough road. "I don't want to have to search through various alcoves for you when I'm ready to take my leave."

"Dash it all, King, if I'd known you were going to spoil my fun, I'd not have agreed to accompany you on this detour before meeting up with Bishop and Rook. I can't for the life of me determine why you're going to all the bother and delaying our amusements with the others. You're not going to marry a chit born out of wedlock."

"Mother has a soft spot for wounded creatures and feared the girl would suffer through the embarrassment of having no one in attendance at this affair where Bremsford is introducing her to Society. Although the twenty thousand pounds he's settled on her is certain to draw some young bucks."

He was also including in her dowry a small estate on the outskirts of London that included several acres of lush land and a manor to serve as her dower house when the time came. Tonight, it was the setting for the grand ball that had been the topic of wagging tongues among the elite for weeks. "Do you know anything about her other than her scandalous beginnings and Bremsford wanting to pawn her off to someone legitimate?"

"She's the daughter of his longtime mistress, who was an accomplished actress, according to Mother. Although she doesn't approve of infidelity, she still enjoys a good love story and apparently Bremsford's was one for the ages. The earl was devoted to the girl's mother and remains devoted to his illegitimate offspring more than to his legitimate ones. I can't imagine any of it has sat well with his countess, his heir, or his other two daughters."

"Do you think any of them will be attending tonight?"

"I rather doubt it."

The coach came to a stop. A footman stepped forward and opened the door. Knight waited until his friend, the duke, had disembarked. While they were equal on many levels, Knight never forgot that until he inherited his father's title, Duke of Wyndstone, King outranked him, and Knight was conscious of showing his friend the deference he deserved when they were in a public arena.

As they wandered toward the manor, a young lady caught Knight's attention and gave him a shy smile. Tipping his hat, he bestowed upon her a grin filled with the promise of a kissing lesson to be given in a secluded corner. She was in the process of pressing her fan to her right cheek, the signal for *yes*, was only an inch away from it, when her mother grabbed her arm and began dragging her along. The lady glanced back. He pressed a hand to his chest, to indicate his sorrow that she'd be watched by a hawk.

"I said no flirting," King reminded him.

"I've not sampled Lady Lisbet yet. A kiss doesn't take that long."

"So you say, but your reputation states otherwise."

"Depends on the lady, I suppose. Where's your sense of adventure, King?"

"Waiting for me after I've seen to this tedious task."

As they climbed the few steps to the open door, several unaccompanied men were making their way inside. Knowing a good many of them, all unmarried, Knight decided they'd been drawn by the pounds. The spares also probably wanted to look around the residence in which they might possibly live—if they didn't have one of their own. No reason for the abode to remain vacant until she was a widow.

He noted the presence of a few other ladies, no doubt their curiosity getting the better of them. Or perhaps they saw an opportunity to contrast themselves against the earl's daughter. At twenty-seven, he had yet to participate in the game of courtship. He was here tonight only because he believed it important to remain in the good graces of every decent lord. One never knew when the support of a particular nobleman—or permission to marry his daughter—might be needed. And Bremsford was a man of influence.

Once they'd crossed the threshold, he and King made their way along the hallway that eventually emptied into a large chamber with a wide stairway on either side, circling around to meet in the middle at the top where an enormous doorway yawned. They reached the stairs on their right. A footman offered them each a dance card. King took one and tucked it inside his jacket, while Knight simply waved off the vellum. They weren't going to be here long enough to partake in any dances. After their ascent, they greeted those standing about whom they knew and took their places in the queue.

"What do you think?" Knight whispered, keeping his voice low and even. "Half an hour?"

"Twenty minutes. A smile here and a smile there, and we'll make our escape."

After the couple before them were introduced and began their descent, Knight glanced down as King handed his invitation over to the majordomo. He recognized Bremsford standing tall, proud, and defiant near the foot of the stairs, his hair having faded from the wheat shade of his youth into silver. The young lady to his right glanced up—

Knight felt like he'd taken a battering ram to the chest. All the air in his lungs had backed up and he could scarcely breathe. "Christ, is that her?"

King looked down. "I would assume so."

She was exquisite. Her hair, the shade of moonbeams, was held in place with pearl combs, a few strands dangling about her face and along her slender neck. She barely reached her father's shoulder. While she was poised, exhibiting grace with her movements, the tiniest of pleats in her brow reflected an uncomfortableness, perhaps even a sadness. Yet, there she stood performing—like her mother, an actress— because the show must go on.

"Sir?"

Her gown was entirely white, the candlelight from the chandeliers sparkling off what must have been a million tiny pearls, making it iridescent, glowing like newly fallen snow under a full moon. His favorite time to walk the moors of the ducal estate in Yorkshire.

Then he could no longer see her because King—with his irritatingly broad back—was blocking Knight's view as his friend made his way toward Bremsford. Had he been announced? Knight hadn't heard it, perhaps because he'd been so focused on the girl that everything around him had ceased to exist, everything except her.

"Sir?"

Leaning to the right in an attempt to catch sight of her again, he heard a harsh clearing of a throat. Then, "Knightly, for God's sake, man, do pay attention."

Glancing over his shoulder, he was greeted by the Earl of Chadbourne glowering at him. He glowered back before hearing the quiet, "Sir?"

Only then did he realize the majordomo was holding out a white gloved hand to him. "Apologies." He offered up his invitation, his name scrawled across it.

The man gave a curt nod before booming, "His lordship, the Earl of Knightly."

Wanting to dash down the stairs, Knight felt rather like an untried youth, which was ridiculous. He'd had women aplenty but something about her drew him, created a need to protect her when it was obvious her father served as her protector. She was a bird in a gilded cage, a girl in a tower. Bollocks but he was having fanciful thoughts. And he did manage not to dash, but to take his time, carrying himself with the confidence honed by generations of warrior ancestors who had engaged not only in battles on the field but in the political arena. A duty that would pass to him upon his father's death, a duty that required a strong woman at his side.

King finally moved on, giving Knight a clearer view of the lady who shifted her attention back to the stairs, her eyes capturing and holding his. Now that he was nearer and could see her more clearly, she didn't appear to be as young as most debutantes. Not fresh from finishing school at seventeen or eighteen. No, he'd wager she was on the other side of twenty, but not by much. Enough so, though, to make her interesting, to have had the opportunity to experience a bit more of life. Although he suspected the circumstances of her birth had already granted her that favor—or disfavor, depending how things had gone.

At last, the final step arrived and after five more strides, he was standing before the Earl of Bremsford. He gave a bow of deference. "My lord."

"Knightly, good to see you here. Your father is well I take it?"

While the question seemed inordinately polite, it carried an undertone of *He'd best be on his deathbed since he couldn't bother to show his face here.* While he hardly blamed the earl, Knight was loyal to his sire. "The duke is well, my lord. I'll relay your concern for his health."

Bremsford gave a little grunt before continuing. "My lord, allow me the honor of introducing my daughter, Miss Regina Leyland."

Had she been his legitimate child, she'd have been Lady Regina. Knight wondered if that lack of honorarium irked her. Bowing, but managing to hold her gaze—her eyes were brown, like the soil that nourished the moors in the spring—he took her hand and pressed a kiss to the delicate fingers, wishing no kidskin separated his lips from her skin. "Miss Leyland, it is indeed a pleasure." Releasing his hold on her, he straightened and offered her the smallest of smiles.

She dipped into a graceful curtsy. "My lord, the pleasure is all mine."

"I wonder, Miss Leyland, if you might have a waltz available?"

"The fourth, I believe." She held up her wrist, from which, attached with white ribbons, her dance card and a minuscule pencil dangled. He hated those blasted pencils; they always made him feel like a clod when he tried to hold one with his gloved hands. Still, he managed to scrawl his name beside the fourth waltz.

When he was done, he gave her a nod. "I look forward to our time together." He turned to go—

"Will you not write my name on your dance card?"

He winked. "I shan't forget."

Then he strode over to where King stood a short distance away.

"Did I just see you sign her dance card?" his friend asked, an edge of irritation in his tone.

"Yes, fourth waltz."

Removing his own dance card from his jacket, King glowered. "That's eight dances away. Need I remind you that we weren't planning to stay long?"

"Since you won't be needing that—" Knight plucked the card from his fingers. "Go on without me, and I'll catch up with you later."

"How will you manage such a feat? You're unlikely to find a hansom around here."

"I'll walk back to London proper and secure one there. Or I'll borrow someone else's carriage. Don't worry about me, old chap. I'll make do."

"I'm not going to abandon you here. What possessed you to ask for a dance?"

Knight shrugged. "I've always had a soft spot for brown eyes."

"You have a soft spot for the shade of any lady's eyes."

"True enough. She's pretty."

"A lot of girls are pretty. There must be more to it."

He didn't know how to explain it. "I find her intriguing."

"Because she didn't find you so?" King studied him. "You're accustomed to women falling over themselves to gain your favor. I didn't see her waving her fan around to convey secret messages."

She'd looked through him as though he hardly counted. Perhaps that was part of it. He wanted to impress upon her that he did count, very much indeed.

FOR THE ENTIRETY of her life, Regina had been whispered about behind her back. It shouldn't bother her so much that the whispers were in earnest this evening, and creating such a low, thrumming din they were nearly impossible to ignore, even if she couldn't make out the exact words being uttered. She knew it was unusual for the illegitimate daughter of a lord to have a coming-out. But her father had never treated her with disgust for being born on the wrong side of the blanket. How often had he told her: *You were a creation of love, not duty*?

Even if duty and his other family had kept him away for long periods of time. He'd provided this residence for her and her mother. And a governess to care for her when her mother performed. And clothes, a pony, and tutors. And now this ball where she should feel like a princess, but instead felt more like the ugly stepsister. Because no matter what he gave her, it was always tainted with the knowledge her mother hadn't been good enough to wed. And by association neither was she. Not without a substantial dowry.

She knew it all to be true because the gentlemen who had danced with her thus far had made it abundantly clear. They'd taken her on a turn about the dance floor because it was expected. A gentleman didn't ask for a lady's hand in marriage without swirling her at least once around the ballroom. She had learned from her mother how to hold her head up high, how not to let it show that all the tiny cuts were a death delivered by a thousand knives. Ah, yes, Mother had been an incredible actress on the stage, but it was her performance in life that should have earned her the greatest acclaim. However, so few saw it because she was hidden away from Society except for the moments when she stepped into a theater.

While Regina didn't doubt her father's affection for her, she'd never been inside his London residence where he resided with his family, had never been introduced to her siblings or his wife. Had never been welcomed at his country estate. He might not be ashamed of her but neither did she feel fully embraced. She was grateful for all he'd given her, all he'd provided. Yet, still there seemed to be a chasm, something missing, that had begun to yawn all the wider since her mother passed two years before.

She'd hoped this affair tonight would begin to fill it. Instead, it only made her miss Mum more, especially as her current dance partner didn't speak at all, didn't even bother to meet her gaze but stared off into the distance. Having noticed him chatting with others, she knew he was capable of speech. But not with her apparently. He was cold and irascible. She wondered if she should make him aware that her father would not accept any offer of marriage without her approval. She certainly wasn't going to commend someone so taciturn, who looked as though he feared his face might crack if he so much as smiled.

Unlike *Fourth Waltz* who was waiting for her when this polka finally came to an end. His smile wasn't large and bold, but was smaller, almost gentle, the one she'd seen a groomsman use when striving to calm a skittish mare. He also locked his blue gaze on her dark one, making it impossible to look away. The man didn't wait for her current partner to lead her off the dance floor but met them partway and smoothly transferred her hand from the arm of the gentleman beside her to his own. "I have her now, Wallop."

Mr. Wallop, the second son of a viscount, gave her a curt bow before marching away.

"Hope he didn't talk your ear off," the Earl of Knightly said, a bit of teasing and knowledge in his tone. She wondered if he'd been watching, knew precisely how many words Mr. Wallop had uttered, or knew the man by reputation and his not speaking while dancing was a common occurrence.

"No, they are still both quite intact."

"And so very lovely."

Disappointment washed over her because he was going to strive to charm her with false flattery. She knew of worse ways to go. She'd just experienced one. The light strains from the orchestra began to fill the air.

"Shall we?" he asked, and she quite suddenly found herself swept onto the dance floor in a manner more graceful than any she'd experienced all night.

Oh, he was good. Accomplished. He had to have spent hours perfecting his steps. He made her feel as though her feet had been lifted from the floor and she waltzed upon clouds. "So are your coffers nearly empty or completely empty?"

The small smile playing over lips that promised the sort of kisses she'd read about in romantic novels didn't waver, but his brow did pleat slightly. "My coffers are full."

"Then why did you ask me for a waltz?"

"I'm not quite sure. Perhaps it was the brown of your eyes. Or the fair shade of your hair. The alabaster smoothness of your skin. The fullness of your bottom lip that begs for a man to cushion his mouth there. Or maybe you had the look about you of a woman who was in dire need of rescue."

That was a little too close to how she'd felt, standing there with her father, smiling, greeting people who without him at her side would snub her. "Fancy your-self St. George do you, slaying dragons?"

"Oh, Arthur Pendragon, surely." He winked. "Arthur is my given name, although no one refers to me as such, of course. Why did you assume I was in need of funds?"

"Because you're titled. I've danced with second sons and seventh sons and every number in between. But no firstborn, no heir. You're the only one thus far. Therefore, I'm striving to determine what you seek to gain."

"Nothing more than a few minutes with a beautiful woman."

She laughed. "Oh, you are a silver-tongued devil, aren't you?"

His smile grew. "You've wounded me to the core. You may have to take a walk about the garden with me to help heal the bruises you inflicted."

"You are a flirt, sir."

"I've told you nothing that wasn't true. Have you met anyone tonight to whom you've taken a fancy?"

"Good Lord, no. I'm not even looking." She prob-ably shouldn't have confessed all that. She didn't trust him and yet he was easy to speak with, especially after spending time in the company of one who didn't utter a word. "My father arranged all this, but I'm only here so he's not embarrassed."

"But you're embarrassed." His smile had disap-peared. However, such depth of understanding resided in his eyes, she nearly wept.

"I know I'm a curiosity. I know if I see any of these

people on the street, they will snub me, pretend to not know who I am. Or worse, let it be known they are very much aware of who I am but find me unworthy of a greeting. His love for my mother has made him blind to—" *What we suffered when he was not beside us.* Why the devil was she blathering on? Why did she want to confess her heartache to him? "Even you, you will ignore me, when next our paths cross."

"I daresay I will not."

She gave as ladylike a scoff as she could muster and arched a brow. "You claim that now—"

"Tomorrow, Hyde Park, half four. We'll put your theory to the test."

She had only another few seconds to ponder him and his words before the music drifted into silence, and the din of conversation took up residence, bombarding her ears and making it impossible to think, to decipher if he was mocking or daring her. Or making a promise, the sort she had little doubt every unmarried lady in the aristocracy longed for, a rendezvous in the park when it would be filled to the brim with everyone anxious to be viewed.

He repeated his earlier smooth maneuver where her hand, suddenly without any effort on her part, found itself on his firm and solid forearm. He escorted her to the edge of the dance floor, lifted her fingers to his lips, and pressed a kiss to the gloved tips so firmly the heat of his mouth managed to make its way to her skin like no barrier separated them. His gaze, intense and unwavering, never left hers. "Tomorrow. I'll find you."

Then he was confidently walking away, leaving her

feeling a bit unsteady on her feet, as though something significantly more than a dance had occurred between them.

KING HAD WAITED. Knight had known he would. He'd been tempted to ask the lovely lady for another turn about the floor, but he'd managed to catch a glimpse of her dance card and noted not a single dance had remained unclaimed. He suspected she had the right of it. Those with empty coffers were striving to fill them as easily and quickly as possible. A daughter with a significant dowry was always the preferred method among noble sons who were opposed to work. Bugger the lot of them.

"I'll leave it to you to explain to Bishop and Rook the reason they had to wait on us for the true merriment of the evening to begin," King said as his coach carried them through London.

"By all means, it should fall to me, although I doubt very much if they'll mind. We have plenty of night left."

"You seemed anxious to leave once you finished your dance. Did it not go as you'd hoped?"

It had gone differently than he'd expected, but he hadn't wanted to watch her dance with others, to discover if she enjoyed being in the company of someone else more. If some other gent had the ability to coax a smile from her. If her eyes would warm for another. "I was merely in the mood for a dance, King. Make no more of it than that."

King issued a little grunt, his equivalent of calling Knight a liar, but it required no response, was merely an acknowledgment. Because it was a lie. He'd been in the mood for a closer association with the woman, had wanted to know her better. Having her in his arms had been sublime. She was light on her feet, wispy as a cloud. Delicate and yet sturdy. But it was what he'd discovered while talking with her that fascinated him. She wasn't like the other women who flung themselves at him, anxious to wield the power that came from being a countess who would one day be a duchess. She'd seemed to have no interest in him at all.

"I detest these balls," King muttered. "I believe I'm going to stop attending."

"You go to few enough as it is."

"But going to none would be even fewer."

"How do you propose finding a wife? The whole purpose of these affairs is to facilitate the arrangement of matches."

"I'm not yet ready to take a wife. When I am, I'll come up with another means to spare me the bother of these tedious social engagements. Perhaps I'll run an advert."

Knight laughed. "Oh, I can't imagine that tactic will go well. Your mother won't take kindly to your lack of participation."

"As she's begun to travel more, I doubt she'll even notice." He glanced out the window. "Ah, good. Almost there."

The coach came to a stop. A few minutes later, they were inside the Mermaid and Unicorn. Located in Whitechapel, it was seldom frequented by nobility, which was one of the reasons they liked it. They were never bothered by people wanting investment advice.

Knight immediately spotted Rook and Bishop

at their favorite table in a back corner. Tumblers of scotch were already waiting for them as he and King drew back the empty chairs and sat. In a ritual from their Oxford days, they each immediately lifted a glass and held it aloft in a salute before tossing back the contents.

Bishop began pouring from the bottle he'd no doubt purchased to save the barmaid being run ragged with all their requests. "What kept you?"

"Knight took a fancy to the earl's daughter and decided to have a dance with her."

"Thought you were going to let me tell them," Knight said, glowering at his friend.

"You'd have lied."

"She must have been pretty, then," Rook said. "He only dances with the pretty ones."

"She was very comely," Knight admitted. "Like King here, she didn't want to be there."

"Hence you thought your company would make the evening more pleasant for her," Rook said, grinning.

"How could it have not?" He took a sip of his scotch. "I'm the most pleasant among us."

His comment received a mixture of groans, laughs, and headshakes. He did enjoy time with his mates. But not nearly as much as he'd enjoyed those few minutes with Miss Regina Leyland.

CHAPTER 3

What he asked of me was simple enough. "Turn around."
His voice was gravelly with need, and I did not hesitate
to comply. Then his mouth swooped in to capture mine.
Of their own accord, my lips parted for him. Soon his
tongue was tangled with mine. Nothing had ever felt so
wicked . . . or so sublime.
—Anonymous, *My Secret Desires, A Memoir*

June 5, 1875

WHEN the coach finally drew to a halt in front
of her residence, Regina was still trembling from her
earlier encounter with Knightly. Blast the man for ruining her evening, tonight of all nights, when she'd
spent a delightful afternoon with Lord Chidding and
was striving to determine if he could provide her with
the protection she required. If he was strong enough,
powerful enough to withstand Society's censure if
the truth of her ever came out. If? No, when, because
the truth always revealed itself, usually at the worst

possible time. Would he stand beside her—or would he bolt at the last minute as Knightly had done?

She'd simply needed a few hours of not worrying about how her carefully constructed life had begun to fray at the edges. Of looking upon her past, of acknowledging decisions made that at the time had seemed so very wise—and all too often had threatened to be her undoing.

And Knightly, damn the man, was at the center of each and every unfortunate decision made. Damn, damn, damn him.

She was reaching for the door when it suddenly opened. Crossing the threshold, she smiled at her butler. "You didn't have to wait up, Shelby."

"I can't sleep until I know you're home safe and sound, miss."

"Well, I'm safe. I don't know how sound I am." As she had no wrap or other item to hand off to him, she merely bade him good night and headed up the stairs.

Once in her bedchamber, she rang for her maid. It wasn't until Millie had assisted her into getting out of her gown and into her nightdress and was brushing out her hair that her most trusted servant mused, "Things didn't go well at the club."

Regina looked up, realizing only then that her focus had been on her hands, and met Millie's gaze reflected in the dressing table mirror. "Whatever gave you such a notion?"

"You look like you encountered a ghost, lass." Millie was only five years older, but she'd always had a motherly, nurturing way about her.

"Not a ghost. Just my past."

"Lord Knightly, I take it."

She gave a barely perceptible nod. "We spoke."

"Did the bounder apologize?"

"I think . . . he may have wanted to. But at first, he spoke to me as though nothing untoward had ever happened between us. He invited me to join him for a libation in the club library."

"Hope you tossed the drink in his face."

Regina laughed lightly. "You are a vengeful sort."

"Not as vengeful as you."

She sobered, grew somber. "No, not as vengeful as I am." She shook her head. "I declined his offer. I learned well the lesson he delivered. I shall decline all his offers should more be forthcoming—which I seriously doubt will happen."

Millie parted the golden strands into thirds and began plaiting them. "Why his sudden interest after all this time?"

"I don't know. He was aware of Lord Chidding's calling upon me."

"Jealous mayhap. Regrets his actions. Recognizes he lost a true gem when he turned his back on you. Did you ask him why he treated you like yesterday's rubbish?"

"I didn't want to give him the satisfaction of knowing any of it meant anything to me any longer. That I'd ruminated about him at all over the years." Of discerning she continued to dream of him every night. And they *were* dreams, dreams regarding what they might have had. Whenever she'd been in his company, she'd been so blissfully happy, had believed he accepted her for herself, flaws and all. He'd found no fault with her parentage. The fact that she had no friends among the nobility hadn't mattered. He'd had friends aplenty and had ensured they always danced with her at balls and treated her with respect when their paths crossed. He'd seemed proud, overjoyed even, to have her at his side. He'd never missed an opportunity to touch her, kiss her, or tell her how special she was. She'd trusted his demonstrations of affection were true. But they'd all been lies. What they had shared had been a lie.

"Mayhap we should return to Europe."

She shook her head. "Three years was long enough. I missed England."

To ensure she always had a place to live, her father had put the manor and its surrounding properties in a trust for her. Unfortunately, she was not allowed to sell it. He'd added that particular stipulation because he'd feared some man would convince her to hawk it and the rapscallion would subsequently abscond with the money, leaving her with nothing. The twenty thousand pounds were also in a trust, and the yearly interest generated more than enough to sustain her. But the conditions of the trust prevented her from touching the principle. Her father, apparently, had little faith in her judgment. Although she could hardly blame him when it had been horrendous at one point. Or perhaps he'd merely known the unscrupulousness of men, even before Knightly had proven himself undependable.

"You should have confronted the scapegrace when you returned."

"There was nothing more to say. We said it all at the church."

Or most of it, anyway. She should have unleashed

the full extent of her fury that morning, but disbelief had numbed her and created a veil of protection. All she'd wanted was to get away from him. And not to give him the gratification of knowing he'd devastated her, torn her heart from her chest, and gutted her as well. She had her pride and a lifetime of sloughing off slights, pretending to be immune to the ugliness often directed her way. That she'd never expected him to fall into the category of cruel was a testament to her foolishness and his ability to forge dreams from fabrications.

She'd not even let her father see her tears, but she'd shed them later, alone in her bedchamber. The crushing weight had nearly destroyed her, but she discovered she was not so fragile as all that. She'd been determined to rebuild herself from all the shattered shards. And she'd done it, although tonight she'd felt the stress on the fragile cracks where she'd pieced herself back together. She'd wanted to feel nothing toward him. Instead, she'd felt everything.

"Bugger him, I say. And good riddance."

"Yes, good riddance." Unfortunately, her tone carried far less conviction than Millie's, because once again she was trapped in that awful morning when so many emotions had bombarded her that she could barely make sense of them.

Her friend-more-than-servant draped the plait over her shoulder, a habit she'd begun years ago to indicate she was finished with the task of preparing her charge for bed. "Will there be anything else, miss?"

"No, thank you, Millie. You've done more than enough."

"Would you like me to help you into bed? Tuck you in?"

Regina smiled warmly at her. "No, I'm going to stay up for a while."

"Not too late. You need your beauty rest."

Regina laughed lightly because Millie always ended the night with those words. Her maid slipped out quietly, leaving Regina alone with her memories.

She'd never forget the redness of her father's face or the bulging of his eyes or the tightness in his jaw when Knightly informed him the marriage would not take place, that he would be announcing the news to those waiting to witness the ceremony. Or the satisfaction she'd experienced when he'd plowed his fist into Knightly's face. Or the flash of worry she'd felt when the man she had loved stumbled back and hit the floor. She'd been horrified watching the blood dribble from his mouth, disgusted with herself because her first instinct had been to render him aid. How could she have cared when he'd been so horrid?

"You will marry her," her father had commanded.

Wiping the blood from his mouth, Knightly had looked at her through hooded eyes. "Do you want to marry a man who can't bring himself to marry you?"

She'd never known a person could survive such heartache. "May you rot in hell."

"I assure you, Reggie, hell is definitely where I am headed."

"I'll sue you for breach of contract," her father had growled.

"I'd expect no less."

"I shall see you ruined." But a man of Knightly's

immense wealth couldn't be brought to ruin or to heel. She'd known even then her father's threats would have as little effect as a fly buzzing around.

Tonight she'd had no difficulty displaying her disdain for him. She hadn't been frozen, wondering why he'd changed his mind. She'd moved on with her life, had chased away all doubts, insecurities, and uncertainties. In their place, she had erected a wall of confidence that now guided her.

Rising from the bench before the dressing table, she picked up the lamp resting on the corner and carried it over to the small desk, with its four spindly legs, near the window. The draperies were pulled aside so she could scratch pen over paper, while periodically gazing out on the meadows through which she'd frolicked as a child.

After settling into the chair, she pulled a blank piece of foolscap from the stack before her, dipped her favorite pen in the inkwell, and then applied ink to paper.

My Secret Desires, Vol. II
Chapter One
The *Gentleman Returns*

CHAPTER 4

❦

April 1870

REGINA was a fool, a right fool, for having any hope at all the Earl of Knightly would keep his word to approach her in Hyde Park and, in so doing, slay all her misgivings and doubts about her father's efforts to forge her a place within Society. Yet, there she was with her lady's maid and confidante, Millie, in tow, promenading over the green as though she hadn't just managed to survive—barely—the most uncomfortable afternoon.

Three gentlemen—the second son of a viscount, the third son of an earl, and the fifth son of a duke—had called upon her at different times and sat in the front parlor, their posture erect as they sipped tea, while Mrs. Dorsett, the woman her father had hired to serve as her chaperone, sat in a corner, the clacking of her rapidly moving knitting needles competing with the ticking of the large standing clock nestled against one wall.

It was a wonder Regina hadn't lost her mind and run screaming from the residence.

She'd tried to be the proper and perfect hostess,

to demonstrate her ability to come across as genteel, even under the most trying of circumstances.

Would you care for tea?

Yes, please.

Sugar?

Two lumps. Three lumps. Five lumps.

Did you enjoy the ball?

Quite. Immeasurably. Enormously.

Lovely weather today.

Indeed.

No April showers.

Silence.

They'd all been so frightfully serious and so remarkably dull. Not a smile among them. Nor much conversation either. And she imagined the meals they would share—should she marry one of them—being equally quiet, with one-word answers to any of her inquiries. She'd welcomed the escape from the residence, although enough land surrounded it that she could have walked—or run—for ages without meeting a soul. She was a glutton for punishment to come to the park. She'd received a few nods of acknowledgment but for the most part she'd been ignored.

"Where did this Lord Knightly state he would meet you?" Millie asked now.

"He didn't. He merely said he'd find me."

"He does realize how large Hyde Park is, does he not?"

Raising her wrist in order to check the time, she nudged the edge of her glove aside and lifted the floral covering of her wristlet watch, a gift from her father on her sixteenth birthday. "We're a little early.

He still has fifteen minutes. If he doesn't show, well, we've spent a lovely hour walking about." And being stared at.

"Is he as handsome as the gossip rags say?"

"Handsomer." Dark brown hair that reminded her of the sable lining the inside of her favorite pelisse, brushed into a fashionable style that revealed his ears. His side whiskers were narrow and ventured no farther than the tips of his lobes. She much preferred his neatness to the mutton chops her father sported, which actually did resemble a cut of meat and she found terribly unsightly. Especially as he also had a heavy mustache joining the two sides, rather like a bridge across his face. But Arthur Pendragon—no, Arthur Pennington—didn't need any sort of embellishments because his facial features had been sculpted by the gods and it would have been a sin for any of them to have been hidden beneath swaths of hair.

"Why, Miss Regina, I do believe you're smitten. You barely said two words about him when I was readying you for bed last night following your ball, but now to hear that sigh in your voice—"

"There is no sigh in my voice. I'm not so foolish as to fall so quickly."

"But you will fall eventually."

She very much doubted it, but like her mother, she could put on a performance when need be. "I wish Father didn't value marriage so much. I don't want to disappoint him. One of his legitimate daughters snagged herself a marquess last Season. The other will soon be presented to the Queen and have her coming-out. I feel as if I'm in competition with her, have been given a head start, and shall still come in last. And I suppose I consider it as a bit of a redemption for Mum. She might not have been good enough to wed, but her daughter is." She shook her head. "Silly, I know."

"It's difficult. You miss her."

"I do." Even with all the servants about, the residence was so incredibly quiet and lonely. Millie was always very conscious of her position in the household. Although they were close, they couldn't go on outings together as equals. Millie viewed herself as the chaperone. Even though Mrs. Dorsett was walking along behind them now. Regina hadn't shared a dozen words with the matronly woman, who usually communicated with only an arched eyebrow, a pursing of her lips, or a clearing of her throat. The throat-clearing reserved for the most offensive of behaviors, such as sitting too near a gentleman. Earlier that afternoon, she'd actually brought out a strip of yarn and stretched it between Regina and one of her suitors, demanding they each scoot over until it could no longer touch either of them.

Regina wasn't certain she was cut out for proper behavior. It was so deuced boring.

She also worried she might disappoint not only her father but her husband as well. She hadn't grown up with an example of how one should behave within a marriage and feared she might have trouble with the obedience portion.

But all her worries scattered on the wind when she caught sight of the handsome man loping on a black steed toward her. Oh, he sat a horse well. As he brought the beast to a halt, she could barely take her eyes from his thighs, hugging the creature, while his trousers hugged him. He swept his hat from his head and grinned at her. A devastating grin, the sort that could topple a woman's resistance, burn to a cinder Mrs. Dorsett's scrap of yarn. "Miss Leyland."

She gave a shallow curtsy. "My lord." Then wondered why she sounded breathless, as though she'd just finished running toward him and they'd crashed together into an embrace that would forever bind them together.

"Would you do me the honor of allowing me to stroll alongside you?"

"Yes. I'd be delighted to have you join me."

While he dismounted, to distract herself from staring at his thighs in motion, she rubbed the horse's muzzle and forehead. "What's his name?"

"Shakespeare."

With a small laugh, she looked at Knightly. In the sunlight, his eyes were such a clear, bright, and stunning blue, a hue that had been somewhat hidden in the rather dim lighting of the ballroom. She didn't know if she'd ever seen such a remarkable shade. "I'd expected Zeus or Thunder or something a bit more warlike."

His grin grew until it formed a small dimple in his right cheek. Oh, Lord, but she wanted to touch it. To skim her fingers, and then her lips, over it. Did every aspect of him have to call to her?

"To be honest, I read a good deal more than I fight." He held out his arm.

As Regina reached for it, a harsh clearing of a throat stopped her movements. Turning slightly, she quickly made introductions. He tipped his head toward the maid and chaperone. "Ladies."

"There's to be no touching," Mrs. Dorsett stated sternly.

"As you wish."

"As her father wishes."

Knightly waved his hand before them with gentlemanly grace. "Shall we?"

Holding the reins, his hands behind his back, he had his horse trailing them and forcing her guardians to walk on either side of them. Fortunately, Millie had rushed forward to take a position on Regina's right, leaving Mrs. Dorsett to walk on the other side of Knightly since he had claimed Regina's left.

"She has excellent hearing," Regina said quietly.

He glanced down at her, mirth in his eyes. "I'm not so reckless as to say anything she'll report to your father."

He hadn't returned his hat to his head, and heavy locks of his hair had fallen across his brow. Her fingers ached to brush them back. "We're being stared at."

"I'm always being stared at. You get used to it after a time."

"They look at you for very different reasons than they do me. They judge me, find me lacking."

"Have they told you this?"

She blinked. "Well, no."

"Then how do you know why they're looking? Could be they are simply enraptured of your beauty . . . as I am."

She bit back her laughter but couldn't stop her smile. "Oh, you're good. You're very good."

His eyes dulled somewhat. "You believe me to speak falsely?"

"I think you flirt. Perhaps you even wish to lead me into your bed, but I know all about you, Lord Knightly. You have a notorious reputation for enjoying the pursuit while taking great pains to avoid the capture. I believe you prefer to love and leave."

"I enjoy women, but I don't view that as a shortcoming." He didn't seem at all offended by her words, which meant they were true. At least he wasn't striving to deny them. "However, perhaps you are the one with the power to convince me to stay."

"I rather doubt it. You will inherit a dukedom. You're not going to take to wife a bastard. I suspect your father has drilled into you the importance of bloodline."

"To be honest, my father fairly ignores me." He lowered his head slightly. "I was not the original heir, you see. He much preferred my older brother, lavishing all his time and attention on him. Until my brother was killed in an accident. My father still doesn't know quite what to make of me."

She'd missed that little detail about him. "I'm so sorry for your loss. Were you close, you and your brother?"

"Remarkably so."

"No jealousy because he would inherit everything and you nothing?"

"I've always been far too independent, determined to make my own way. Even now, I take nothing from my father."

She staggered to a stop and stared at him. "Are you implying you . . . *work*?"

He laughed, a deep, booming rumble that for some reason brought up an image of velvet intertwining with silk. "I don't engage in honest labor that creates a sweat—although I certainly don't fault those who do. Unfortunately, there exists unpleasant tasks someone must see to if society is to carry on. I do, however, invest in various enterprises. If you won't judge me a braggart, I'll confess most have proven extremely profitable. Therefore, I enjoy autonomy and am quite liberated from having to do whatever my father might wish in order to retain an allowance as I've no need of it."

"How fortunate you are. I worry far too much about what my father might wish. And not because of the money." But she couldn't tell him it was because she craved his approval and feared she fell short. Unlike his other daughters, she would not be introduced to the Queen or accepted by the *ton* based on her own merits. Without him at her side, without her dowry, she was of little consequence.

"Does pleasing him make you happy?"

"It did when I was younger. Very much so. But his latest request of me, to marry . . ." Her voice trailed off, and she shook her head. A quick burst of laughter escaped. "However, if not for his determination to see me wed, we wouldn't now be walking through the park."

"Don't be so certain. You intrigue me, Miss Leyland."

"According to the gossip rags, you are intrigued by a lot of women."

"Do you blame me for my interest?"

"I think you grow easily bored. I want a man who is above all else loyal. I am not my mother's daughter. I will not settle for being second—not for any man."

He studied her for a long moment. "My condolences on the recent loss of your mother. I saw her on the stage once, you know."

For some reason, it had never occurred to her the people she was meeting now, those she might possibly visit with at some point, had enjoyed a performance by her mother. "Did she bring you to tears?" Mother had often told her making people experience emotions, especially those they'd rather not, was her strong suit.

He grinned. "She made us fall in love with her. I was only fourteen or so at the time, and at that age, a boy most certainly does not weep. Some mates and I snuck away from school one night. I'd purchased a flower from a flower girl. A rose. As it was early evening, it was rather wilted. During the performance, I clung to it near the bud to avoid the thorns. We went backstage afterward, just for a glimpse of her. It was remarkably crowded. She had so many admirers. We were jostled about. I guess someone must have bumped into the flower, broken it, because when we were finally near enough that I could present my gift, she held out her hand and the blossom toppled into it. Left holding the stem, I was mortified, my face burning with embarrassment. It's a wonder I didn't suddenly ignite. She must have understood what I was going through, because she smiled warmly and said, 'You've given me the best part, and that's all that matters.'"

Had her mother felt the same way about the earl? He might not have given her marriage or even respectability, but he'd given her the best part of himself, he'd given her his love. "Thank you for sharing your story with me. Other than with my father, I don't know if I've ever talked with anyone else about her at length."

"My pleasure to share it. I hope it brought you some comfort."

"It did indeed. What of your mother? Is she still alive?"

He looked off toward the horizon. "To be honest, I'm not sure."

His gaze came back to her, and she couldn't read exactly what was reflected in the blue depths, wondered if she should leave it at that, but her curiosity got the better of her. "How can you not know?"

"When I was seven . . . one night . . . she . . . went away. I haven't seen her since."

"I think the not knowing would drive me mad."

"It was hard at first, but loss, any loss, always is. Will you be attending the Wolfford ball?"

It was an abrupt change in subject, no doubt to avoid a painful memory. She nodded. "Yes. I'm rather nervous as it'll be my first appearance at something hosted by the *ton*. My little ball certainly didn't count."

"Don't be nervous. I'll be there. Now that you know I am dependable, save your first waltz for me."

She smiled. "It will bring me joy to do so."

"I must be off. I have an appointment. Thank you for gracing me with your company this afternoon." He settled his hat on his head and nodded at her chaperones. "Ladies, it's been a pleasure."

He gave his attention back to Regina and lowered his head slightly. "You've also learned I keep my word, so know I will be kissing you at some point during the evening of the Wolfford ball."

Before she could respond, he was swinging up into the saddle. Mutely, she watched as he trotted away, every aspect of her growing warm with anticipation. In five days, she'd be receiving her first kiss.

CHAPTER 5

*His mouth left mine to glide slowly and provocatively
along the column of my throat, leaving heated dew in
its wake. Farther down he went, until he reached my
décolletage and the shallow swells. As he skimmed his
warm lips over them, he released a soft purr. It was a
sound of satisfaction and approval. At that moment, I did
not feel at all lacking—in any manner. It was an incredibly
liberating sensation. And rewarding. To know within his
eyes, I was perfection.*
—Anonymous, *My Secret Desires, A Memoir*

June 8, 1875

KNIGHTLY urged his horse into a more urgent gallop, a punishing pace, because he possessed an obses-
sive need to outrun the past. Odd that, as he was, in
fact, heading straight for it.

He'd left London proper behind, traveling a route
he'd journeyed along countless times, when good
folk—including Regina's chaperone—were abed. When
she would slip out of the residence to meet with him

for a midnight stroll into the forest where he would lay her down on a bed of moss and leaves . . .

Although on some nights, when he was feeling particularly bold and daring, he would climb the towering elm outside her bedchamber window and tap on the glass until she scurried over and released the latch, inviting him in. On the most wicked of nights, he'd take her to London, to his bed.

He'd spent five years striving not to think about her, but ever since their encounter at the Dragons, every rendezvous, every caress, every whispered word, sigh, and groan had flitted through his mind over and over. Reading the bloody book certainly hadn't helped.

He neared the property, enclosed by a tall wrought iron fence. The gate was open, an indication she might have gone out in the carriage. No matter. He would wait for her return, whether it be today, tonight, or tomorrow. He would confront her and get the truth from her if it killed him.

He slowed his gelding to a trot, then a walk. No need for Regina to witness his desperation to set eyes upon her, should she be about. Besides, he needed a few more minutes to regain his calm, his control. He wasn't quite certain what game she was playing, but he would figure it out and determine the best way to win. Strategy required clear thinking, and he'd long ago mastered it. It was part of the reason he was so very skilled at investing. Emotion was never part of the process. He'd become more successful since he'd been forced to betray her because he'd buried all sentiment completely. He existed to make sound business decisions, to make amends for what he was and what he'd been given.

The manor came into view, and he fought not to remember his first visit, and how she had captured his interest. And eventually his heart.

He brought his horse to a halt near the steps, dismounted, and secured the reins through the metal ring hanging from a post with a black iron horse's head to clarify, unnecessarily, the object's purpose. After striding up the steps, he grabbed the knocker and used it to make his arrival known. A few minutes later, the butler who'd greeted him numerous times in the past opened the door, and Knight formerly presented his card, even though he was known here. "Lord Knightly to see Miss Leyland."

"She is not at home."

To you, he could almost hear the man mumbling beneath his breath. "Then I'll wait."

He gave the butler a stern look until the gent finally relented and stepped back. Knight edged past him and marched into the drawing room, aware of the echo of the butler's retreating footfalls as he no doubt went to tell the lady who was "not at home" that they had a visitor.

Knight came to a stop beside the rust-shaded velveteen sofa where he'd once sat while she served him tea. A proper afternoon visit with a proper gentleman. An indication he'd been calling upon her. They'd had a few respectable meetings to distract others from suspecting they were having several disreputable ones. Odd thing, that even when they weren't engaged in doing what they ought not, he'd enjoyed being with her. Quiet conversations about mundane matters, shy smiles, reading to each other. The rainy afternoons were the best, when they would sit by the window in silence, watching the droplets roll down the pane, their fingers interlaced, while a contentment he'd never known—

A scuffling sound caught his attention and had him jerking his head in the direction of the far side of the large room, where a wall of books provided a pleasing backdrop for a rosewood desk. Between its curved, intricately carved support, a small girl, resting on her stomach, was busily scratching pencil over paper. Her legs were bent at the knees, her feet sticking up and swinging back and forth so the skirt of her blue frock no longer properly covered her, and yet her innocence made it not matter. Her dark hair was a wild abandonment of curls.

After taking a few quiet steps nearer, he crouched. "Hello."

She looked at him, her brilliant blue eyes huge and her smile bright. "Hello."

"Who are you?"

"Ari. I wrote a story. Do you wanna read it?"

She apparently had no misgivings when confronted by a stranger. Because she believed her world safe? Because an unknown gentleman appearing in the parlor was not an odd occurrence?

He had a thousand other questions. What was a child doing here? To whom did she belong? The shade of her eyes was his, but the oval shape of them was all Regina. Coincidence? How old was she? Three, four, five? Not as much as six, he didn't think, but he paid little enough attention to children and hadn't the slightest talent for adequately ascertaining an age. However, he was very much aware that he didn't wish to disappoint her. "Yes, I would very much."

She popped up, grabbed her piece of paper, crouched, and waddled beneath the desk until she reached him. Then she promptly plopped down onto her bottom, which he supposed meant they weren't going to move to more comfortable furnishings, so he lowered himself to the floor, reached into his jacket pocket, removed his spectacles, and settled them into place. He held out his hand and marveled at how small hers was when she gingerly placed her treasure on his palm.

Her story was nothing but lines and scribbles, curls and loops.

"Oh, dear," he said gravely. "I brought the wrong spectacles. These aren't able to read writing as elegant as yours."

"I can read it to you."

"Thank you. I'd enjoy that." He returned it to her. Then, to his surprise, she scooched nearer until she was nestled against his side, warm and tiny, and yet remarkably overwhelming, as though she encompassed all the space around him, claimed it, and made it hers.

"The dog was lonely. He wanted a friend. The girl was lonely. She wanted a dog." She looked up at him expectantly.

"Does she get a dog?"

Mulishly she pressed her lips together and shook her head. "Not until she's six."

"How old is she now?"

She held up four fingers, then pushed her tiniest one down. "This many."

"Three."

She nodded, before grinning mischievously and letting the tiny finger pop back up. "Until next week." She frowned as though trying to determine precisely when that was, perhaps because she'd merely repeated by rote what she'd been told. Then her face became illuminated as if the sun had shifted out from behind dark clouds for the sole purpose of shining upon it. "Do you wanna come to my cel-bration?"

He wasn't quite certain how to respond to that, especially as he was occupied running months and numbers through his head, calculating the passage of time and the possibility that his not going through with the wedding may have been a far graver affront to Regina than he'd possibly imagined.

Although it seemed the little sprite didn't need a response. She jumped up and returned to where he'd first seen her. With pencil in hand, she began scribbling on another bit of foolscap. When she was finished, she rushed back to him and held it out proudly. His invitation, he assumed, although it very much resembled the story she'd written. Taking it, he carefully folded and tucked it inside his jacket. "Thank you very much."

"We're gonna have cake with strawbries."

"Do you like strawberries?"

She nodded. "And dogs."

He grinned. "You seem rather obsessed—"

"Arianna!"

Somewhat guiltily, both he and the child swung

their heads around to be greeted by Regina trudging toward them like a warrior marching into battle.

"We've been looking everywhere for you, young lady." The tone was implacable, and he had the absurd notion that he wouldn't mind her directing it at him, ordering him into her bed, but then he'd always been at her beck and call until he wasn't. Unfolding his body, he rapidly shoved himself to his feet.

"I wrote a story, Mum."

At her address, at the implication that tiny word confirmed, his gut tightened and clenched, nearly dropping him to his knees. Regina had a child. He'd suspected but hadn't truly wanted to believe the reality of it. He'd once dreamed of a future with her that included children.

The lass raced to the woman with the mien of an avenging angel and offered in tribute the original piece of paper she'd shown him. With a soft smile, Regina lowered a hand to the dark curly head. "We'll read it later, shall we? Now you need to go with Nanny."

Only then did Knight realize another woman had entered the parlor. Easing forward, the servant curled her fingers over the girl's slender shoulder and began guiding her toward the doorway. The lass turned and waved at him. "Don't forget my birthday."

It took every bit of training he possessed to force out the words without giving away the varied emotions rioting throughout him, causing strange sensations to rampage his entire being. "I won't."

Once the girl and her nanny had disappeared into the hallway, Regina turned her attention back to him. "What the hell are you doing here?"

Her curt, accusing tone implied she was not at all pleased by his presence. Not that he'd expected her to be, but still reeling from the revelation that she had a child, he felt like everything was coming to him from a great distance through a thick fog. "She read me her story."

Her features softened slightly. "About a dog, I imagine."

"Is she mine?" He hadn't meant to ask so bluntly or abruptly. He'd planned to work his way around to it. But he'd been unable to contain the words when they'd been bombarding him, insisting on being set free.

"Since she apparently shared with you that her birthday is coming, I would think you could do the calculations based upon the last time we were together, which was also a June. I assure you that I didn't carry her for twelve months."

"She has blue eyes."

"You don't believe yourself to be the only man with blue eyes, surely."

"Considering my . . . lack of carrying through on a promise, I'd have thought you'd have avoided them."

"Have you avoided women with brown eyes?"

At first, he'd drowned himself in them, searching for the adoration, love, and admiration he'd seen in hers. Then he'd begun to eschew them like they carried the plague because they did nothing to diminish the memories of hers that haunted his dreams. "Who is her father, then?"

She shrugged. "Could be the Spanish matador, I suppose. Or the Italian sculptor. The Parisian artist. The German clockmaker."

With each mention, his jaw had clenched tighter, and he had to force it to relax so he could speak, striving for a neutral tone so she wouldn't realize her words had any effect on him, were in fact painful blows. "I'd heard the rumors that while you were in Europe you'd sampled as many men as you did the variations in cuisine." Each tale had been a slice to his heart, and he'd believed with enough of them that he could eliminate his heart completely. Without it perhaps he'd at least find peace.

She gave him a smile, the sort a well-sated woman delivered in bed as her lover rolled off her. Triumphant and knowing. Fully aware, however, that in this case, he'd suffered. Greatly. And she was glad of it. Not that he blamed her. He deserved whatever punishment she meted out. "Why are you here, Knightly?"

"I know, without reservation or any doubt, you're Anonymous."

As soon as she'd seen at the Twin Dragons that he had acquired a copy of the tome, she'd known he'd deduce that she was the author. Her only surprise was that it had taken him a few days to arrive on her doorstep. She was also well aware he wouldn't leave without having his say. Perhaps he'd come to blackmail her, although she couldn't see him engaging in such a reprehensible act. She straightened her spine and angled her chin haughtily, giving the impression she was looking down on him when he stood several inches taller than she. "What of it?"

"You lied. You have read the book."

"Actually, I didn't lie. I've not read the book, only

the manuscript." Its contents and what she knew of them, yes, those she had lied about. But then he'd lied as well, claiming to love her when he hadn't.

He laughed loudly, almost joyfully, a sound that had once sung to her soul. When the echo of it faded away, he remained smiling, a touch of affection in his eyes. "Only you would sparse words so carefully."

Her heart ached with the reminder of how well he'd come to know her, how much they'd shared, how often he'd made her feel treasured. "What do you want, Knightly?"

"Does Chidding know about her?" He jerked his chin toward the doorway.

Other than the servants and her father, no one else yet knew about Arianna. However, only Regina and the ever-faithful Millie knew the lass had actually been born in March, nearly nine months to the day after Regina should have wed. They'd vowed to claim June as the girl's birth month to eliminate any suspicion that Arianna was Knightly's. Regina had made the decision as a means to protect her child from possible hurt and to prevent Knightly from learning the truth of her. He didn't deserve her. In the end, he hadn't wanted Regina. Why would she think he'd want his daughter?

Slowly she shook her head. "I've yet to determine if he can be trusted with the knowledge, how he might react to it. Once bitten, twice shy, or so they say. Will you tell him?"

"What do you think?"

"That I don't know you. The man I thought you

were wouldn't have cast me aside on the morning we were to wed. Why exactly did you?"

Turning his back on her, he walked to the fireplace, pressed his forearm against the mantel, and stared into the empty hearth. "To protect you."

"By breaking my heart?"

He visibly stiffened, then sighed. "It seemed the lesser of two evils." He faced her. "I assume he also doesn't know you're the author of that scandalous *memoir*."

"He does not, nor do I intend to ever tell him. I will deny being the author with my last breath."

"Then why even write it?"

She'd decided that revenge was not best served cold, but rather hot—with heated words and searing passages designed to torment and tease the curious. With truth, conviction, and knowledge. When she'd submitted the manuscript to a publisher, she hadn't even cared if all the world knew she was the author, but at the last minute, she'd made the decision to send it in anonymously through her trusted solicitor, who also collected her earnings. Now people debated whether it was truly a memoir or a novel. Surely it was fiction, the result of a wicked imagination. But if it was true, it had to be the product of a woman scorned. She'd been scorned.

"I grew up the object of unkind gossip and speculation. It turned savage when I was jilted. I was raked over the coals, my unworthiness proven when you announced I'd changed my mind."

"I apologize for that miscalculation, Regina. I

thought it would go easier on you if people thought you'd found fault with me rather than my finding fault with you."

"What fault did you find?"

"None. I told you that. My reasons had naught to do with you."

Shaking her head, she scoffed. "It doesn't matter. However, I wanted you to feel the pain of the bite that was inflicted upon me." Although she hadn't expected the tale to be labeled indecent. Granted, the writing might be provocative, might hint at fornication, but she hadn't described the actual bedding in detail. *That* she had kept to herself, unable to share the intimacy of it because it had encompassed the whole of her.

"Well, the bite has been sharp, and I can hardly go to my club without hearing the nattering going on behind my back, much less conduct business with the success I once enjoyed when entrepreneurs are presently more interested in discussing if I'm Lord K. The speculation is getting tedious. I want you, as Anonymous, to write a letter to the *Times* declaring I am not Lord K."

"We all want things, Knightly. We don't always get them."

A muscle of irritation ticked in his jaw. Unfortunately, it was the same muscle that ticked when he spilled his seed inside her. When she'd loved him, she'd memorized every aspect of him, and now she hated suffering through all the reminders.

"It's a simple enough task, Regina. It's not as though I'm asking you to scale a mountain."

"I'd rather scale a mountain." She smiled sweetly.

"As a matter of fact, I have and found it much to my liking. Penning letters not so much."

"You wrote a blasted tome."

She did little more than arch a brow. "Your point?"

A corner of his mouth hitched up, creating the solitary dimple that had always fascinated her. Once she would have pressed a kiss there. She suspected a change in tactic was coming, a cajoling mayhap since she wasn't conceding to his demands.

"You do realize your gent's prowess along with your not-so-subtle hints Lord K is in fact based upon me is making me somewhat . . . legendary."

She had, unfortunately, misjudged that aspect of it. "Completely unfair. You're viewed as a hero and me as a harlot. That is if the lady of the tale was based upon me, which she is not. She is purely a figment of my imagination."

He took two long strides away from the fireplace, so if he stretched out his arm and she leaned forward the smallest fraction, his long, tapered fingers would be able to graze along her cheek. "So you wouldn't do anything Lord K asked of you?"

"Once perhaps, but no longer." Hot anger began pouring through her, and she was surprised he didn't see sparks shooting out of her ears. It was so like Knightly to lure her in, to be so easy to talk with, to make her forget he was a scoundrel extraordinaire. To make her believe his promises of a lifetime of love and happiness. "Do you not understand you are the villain? You used your charms to seduce an innocent into falling in love with you, in giving to you everything she held dear, without remorse or shame.

Then you deserted her, left her to suffer her shattered heart alone. Now begone and leave me in peace."

She turned for the door.

"If you didn't want me in your life, you wouldn't have written the book in such a manner that it couldn't escape my notice."

She swung around. "I wrote the book to exorcise the last remnants of what we had that continued to plague my hopes and dreams. And it worked. Every word dripped with the loathing I hold for you. Every sentence scored you from my heart. Every paragraph bludgeoned my soul. Every passage served as a reminder of the fantasy you created for us, a love that did not truly exist. I poured every memory of you onto paper until not a single one holds sway over me any longer. I require no apology, no explanation, no repentance from you. You are no longer my reality. I don't think of you, dream of you, or yearn for you. I am free of you. Utterly and completely. Good day, my lord."

Spinning on her heel, she walked out as regally and with as much dignity as she could muster before he could decipher that every damned word had been a lie. Because instead of walking away, she'd very much wanted to walk toward him and straight into his arms. Stupid, silly girl.

CHAPTER 6

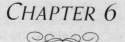

*"I want to lay you down on the grass and have my way
with you," he whispered seductively, his breath a rush of
heat against my ear. I imagined how wonderful it would
feel to have the cool green against my back and the fire of
his flesh pressed against my bosom.*
—Anonymous, *My Secret Desires, A Memoir*

June 12, 1875

REGINA seldom received invitations to balls—not
since her father's death a little over a year earlier, not
since he was no longer present to throw his influence
around in order to secure them for her. As a matter of
fact, she was rather certain his heir, her half brother,
had let it be known he wouldn't attend any affairs to
which she'd been invited and would look unfavorably
upon anyone who extended an invitation to her.

The Duchess of Thornley, however, as an infant
left on the doorstep of a baby farmer, was not one
for playing political games or being intimidated. Regina had met her two years earlier, when her father,

in spite of his failing health, had brought her to the Thornley ball. After she'd returned from the Continent, he'd set about once again striving to find her a protector. If not for Arianna, Regina would have dissuaded him, but she'd also known he could more peacefully leave this world if he was providing her with resources.

She was not fool enough to refuse an invitation that arrived at her door, especially when it might provide an opportunity for Viscount Chidding to pursue his courtship of her in a more public setting.

Hence, this evening she was at the well-attended affair, speaking with Lady Rosemont, the duchess's sister and wife to the Earl of Rosemont, and Lady Aslyn, who had married Mick Trewlove, the duchess's brother.

"Fancy, you own a bookshop for goodness' sake," Lady Aslyn was saying to her sister-by-marriage. "How can you not obtain a book I want to read?"

"Aslyn, no copies are to be found anywhere. Before I could get word to my shop manager that I wanted some put aside for us, she'd already sold all our copies of *My Secret Desires*. Honestly, this book has unexpectedly taken the country by storm. I've spoken with the publisher, and he's assured me he will print more . . . once it's safe."

"Safe?"

Fancy glanced around before revealing in a lowered voice, "He fears being arrested for printing obscene material."

Regina refrained from rolling her eyes. Through

her solicitor, she'd already been informed of the publisher's concerns. They were barely two months in, and it would be the fifth printing—apparently, he'd grossly misjudged the book's potential popularity—and if he'd not been arrested yet, surely he was not in any true danger of being so. Perhaps he was merely sharing nonexistent fears in an effort to add to the story's mystique, so more people were clamoring to read it.

"How obscene is it?" Aslyn asked.

"Not very," Regina answered without thinking.

"You've read it, then?" Fancy asked.

"No, I've not read the book, but I've heard it's not terribly detailed when it comes to describing the more intimate encounters. It's the journey of a woman falling in love . . . with a rake. Apparently."

"Having fallen in love with one myself," Aslyn said, "I can well imagine such a telling has the potential to provide an absorbing read. I suspect the staider and more boring among us are the ones raising the fuss about it."

"On the contrary, I suspect, they're the ones reading it and making it so dashed difficult to find," Fancy said.

Regina released a small burst of laughter. "Do you truly think so?"

"Absolutely. We all have things for which we secretly yearn. Books open worlds to us, and a person shouldn't be made to feel ashamed of their reading choices."

"I quite agree."

"We have one patron who will only write down the title she wishes us to find for her. She'll never say it out loud. Embarrassed, I think, for anyone to hear what she wants to read. I find it remarkably sad that she's not comfortable sharing her joy of the material with others."

"But at least the material is available to her," Aslyn said. "The book I want to read is not available to me and that's upsetting. It has piqued my curiosity even more to discover what is in it that others find offensive."

"From what I understand," Fancy said, "some view it as a danger because the heroine is unwed and carrying on as though she were, having relations outside the boundaries of marriage. As you are well aware, among proper society, that sort of behavior is not to be tolerated. Some fear the book might encourage people, in particular single ladies, to engage in illicit liaisons."

"People aren't supposed to murder either," Regina said, "but no one is shouting 'Oh, the obscenity of it,' when it comes to detective novels."

"I'd never thought of it that way," Fancy said. "Can you imagine how my brother Beast would react to having the detective novels he pens banned? I daresay he'd have a word or two to say about that once he finally takes his seat in the House of Lords."

"I am more intrigued than ever," Aslyn said. "Fancy, you absolutely must secure me a copy."

"I shall speak with the publisher again. Perhaps he has one hidden away somewhere. If not, well, I do know of some shops that sell that which is not to be sold."

"Are you referring to an underground market?" Regina asked.

"Quite. I don't dabble in it. My family has worked too hard to earn respectability, and I have no desire to have my shop invaded or torn apart by a well-intentioned constable or whoever is charged with enforcing these laws."

"Any destruction of your property would be such a shame," Aslyn said. "It is the loveliest shop and so welcoming. Have you ever visited, Regina?"

"I've not but have decided I must in the very near future."

"I'm hardly ever in the bookshop these days," Fancy said, "but if you let me know when you're coming, I'll make a point to be there."

Regina smiled. It was so lovely to have friends. She wished she'd known these ladies when she was younger. They were incredibly accepting, but then she'd yet to meet a Trewlove who sat in judgment of anyone. "You're so very ki—"

A warm sensation settled along the nape of her neck, causing the fine hairs to shimmer pleasantly, and she knew, *knew*, who had quietly approached even before he spoke. She had always, somehow, instinctually sensed when he was near, drawing her toward him, just as the moon did the tides.

"Ladies. Miss Leyland."

She understood Knightly intended no insult with his forms of address but was merely exhibiting proper etiquette by giving each the respect due her. The other two were ladies—one by marriage, the other by birth. And Regina was a *miss* by lack of marriage and questionable birth. She didn't know why their forebears had decided distinctions were necessary. Or how they had determined what was polite behavior. At the moment, she had a desire to be incredibly impolite and simply ignore the scoundrel. However, doing so might give him the impression he was of consequence. Better to face him with disdain so clarity reigned, and he understood he mattered not at all.

"My lord," her two companions said in unison, while she slowly turned, arching one eyebrow and holding the rest of her features immobile, showing no other reaction to his presence. Although inwardly, she cursed soundly. The man was handsome enough in ordinary clothes, but when wearing his black evening attire, he was gorgeous. And well he knew it.

His cerulean gaze was homed in on her, and she began to grow warm under his intense perusal. It seemed to last a lifetime, but it couldn't have been more than a few seconds before he spoke, with a slight lowering of his head. "Miss Leyland, would you be kind enough to honor me with a waltz?"

"I would not."

His eyes flared briefly. Obviously, he'd not been expecting her to rebuff his invitation, especially in view of witnesses. He shifted his attention to the other two. "I don't suppose you'd give us a moment."

"No need," Regina said, "as I can't tolerate the fetid air that blew in with your arrival."

She'd barely taken a step before he moved in front of her. "Please. One dance."

"You are under the misconception that I would be

willing to give you anything at all. Why this sudden urge of yours to continually approach me is beyond my ability to comprehend. I don't know how to make it any clearer, my lord, but I want nothing at all to do with you."

"Regg—"

She shoved on him, cutting off his use of the shortened version of her name that only he had ever used, and sent him staggering back a few steps. She hated to have lost control, to sense the heat of her anger beginning to burn brighter. "I am done with you. And I have been for years."

Lifting her skirts, she made haste to reach the open doors leading onto the terrace and from there into the gardens. She desperately needed the cooler air and hoped Chidding had not witnessed her display of temper. She'd already waltzed with him once, and he'd reserved the final dance of the night for her. He was charming and witty, with hair the shade of burnished red and eyes the darkness of brewed tea. He reminded her nothing at all of Knightly.

Finally, she was outside. Raising her skirts higher, she raced down the steps and then slowed her pace so as not to give the impression she was in fact running away. She wasn't. Damnation but she was. From the memories that still plagued her. Putting them to paper had only temporarily rid her of them. Knightly approaching her had brought them and the emotions surrounding them back to life. The joy. The humiliation.

The humiliation had torn her asunder. But the joy

had been exquisite. The kind that served as the impetus for sonnets being penned, songs being sung, books being written. She dearly wanted to experience it again but was fairly certain it was allowed only once in a lifetime. While she liked Chidding quite a bit, was comfortable with him, she knew she'd never fall madly in love with him. Nor would he with her. While she experienced moments when the realization saddened her, she understood the need for sacrifices.

A good bit of her life had been comprised of them. What was one more?

Her thoughts traveling darker paths, she decided to take her feet in the same direction and left the lighted pathway through the gardens, making her way over ground carpeted by thick grass. The distant glow provided enough illumination she was able to wend her way between the blacker shapes and shadows and avoid stumbling over foliage or snagging the silk of her gown. The very last thing she needed was to return to the ballroom looking as though she'd been involved in a tryst.

She came to a stop beneath a towering elm. Before her a brick wall enclosed the duke's parcel of land in London. A brick wall similar to one against which Knightly had once pressed her as he'd devoured her mouth. Why did every blasted thing she encountered have to remind her of him?

Even the blossoms in this area of the garden smelled of sandalwood—bloody hell, the scapegrace had followed her. She wondered, if she sprinted fast enough, if she'd create enough momentum to propel herself over that wall. But then running from him wasn't the answer. It never had been. "Why will you not leave me in peace?"

"I owe you."

"An explanation regarding the truth of that morning?" Neither his words nor his actions had ever made any sense to her. She swung around. "After all these years, it had better be damned good."

"I remember a time when you didn't use profanity."

"I used to *not* a lot of things. I was a child then. No longer. So why precisely did you change your mind about marrying me?"

"*That* I cannot explain."

"I am past the point of having my feelings hurt because you found fault with me. So list out all the reasons you changed your mind, all the details about me that you decided made me unsuitable."

"Christ, Reggie, is that what you thought all these years? Trust me, my not going through with the marriage had nothing at all to do with you."

"Ha!" She slapped a hand over her mouth at the unexpected burst of a scoff. She certainly didn't need for anyone to find her hidden away here with Knightly, for Chidding to hear of it. Curling her fingers into fists at her sides, she took a step forward and said scathingly, "Perhaps it was your plan all along to publicly bring me shame, to show all of London I was not worthy of dreams, was reaching for something beyond my grasp."

KNIGHTLY SHOULDN'T HAVE followed her, should have left the ball the moment he realized she was there.

She'd made her point during their last encounter, but to hear the justifiable rage slithering through her voice, the pain causing it to rasp, the humiliation making it tremble—he felt as though he'd been catapulted back to that morning when he'd broken her heart. She, too, was there again, bombarded by all the emotions that should have been absent that day. The years had brought her no solace, hadn't washed away the memories or caused them to fade. He hated how she continued to suffer.

If only he could have spared her the cruelty of being caught in the web of deceit that unceasingly held fast to tear at them.

He needed to free her, and he knew of only one way to accomplish that task. In the darkness, it would be easier to face the past, to explain to her when she was lost to the shadows how he would make everything right. He couldn't undo what had transpired that day, but by God, he could make it right for her, just as he'd made it right for another.

"I unexpectedly learned something about myself, and I knew with me, you would never achieve true happiness. I sought to spare you a future that would have involved far more tears than smiles."

"Well, if that's what you considered sparing me, then you're correct. I would not have remained happy with you." In spite of the fact that he couldn't see her clearly, he was very much aware of her penetrating perusal of him. "What did you learn of yourself? That you're a coward?"

He couldn't help it. He grinned. He'd thought her formidable before, but she was more so now. He wanted to confess everything, but he'd sworn to take the secrets to his grave. The well-being of others depended upon his discretion. "Close enough."

She sighed with apparent frustration. "I've been gone from the ballroom too long. I need to get back." She made a move to leave.

"How badly do you want Chidding?"

Her gaze swung back around to him, landing on him like a harsh thud to punctuate his words. "I beg your pardon?"

"At the Dragons, you didn't seem at all bothered by his impoverished state. I suppose he could be classified as handsome."

"I don't give a fig about his appearance. I need respectability for me and for . . . Arianna. I don't want her growing up ridiculed and mocked as I was. I don't want her hidden away." She slammed her eyes closed and shook her head. "I realize that is precisely how she is living now. A secret. The staff is exceedingly loyal. They won't betray her, but as you witnessed, she is of an age where she tends to get into mischief and rebels against the boundaries I have set for her." Opening her eyes, she met his gaze straight on. "In spite of his impoverished state, Chidding's reputation is unblemished. He amassed debt striving to keep his estate maintained. I find him quite admirable. The few times we've been together, he's been kind, hasn't attempted to take advantage." She rolled her eyes. "We haven't even kissed yet. And I don't know why the bloody hell

I'm telling you any of this when it most assuredly is none of your concern."

"I can deliver him to you."

She growled, and he was reminded of a dog straining against its tether. "I don't need your interference. I don't need *you*. I've gone five years without you in my life and managed quite well, thank you very much."

"Then let me ask you this: How quickly do you wish to marry?"

"If that's a proposal, you can rot in hell."

He chuckled low. He'd loved her before she was this feisty. If he was wise, he'd make himself scarce around her rather than risk falling more deeply in love with her, but then where she was concerned, he'd seldom shown wisdom. "Do you know what his best mates call him?"

She released an impatient breath strong enough to stir the leaves in the tree. "I'm certain you're going to tell me."

"Tortoise. The man is remarkably slow at making decisions. I assume for your daughter's sake, you'd like him speeded up."

"You have a plan for accomplishing that end?"

"I do. After we return to the ballroom, dance with me."

"For what purpose?"

He didn't blame her for the suspicion reflected in her tone. "To make him jealous."

She scoffed—quieter this time so no one else would hear—and he was reminded of the many times he'd muffled her cries of pleasure. To protect her reputation. All he'd ever wanted was to protect her. Instead, he'd ruined her.

"Our past is well-known. No one is going to believe you have an interest in courting me."

"They will if I appear . . . regretful . . . and still enamored of you."

"Well, I'm certainly not going to give the impression I have any interest in you at all."

He took a step toward her. She stood her ground. "In spite of how things ended between us, the smoldering embers of desire haven't been completely snuffed out, surely."

"As though several buckets of cold water had been doused upon them, leaving nothing but ash."

Ah, but the phoenix arose from ashes. He tamped down the thought because nothing had changed, and he still couldn't give her what she deserved. "Then waltzing with me should hardly affect you."

"I don't understand what you gain."

"An easing of my guilt."

"As if I should have any interest at all in lessening your suffering."

"Dancing with me will increase it. If the book wasn't enough, you could have a little more revenge."

"I don't trust you."

"Who's the coward now?" he goaded, knowing he was backing her into a corner, one in which she would not stay.

"Fine. One waltz. I'll return to the ballroom first."

She didn't wait for his response, but simply edged past him, her gardenia scent wafting toward him. He inhaled deeply as though he could bring all of her nearer, but she disappeared into the shadows.

He held still, counting the seconds before he could

follow, detouring around the gardens so he emerged from another direction.

While she might not acknowledge it, Regina needed his protection more now than ever. As did her daughter. He intended to ensure Regina was married by Season's end.

CHAPTER 7

"You deserve more than the cold ground," he said. "You deserve a warm bed. One heated by the fires of our passion for each other."
—Anonymous, *My Secret Desires, A Memoir*

June 12, 1875

SINCE her return to England's shores, Regina had grown accustomed to the fact that her dance card would not be filled on the rare occasion when she attended a ball. In spite of her father's attempts to marry her off, Knightly's actions had deemed her a risk—either way. Those who believed he'd spoken true and she'd changed her mind found her audacious, and who was to say she wouldn't change her mind again? Those who thought he was in fact the one who had decided the marriage was not to happen believed something to be amiss in her.

In spite of her manor and yearly income, she was considered soiled goods. It was a descriptor with which she'd never argued because it was the truth.

Arianna was proof of it. To claim she was pure and then to prove otherwise to a man who intended to ask for her hand would only serve to ensure he didn't propose, would label her as a deceptive wench. Hence, she'd learned to pick her battles.

She should have chosen the one with Knightly in the garden, should have fought with more determination to win. Instead, she had lowered the flag. But that didn't mean he still wasn't in a position to lose. She would be irascible and unpleasant during their waltz. A direct contrast to how she would behave when she danced again with Chidding.

Knightly had obviously observed her time with the viscount. Had he been jealous? Was that the reason behind this elaborate ruse to get her to the altar with another man? Did he want to put himself in a position to spend time with her, to woo her? He couldn't really be interested in assisting her in her quest to achieve a more secure home life for Arianna. Could he?

As for those smoldering embers of desire he'd mentioned—she'd see them banked. Most certainly, she wasn't experiencing them. They were in her past, not her present. They were not the reason she kept turning her gaze toward the terrace doors wondering when the devil he would emerge through them so they could get their dance over with.

Then she felt his presence, at her back, and she wondered how long he'd been watching her. He stepped up beside her. "I didn't see you enter," she stated tersely.

"I came in through a side door that led into the cardroom."

"At least you're finally here. Let's get this done, shall we?"

"The tune is a few stanzas in. We'll wait for the next one. It's a waltz as well."

"Perhaps you could walk away then."

"It would help your cause if people thought we were on a path toward reconciliation."

"But we're not." With a sigh, she closed her eyes. "I was rid of you, Knightly. I want it to stay that way." Opening her eyes, she faced him. "Do you not understand how hard it was for me?"

True remorse in his eyes, he lifted his gloved fingers to her cheek. "I do, Reggie. More than you'll ever know. If I'd realized sooner that we could not be, I would have spared you that morning of devastating disappointment. I would have spared you the tears and the shifting of your feelings for me from love to hate. I can't undo the past, but I can ensure the next time you take a walk toward the altar, the right man will be waiting for you."

Easing her face away from his touch, she shook her head. "I don't know how you can ensure the actions of another when you couldn't even ensure your own. Maybe he'll change his mind at the last minute as well."

"He won't."

"How can you be so bloody sure?"

"Because I suspect my situation is quite unique."

She was becoming irritated that he continued to speak in riddles. What had he learned about himself that made their being together impossible?

The music drifted into silence, and he held out his

hand. When her gloved palm touched his, she realized she'd been wrong. The embers hadn't completely died, and they gave a little spark as though a soft breath had been blown upon them. But she was going to ignore them, deprive them of oxygen.

However, it was terribly hard when he glided her across the parquet floor. Besides Chidding, she'd danced with a couple of other gents earlier, but no one moved as elegantly nor as smoothly as Knightly did.

"Do you like the way I knotted my neckcloth?" he asked after a while. "Or are you trying to determine the quickest way to rid me of it?"

She jerked her head up. He smiled. "I thought that would get your eyes on mine."

"I agreed to dance with you, not to carry on a conversation, and certainly not to flirt."

"You're more beautiful than you were five years ago. Maturity agrees with you."

He was more handsome, with deeper lines in his face, but they were not lines cut by happiness or joy. She wondered what challenges had carved them. Then cursed herself for wondering anything about him at all.

"Was it difficult traveling through Europe alone?" he asked.

"I had my maid with me." She tilted her head slightly, unable to prevent a small smile. "And I was rid of the termagant."

He grinned. "Mrs. Dorsett."

"Indeed. Therefore, no chaperone, which gave me a great deal of freedom. But more, I could be whomever I wanted. No one knew me. It was a chance to explore various aspects of myself, some I wasn't even aware existed." She'd discovered she possessed more inner strength than she'd thought possible.

"How did your father react to . . . the gift you brought him?"

She didn't need clarification regarding the nature of the gift, nor did she like the way her heart softened toward him with the word he'd applied to Arianna. She had been a gift. From the moment Regina had realized she was with child, she'd felt immeasurable happiness. A bit afraid, but never burdened. She wondered if her own mother had felt the same, had been delighted at the prospect of having a child. She also wondered how she might have felt seeing history repeat itself with her own daughter. There were times when Regina certainly would have welcomed the advice of someone who'd had a similar experience, although in some ways Regina was traversing uncharted ground because her mother had at least had the support of the man she loved. "He was overjoyed."

She remembered his elation and the light that had sparked within his eyes. He'd been ill for a while by then, and the sight of Arianna had seemed to revitalize him. But only for a short time. His illness was such that nothing could prevent it from having its way with his body. "My father believed every child was to be treasured, whether born within the bounds of a marriage or out of it. He spoiled her while he could—just as he did me. I wish only that he'd had more time with her, with both of us. But then I don't think we're ever ready for someone we love to be taken from us. You lost your mother at an early age, as I recall."

"Life is seldom fair or without challenges. I do admire how well you face them."

"I don't want your admiration. I want your absence. I already regret agreeing to this waltz."

That damned dimple appeared again. "I shall strive to lessen the regret. When did Chidding first approach you?"

She supposed no harm would come from telling him. "Shortly after my father passed, Chidding came to the residence and offered his condolences. Then six weeks ago, when my official mourning period ended, he returned and brought me a book of poems. Read me some. In the garden." It had been a lovely day, heralding the completion of spring, the start of summer. Flowers had been in bloom. Birds had been twittering in the trees. A slight breeze had cooled the air and toyed with her hair, working a few strands free of their pins. Chidding had slowly, cautiously tucked them behind her ear. And then blushed.

She couldn't imagine Knightly's cheeks turning pink with embarrassment. Certainly, she'd never seen them do so.

"So he was counting down the days to be with you."

That assessment seemed rather melodramatic, and yet it gave her a great bit of satisfaction to be able to reply, "It would seem so." *He fancies me, has an interest in me.* Only then did she realize she wanted Knightly jealous, to fully comprehend that another gentleman desired her.

"Since then?"

"We met at Hyde Park one afternoon and strolled along the grounds."

"You didn't tell him you prefer riding through the park?"

Riding was something she'd done with Knightly, and she hadn't wanted to replace the memory, a memory she didn't want to remember. Nor had she wanted the opportunity to compare the two men, because she'd known her heart would find Chidding lacking. But on this matter of what was best for her and Arianna, her heart had no say. "I've discovered strolls are more conducive to carrying on a discourse. I enjoy conversations with him. He is well versed on many topics."

"A reader no doubt, then. I wonder if he's read your book."

Her cheeks warmed. She'd never given thought to a particular person, especially one of her acquaintance—other than Knightly—perusing the words she'd written. "The subject has not come up."

Nor would it. At least not through her prompting. She wasn't ashamed of what she'd committed to paper, but she suddenly realized books created a rather intimate exchange between author and reader. How could any writer not put a portion of herself into the work? Unexpectedly she felt a sense of vulnerability. "You never told me what you thought of it."

Could she have not bit off her tongue before voicing those words? She didn't give a fig regarding his opini—

"You were born to be a writer." His eyes reflected complete honesty. "You made me *feel* what those characters were experiencing. The fact that I had actually lived through the moments had no bearing on the sensations that swept through me. I was enthralled. You write with an honesty few have the courage to emulate. Although you did change the conclusion of our tale."

"I wanted you identifiable, not myself. And who is to say that you never abandoned a lady at a railway station after promising to run off with her?"

He studied her for a long moment. "I felt every crack running through her heart as it was crushed by his betrayal. You should have put your name on the book."

"Considering the reception it has received from some, it's probably best I didn't." Especially as she didn't know how Chidding might feel about it. "Besides, you once told me you were an anonymous partner in some of your investments. Where's the harm in a bit of mystery? It might have added to the book's popularity as people strive to determine the identity of the author . . . or Lord K. If I may be honest, they seem more interested in knowing exactly who that character is than anything."

"You made him an extremely appealing fellow. Until the end, when the truth of him—as you saw it— bears out."

"I don't think the truth of him could be viewed in any other way. He showed no honor or decency when forsaking her on a cold winter's night." She'd also altered the months during which the story occurred, so they didn't match their time together exactly. "I've begun penning a sequel in which I will reveal his demise."

He grinned broadly, and she remembered how she'd

once lived for those smiles. "Something horrible, I wager. Painful and slow. You'll want him to have ample time to experience true and deep remorse, to recognize the error of his ways, and to know he hasn't time to right his mistakes."

"Is that what you're doing now? Attempting to right your mistakes?"

He grew somber. "Sometimes, we're faced with an impossible choice."

As if she didn't half know that. Chidding would be such a decision. Giving up the chance to experience another grand love in favor of ensuring her daughter would be more accepted by Society than she. "Do you ever regret the choice you made?"

"Only in that it hurt you. But if I were faced with the same dilemma at this moment, I couldn't choose otherwise."

"What did you choose, Arthur?"

The music drifted into silence and their movements ceased. His hand still wrapped around hers, he brought it to his lips, his gaze never leaving hers. "Good night, Reggie."

"You're leaving?"

"My work here is done."

Rather than escort her to the edge of the dance floor as she'd expected, he merely turned slightly and offered her hand to another, to Chidding, who then stood beside her, watching as Knightly strode away.

"I was rather surprised to see you dancing with him," Chidding said, as the next tune began to play, and he took her into his arms for an unexpected turn about the room, which would no doubt have tongues that had begun wagging when she'd danced with Knightly continuing to wag.

"It was simply for old times' sake."

"Not many women would be as magnanimous as you."

"My mother once told me that holding grudges causes wrinkles. Besides, he means nothing to me any longer. Waltzing with him was rather like having a tooth extracted. Painful while it lasts, but a relief when it's over."

He flashed a grin. "Then I need not be jealous."

She winked. "A little perhaps, but rest assured, he is in my past. And I intend for him to remain there."

UPON REACHING HIS carriage driver, Knight issued the order, "Home, as fast as you can."

Because he needed to get as far away from her as quickly as possible before he began to regret a choice he'd been obligated to make—out of love, out of kindness, out of decency—because the man who'd forced him to choose was anything but loving, kind, or decent.

As the vehicle raced toward London, Knight closed his eyes and inhaled her gardenia fragrance that clung to him. It would probably dissipate before he entered his residence, but it was with him now, faint and yet with enough power to haunt his thoughts and cause all his memories of her to bombard him. Holding her in his arms again had been both heaven and hell. Handing her off to Chidding the very depths of hell.

He'd hoped by dancing with her that he'd demonstrated he still held respect for her, favored her. He wanted those in that ballroom to understand she was worthy of their attention and courtesy. He'd noted only a couple of gents had danced with her, unlike her first ball when every unmarried man in London had been clamoring for her. Knight had done that, made her a pariah. When she deserved to be a queen.

The carriage finally came to a stop in front of his residence. He leapt out of the conveyance, dashed up the steps and through the door. He didn't even bother to stop as his butler approached, but handed off his hat, walking stick, and gloves as he passed by the servant. He strode briskly down the hallway to his favorite room, his library, where she had marveled at all his books. Where she had read to him romantic tales and he had courted her with sonnets.

Reaching the sideboard, he splashed scotch into a glass and quickly downed it, relishing the warmth burning his throat, penetrating his chest, dulling the ache that resided there. After refilling the glass, he walked over to the fireplace and lowered himself to a thickly stuffed chair. Slipping two fingers into the small pocket on his waistcoat, he rubbed the green ribbon he'd once taken from her. It had begun to fray. Eventually, he supposed it would come apart. Perhaps when it no longer existed, the memories of her would fade away as well and his torment would abate.

But he'd learned that life seldom went as one expected.

He'd been born the spare, second in line to a dukedom. He hadn't minded because it meant for the most part his father ignored him, except for the rare occasion when he was summoned into the library where his cheek met the duke's palm, and then he was dismissed without ever learning what he'd done to displease his sire.

He'd never told his mother about the slaps, fearing his father might deliver one to her, because the duke gave her little attention as well. Perhaps it was because she was so quiet or maybe because she had the mien about her of someone who wasn't quite of this world. She was always staring off into the distance, the corners of her lips turned up into a small smile as though she'd ascended to a place of joy. When she tucked him into bed—after his nanny had already tucked him in—she would sit on the edge of his mattress and tell him a story about a princess who fell in love with a stablemaster or a gardener or a keeper of the hounds. Those were his favorite moments of the day because she brought with her such serenity.

His brother, Francis, four years his senior, was styled the Earl of Knightly, carrying one of his father's titles as a courtesy. Frank received the lion's share of their father's attention because he would one day inherit—even though he struggled with the numbers and letters that so fascinated Arthur. For some reason, it angered the duke that Arthur was advancing in his studies faster than Francis. Arthur tried to explain to Frank how easy everything was, shared little tips for making hasty calculations and for recognizing words on sight. But Frank preferred riding, chasing the hounds, and swordplay. Even if the swords were only wooden.

When he was seven, Arthur was awoken in the middle of the night by his mother's cries. He slipped out of bed, tiptoed across his room, opened the door, and peered out. He saw two men dragging his mother—in her nightdress, kicking and screaming—down the hallway toward the stairs. He would have rushed out to help her, but the duke stood there, his arms crossed over his chest, watching. He feared the duke more than he feared what was happening with his mother. Surely if she was in trouble, the duke would step in to help her. He quietly closed the door, returned to his bed, and stared at the ceiling while tears gathered and rolled down his face for the remainder of the night.

The following morning, during breakfast, while dipping his spoon into his boiled egg, the duke announced, "Your mother has fallen ill. You'll not be seeing her again."

Arthur opened his mouth to ask for more details, but Frank caught his attention with a widening of his eyes and a shaking of his head. Therefore, Arthur held silent. He knew people often died when they became sick. Had his mother died, then?

Later, Frank told him her illness was the reason she often looked like she was awake but not really there. Mentally, she'd gone someplace else. "She's not well, but they can't do anything for her. It's her mind, you see, but it's not something to be talked about."

He didn't see. Nor did he ever again talk about it.

When he was sixteen, his life took another drastic turn. He'd advanced far enough into his studies to be accepted into Oxford. The night before he was to leave, Frank introduced him to gin and then convinced him to go on a midnight ride. Galloping over the moors with abandonment and recklessness, urging his horse to jump over stone walls, Frank eventually lost his seating, tumbled from his mount, and broke his neck. The heir apparent was dead.

Long live the new heir apparent. Arthur Pennington, styled the Earl of Knightly.

It should have been you, his father had grumbled the morning Frank was laid to rest in the family crypt on the ducal estate. *Why couldn't it have been you?*

Arthur wished it had been. For so many nights, so many days, he wandered around Oxford much as his mother had roamed through the house, in an absent sort of state. He didn't want to be an earl, didn't want to be a duke. But the law didn't allow his father to replace him. It didn't allow Arthur to turn his back on his responsibilities.

One night, however, he decided if the duke wanted nothing to do with him, he would have nothing to do with the duke. He would study even harder than he had in the past. He would make his own way in the world. Earn his own money, accumulate his own wealth, have his own residence. He would ask nothing of his father ever again.

Then he met three chaps who also wanted to be independent of their fathers. They began strategizing their course. And the Chessmen were born.

Now Knight took another sip of his scotch and stared at the empty hearth. As much as he trusted the Chessmen, there were things he hadn't told them, things he'd done that he couldn't bring himself to voice aloud. Things of which he was guilty. Things he needed to make right. Hopefully tonight he'd taken a step toward making amends.

"You're home early."

Glancing to the side, he smiled at the silver-haired woman in her nightdress and wrapper. She was still too thin for his liking. "Good evening, Mother." Setting his glass aside, he stood and began walking toward the sideboard. "Brandy?"

"Yes, please."

By the time he'd finished pouring it, she was settled in the chair across from the one in which he'd been sitting. After handing her the glass, he returned to his place and took a swallow of his scotch, watching as she sipped on her brandy, a small smile of contentment playing at her lips. It brought him satisfaction that something so simple could bring her such joy.

"Back in my day," she said, eyeing him mischievously, "balls did not end until long after midnight, sometimes not until dawn."

"They've not changed. Tonight's is still well under way, I'm sure." He shrugged. "But my purpose in attending had been fulfilled."

"What purpose would that be? If it is to gain a wife, I'd have thought you'd stay until the end."

"Why are mothers always so anxious to see their children married off? You should accompany me some time."

She shook her head. "I've been too long away from Society. Besides, I have no wish to encounter your father."

"We do not attend the same affairs."

"How do you avoid doing so?"

He took a long swallow of his scotch and then tapped a finger against the glass. "I send him a missive alerting him to the ones I'll be attending."

"He's a duke. He's expected to make an appearance."

"Look around you, Mother. My London residence is larger and posher than his. My coffers are fuller. Do you not think my influence is greater?"

"I think he has made you hate him with a vehemence equal to my own, and I worry it is spurred by more than his treatment of me. I wish you'd tell me how you managed to secure my freedom from that awful place."

That awful place. An insane asylum. Knight had been appalled to learn how easy it was to have someone, especially a woman, committed for the slightest unwelcomed behavior. Too quiet, too loud. Caught pleasuring herself. He had no idea what action his father had cited to necessitate removing her from society. Until a few years ago, he hadn't even known she was still alive.

"My being released couldn't have happened without his approval, for he is my husband still."

"You shouldn't concern yourself. It was a price I was willing to pay." Although not at first. At first, he'd hesitated. He still harbored guilt for the hesitancy, for considering his own selfish wants and desires, and nearly placing them ahead of hers.

"Does it have anything to do with the reason you don't stay long at balls?"

It had much to do with the reason he did a lot of things. "I didn't liberate you from the other place simply to have you lock yourself away here."

She gave him a little laugh. "Then you shouldn't have made this place so comfy."

It was a game they played. Each of them changing

the topic when they didn't want to answer a particular question or address an uncomfortable subject. Secrets. They both harbored secrets.

Regina did as well, although he was fairly certain he'd figured out hers. Although she could have others hidden away.

Sipping his scotch, he settled deeper into the chair. He couldn't deny he had comfortable furniture, that his residence was a bright spot, even if on occasion it felt somewhat lonely. As long as he owned it, the hallways would never ring with the laughter of children or a woman's soft murmurings in the dark after he'd made love to her. He'd never bring a paramour here, because the memories of time spent within these walls with Regina had worked their way into the very fabric of the foundation. There were moments when he could swear he still caught a whiff of her fragrance in his bedchamber. Impossible to be sure. Linens were changed daily. Flowers were replaced, their scent strong until they wilted. Furniture was polished. Floors were scrubbed. Nothing of her could possibly remain after all these years.

Yet, he couldn't enter a single room without thoughts of her greeting him. He wondered if Chidding would one day claim the same—if memories of her would encompass his life. Only he wouldn't need to rely on memories because he'd have the reality of her. Her presence. Her passion. And perhaps even her love.

If Knight hadn't irrevocably shattered her heart when he'd demonstrated a callous disregard he'd not felt. He'd hoped to make her angry enough, to fuel a hatred for him that would allow her to survive the devastating pain of betrayal he'd been forced to inflict upon her.

"Are you Lord K?"

With his thoughts traversing along a path that brought Regina to the fore of his mind, he'd forgotten his mother was there. How often had he caught her staring off into the void—or what he'd believed to be the void? It occurred to him now that perhaps she'd simply been examining a kaleidoscope of memories, a journey that had brought her more happiness than her actual world. Her question, however, sent his reflections scattering like leaves caught up in a gust of wind. "What the devil do you know of Lord K?"

"I might not be making the rounds through Society, but I do keep up with it through the various gossip sheets and newspapers. Why just the other day, someone in a gossip column wrote, 'Those who have known him intimately say it can be no other than the Earl of Knightly.' The piece went on to say you were quite a notorious flirt some years back, known for breaking hearts. Your reputation makes it difficult to identify the author apparently. Then there's the book, of course."

"What of the book?"

"I started reading it and was quite enamored as I do enjoy a good love story, but *the* gentleman began to remind me far too much of you in appearance and behavior, so I set it aside, deciding ignorance of the details might be bliss. This Anonymous. Is she a former . . . paramour?"

"How did you even obtain a copy?"

"I have a standing order with a nearby bookshop to put aside anything new that I might fancy. I so love to escape into a book. I missed reading while I was away."

Away. Her euphemism for the twenty years when his father had seen her disappeared from his life, Society, the world.

"So, are you?" she repeated.

He wanted to deny it but the last thing he desired was for his mother to read the remainder of the book. The very thought made him want to squirm. He didn't expect her to believe him a eunuch, but for God's sake, she didn't need to know the details of him seducing a woman. "It was years ago, when I was young and foolish."

"Did you love her?"

With all my heart. With all that I was at the time. What a lie. He loved her still. Because of the way she faced him, making it clear she cared nothing at all for him anymore. Because Society might think the circumstances of her birth made her beneath them, but she didn't accept it. She went to their gaming hell and took their blunt. She didn't shy away from attending their balls. Her father was no longer there to offer her protection, but she'd learned to stand on her own two feet. To know what she wanted and to go after it.

What she wanted was to provide her daughter with a life far different from hers as a child, and she would do whatever necessary to ensure the lass was accepted. He may love her most of all for that care, for her ability to understand the veracity of a situation and to go about changing it because the alternative was unacceptable.

"It was a long time ago," he reiterated, rather than respond truthfully.

"That's not an answer, Arthur."

"I have no answer that would satisfy." *You or me.*

"I read enough of the tale to know she did not conform to Society's expectations regarding the sort of woman a lord should marry."

He couldn't stop a corner of his mouth from curling up. "No, she did not conform."

"Would you have married her if you weren't the heir?"

Yes, gladly.

But then his mother would have paid the steep price because if Knight hadn't been the heir, his father never would have offered him a devil's bargain.

CHAPTER 8

He cupped my cheek with his warm hand. He'd removed
his gloves, in anticipation of touching me, I suppose. Even
the surrounding darkness could not prevent our gazes
from clashing. I wondered if within mine, he could read
the temptation to give in to my desires.
—Anonymous, *My Secret Desires, A Memoir*

June 15, 1875

STANDING in the garden, Regina couldn't help but
smile at Arianna's excitement as the hour of her party
approached, although it did sadden Regina that other
than herself, Ari's guests—currently being arranged
by her daughter on chairs at the smallest of tables
in the garden—were an assortment of dolls. She felt
guilty for keeping the lass hidden away, but presently
it was for Arianna's own protection, because Regina
didn't want her to publicly carry the burden of being
born out of wedlock.

And she would until Regina took to husband a man
who would treat her as though she was his own flesh

and blood, would stare down anyone who arched a brow at her, would call out anyone who uttered an unkind word. Who would ensure she was educated in the best schools, invited to affairs where she would frolic with his contemporaries' children, and accepted by Society so she was fawned over, not for her dowry, but for herself. *As I had not been.*

As long as Regina's father had been alive, she'd known he would shield his granddaughter from the harsh reality of her birth, but when he'd passed away, everything had pretty much gone to hell. His heir wanted nothing to do with her and wasn't even aware she had a child. Her options were limited. Move elsewhere and claim to be a widow or stay here and marry.

When Lord Chidding had recently called upon her, she'd viewed him as an answer to her prayers. Although her relief would have no doubt been dashed had he discovered Arianna in the parlor as Knightly had done. She didn't want to admit how right it had looked to come upon him, his long and lean body perched on the floor, alongside her daughter. Wearing his spectacles, no less.

They'd always had the power to twist her stomach into knots. Without them, he was as handsome as sin, but with them perched on his nose, enlarging his blue eyes, he was mesmerizing, a sage who knew all the answers, a wise man who would never be taken for a buffoon. Someone to whom she could bare her soul . . . and her body.

She'd revealed both to him, and he'd taken them with such care and treated them so tenderly that she'd dared to hand over her heart. Without fear of rejection or being made to look the fool. He'd filled her with the sort of joy designed to make her feel she would simply float through the remainder of her life without troubles or worries—until he'd burst the bubble of her happiness and she'd crashed back to reality, bruised and broken.

The wounds had managed to heal until he'd danced with her at that damnable ball. She'd felt the remnants of the injuries striking again, but they'd hurt even more than when freshly inflicted because they'd been accompanied by an intense yearning to have him in her life once more.

Had he been correct? Had she written the book to entice him from the periphery of her existence back into the center of it?

No, she didn't want him there. Even if being swept over the floor by him had been like rushing through a roaring fire, while waltzing with Chidding had been like walking through cool ashes. Chidding was not exciting. He'd never set her heart to thundering. But he was reliable. He'd come to her aid, concerned she might need him after being with Knightly. He'd spoken kindly and with deference. Later, he had claimed his last dance and his gaze had never left her. Appreciation, respect, duty. He offered all three. He would be—

"You came!" Ari suddenly shouted, catapulting Regina from her thoughts.

Her daughter rushed off, and Regina swung around to follow her but came to a bracing stop, rooted to the spot, unable to go any farther because the *you* in question was a *you* she didn't want to encounter.

Knightly. One hand holding the handles of a small, closed wicker basket.

His strides were long and confident, but he came to a halt just as Arianna reached him, wrapped her arms around one of his legs, and gazed up at him adoringly. Regina had forgotten how easily he could charm any female. "What the devil are you doing here?" she asked smartly.

He had the audacity to bestow upon her one of those devastating smiles while reaching with his free hand into his coat before extending a slip of paper toward her. "I was given an invitation."

She didn't have to grab it from him in order to view Ari's familiar scrawl and swirls. When she didn't take it, he tucked it away and looked down at her child as though she was comprised of the moon and stars. "I have something for you."

He lowered himself to one knee, a knight paying homage, which was exactly what she'd thought when he'd done the same for her before asking her to honor him by becoming his wife. The memory had her sucking in her breath. The warmth and hope in his eyes. The love—or what she'd mistaken for love—with which he'd watched her had convinced her that happily-ever-afters occurred outside of fairy tales.

Clapping while dancing on her toes, Ari asked, "What is it?"

He folded down the handles and tapped the wooden top. "Open it and see."

But Regina didn't need for it to be opened to hear the scratching or light whining. She wanted to snatch the basket away, knew it would make her daughter fall in love with him as easily as her mother had, but she didn't have it within her to deny her child this small measure of happiness when only a few minutes earlier she'd been lamenting the absence of any guests with the ability to move themselves around.

Her throat clogging with unshed tears, she watched as Ari's tiny fingers took hold of the lid and slowly, carefully lifted it. Then a black nose, large black eyes, and brown fur were poking out. Ari's eyes widened with her delight as Knightly took hold of the lid and dropped it all the way back. "A dog!" She looked at her guest. "Who does it belong to?"

"You, moppet. Happy birthday."

Ari jerked her head around to look at Regina. "Mum?"

A thousand questions were encapsulated in that one word that ended on an unsure note. "It's a gift, Ari. It's all right to accept it but do thank the gentleman."

"Thank you," she gushed as she reached in, gathered the wriggling puppy—based on its small size it couldn't have been more than a few weeks old—into her arms, and lifted him free of his prison.

Regina wished she could as easily free her daughter from hers.

Ari dropped to the ground, released her hold on the spaniel, and giggled as it pounced on her. "What's his name?"

"It's a girl," Knightly said.

"How *do* you know?"

"Yes," Regina stated succinctly. Perhaps she could make him blush like Chidding after all. "How do you know?"

But then, of course, anything associated with sex or bodies wasn't going to make the notorious Lord Knightly blush. He merely flashed an all-knowing grin, the bugger. "She told me as we journeyed here. We spoke of all manner of things. Her name can be whatever you want it to be, sweetheart."

She wanted to scold him for using that endearment with her daughter, and yet it was innocent enough, even if it brought pain in ways it shouldn't, a reminder of all the times when Ari would not hear her father gifting her with special names.

Ari looked up at her. "Mum?"

"We'll discuss it while we're eating your cake."

She kept her gaze focused on her daughter, but out of the corner of her eye she sighted Knightly unfolding that magnificent body of his. She'd gone too long without a man's intimate touch. Until that moment she hadn't realized how much she needed another fellow to serve as a deterrent to wanting Knightly.

He approached, his wonderful sandalwood fragrance wafting around her. "You can hire someone to care for the dog. I'll pay for it."

"No need. We'll use it as an exercise in learning the importance of responsibility."

"A lesson you no doubt think I never learned."

"You obviously hadn't learned it five years ago."

"How long before we leave the past behind us?"

She raised a slender shoulder, dropped it. "Oh, a hundred years or so."

He chuckled darkly, as though he'd expected no other response from her. "Can we not at least call a truce for today . . . for her sake?"

"I can't believe you came. She's nothing to you," she whispered harshly.

"She's something to you."

"God." She buried her face in her hands, moved her palms up, and pressed the pads at the base of her thumbs to her temples. "Your smooth words no longer have an effect on me. Don't you dare hurt or take advantage of her, Knightly, else I shall see you destroyed."

Her words carried utter conviction, and he didn't seem surprised by them either. "Was I to ignore her summons? Would a rebuff not have caused her harm?"

"She's only four. I doubt she even remembers inviting you."

"How could I be sure? Better to err on the side of caution, don't you think?"

She didn't know what to think. Except that her daughter appeared remarkably happy playing with a bundle of fur. Regina had wanted to put off getting her a dog until they were situated with a secure future—just in case whomever she took to husband wasn't fond of pets. But as it would no doubt be her dowry responsible for causing him to propose, she supposed she could have a say in whatever menagerie accompanied them to their new home. And if they happened to reside here, well, Regina would certainly reign over the household and all its occupants—furry and not—then.

"You should have checked with me before bringing that creature," she scolded.

"You'd have said no." He leaned toward her, mirth dancing in his eyes. "She'd already told me she had to wait until she was six."

"I'll not have you being a bad influence upon her."

"What about upon you? Could I be a bad influence upon you?"

"Your days of having any influence upon me are behind us."

"Is that a challenge?"

"If it were, are you cruel enough to accept it?" She knew the answer before she'd asked the question. Or at least she'd once known the answer. The man she'd previously assumed him to be, the one with whom she'd fallen so desperately and maddeningly in love, had not shown a scintilla of cruelty—until the morning they were to wed. Why then? How had she so vastly misjudged him?

His jaw taut, he looked at her daughter gathering grass stains upon her skirts, the ribbon holding her hair back loosening as she tumbled about with the rambunctious pup. "No," he said quietly, but it was as though the word traveled through the distance of years to reach her.

CHAPTER 9

June 1870

It was not in his nature to be cruel, and yet he'd been given no choice except to be.

Staring at the entrance to the church, Knight thought that with enough time, perhaps he could have determined another way out of this diabolical situation in which he'd been placed. But time didn't favor him.

In only a few minutes he was to exchange vows and take a wife.

But she deserved better than what he could now offer her. And she most certainly didn't deserve the heartbreak he was going to inflict upon her. But, again, he'd been given no choice.

He couldn't ask her to give up legitimacy and respectability. Not when she'd already lived twenty-two years without either. He couldn't ask her to sacrifice everything she desired and deserved, everything he could no longer give her.

He'd always surmised with enough coins in his coffers he would obtain complete freedom from his father's influence—and yet the vile creature all of

London knew to have sired him was more odious than Knight had ever given him credit for being. Over the years, he'd made excuses for him. It couldn't have been easy to lose his firstborn son. But now he understood the man possessed a depth of brutality that was unconscionable. One Knight possessed no weapons to conquer. He was a solitary figure standing on a battlefield, caught in a war he'd been too distracted to comprehend was coming.

A war that would take an innocent if he stood his ground, would take an innocent if he retreated. He'd been commanded to choose which to leave on the field bloodied.

An impossible choice.

Yet, he'd made the decision at once, demanded the duke go straight to hell as he had an appointment to keep. In an almost blind rage, he'd made his way to his carriage. But as the wheels had spun and the horses had clopped, remorse, regret, and guilt had settled over him. By the time he'd arrived at his destination, he'd known he had to reverse his stance in order to live with himself. He also knew if he didn't, any happiness that greeted him in the years ahead would be tainted and lacking in true joy. How could he subject his wife to a lifetime with someone suffering through a penitence?

He had to set Regina free without telling her precisely the reason for it. Holding his tongue was the only way to protect her. The duke had made that clear enough. He knew no words to utter that would ease the devastation he was about to inflict upon her.

Although perhaps he'd misjudged her feelings.

Christ, but he hoped he had. That she wanted him only for the position he would grant her within Society. Still, she'd be hurt, angry, and mortified. He couldn't lessen the blow but could ensure he took the brunt of it.

After taking a deep breath, he marched up the steps, pushed open the door, and entered the vestibule.

"You're late," King said in a harsh whisper that still managed to echo somewhat through the antechamber.

He turned to find his best mates standing there, brows furrowed.

"What kept you?" King asked.

"I'm not going to marry her."

King, usually so in control of his emotions, gaped. "Little late for that. The church is packed to the rafters."

Of course it was. Everyone having arrived early enough to get a good seat. It wasn't every day a lord married a woman born on the wrong side of the blanket. He wondered if they'd come hoping to behold a debacle in the same manner that people gathered around to watch someone walking across a tightrope, not really to be amazed by the skill but anticipating watching the blighter fall. He despised the thought that they were here in hopes of seeing her fail—

And he was on the verge of giving them precisely what they'd come to witness.

"Why the change of heart?" Rook asked.

His heart hadn't changed, even as he could presently feel it growing cold and brittle. What of her heart? Would it shatter into a thousand shards? Who would piece it back together? Surely, someday someone would. And that man would be the luckiest on earth, and Knight already despised him with every ounce of his being, even as he was grateful the man would have the power to bring her joy. "I came to the conclusion we wouldn't suit, at least not for the long term."

"Yet you are dressed in your wedding finery, as though you intended to carry through on the matter." Damn Rook for noticing. "Hence, the decision had to have been made on the way here."

True enough, but Knight kept silent, his jaw aching from the clenching of it necessary to hold back the truth.

"You're not prone to cowardice, but could you be experiencing simply a sane man's hesitancy at losing his freedom? A hesitancy that will pass when you catch sight of the lady walking up the aisle?"

"My mind is set. If you'll excuse me, I need to have a word with her."

He headed down the vestibule, rounded a corner into a hallway, and slammed to a complete stop at the sight of her standing outside of a door, talking in a low voice with her father. He didn't know where her maids of honor were. They were apparently girls with whom she'd gone to school. She wasn't close to any of them. Perhaps they were off somewhere tittering about their chances of landing a lord. Not that he cared; the fewer witnesses the better.

She must have sensed his presence because she turned her head and delivered a brilliant smile capable of possibly melting his father's rock-hard heart. Her eyes were filled with warmth and mirth. "It's bad luck to see me before I enter the sanctuary."

He was going to lay at her feet the worst, rottenest luck of all.

"What the devil are you doing, Knightly?" her father asked. "You should be at the altar. It's time we got on with this matter."

Everything within him screamed to spin about on his heel, grab his friends, and get to the altar. "Can you give me a moment alone with Regina?"

The earl glared at him, but his eyes softened when he glanced at her, and she nodded. Of course she'd agree. She was expecting a final declaration of love, a private vow, perhaps even a gift to demonstrate the depths of his feelings for her. Instead, he was going to destroy her, and how in the hell was he to live with that knowledge?

"Make it quick," her father commanded before striding off and disappearing around the blasted corner that seemed to be a demarcation of his life. The before-he-destroyed-her moments and the after-he-destroyed-her moments. Knight very much doubted he'd ever again set foot in this church, in any church for that matter.

Her lips quirked. "Couldn't stand to go so long without seeing me? It's been only a few hours."

Since he'd slipped from her bedchamber after making love to her in sin for what he'd thought would be the final time. When next they came together, it was to be within the boundaries of the law as man and wife.

He took several steps until he was near enough to

draw her into the circle of his arms, inhale her fragrance, and simply hold her, this woman who was so incredibly precious to him. And it was because of those feelings that he had to rip them asunder.

"Arthur?" Her voice was laced with worry. "What is it? What's wrong?"

He slipped a forefinger beneath her chin, tilted up her face, and pressed a kiss to her forehead. Then, after releasing his hold on her, he stepped back. "I can't marry you."

A tiny pleat appeared between her brows. She blinked. Blinked. "Pardon?"

Pushing the words out once had been difficult enough, but to do it again . . .

Christ, he wished he'd had time to devise an elegant exit from this mess. He was a planner, never acting in haste. Every action thought out, but he was too numb by what he'd learned and the pain he was causing her to truly think at all. "I can't marry."

Not only you, but anyone. However, he wasn't going to tell her all that because she'd want to know everything, and *everything* had to go to the grave with him. Nor did he want to burden her with his own struggles.

"I don't understand. Whyever not?"

Tell her the truth. The truth. The truth. But the shock of it was still rumbling through him, tearing apart the very fabric of his being, like an earthquake that was rapidly destroying all in its wake, leaving behind gaping holes into which souls fell, never to be seen again. He was not who he'd always thought himself to be. He was not *what* he'd always thought himself to be. The revelations had left him floundering, tossed about in a raging tempest at sea with no hope of reaching the safety of land.

The one solid aspect of his life . . . he was having to shove beyond reach, because if he grabbed her, she would drown as well. The marriage she dreamed of would not be. Not filled with happiness and joy. He could already sense the bitterness moving in to inhabit his soul. And the children she wanted could never be. Not if she remained with him.

He wanted to be gentle with her. He wanted to be kind. But he needed to destroy all hope. Needed her to hate him more than she mourned the loss of him so the fires of her animosity would burn to cinders any remnants of sorrow. He needed her angry if he wished to leave her with a portion of her heart that she could someday give to someone else.

He released a low, dark scoff, the effort nearly strangling him. "I awoke this morning and wondered what the bloody hell I was doing, to shackle myself to one woman for the remainder of my life when there are so many to be had."

The pleat between her brows deepened into a furrow. Another blink. "I don't understand what you're saying. You love me. I love you. Why would either of us ever want to be with another?"

Then he knew what he had to say, the words that would tear her from him forever. "I don't love you. I merely got caught up in the fantasy. You're so beautiful. Certainly deserving of the words. And I liked the way you looked at me after I uttered them. And the things we would do after I said them."

In her expressive eyes, the devastating hurt and

anger burned into an explosive fury. "You couldn't have decided this yesterday? Or last week? Or before you even asked for my hand?"

No tears were welling in her eyes, and he might have taken comfort in that if it weren't for the fact he heard them in her voice. But the answer to her question was a resounding no because the duke he'd spent his early years striving to please had waited until he knew he'd inflict the most damage to his son's reputation—with no care at all for the agony and humiliation he'd cause this lovely woman who was deserving of none of this—to reveal the truth of the matter and offer his damnable bargain. A bargain Knight had originally tossed in his face and now would have to humble himself to accept. But what choice did he have really?

"You can't be surprised. You once claimed to know my reputation for loving and leaving."

The sting of his cheek as her palm met it shouldn't have taken him by surprise, and yet it did. But more, the blow had been effectively delivered to his heart as well. He wished she'd smack him again, wouldn't stand there so stoic and proud and determined not to let him see the agony, but it was there, mirrored in the brown depths of her eyes. The disbelief, the fury, and yes, even the hatred. He'd never felt more despicable or disgusted with himself. No doubt another reason the duke had waited until the last minute to pay his heir a visit—to give him reason to loathe himself as the duke loathed him.

Tears were suddenly pooling in her eyes, and while he'd hoped to be spared the sight of them, he knew he deserved to see them, to have them haunting him for the remainder of his days.

"I hate you," she rasped as she turned away from him. "I never want to set eyes on your face again."

Of course she wasn't going to beg him to marry her. It wasn't her way. Proud girl.

"I'll give your father time to escort you away from here. Then I'll go out and announce to those who've gathered in the church that you changed your mind," he said.

"So they'll despise me for spurning one of their own?" She was studying her fingers, knotted together, and he suspected she'd intertwined them to stop from striking him again.

"I'll make it clear the fault rests with me. That you came to the conclusion, rightly so, I would not make a good husband."

She glanced over her shoulder. "How could I have judged you so erroneously? The man standing before me now is not the same one who was in my bedchamber only a few hours ago. Was it a performance from the beginning? For what purpose? To humiliate me . . . and my father?"

"No . . . I . . . you wouldn't be happy with me, Reggie, not in the long run. Believe it or not, someday you'll look back on this moment and be grateful you didn't take that walk up the aisle with me."

"I shall never look back upon this day . . . or think of you. You are dead to me."

CHAPTER 10

❧

I had never wanted as I wanted now, his hand resting
against more than my cheek, but gliding over other areas,
causing little eruptions of pleasure wherever he touched.
—Anonymous, *My Secret Desires, A Memoir*

June 15, 1875

He'd come because he hadn't wanted to disappoint the child. Not as he'd once disappointed her mother. Regina's father had been furious, justifiably so, when Knight had instructed him to take her away from the church before he announced to the gathering that no marriage was to take place. The earl's fist had landed against Knight's jaw with a force he'd not expected of the older gent. He'd wanted an explanation that Knight had refused to give. Her father had threatened to ruin him, to ensure no father gave him permission to wed their daughter. Knight had been more than willing to give him that victory.

He imagined, if her father were still alive, he'd object to Knight's presence here today as much as Regina did. But ever since the little sprite had handed him the invitation, he must have glanced at it a dozen times and traced his fingers over the intricate loops. Now standing beside her mother, he could barely take his gaze from the girl as she played with his gift.

"How did things go with Chidding after I left?" he asked, striving to retain a neutrality in his tone he absolutely did not feel. If it hadn't gone well, he'd bear the brunt of disappointment. If it had gone well, the answer would slice into his heart as effectively as a cat-o'-nine tails.

"Well. We waltzed. He brought me a lemonade. To be honest, he barely left my side until the final dance."

"Laying claim to you, then. He didn't do that before we danced."

"Are you taking credit?"

He fought against smiling at her incredulous tone. Since he'd sat at the table that night at the Dragons, getting a rise out of her was fast becoming his favorite thing to do. He'd always thought her worthy of sitting at the side of any lord, but now it was a matter of only a few being worthy of sitting at her side. He shifted his gaze over to her. When her hackles were raised, she was a gorgeous sight to behold—but then she was under any circumstance. "When will you see him next?"

It was difficult to tell if she was piqued because he'd ignored her question to ask one of his own, but she'd pursed her lips, obviously not wanting to answer.

"Nothing formal has been arranged," she finally responded.

"Mmm."

"What does that little condescending groan of disapproval mean?" she asked tartly.

"I'm simply surprised he didn't arrange for you to be in each other's company. At the park or a museum. Or a ride over your grounds. Do you still do that in the mornings?"

On more than one occasion he'd been waiting for her beyond sight of the manor, and they'd raced over the meadows and through the forests.

"I don't think he's much of a horseman."

"What about your daughter? Does she ride?"

"Not yet. But she will."

"Does she have a pony?"

"Is there one in your basket?"

Grinning, he wondered if she might ever address him without a cutting edge lacing her words, her tone. Yet, he couldn't help but admire the strength she projected. He'd once thought her in desperate need of protecting, but the woman standing before him now protected herself—and all she held dear.

Which obviously was no longer him. The sense of loss that washed over him threatened to take him under. He'd thought he'd known the price he was paying. What he hadn't considered was the value that years added to a masterpiece. She was precisely that. Rare and remarkable.

"I know a horse breeder who is skilled at matching equines with the appropriate rider. When you're ready for her to have a mount, I'd be happy to provide one for her through him."

"Just because she gave you an invitation, don't think you'll be remaining in her life."

"Once you are wed, I suspect you—and she—will never see me again." It would be too painful to watch another man enjoying the fruits of a family Knight so desperately longed for and would forever deny himself.

REGINA REFUSED TO be charmed by the sight of Knightly sitting on the tiny chair, his legs splayed so he was within easy reach of his platter and glass, his knees nearly touching his chest. She'd taken great delight in the horror crossing his features when a footman had brought out the cake and set it upon the miniature table and Knightly had realized they'd be celebrating Ari's birthday with the dolls.

"Did your invitation not mention the dining arrangements?" she'd asked smugly.

"I somehow overlooked that particular detail."

He had, however, been incredibly gracious when her daughter had pointed out that he was to sit in the chair beside her. Because of his cordiality she'd ordered a footman to "fetch his lordship a glass of scotch."

"So you've agreed to a truce," Knightly had murmured, leaning forward to where she sat across from him.

"For an hour."

Ari had introduced him to her dolls, and he had assured each one that he was pleased to make her acquaintance. Regina was left with the resounding conviction he would make a wonderful father, and that perhaps she should have had Chidding on hand to compare them. But such a contest would serve only to leave her discontent with a choice that must be made.

She needed a man upon whom she could rely, not one who even now still possessed the power to make her yearn for his touch, his scent, his kiss.

The pup, no doubt striving to recover from the earlier exuberant play, slept at Ari's feet. She'd fair worn her out, although she still maintained an abundance of energy. "Sir, what should we name her?" she asked, just before shoving cake into her mouth.

While she hated to do it, Regina knew it was never too early to begin teaching manners and etiquette. "Ari, you should address him as *my lord* rather than *sir*. He's an earl, you see."

"What's an earl?"

"It's a rank within the nobility."

"What's nobility?"

"It's . . .." *Something you should not have been denied.*

"I give you permission to call me Knight," her guest said.

"Knightly—"

"She's four, Regina. And she invited me to her party, so we're friends. It's acceptable. Unless you want to spend the afternoon explaining the peerage."

She sighed. The man always complicated matters. "We'll make an exception for the day."

"Very good. Regarding the name for your pup, whatever you like."

She was not going to weep at the way Knightly placed an elbow on his firm thigh and bent toward her daughter so they could discuss and discard various names, as though Regina had no say in the matter. It didn't help the situation that from the moment she'd realized she was with child, she'd only ever been able to envision Knightly cradling the babe in his strong arms, offering his protection . . . and love. She'd have moments of despising him followed by hours of thinking no one else would ever treat her daughter as well. Chidding would. Certainly. Had she ever asked him about children? He would no doubt want her to deliver to him an heir and a spare. But surely the kindness he'd bestowed upon her thus far, in spite of her lack of proper parentage, was an indication of his benevolence toward all creatures.

"Princess!" Ari shouted.

With a start, Regina glanced around wildly. With Knightly's appearance, she most certainly wouldn't be surprised to find someone from a royal household had also arrived. "Where?"

Ari laughed delightedly. "The puppy. We're gonna call her Princess."

Regina clapped a hand against her breast, to stop her heart from striving to push through her ribs. Then she chuckled low. With this child, there was never a dull moment. "Oh, the dog."

The dog that had awoken and was now licking cake off Ari's fingers. "Do you like it?" Ari asked hopefully.

"Your grandfather used to call me his princess." Reaching out, she tweaked her daughter's nose. "You probably don't remember but he called you that as well." Just as her father had made her a princess in a tower, so she was doing the same for her daughter. But only for a short time, and then they would climb out of the tower together. "I like it very much."

"It was his idea." She pointed at Knightly. He appeared neither smug nor haughty, but rather subdued. Odd when he'd obviously won the naming game, and he was very fond of winning. But in some strange way, he almost looked as though he'd lost.

"Of course it was. Splendid name." She gave her head a little bow. "Well done."

"A compliment. I like this truce," he said.

"Don't get used to it."

"What's a truce?" Ari asked.

Regina smiled fondly as she tugged on one of her daughter's earlobes. "Little ears hear everything, don't they? And little girls need an afternoon nap."

"Can he nap with me?" Once more, she directed her tiny finger Knightly's way.

He seemed as surprised by the request as she was. "Absolutely not." Before her daughter could object and cause a row, she added, "But the puppy can."

Regina looked past Ari to where the nanny waited patiently, having arrived only a few minutes earlier. "Have a footman assist you with Princess. Perhaps she can sleep in the basket." She turned her attention to Ari. "Now, come give me a hug."

Her daughter did, and Regina gloried in the small arms tightening around her neck. Nothing was more magnificent. When she was finished, Ari ran around to the other side of the table and flung her arms around Knightly's neck. "I love you," she declared.

His look was one of pure devastation as his arm came around her, holding her close. "I love you, too, moppet," he rasped, and Regina hated him all the more at that moment for the ease with which he could speak words he didn't mean.

She wanted to reach across the table and free her daughter from him. Wished she could be completely rid of him. Marriage. He'd said once she was married, he'd be gone from her life permanently. She needed Chidding, desperately, now more than ever, because she couldn't have this man near her daughter. Because one day he would disappoint her, hurt her.

She didn't know what expression marred her face, probably loathing, because the nanny came over and eased her charge away from their guest. "Come along, little one. Let's show this puppy all the joys of the nursery."

"Oh, yes! Let's!"

Any other time, Arianna might have balked at a nap, but now she had someone with whom to share it. As she went with Nanny, she was chattering away, whether to the woman or the dog, Regina couldn't be sure, but she held still, unmoving, until her daughter was in the residence and then she shoved herself to her feet. "The party and the truce are over. Get the hell out of my sight."

Slowly, so very slowly, he stood. "Go for a ride with me."

She wanted to shriek to the heavens. "Can you not get it through that thick skull of yours that I want nothing to do with you?"

"But you do want Chidding. We need to strategize, speed up the tortoise."

She laughed, almost maniacally. "Are you not familiar

with Aesop? Slow and steady wins the race. You were the hare and you lost. Don't ever come here again."

She spun on her heel and began marching toward the residence.

"Was she a difficult birth?"

Having taken only a half dozen steps, she swung back around. He'd not moved from his spot. "Why do you care?"

"I can't stop thinking about you being alone. I want to put my fist through her father's face, for how hard his absence must have made everything for you."

Damn him, for the true remorse she heard in his voice, the anger, the understanding of what she might have endured. "I assume you rode here."

"I did."

"Shakespeare?"

He gave a small nod.

"I'll need to change. Meet me at the stables."

If he'd grinned with triumph or gloated, she'd have gone to the residence, locked herself in the library, and buried herself in a book, leaving him to wait hours for her. Instead, he merely said a quiet "Thank you," and walked away.

HE'D HAD HER horse readied and waiting by the time she'd joined him at the stables. While he'd known she'd probably hate it, he'd ensured the grooms were nowhere about, so he had the privilege of placing his hands on her waist and lifting her onto the saddle, even knowing she would take advantage and send her horse into a gallop before he himself was mounted.

He hadn't wanted to hoist her up. Instead, he'd

wanted to draw her nearer. But he'd given up the right
to those lips, her throat, her murmurs, and her sighs.
However, he had taken his time, raising her slowly,
relishing the feel of her waist against his palms.

Now they raced over the open fields and through
the occasional copse of trees. If he put more effort into
it, he could probably beat her, but he wasn't quite himself, not since her daughter had uttered *I love you* with
such uncompromising conviction. The words coming
from her had undone him to his very core.

He had planned to leave as soon as the party was
over. Party. It had been no such thing. A party was
jubilation, crowds, friends, and family gathered about
in celebration. Not dolls with lifeless eyes. Not her
mother only.

Her mother. A fierce goddess, a warrior, a queen.
Who had threatened him with destruction if he
harmed her precious child, and her tone had left him
with no doubt she would indeed keep her vow. Not that
he had any intention of hurting the girl. Quite the opposite. He wanted to protect her as much as he wanted
to protect her mother. Even if the woman needed no
guardian.

And was in danger of outdistancing him by a
great deal.

Turning his attention to the matter at hand, he urged
Shakespeare to increase his speed, and the gelding
didn't disappoint. Knight had always enjoyed these
races against Regina. She was a fine horsewoman
and provided competition. Normally their encounters
ended in a draw, but this afternoon, she was going to
win. Even if he hadn't been initially distracted with

thoughts of her daughter, he could tell by the manner in which she rode she was determined to best him.

REGINA DIDN'T KNOW if she'd ever ridden so hard in her entire life. She needed to escape the feel of Knightly's hands closing around her waist before he lifted her onto the saddle. The wondrous sensation of her hands cupping his strong shoulders for support just as her feet left the ground.

Slowing, she guided her mare to the left, toward an area where the trees grew thick, nourished by the waters of the nearby stream. She shouldn't lead Knightly there, and yet it seemed to be calling to her. Or the memory anyway. A night when a full moon had reflected on the dark waters, and then the moonbeams had encompassed them as they swam naked.

When the stream came into view, she drew her horse to a halt and waited. Until he arrived, dismounted, and came to her. Once more his hands were upon her waist and hers upon his shoulders. Slowly, so very slowly, as though he possessed the strength and power to extend the moment into an eon, he lowered her down. They stared at each other, their breaths coming quickly from the exertion of riding. And quite possibly something more.

"Reggie—"

She broke free of his clasp and walked to the water's edge. He joined her there, to stare at the flowing stream. Somewhere birds tittered. A couple of robins seemed to be arguing. She didn't want to consider that perhaps they were mated, that they'd once loved and filled a nest with eggs and were now at discord.

Squirrels chatted. A fish splashed. Life carried on, even when she was in turmoil, hating and loving at the same time. She dared to shift her view slightly until she could appreciate the cut of his profile. Smooth lines, but bold.

"It wasn't difficult," she finally said quietly.

Slowly, he turned his head toward her as though fearful if he moved too fast, she might stop speaking.

"The birth," she clarified. "It wasn't difficult. I don't think. My experience is somewhat limited. Certainly, I couldn't mistake it for being on a picnic, but when I held her . . . I would do it all again."

His gaze was intense as he studied her, and an emotion she couldn't read resided within the blue depths. "I'm sorry you went through it alone, more than I can ever express."

"My maid, Millie, was with me. And I had a midwife."

"Still, her father should have been there to care for you."

She offered him a wry smile. "Men have avoided the birthing bed since the dawn of time."

He dipped his head slightly, his lips twitching. "I didn't mean quite that near."

She released a small laugh, then abruptly cut it off. She wasn't going to allow him to lighten her heart or charm her. "I noted your surprise when Ari gushed her love for you, but you should know she tells everyone she loves them. It's a child's openness and acceptance, I think."

"Would that adults were the same."

"I wish I could spare her some of life's lessons that will serve only to make her less exuberant. But a parent can't shield her child from all hurt . . . and that knowledge pains me immeasurably."

"I can't even imagine." He cleared his throat. "I don't know much about young children, but your daughter seems particularly astute for all of her four years."

"She is incredibly smart . . . much like her father."

"I didn't think you knew who he was."

She knew exactly who he was, because he was the only man with whom she'd ever been intimate. "I'm not in the habit of taking stupid men to my bed."

That muscle in his jaw fairly throbbed. She should have found satisfaction in raising his ire, in making him believe there had been others. In perhaps causing jealousy. No, not jealousy. If he felt that at all, he wouldn't be striving to marry her off to Chidding. Although perhaps he experienced a bit of envy.

"Only those four?" he finally bit out.

He *was* jealous. Could he be if he didn't hold feelings for her? His attempt to marry her off made absolutely no sense. But then neither had his actions on the morning they were to wed.

"The number isn't really your concern. I don't ask how many women you've bedded."

He released a long, slow breath that she was surprised to find wasn't comprised of flames of anger.

"You're different," she said hesitantly.

He arched a dark brow.

"From how you were before. You're more serious. I sense no joy in you."

Looking back toward the stream, he sighed. "I suppose maturity does that to a man."

It wasn't the years or the aging. She didn't know what exactly it was. What she did know was that the man standing beside her now was not the one who'd snuck into her bedchamber through the window the night before he was to take her to wife. Who'd whispered naughty things in her ear and promised her a lifetime of happiness.

"Which ball will you be attending next?" he asked.

"None. I've received no invitations."

He swung around then to face her fully, his face a mask of near rage. "Damn the snobbery of the aristocracy."

Good Lord, was he, of all people, defending her? After what he'd done, the irony of it took her aback, but she was weary of striving to determine the truth of that long-ago morning, so she refrained from pointing out his own guilty behavior. "With my father gone, I have few to speak out in my defense."

His scowl was likely to deepen the creases that had already begun making a home in his features. She wondered at the burdens that had formed them originally, hated being curious regarding all that had transpired within his life since their encounter at the church. "I'll ensure you begin receiving invitations."

"My father's son has seen to it that I don't."

The smile he bestowed upon her was naught but arrogance and confidence. "Bremsford is no match for me, Reggie."

Few men were, certainly none she knew personally. Not even Chidding, but then he would never be forced to battle it out with Knightly. She and he would no doubt live a quiet, peaceful existence. She longed for the dull and mundane. "You confound me. I can't determine why you care."

"Would you believe me if I told you I never stopped caring? That all I want, all I ever wanted, was your happiness?"

"You have a damned atrocious way of demonstrating that."

Reaching out with one hand, he cradled her cheek against his palm. She should pull away; yet late-afternoon shadows had fallen to blanket them in the sort of intimacy that called to lovers. Even if they were no longer so defined, once they had been. Once she had been desperate for any hint of a shadow where they could take refuge to experience what they were not allowed to display in the light. Therefore, she remained as she was, with her chest working like a blacksmith's bellows, straining to take in and release the very oxygen it required to do its job.

"For five years, I fought to forget every moment spent in your company," he said, his voice low, an intimate caress. "I very nearly succeeded, and then you published that damned book, and while the various true aspects of it are not as I exactly remembered, some are familiar enough to stir back to life what I thought I had finally put to rest. And they were all written with such passion."

His thumb dropped down to skim over her lower lip. "Do you know I've not kissed a single woman since you?"

His intense gaze held her mesmerized, until she doubted she could have pulled away if she wanted. Damn him. Chidding would never look at her with naught but hunger and need. Damn her because she would never respond to his perusal with ravenous desire. It had been a mistake to put herself in a position to be alone with Knightly, to believe her body would not react in the manner he had taught it. Even now she was aware of the dampness gathering between her thighs in anticipation of what he would deliver.

"Bollocks," she forced out. "I don't believe you've been celibate all these years."

"You're right. I'm no saint. I didn't say I hadn't bedded a woman. I confessed to not kissing one. Because I knew none would taste as flavorful as you. Because kissing you had become one of my greatest joys, and I knew no other could ever compare."

She'd not forgotten how his seduction always began with words but had mistakenly believed she'd become immune to their mesmerizing sway. Instead, she was incredibly aware of them sparking a fire within her, a fire only he possessed the power to douse. She hated the temptation threatening to undermine her resolve to resist his allure.

"Did you kiss your Spaniard?" he asked.

"Yes."

"Your Italian?" His voice went an octave lower.

"Yes." Her response was slightly more breathy.

"Your Parisian?" Lower still.

"Yes." Breathier.

"Your German?" Hardly audible.

"Yes." All breath.

He dipped his head a minuscule fraction. "Then end my torment, my abstinence, and kiss *me*. For old times' sake. Afterall, a kiss is only a kiss."

With him, a kiss had never been *only* anything.
"You're a fool if you think it will be as it was before."

"Then prove me a fool." He dared her with a voice
as smooth as silk, as warm as velvet.

Oh, she wasn't half-tempted, to show him exactly
how little he meant to her now. Nothing. Nothing at
all. Not even as much substance as a mote of dust.
Strange, how she sometimes reminisced about their
last kiss, not realizing when it had occurred it would
be their last. It had been a quick brushing of the lips
in parting because in a few hours they'd have been
married and every night thereafter was to be filled
with an abundance of kisses. And every morning as
well. She'd been beside herself with joy and anticipation at the thought of awakening in his arms with the
first rays of the morning sun teasing the day. No more
stealing out of each other's beds in the dead of night,
no more sneaking around desperate not to be seen. No
more feeling guilty for doing what they ought not. For
her sake, perhaps she required a proper ending, a final
goodbye, one filled with loathing, one to demonstrate
when her heart was no longer involved, a kiss was
nothing at all.

Licking her lower lip, where his thumb still lingered, tasting the salt of his flesh, she gave one barely
perceptible nod. But she knew he detected it because
his eyes darkened with promise and passion.

His thumb slid away. He lowered his head and that
damn heavy forelock brushed across her brow, just
before his lips touched hers, gently at first as though
testing the waters. She almost smiled, wondering if
he'd expected her to bite. Then his tongue outlined the

seam of her lips, and her traitorous mouth opened to him. He delved within and she became incapable of smiling or wondering, but only feeling, as he brought back to life all the sensations she'd forced to lie dormant since the day he'd broken her heart.

Of their own accord, her arms twined around his neck, her fingers scraped along his skull, beneath the thick strands of his hair, welcoming their softness as they greeted her after so long. His arm came around her, pressing her against him, and then he proceeded to devour her. His mouth was that of an untamed beast, ravenous and wild. *He* was a beast, growling low, clamping her to him as though to never release her.

While she knew she shouldn't, she seemed incapable of not relishing the urgency with which he partook of their joining. She knew him well enough to sense the tension in him, to be acutely aware of the restraint he wielded—he wanted more, wanted it all. But he limited himself to only what she was offering.

He brought his hand up to cradle her head and tip it back, giving him easier access to plunder, to conquer. Except she was no longer the young innocent to be vanquished. While she had planned to hold completely still and give nothing back and prove she was completely free of him . . . well, that ship had already sailed since she was presently clinging to him like some sort of vine capable of finding purchase over the most challenging of surfaces. Later, she would curse herself for her lack of resistance.

But for now, she determined her best course was simply to make him suffer, to be bolder, more enthusiastic, more daring. To remind him of precisely what he could have had. To make him regret this was indeed their very final kiss.

With a low moan, she clamped his head between her hands and angled it so she could deepen the kiss with a fervor that far outdid his. Their tongues tangled. Then she sucked on his until he released a tortured groan, the rumblings of which she felt traveling through his chest. In spite of all his clothing. She stopped short of removing it, of imagining how five years might have changed his body's contours. He'd certainly not gone to fat during that time. If anything, he felt firmer.

While he tasted of cake, strawberries, and scotch, woven throughout the mixture of sweet and dark was his familiar tantalizing flavor, one to which she'd once been addicted. But then every aspect of him had called to her, had seemed right. Only it had all been a lie.

Breaking off the kiss, she clutched his head to hold it in place while leaning back to see him more clearly. His cerulean eyes were smoldering with need and want. His breaths came in short pants. His arm loosened its hold. His fingers barely touched her cheek now, as though he was awakening from a long laudanum-induced sleep and just beginning to stir.

"In case it missed your notice," she began, grateful her voice didn't betray all the emotions rioting through her, "that was farewell."

Separating herself from him completely, she spun on her heel.

He grabbed her arm. "Reggie—"

She broke free of him and gave him her most haughty glare. "Never touch me again."

She'd deliberately chosen this bend in the stream because many years before a storm had toppled a tree, leaving in its wake a stump that rain and wind had somewhat smoothed. Now she led her horse over to it, stepped onto it, and pulled herself, not as elegantly or gracefully as she would have liked, into the saddle. Without bothering to look at Knightly, she set her horse into a trot.

She'd been wrong. Knowing when the last kiss would be hadn't made anything any better. All it had accomplished was to leave her longing for one more.

CHAPTER 11

*His mouth returned to mine with a fervor and hunger that
stole my breath and probably should have frightened me.
Instead, I welcomed him, knowing it would be impossible
to ever have enough of him.*
—Anonymous, *My Secret Desires, A Memoir*

June 15, 1875

$\mathcal{S}$ITTING at the Twin Dragons while his mates had
carried on a conversation regarding an investment
opportunity with an American firearms manufac-
turer, Knight had been unable to stop contemplating
the time he'd spent that afternoon with Regina. Every
word uttered, every glance, every touch, and then that
damned kiss.

He'd fully expected her not to respond to the kiss,
to rebuke him by not reacting at all. Instead, she'd
poured all she was into it, and by doing so, although
it might not have been her intention, she'd punished
him tenfold by reminding him of what he'd never
again fully possess. He'd been like the character in

her book, willing to do anything Miss Regina Leyland asked of him. What she asked—nay, demanded—was that he never touch her again.

Which he'd never intended to begin with. To ever touch her again. But having done it that afternoon, the thought of never having that particular pleasure for the remainder of his life was pure torment, the pain most assuredly deserved.

"You mentioned you had a favor to ask of me?" King prodded.

Knight glanced over at his friend. When the others had begun to take their leave, he'd asked King to remain behind for a few minutes, and as he'd settled back into place, so Knight's thoughts had begun to drift into the occurrences that afternoon instead of remaining transfixed on the reason he'd asked King to stay. He fought to refocus his attention on the matter at hand. "Yes. I'd like you to invite Miss Regina Leyland to your ball."

King released the tiniest huff of disbelief before leaning forward and bracing his forearms on his thighs. "You're no fool, Knight. You must know that particular woman from your past is most likely the one who penned the book that is now on everyone's tongue. I swear, since we were last here, I've not had a single conversation with a solitary person in which that damned tome has not come up and I've not been asked if Lord K is my firm friend Lord Knightly. It's deuced irritating."

"How do you respond to such impertinence?"

"I tell them I haven't a bloody clue." Looking abashedly guilty, he glanced around before leveling his gaze back on Knight. "However, my Penelope managed to obtain a copy—"

"I thought the book had become available only in a shop's secret rooms reserved for pornographic materials."

"My Penelope is exceedingly resourceful. Why do you think she made such a superb secretary? But more importantly, she's been reading it aloud after we've retired to bed." He cleared his throat. "It is quite titillating. That aside, the descriptions of this Lord K—both his physical appearance and mannerisms—it's as though you stepped onto the page in all your arrogant glory."

Knight chuckled low. "Arrogant? Why not merely confident?"

"That as well."

Knight shrugged. "The author could be a lady who merely lusted after me from afar and simply penned her fantasies. I've had many admirers over the years."

"Do you truly believe that?"

He trusted no man more than he did King, but still was reluctant to confirm the author's identity to anyone. "Chidding has an interest in Regina. She deserves a good man and happiness. I'm striving to provide an avenue that will lead her toward the altar with someone worthy of her."

With an insolent grunt, King settled back against the thick leather cushion. "You obviously still have some feelings for her. Why not marry her now?"

"I vowed never to marry. We'll leave it at that. Will you invite her to your ball?" He fought not to squirm under his friend's intense scrutiny.

Finally, King shoved himself to his feet. "Consider it done. Now, if you'll be kind enough to excuse me, my wife and chapter four awaits."

Knight laughed low and darkly as his friend took his leave. He didn't know whether to be chagrined or elated with pride at what that particular chapter would reveal about him. The author hadn't gone into minute detail, but she had admitted how much she'd enjoyed his mouth gliding over her skin. However, threaded throughout the tale were the hints that none of it had been real, that it had been seduction with no substance.

Which made it fiction.

Although she didn't realize it. Her perception, in hindsight, of what had transpired between them from start to finish could have been nothing other than devastating, believing he'd made a fool of her. She'd not heard his keening wail when he'd realized he couldn't have her for eternity. She'd not seen the gaping hole his fist had battered into the wall. She'd not brushed the tears from his cheeks. She'd not been witness to his despair—not only for what it had cost him, but more for what it had cost her.

"My lord?"

He glanced up to find himself staring at her brother, hovering, slightly bent, like a troll lurking beneath a bridge. "Bremsford."

"May I join you?"

Having never much liked the man, he was tempted to reply, *No you bloody well may not*. But curiosity had him nodding toward the chair King had recently vacated. The earl settled into place. He had Regina's blond hair and brown eyes, but there the similarities ended. He was a mismatch of features: his father's hawklike nose, his mother's near-absent lips. And his narrowed eyes were far too calculating.

A young footman approached and set a glass of scotch before each of them. Knight experienced one of the rare moments when he wished this club wasn't so accommodating to its members, because if he were in his own residence, he wouldn't have been hospitable and offered the man, only a couple of years older than himself, a glass of anything. He'd have simply waited for him to reveal his business and be gone.

Bremsford took a sip and smacked his lips with what Knight assumed was a show of appreciation for the fine liquor. But his own glass remained untouched. If the earl noticed the slight, he ignored it.

"I was wondering if you might confirm for me that you are in fact Lord K."

Glaring, Knight shook his head while releasing an impatient gust of air. "Christ, Bremsford, you are not listening to gossip, surely. How the devil would I know?"

"It's just that I heard you were brandishing a copy of that disgraceful book around at the gaming tables the other night, so I assumed you'd read it."

"It was given to me while I was here, and I didn't have a pocket large enough to accommodate it, and therefore I was forced to carry it about. I certainly wasn't brandishing it."

"But have you read it? For if you have, perhaps you can confirm that the author is my father's by-blow. She was always a bit rash."

"How would you know how she was, my lord? As I understand it you did all in your power to avoid her." He remembered the night Regina had spoken about her half-siblings. How she'd never met them. Her voice had been laced with a deep sadness, her tone one of immense loss, but even then, she'd had too much pride to weep.

"I've heard enough about her over the years, know she wrote lengthy letters to my father whenever responsibilities kept him away from her whore of a mother. When you—rightly—jilted her, she became a woman scorned. And she has no shame. I am not the only one to suspect it is she who has boldly written about intimacy—yours and hers. What better way to exact her revenge than by bringing notoriety to your door? To ensure you are no longer held in high esteem by your peers and others among the aristocracy?"

"If she was going to go to such bother, why not do it soon after she was scorned? Why wait nearly five years?"

"Because Father was still alive, and she wouldn't dare risk embarrassing him. She couldn't guarantee her identity wouldn't be uncovered or that the gossips wouldn't point the finger to her. No, she would have waited in order to avoid his censure. But now he is gone. You are the only one to suffer the embarrassment, at her whim. Who is to say it will be the last book she pens? She may have decided to pursue a career as a writer in order to supplement the substantial allowance my father arranged for her. She is greedy that way."

It was a very good thing Knight had not picked up

his glass of scotch because the force with which his hand closed into a fist would have shattered the crystal. "I never knew her to be greedy. If anything, I've found her to be far too generous."

"In your experience . . . with her spreading her legs wide for you."

Knight barely remembered catapulting out of his chair, but suddenly—with one hand fisted around Bremsford's shirt, near his throat—he was hauling the man to his feet, his other hand knotted tightly, prepared to deliver a blow to the man's gut. "You will speak of the lady with respect, or I'll beat bloody manners into you until you do."

"Don't be a hypocrite, Knightly. You saw the rancid truth of her and came to your senses before making the fatal mistake of marrying her."

"As I explained at the church, she is the one who came to her senses, recognizing the truth of me, and that with me she'd never know true happiness. She is all that is pure and good, and deserving of nothing but admiration."

"No one believed that poppycock you spouted. Through you she gained everything: prestige, power, wealth. She brought nothing to the marriage."

"She brought herself and that was worth more than anything I had to offer her. But I couldn't give her the amazing life she so rightly deserves."

"Regardless, I am convinced she is Anonymous."

"She is not." He flung the man back into the chair with enough force to nearly topple it. However, it did scoot back several inches and Bremsford clung to its arms as though he was aboard a ship being tossed about by a tempest. "Nor am I Lord K. Spread rumors to the contrary and I'll see you destroyed. By the by, if you received an invitation to the Kingsland ball, disregard it; otherwise, my fist will do the welcoming when you arrive."

He spun on his heel. Ignoring all the gentlemen who'd come to their feet, eyes wide, mouths agape, he stormed from the library that had once served as a calming sanctuary and wondered if he'd ever find enjoyment in this room again.

CHAPTER 12

*In the darkness of that garden, as his mouth
plundered mine and his hands journeyed possessively
over me, I became lost to all the glorious sensations
he brought to life.*
—Anonymous, *My Secret Desires, A Memoir*

June 18, 1875

The Kingsland ball was an incredibly formal affair—
he was a duke after all, and his duchess was extremely
skilled at arranging matters—and so guests were announced at the top of the stairs when they arrived.
Hence, Knight knew the moment Regina crossed the
threshold from the hallway into the ballroom. Not that
he'd needed to hear her name booming out to know
she'd arrived. He'd sensed her presence, always would.
Of course, staring at the doorway had also helped. Because he was here for only her.

If he hadn't managed to garner her an invitation,
he would have made an appearance, but his heart

wouldn't have been in it. Tonight it was fully engaged, the first time in a long while since it had been stirred to feel anything at all when he'd attended one of these aristocratic affairs. Earlier, he'd been tense with concern that she'd ignore the gilded card delivered personally to her by one of the duke's footmen. He'd almost sent her a missive alerting her that she'd be welcomed.

But then she'd arrived, and he'd taken a full breath of relief. He should have known she'd not let the possibility of receiving cuts dissuade her from placing herself in a position to walk gracefully down those stairs, her head held high, daring anyone to object. The woman was magnificent in a pale green gown that bared her shoulders and hinted at the way her breasts would fill a man's palms, had filled his. At his sides, his hands clenched and unclenched as he fought off the memories of warm silken flesh against his skin.

Standing with Rook and two other gentlemen, ignoring their chatter, he surreptitiously watched as she gracefully curtsied before the duke and his duchess, the warm smile they each bestowed upon her indicating they were truly glad she'd come. Knightly had chosen his friends well, and he would make a point of thanking them later for their graciousness.

She'd taken only a few steps away from her host and hostess when Chidding approached her, his smile tentative and awkward, and Knight couldn't help but wonder, as the man signed her dance card, if Chidding would have done the same if he had coins in his coffers. She deserved a man who was more interested in her than in the easier life she could provide. Perhaps he should strive to secure such a gentleman for her. Although he suspected she wouldn't appreciate his finding fault with her current suitor and seeking to replace him with someone more worthy. Chidding wasn't a bad fellow, but neither was he particularly exciting. On the other hand, maybe Regina felt she'd had her fill of excitement. Perhaps she yearned for a quieter, calmer life, one in which she wasn't constantly the object of gossip or conjecture, one within which she was fully accepted, and the circumstances of her birth mattered not at all.

"What do you make of it, Knight?" Rook asked.

He turned his attention away from his musings. She was no longer his to worry over. She wanted Chidding, so Chidding she would have. "Apologies. I was distracted for a moment there. To what were you referring?"

Rook's smirk indicated he knew precisely what had distracted him, damn the man.

"Granard here was saying Bremsford has offered a thousand-pound reward to anyone who can confirm the identity of Anonymous."

Knightly glared at the gray-haired earl, more his father's contemporary than his own. "Has he gone mad? Why the devil would he care who the author is?" Although based upon his encounter with Bremsford only a few nights earlier, he suspected the earl was seeking to wreak havoc for Regina out of spite or jealousy or . . . simple unkindness.

"Because he is a man of firm convictions and understands the danger posed by such salacious writings. The things this fallen woman allows this man to do to her." He slowly shook his head as though crimes had been committed and he lacked the ability to comprehend what was to be gained by such abhorrent behavior.

"You've read it, then?"

His ears and cheeks turned beet red. "Only as a study in how we might need to amend the Obscene Publications Act. The thoughts this author puts into a woman's head are indecent."

"What? That she can find pleasure? Should, in fact, glory it?"

"It has not been my experience that a woman takes any joy in bedding at all."

"Then, my lord, you are not doing it properly."

The man's eyes went so wide, Knight was surprised they didn't have to actually be placed back into their sockets. "How dare you, sir! I know what I am about. But then you would say such a thing, being Lord K and all."

"I say such a thing because I appreciate that women are capable of enjoying a great deal of pleasure. In fact, they are deserving of it. They aren't chattel, man. They don't exist to provide us with a vessel in which to slake our lust or to deposit our seed in order to merely provide us with children. They have thoughts, feelings, needs . . . and desires. Why, in God's name, would any of us want to be with a woman whose passion does not equal our own?"

"They . . . it's not . . . we aren't . . . this is not the place for such a sordid discussion. You, my lord, are disgusting. Little wonder your father has naught to do with you." His face having gone red and blotchy, Granard marched off. The lord who'd arrived with him stood there startled for a few seconds, before following his friend's example.

"Brilliantly done," Rook murmured with an edge of sarcasm. "I have a feeling you've read the book to which you claimed to have no interest, recognized the tale, and determined it is as most of the nobility have surmised: you are indeed Lord K and the author is a vindicative woman you scorned, determined to prove that hell hath no fu—"

"It's all conjecture," Knight interrupted, "not a bit of truth to any of what you or others are alleging. The story is fictitious, not a shred of my exploits to be found within its pages."

"Why are you so vehemently opposed to being the archetype for Lord K?"

"I'm not opposed to being the inspiration for the handsome and seductive fellow. I'm opposed to people drawing conclusions about the author based on their attempt to identify Lord K."

"There's a wager at White's that Regina is the author."

Beneath his breath, Knight cursed soundly. "You think that's the reason that Bremsford, the dashed idiot, offered the bounty? Because of a wager he's made?"

"Perhaps. Or like so many, maybe he's merely curious. Seeking to solve a riddle."

Whatever the reason, Bremsford posed a danger to Regina's happiness—and to her daughter in every manner conceivable. Knight wasn't going to allow that to stand.

REGINA HAD ALWAYS felt a trifle awkward when her name was announced and she proceeded into a ballroom, whether by descending stairs or simply emerging through a doorway. The Thornley affair had not announced its guests as they arrived, and she'd wondered at the time if it was because the Duchess of Thornley, a child of the streets, wasn't comfortable with all the pomp and circumstance.

But the Kingsland ball was handled in a manner fit for a king and his queen with an abundance of grand gestures. She'd read in the gossip sheets about one ball hosted here where a giant gong had sounded when the duke wished to have his guests' notice before announcing the name of the woman he intended to marry.

When Regina's arrival had been proclaimed, she'd rather felt like one of those gongs had been struck so its vibrations echoed out over the room and drew everyone's attention to the stairs. Music continued to play; couples continued to dance. Still, she had the uncomfortable sensation of every pair of eyes turning toward her, their owners judging her. It was the first time she'd made an entry into a ballroom after her name was announced without her father at her side.

She'd felt at once conspicuous and uneasy, yet determined to make him proud. If she'd learned anything at all from her mother, it was how to bury her apprehension, step onto the stage with an air of confidence, and give a performance that would bring the audience to their feet. And to imagine everyone without clothing.

Therefore, she'd made her grand entrance with her chin up and a smile hinting that she knew everyone's secrets. She didn't give away that against her kidskin her palms were damp or how her pulse thrummed with the ferocity of a drummer pounding his instrument to send out a commander's orders in the midst of a skirmish. Or that she did indeed feel as though she was headed into battle.

Through Knightly, she knew the Duke of Kingsland, but was only now being introduced to his duchess. She suspected it was at Knightly's urging that she'd received an invitation. She'd considered declining, to prove to him that she didn't require his assistance and wanted naught to do with him, but she was no fool. Invitations were scarce, and she needed to make the most of each one received. Therefore, she'd swallowed her pride, washed down the bitter taste with a perfectly aged cabernet, and drawn on her finest gown.

At the duke and duchess's kindhearted, sincere welcome, she was glad she had. She hadn't been certain of the duke's regard for her, because she didn't know what Knightly might have told him regarding his reasons for not carrying through on his promise to marry her.

She'd taken only a few steps away from her host and hostess when Chidding greeted her with a warm smile, bowed over her hand, and touched a light, barely whisper of a kiss to it. She imagined he might do the same before climbing into bed with her. He was incredibly formal, but it was the way he'd been brought up. He would never be the object of a salacious book or have his name associated with scandal. But then she would provide enough scandal for them both. She need only determine if he was willing and capable of weathering the storms her mother's misguided heart and her own impetuous one would be sending their way.

Straightening, he said, with true joy in his voice, "I'm frightfully glad you're here. Will you honor me with your first waltz and your last?"

"I would be delighted."

He complimented her loveliness, as though it was something over which she had control, commented on the pleasant evening air, but stopped short of asking her to take a stroll about the garden in it.

After he left her to make her way through the crowded ballroom, she took a coupe of champagne from a passing footman and wandered along the edge of the dance floor. To a small group of four women she recognized from her first Season because they, too, had debuted that year, she offered a small smile that was not returned by any of them. As a matter of fact, in unison, they managed to give the appearance of presenting their backs to her, even without a single one of them actually turning around. She recalled each had gained a husband, but before they'd achieved their good fortune they'd viewed her as competition—even if they'd all been courted by firstborn sons while she'd had the attentions of the lesser ones.

She hated that terminology, because it implied one son was not as important as another. Why should only one son inherit? Why should so much stock be placed

in him? She'd become so involved in inwardly arguing
the unfairness of the untenable situation, she nearly
jumped out of her skin when a hand landed briefly on
her bared upper arm. When she spun around, a bubble
of laughter escaped. "Lady Letitia."

The young woman smiled brightly. "You looked as
you do when concentrating deeply on your cards at a
gaming table at the Dragons."

"Merely contemplating the hard row non-firstborn
sons are forced to plow."

"You have a firstborn interested in you, though.
Viscount Chidding's face quite lit up when your name
was announced."

More than a hundred people had to be circling
about this room, and the lady noticed one gentleman's reaction? Why had she been studying Chidding
to begin with? Had she a tendre for him? "He has
shown me some kindness, yes. Not everyone does."

"Probably because you best them at cards. You
took most of my allowance the last time I sat at a table
with you."

It was silly to be grateful to this girl for drawing her aside, for actually speaking with her, and to
feel a need to show a measure of appreciation after
the rebuffs she'd suffered thus far. Regina placed her
hand near some curling strands of her hair that dangled against her neck and began coiling the tresses
around her index finger. "You always play with your
hair like this when you're holding a pair of jacks or
better."

The girl's eyes widened. "I do not!"

Regina shrugged. "As you wish."

"Do I really?" Lady Letitia furrowed her brow and gnawed on her lower lip.

"And you do that—worry your teeth on that lovely lower lip I'm certain some gent wishes to kiss—when you've been dealt nothing of consequence."

"Devil take it. I think I do. Is that how you manage to win?"

"The players always reveal much more than the cards."

"What about Lord Langdon? How do you know what sort of hand he's holding?"

"Ah, he gives no hints whatsoever. He is a formidable player, although I suspect it is because his family has a close association with the club owner, and he's spent many hours at the card table, perfecting his ability to give nothing away. From what I understand, his family's origins are almost as scandalous as mine."

"Much worse to be sure. His father was known as the Devil Earl. While yours, in spite of his sins, still managed to be respected by most of the *ton*."

His sins. Of which she was the result of one. No matter how fancy she dressed or how warmly she was greeted, she couldn't remove the stain of her birth. She'd condemned her daughter to a repeat of her mother's life. Would Chidding be able to spare the child at least some of the worst of it?

"What of Lord Knightly?"

With a mental shake to turn her thoughts from her worries, she studied the young woman standing before her. "What of him?"

"Does he provide any clues regarding his cards?"

When he knew he had a chance of winning, he

brushed back those forelocks that never wanted to stay in place. She offered the lady a coy smile. "I can't share all my secrets. It would place me at a disadvantage, and I do so love winning."

"Who doesn't?" Lord Lawrence asked as he smoothly stepped into their circle. He bowed his head toward her. "Miss Leyland, I hope you're enjoying yourself at my brother's soiree."

"I am indeed, my lord."

"Good. I hate to deprive you of conversation, but"—he offered his arm to Lady Letitia—"this lovely lady promised me the next dance."

As Lady Letitia placed her hand upon his forearm, she also began twirling strands of her hair, so her habit extended beyond the gaming table to signal anything she truly liked or took pleasure in. Or perhaps she thought she was on the verge of winning Lord Lawrence. Regina decided she didn't need to make the lady feel self-conscious by telling her what she'd noticed. "Enjoy the quadrille," she said instead and then watched them walk away.

"I think she rather fancies him," a soft feminine voice mused.

Regina spun around and immediately dropped into a curtsy. "Your Grace."

The Dowager Duchess of Kingsland smiled at her. "Miss Leyland. I've not seen you in a good while, m'dear. How are you faring?"

"I'm well, Your Grace, thank you for asking. And you?"

"Returned yesterday from a lovely month in Italy. Overall, however, I am much happier since my elder son wed. Now, if I can just get Lawrence to walk up the aisle. Did he ask you for a dance?"

She considered lying, but knew a chance existed she'd ask her second son for confirmation. "No, he hasn't, but he seems smitten with Lady Letitia."

"He's smitten with them all. I'm sure he'll ask you. He probably just didn't want to do it in front of the girl because he likes for each lady to feel she is special and has his undivided attention when he is with her. But he enjoys dancing. Unlike Lord Knightly."

"Lord Knightly?" He loved dancing. In addition to circling her about dance floors, he'd waltzed with her in gardens and in the moonlight along the stream on her property.

"Hmm," the dowager duchess murmured. "At these affairs, he's more ornament than use. No matter that women far outnumber men. He never dances. Although I did hear he once danced with Penelope before she married my son, but I'm fairly certain that was just to tease my boy, to make him jealous." She furrowed her brow. "Although he danced with you, didn't he? Years ago, of course, and then based upon the nattering of matrons tonight, more recently."

She very nearly cursed aloud. Did they have to always be the object of gossip?

As though speaking about him had conjured him, looking past the duchess, she spotted him standing in a circle of men, but he hardly seemed to be paying any attention to them. His gaze captured hers, and she felt as if he'd suddenly shackled it in irons because she couldn't look away. Then he did the strangest thing. He reached up and tugged on his left earlobe. A signal. A signal they'd devised for communicating. *I'll be waiting for you in the gardens.*

The audacity of the man. After what had transpired by the stream, did he really think she was going to rendezvous with him in a darkened place?

"Handsome devil, isn't he?"

Regina jerked her attention back to the dowager duchess. "I was simply admiring the beauty of this chamber, the wallpaper, mirror, and elegant chandeliers."

"M'dear, I may have some years on me but I'm not dead, and I can certainly detect a spark of interest in a lady's eyes."

"I promise you I have no interest in him at all."

"I suppose I can hardly blame you when he didn't do right by you. Your father shared with me the truth of things. Shocked me down to my toes as I'd considered Knightly a man of honor. Your father suing him for breach of contract made it very clear he was not."

Unfortunately, it had also served to give fuel to the speculation that Knightly had lied when he'd declared she'd changed her mind, especially after Knightly paid without a single objection. The money had gone into her trust, increasing the amount of interest and thus providing her with a little more income each year. She knew the exact amount down to the penny because when she'd returned from Europe, she'd set up a trust for Arianna and ensured the additional earnings from Knightly's contribution were deposited into it.

"Better he decided we didn't suit before we were married than after," she said.

"How gracious of you, m'dear. If it had been me, I think I'd want some sort of revenge. Although they do say it can be a double-edged sword." She lightly patted Regina's shoulder. "But it appears you have a new suitor. Good luck to you."

The dowager duchess greeted Chidding in passing as he came to claim his waltz. Regina liked the way his eyes warmed at the sight of her, the small smile he bestowed upon her that revealed one tooth in the front charmingly overlapping the other.

When he circled her over the floor, he ensured they remained a respectful distance from each other. Proper. They would lead a very proper life, very different from the improper one she'd lived from the moment she was born.

"Do you find it difficult being at these affairs?" he asked, to her surprise. She'd expected him to comment once more on the weather.

"I'm accepted by some, not by others, but that is the way of the aristocracy."

"Do you want to live among them?"

She wanted it for her daughter, and she supposed in a way, for her father, to prove she was worthy of the notice, respect, and elevation. As redemption for her mother as well. She wanted to be welcomed into ballrooms where her mother had been denied entrance. But mostly, she wanted to be accepted for herself, for people to look beyond the circumstances of her birth and to find her worthy of their admiration because of who *she* was within her heart and soul. But that was so very hard to admit. "My father set me on this course. I suppose I don't want to disappoint him."

"I can't imagine you ever disappointed him. I also imagine it was difficult coming by yourself. I'd not realized you'd been invited as . . ." His voice trailed off.

"As?" she prompted.

The tips of his ears turned red. "I knew your brother had been."

"Did he tell you that?"

He nodded gravely. "At the club, when he approached to tell me I should cease giving you attention."

She couldn't have been more surprised if a unicorn had suddenly galloped in through the doors leading onto the terrace. Not at her brother's actions, but at Chidding's disregarding the instructions. He was such a quiet, unassuming man she was embarrassed now to acknowledge she'd been unsure of his backbone. "Yet here you are dancing with me."

He grinned. "Here I am, dancing with you."

Because he liked her or because he was incredibly desperate for her funds? Why did she have such doubts? Because she'd once trusted unconditionally and been deeply hurt. "Is he in attendance?"

She'd not spied him but then with so many people roaming about in this large chamber, as well as the adjoining refreshment room, she might go all night without noting the identity of every guest.

"No. Apparently, he had an altercation with Knightly at the club and was threatened with bodily harm if he showed."

Did that encounter with Bremsford have any bearing on why her former lover wanted to meet her in the garden? "Still, you're disregarding the advice of my father's son and dancing with me. He's bound to hear of it."

He gave her a gentle smile. "I'm not one to strut about, but neither am I one to be intimidated. I have a mean right hook when I put my mind to it."

Releasing a bubble of laughter, she looked at him through a very different lens. "Indeed?"

"I admit to being timid, and I'm not particularly bold, but you may rest assured I do protect what is mine."

"I'm very glad to know that particular fact about you, my lord." Now, she just needed to determine if he would consider her—and Arianna—his.

"I admire you greatly, Miss Leyland. It cannot have been easy to arrive here unescorted. Yet, you braved the censure. Perhaps, if you plan to attend another ball, you could send word, and I might accompany you, with a widowed cousin serving as chaperone."

"You've made an incredibly generous offer, my lord. I'll certainly keep it in mind."

The music ceased, and they came to a stop. Once more, he placed a kiss against her knuckles and held her gaze. "I shall count the minutes until the final waltz."

Suddenly she found she would be counting them as well.

Still, a little while later, with guilt eating at her, she slipped out through the opened doors and onto the terrace. Had her father considered himself as traitorous when he'd left his wife to visit his mistress? How did one carry on with another without acknowledging the burden of betrayal? She wasn't even betrothed to

Chidding; yet still she feared he'd be immensely disappointed in her if he discovered her present journey.

The cool night air had drawn people out. Many stood about the terrace conversing. Some had gone down the wide steps to meander about the gardens that were visible because of the tall gaslights that must have cost a fortune to install. Her residence beyond the city had not yet been modernized, and they depended upon oil lamps and candles to guide their way through the manor after sunset.

She skirted past a couple of people who ignored her because they were too absorbed with each other to pay her any attention, thank goodness, and dashed quietly down the steps. Reaching the clearly marked garden path, she kept to the shadows. When she was a good distance into the abundant foliage, Knightly stepped out of the darkness and joined her. She'd been expecting his sudden appearance. It was how they'd managed things before. He always seemed to know precisely where to find her. Perhaps he followed along in her wake. She hadn't cared then; she'd been too overjoyed by the notion he wanted to be with her. Now she was a bit cross because she felt disloyal to Chidding.

"I wasn't certain you'd heed my request," Knightly said. He took her hand. His was bare. He'd always removed his gloves when he entered the garden because he would take advantage of any opportunity to touch her, even if it was only her cheek, and he wanted nothing separating his skin from hers. "Let's go farther in where we can be assured of more privacy."

"I do hope you're not expecting a rehash of what I granted by the stream. I assure you I'll never grant it again. It was the final kiss for all time." Even as she said it, she mourned the words. She hated him for continuing to have this hold over her.

"We need to talk, and I want to ensure no one will overhear."

They held silent as he led her through a maze of hedges, flowers, bushes, and trees. She assumed he'd walked through these gardens with Kingsland dozens of times, so he was familiar with every nook and cranny, every bend, every curve. Finally, he brought her to a halt near what appeared to be a trellis awash with roses, if the scent was any indication. The barest of faraway light allowed her to discern only outlines and silhouettes. When he didn't release his hold on her, she shook herself free of him. "What is it you want of me?"

"I heard tonight that Bremsford has offered a thousand-pound bounty for proof of the identity of Anonymous."

His voice came out low and secretive, but still she glanced around, fearing they weren't far enough away from prying ears. After swallowing her trepidation, she nodded, although he probably couldn't make out the motion in the inky obscurity. "I'm aware. My solicitor called upon me most discreetly this afternoon to alert me to the fact that my father's son had paid a visit to my publisher, insisting he reveal the identity of the writer of that *salacious* book."

She'd wanted to hide, build a moat around her residence, lock herself away. She'd certainly considered not making an appearance tonight but had decided it was imperative not to cower. If she gave the impression she feared discovery, Bremsford might decide he was on the correct track.

"I assume your publisher guarded your privacy."

"Only my solicitor knows I penned the book." She shrugged. "And you, of course."

"Why does Bremsford bloody well care who wrote the damned story?"

"Because he's hateful, and he suspects it's me."

"What does he hope to accomplish? It seems the very last thing he'd want is to bring notoriety to his father's daughter. To give you any sort of acknowledgment at all. To have you recognized as someone who has created a piece of work that has captured the imagination of so many."

She wove her fingers together and clenched them tightly. It was really none of his business, and yet at the moment the weight of it seemed incredibly heavy. She had no one else with whom to share the burden. He'd shown such kindness to Arianna. In addition, his concern touched her, made her want to relieve herself of some of the pressure suddenly bearing down on her. She sighed. "The residence and the land surrounding it—my father did not deed them outright to me but placed them into a trust for safekeeping. As he did with the twenty thousand pounds originally set aside to serve as my dowry. But the trusts come with a stipulation of which I was unaware until today. I don't think my solicitor ever gave it any credence because it was so ludicrous. And he didn't read the manuscript before taking it to the publisher at my request." She found it difficult to go on, to realize what a fool she'd been. But Knightly, of course, had no such misgivings.

"The stipulation?"

She cleared her throat, wishing the noise didn't sound so loud in this quiet part of the gardens. "If I'm ever arrested, simply charged with—not necessarily convicted of—a crime, such as indecency, or even proven to be of questionable character by those who now oversee the trusts, the contents will transfer in whole to the current Earl of Bremsford."

"Bloody hell." The words were uttered in a harsh and heated growl beneath his breath that no doubt scorched the surrounding fauna.

"Yes, quite," she agreed, more softly, in resignation because she didn't know how she was going to avoid holding this secret forever. Secrets always made their way from the darkness to the light. Her mother was supposed to be her father's secret lover—and then she wasn't. Everyone learned about her. Her father's by-blow was to be a secret. Eventually, she, too, was found out. Just as Arianna would be.

"Questionable character," he muttered. "If Bremsford were to learn about Arianna—"

"Fortunately, he can't hurt me there. The stipulation is carefully worded to apply only to behavior that occurs since my father passed. Anything that happened before his death, he excused."

"You told me your father was overjoyed to have her in his life."

"He was. However, as much as he loved her, he was terribly disappointed that I'd placed myself in a position to have a child and no husband. He was also quite irate that I refused to tell him anything at all about who might be her father. But to have punished me with anything other than expressing his ire would have made him a hypocrite, since he also had an illegitimate child."

"You neglected to mention that he wasn't happy with you."

She shrugged. "You asked what he thought of Arianna."

"Therefore, this ridiculous addendum to the trusts is his attempt to bring you to heel . . . from the grave?"

"Yes, I suppose it is."

Learning about that clause in the terms of the trusts had gutted her. She'd always thought his love had been unconditional, but his words had put a condition on her survival. She'd never thought he had it within him to be cruel, but now she was left to wonder if she would ever know a man who wouldn't disappoint her.

"Without the trusts, I would not be a good prospect for marriage to a lord who is in need of the funds that one of those trusts can provide." She chuckled darkly. "Because I was born out of wedlock, my entire life my parents insisted I must be above reproach . . . and I've failed miserably. First because I lost my head to your charms and then for want of revenge. The latter, however, is now a threat to my future. Ironically, tonight the Dowager Duchess of Kingsland told me revenge is a double-edged sword, and already I feel it pricking my skin."

While it was unfair, she hated Knightly for it. He'd torn her heart asunder, and in so doing, had ruined her life. Was it unfair of her to want to ruin his a bit?

His warm palm came to lay gently against her

cheek. "You penned a book, Reggie. It's not as though you committed murder."

She did wish he wouldn't use his pet name for her. It brought to mind far too much intimacy shared between them. "I know I should tell Chidding because he needs to understand precisely what he'll be stepping into if he marries me, but a thousand quid could be incredibly tempting to a man in his dire straits."

"A man can't live on a thousand pounds for the remainder of his years."

"You started with less and look where you are now."

"Be honest with yourself. You don't trust him completely. How can you marry a man you don't trust?"

"I went to a church to marry a man I did trust and that didn't turn out so well, did it?"

His hand fell. "No, I suppose it didn't." He turned away.

"Don't turn your back on me," she fairly hissed through clenched teeth.

He spun around, and even with all the shadows surrounding them, she could make out him plowing his hands through his hair. "I meant no insult. I was striving to determine a way out of this mess."

"You can't do it facing me?"

"You've always served as a distraction." He flashed a grin. "But you're correct. We need to work on this together. He suspects you of being Anonymous because he suspects me of being Lord K. He also knows I have a copy of the book and have no doubt read it. At the club the other night, he wanted me to confirm it was our story—yours and mine."

Was that what had led to the altercation? "Chidding mentioned an incident at the club."

"I took exception to some things he said, but I didn't confirm you were the author, which is no doubt one of the reasons he's offered the bounty. He thinks it's you and seeks proof. If we continue to pretend a reconciliation, perhaps he'll be convinced it must be someone else. The furor over the book will eventually die down. Another scandal will replace it, and Bremsford will give up the hunt. If I were you, however, I would reconsider the wisdom in penning that second volume."

She wondered if he could see her wicked smile. "But plotting your horrific demise has brought me such joy."

"It could put you at further risk, Reggie."

He sounded so deuced serious, and she knew he made a valid point, but at heart she was a writer, and she wasn't going to grant Bremsford complete power over her life. "It's mostly fiction, anyway. If I continue to publish as Anonymous, and the story has no basis in fact, perhaps that, too, will convince him that he's barking up the wrong tree. But if I stop writing, cease doing something I so enjoy, then in a way he's still won."

"Well, we can't have that. Giving him any sort of victory." His grin was impossible to miss, captured by the light of the moon and stars. Of course, he had the power to command nature to illuminate him when necessary. "Tell me, do you grant Lord K at least one more night with the lady he wronged before you do him in?"

"Why would he want it?"

His smile diminished as he shook his head. "We should probably retire inside now. Do you have an available dance?"

She nearly scoffed. "They're all available except for the last."

"Then I'll take the honor of the next waltz."

"I'd rather you not."

"Do you want to convince people the book has nothing to do with us? Besides, it'll keep Chidding on his toes. Go on. I'll meet you inside."

She shouldn't. She should declare she could avert disaster without his assistance, but her father's son was hemming her in, threatening harm to the one person she held dear. She was willing to try anything to protect Arianna, no matter how abhorrent it would be. She suspected Knightly was very much aware of that. But she couldn't imagine he was seeking to take advantage, because he couldn't want to be with her any more than she wanted to be with him. "One dance," she stated concisely.

"One dance."

"This changes nothing between us."

"You've made your position regarding me quite clear. I'm not likely to misinterpret it."

"Very well, then. The next waltz."

With a huge gust of a sigh, she headed back to the residence. How was it that a need for retribution had managed to so complicate her life? If she'd only realized before she submitted it for publication that Chidding had an interest in her, perhaps she wouldn't have done it, would have viewed finding contentment with him punishment enough for Knightly. Or if she'd known about the blasted terms included in the trusts, perhaps she could have produced a tamer telling of the tale. But then it wouldn't have been the story that had poured from her soul.

Bremsford would soon grow weary of the chase, however. She was rather certain of that. Her father's son had never been faced with a challenge that tested his mettle. While Regina had survived numerous ones. She'd survive this one as well.

KNIGHT HAD ONCE considered love to be paradise. Now it was hell, plaguing him whenever he was in the vicinity of Regina. Plaguing him when he wasn't.

He knew in order to win, often sacrifices were required. However, Christ, the ones he and Regina had been forced to make were too damned much.

Tonight he waited until the first notes for the waltz struck before approaching her and offering his arm. Her lukewarm smile was far better than the icier ones she'd been bestowing upon him. He wondered what it might take to be the recipient of the one that had always lightened his steps and his heart when in its presence. She was no doubt reserving them all for Chidding. As it should be.

Still, it didn't mean he wasn't experiencing a touch of envy. Although at least she wasn't striving to undo his neckcloth with her eyes.

"How are you getting on with the puppy?"

Her face softened as he'd hoped it would. "Dare I admit that a certain girl was in need of a pet now rather than when she turned six? They've become fast friends."

"Well, I did have an advantage in determining that might be the case. From the moment she and I met, it was all that was spoken of. I don't suppose she's asked after me."

"Every single day."

"What do you tell her?"

"That you're an extremely busy man."

"I could make time—"

"I don't think it would be wise."

He nodded in understanding. With Regina's marriage, the girl would acquire a father, and it wouldn't be in Ari's best interest for Knight to interfere, as he might very well be tempted to do.

Although a good many people were enjoying this dance, they never stayed long in the vicinity of anyone for even snippets of a conversation to be heard. However, he did glance around to ensure no one seemed to be paying attention to them before he said, "If only three people know the truth of Anonymous, I should think the author is safe from Bremsford's machinations."

She nodded. "I should hope so, but he does seem rather determined to see me ruined. I've often wondered if I'd been the legitimate one and he not, if I'd have hated him as he does me. All I've ever felt is a measure of sadness and loss that we couldn't at least have tolerated each other. And I've regretted having no relationship with the duke's other daughters. I suspect they might be around here somewhere, but I've never met them."

"You were playing cards with one of them the other night at the Twin Dragons."

Aware of her losing her footing as her eyes widened, he held her more tightly, steadying her without his own steps faltering.

"Not Lady Leticia, surely?"

Based on the tone of her question, he had the impression she rather liked the girl. "No. Lady Warburton."

"I suppose she married while I was away. My father never mentioned her new name. However, she gave me a heated look every time I won. I assumed she was simply a sore loser. But why would she sit at the table? I was there first."

"Maybe she didn't recognize you either."

"The dealer called me by name. Why didn't she leave in a huff once she knew who I was? I wonder if she was spying for Bremsford." She sighed. "I don't know if I'll ever become accustomed to being disliked for something that wasn't my fault."

"It's not an easy thing with which to deal, to be sure, but I found it helps to recognize that the shortcoming is in the person who has no valid reason for the disliking."

She tipped her head slightly. "I recall your father didn't favor you."

"Can't stomach the sight of me."

"Because you're a reminder of the son he lost?"

"Among other things." Things he wasn't going to discuss with her. "As people are seeing us conversing more than we did the last time we danced, I think we may be off to a good start with our scheme. In order to make our reconciliation more believable, we should probably make an appearance together at the park."

"I'm not sure that's really necessary."

"Are you willing to risk it, Reggie? Where's the harm in one afternoon where many will view us together?"

She rolled her eyes in obvious frustration. "Very well."

"Excellent. Why don't you have your driver deliver you to my residence tomorrow afternoon? Dress appropriately for a ride. I'll have a horse ready for you."

"And one for my maid, Millie. She'll be serving as chaperone."

"Your maid rides?"

"She was raised on a farm, and I've never objected to her taking a horse out for a trot now and again."

The music faded, and they slowed to a stop.

"Any particular time?" she asked.

"Whenever it is convenient for you."

After escorting her to the edge of the dance floor, he walked away feeling triumphant, a condemned man who'd just been granted a reprieve.

CHAPTER 13

I could not help but touch him in return. His dark hair. His broad shoulders. His strong back. His taut buttocks. Yes, I even dared to squeeze there. His attentions were setting me free from any inhibitions.
—Anonymous, *My Secret Desires, A Memoir*

June 19, 1875

THE following afternoon, as her coach carried her into the heart of London and Millie sat opposite her, a weariness deep enough to make her bones feel as pliable as melting wax settled over Regina. As much as she enjoyed riding, she wasn't looking forward to this outing. She'd not slept after returning home from the ball. Every time she closed her eyes, Knightly was over her, his hair brushing her forehead, his eyes heated, his voice rough as he assured her, *Everything will be all right.*

And her body would grow warm and ache in places that longed for a man's attentions. She tried to think of Chidding. Why couldn't visions of him come to her when she had these dreadful yearnings? Because he'd yet to kiss her? Because she had no sexual experiences with him to draw upon?

The very last thing she wanted was to spend time with Knightly.

No, the very last thing she wanted was to lose her trusts. She could find employment somewhere, surely. For a newspaper perhaps. Although she was fairly certain the income wouldn't be nearly as generous as the yearly amount she was presently accustomed to receiving. She'd be unable to afford servants, except perhaps for Millie who might be content with a roof over her head and food. In exchange for which, she could watch over Arianna. Regina would need someone to care for her daughter if she herself had to be out searching for stories.

Then there was the matter of someone learning she'd given birth to a child out of wedlock. That sort of situation was terribly frowned upon. No one would hire her under those circumstances. She could claim to be a widow. She'd considered it when she'd first returned to England, but the deception didn't sit well with her—now, however, she was turning to deception at Knightly's urging in order to protect herself and her daughter.

She could devote herself more enthusiastically to her writing. She had earned a tidy little sum on her first book, although *little* was the important word there. But if she wrote novels of romance and adventure, with heroines to capture ladies' imaginations, perhaps she could eke out a modest living. She'd received several letters sent to *Anonymous* or *Author of My Secret Desires* via her publisher who had passed them on to her solicitor who had, of course, delivered them to her. Most praised her writing and encouraged her to write another tale. Oddly, she'd not had a single woman complain about *My Secret Desires*. Only the men. Perhaps they were threatened by the notion of a female protagonist who would not be cowed.

In spite of the current upheavals, she was making good progress on the second volume. Writing the first had been draining, but the second, because most of it was indeed fiction, was a more joyful experience. She could shift the story's focus, so it didn't relate to the first at all, so it was clearly a novel. It was something to ponder.

She might ask Knightly for his opinion on the matter. No, she absolutely would not. He was not a confidant for God's sake. He was a fellow conspirator, and nothing more. Once this Bremsford business was behind her, she'd never engage with him again.

She hated the sense of loss that thought brought with it. Damn the man. Even when she didn't like him, he had the ability to occupy far too many of her musings.

The carriage finally turned into his drive, and she tamped down the excitement that arose from a past habit of when she'd always anticipated moments with him. Now they were merely to be endured. She didn't bother glancing out the window, but rather studied her knotted hands, striving to bring a calm to her erratic heart and a neutrality to her features. While she appreciated his willingness to assist her, she wanted to make it clear she felt nothing even remotely joyous toward him.

After the vehicle came to a stop, the door immediately opened, and he was there extending his hand toward her. Had he been waiting for her out here? No, he'd probably had someone watching to notify him of her arrival. "I trust you had a pleasant journey."

"Yes, thank you." She placed her hand in his and, as he closed his fingers around it, commanded her heart to still itself. While he wasn't wearing gloves, she was wearing leather ones, so it wasn't as though it was skin upon skin, but just like last night, it felt magical all the same. Damn, the man.

Gracefully, she alighted, and he released his hold quickly, no doubt because Millie hovered in the doorway. Regina watched as he greeted her maid before helping her to clamber out. Millie was adept at blending in. She wouldn't expect to be included in conversation. However, she'd be vigilant in watching her charge, but unobtrusive. Certainly, she wouldn't bring out a scrap of yarn and measure the distance between Regina and Knightly, who at that moment swept a hand off to the side. "I've had the horses readied."

Regina looked in the direction he indicated, and her breath backed up in her lungs. His horse she recognized, but standing beside the gelding was a glistening black mare with a pure white mane and tail. In awe, she slowly began walking toward her. "Oh, my word. She's gorgeous. I've never seen the like. Wherever did you find her?"

"I told a breeder I know that I was in search of something unique. He found her for me."

When she was near enough, she took hold of the

bridle and rubbed her hand along the horse's forelock.
"What's her name?"

"Queen. She was meant to be your wedding gift."

She jerked her head around to stare at him, but he
was watching his hands as he tugged on his gloves.
Was this horse proof he had intended to marry her,
that as he'd divulged, she wasn't the reason he had
changed his mind?

He lifted his gaze, pinning her to the spot. "You
can take her with you when you leave, if you like."

"I'm not going to accept a gift from you."

"You'd be doing her a favor. She doesn't get ridden as much as she'd like. She's gentle. Your daughter
could ride her."

Queen nudged Regina's shoulder, and Knightly
smiled. "She likes you. She knows where she belongs."

She hated him even more for this, for making her
want the mare, for making her wonder what had truly
transpired all those years ago. "I wish you would tell
me the truth of what happened."

"Shall I hoist you in the saddle?"

For a moment it was as though he'd asked if he
could put her in his bed, and she wasn't altogether
certain she'd have said no. She wanted him to touch
her, with his hands, with his lips, with his words.
She longed to understand how he could go to such
trouble to find her the perfect present, knowing how
much she loved to ride, and yet subsequently break
her heart. It made no sense whatsoever, but his quick
deflection of the question indicated he wasn't going
to tell her anything. What was the secret he held so
close, so tightly? Did it choke him as hers did? She

wasn't going to beg or nag or goad him into telling her, because she, too, was keeping things from him. "Yes, please, if you don't mind."

She shifted into position and realized the saddle, too, had been made for her. An *R* within a circle of flowers intricately carved within the leather. What did it all mean?

"Turn about," he said.

Then she was looking up into his deep blue eyes, trying to decipher all the emotions they seemed to be conveying.

"As I mentioned before, it had nothing at all to do with you. I'm incredibly sorry, Regina, that I've brought you such trouble, but I promise you will not pay any other price for it. Bremsford will not learn the truth. Speculation will soon cease. You will have the wedding and husband you deserve."

"You never call him my brother."

"Having had a brother myself, I know Bremsford is not worthy of the distinction. A brother doesn't seek to destroy his sister."

"I guess we'd best get on with the . . . pretense."

With a nod, he closed his hands around her waist and lifted her into the saddle. It was perfection, fit her like it had been made for her and her alone, because of course it had been. She didn't want to consider how life with him would have been a series of surprises, like this. How often he might have brought her tears of joy. All the mornings she may have awoken grateful to have him lying beside her.

While he assisted her, a groom—who'd been waiting nearby—helped seat Millie.

Now Regina watched as Knightly mounted, his breeches pulling tight across his thighs and buttocks—mouthwateringly so. When settled, he offered her a small smile and guided his horse toward the gate. She mimicked his actions and drew parallel to him, while Millie followed at a short distance. "Do you really think this is going to work?"

"If nothing else, it'll shift the gossip away from the book to us specifically. There's bound to be some speculation that I've rethought matters and am after your hand."

"But you haven't and you're not."

"Would you want it any other way?"

"My father once told me that trust lost is difficult to regain."

"I'd say he was a wise man, but he put that stupid stipulation on your trust. He had to know his son's feelings toward you."

"Sometimes I think my father had the ability to divide his life into distinct parts. He had two separate families. I suspect—or at least hope—he loved them equally. I knew his love and hope the others did as well."

"You're a remarkable woman, Reggie, to be so generous. I think Bremsford would rather destroy you than wish upon you any measure at all of your father's devotion."

"Do you know I've never even spoken to him? The current Lord Bremsford. My half brother. I've seen him from a distance, but that was some years ago. I doubt I'd recognize him if we crossed paths now."

As they entered the park, she could sense him

studying her. "Then Bremsford doesn't know you at all, does he? He knows only of your existence, not the woman you are."

"I very much doubt he'd like me anyway."

"He'd adore you."

She laughed lightly. "You can't help it, can you, Knightly?"

"Help what?"

"Flirting, issuing compliments."

"I never say anything I don't mean." He shrugged. "Well, except when I claim I'm not Lord K and have no idea who is Anonymous."

Had he loved her five years ago, then, when he'd regaled her with words of love? Did he loathe her now? His actions to assist her with her current trials certainly didn't make it appear he suffered while in her company. Although perhaps his support was all simply guilt. She wondered if she'd ever know the truth of things.

REGINA LOOKED MAGNIFICENT sitting astride Queen. Knight had known she would. It was the reason he'd purchased the mare for her. Over the years, he'd considered sending the beast to her as an apology but hadn't been certain she'd accept the mare or appreciate the gesture. She'd been furious with him, rightly so, hatred reflected in the tears brimming in her eyes. He knew she wouldn't have taken her feelings out on the horse, but he'd been unable to imagine she would have loved the steed either. Animals deserved to be adored.

However, after having placed her on the horse, he

was rather certain they were growing fond of each other, and he hoped she'd take Queen back with her when their journey through Hyde Park was completed. It was where the horse belonged, with the woman who was born to ride her.

He remembered the pride he'd always experienced having Regina at his side. It was with him now, swelling his chest, his head, and another part that it shouldn't, but how could he look at her and not want her? He felt like a withered field in want of rain—desperate for it. He thought he'd schooled his emotions, tamped down his desperation for her, but having her near was torment, and yet he couldn't seem to mind it. He did wish for the ease they'd once shared to return, to hear her laugh fully and completely, not with the caustic bark she now occasionally tossed his way. Sometimes she did forget her hatred of him when she smiled, and he relished those moments when her lips curled up and her eyes reflected joy.

As their horses trudged along Rotten Row, he couldn't stop himself from saying, "You spend quite a bit of time in your book describing our first kiss." That damned garden scene everyone was on about went on for pages.

She gave him a sidelong glance, those lush lips of hers hinting at a smile but not fully committing to granting it to him. "For me, it was a moment of awakening. I'd never imagined it could be so all-encompassing. I suppose a small part of me wanted to alert women to how it should be, how it overtakes all your common sense."

"It's not like that for everyone."

"Because every man is not as experienced and skilled as you?"

After sidling Shakespeare a little nearer to her, he removed his hat because he wanted no shadows to prevent her from reading the truth in his eyes. "I'm not boasting here. What I'm about to say is simply to make a point. But I had kissed . . . several women before you, and yet that night was a revelation for me, a shock clear down to my boots. You owned me that night." *And every night since.*

She stared at him as though he'd knocked her off her horse, and she was unable to catch her breath. He settled his hat back into place. "Was that not your experience when sampling all the men you fancied in Europe? That I was somehow different?"

She looked ahead, to the side, and back at him. "No one has ever made me feel as you do, Knightly. That realization might have fueled my need for revenge."

He wanted to ask her more about those men, but they weren't his business. Just as the women in his life weren't hers. But not a one could measure up to her.

"Lord Knightly! Miss Leyland!" Lady Letitia drew her horse to a halt near them, causing them to stop as well. Two ladies were with her, and she quickly made introductions. After which she said, "That's a gorgeous horse, Miss Leyland."

Regina blushed. "Thank you. She belongs to Lord Knightly."

"But Miss Leyland may have her if she wants her," he said.

Lady Letitia wrinkled her nose and smiled cunningly. "Are you courting her again?"

"No," he said.

"Absolutely not!" Regina insisted with firm conviction.

Lady Letitia laughed. "You do make a handsome couple."

"We're striving to put the past behind us," he said.

She leaned so far forward toward him that he was surprised she didn't topple out of the saddle. "You'll never guess what I got my little hands on."

"*My Secret Desires*?"

Her face fell. "Well, yes, but it's rude to guess correctly and ruin my surprise."

"It was a lucky guess, I assure you."

She brightened. "My friends and I were discussing it over tea yesterday, and I think I should warn you that some ladies are determined to lure you into gardens for a bit of mischief in an attempt to determine if you are indeed Lord K."

He chuckled low. "They shall leave the garden convinced I am not."

"But will they leave it kissed?"

"I very much doubt it. I read the book as well, Lady Letitia. It is the passion of the woman he is kissing that he reacted to, that swept him away, that silenced his voice of reason, that made him want with a desperation that is near impossible to satisfy. It was more than merely a kiss. It was breath, life, and love. It was a world where dreams dared to exist and yearned to become reality."

"But in the end, he abandons her. Not at the altar. Otherwise, I might suspect Miss Leyland here of being Anonymous. But he simply disappears, leaving her waiting on the railway platform, all her hopes for a life with him dashed."

He shrugged. "Some dreams are not meant to be."

"That is my only fault with the story. I dearly wanted them to be together at the end."

"Instead, he was a rotter," Regina said.

And Knight refrained from glaring at her.

"Did you secure a copy as well?" Lady Letitia asked her.

She smiled with a touch of irony in the twisting of her lips. "I did manage to find a copy."

"Didn't you think it was brilliant?"

"I suppose it was somewhat entertaining."

Lady Letitia placed a hand over her heart. "I want Lord K to return to her. I believe they are destined for each other. I do hope Anonymous will continue their tale." She glanced back at her companions. "Well, we must be off. It was lovely to see you both. And together as it were, considering your tumultuous past. Gives me great hope that Lord K could be forgiven."

"You speak of him as though he truly exists," Knight said.

"To me"—she looked at her friends—"to all of us, he does. Good day."

The trio trotted away, and Knight glanced over at Regina. "You might have to reconsider the demise of Lord K. Perhaps you should give him and his lady the happy ending Lady Letitia wants."

Her smile was wickedly frightening. "Oh, his lady will get her happy ending—she will find his horrifying demise incredibly rewarding."

HIS DEEP LAUGHTER rang out over the green, drawing attention to them. Regina wasn't certain if he'd taken joy in her scathing retort or had simply wanted to ensure people noticed they were riding through the park.

The story she was writing was not going precisely as she had envisioned it. She thought it unlikely *the* gentleman was going to meet a tragic end, because he and the lady were reconciling. She was deuced irritated by that. Every time she began writing a scene in which he would endure something horrible, it ended with them kissing. An encounter with ruffians. Kiss. A knife wound. Kiss. A bullet lodged in his shoulder. Kiss. As the author, she believed she should have more control over her characters, but they seemed to disagree, and she'd find herself scrawling words she'd never intended to put to paper. It was frightfully vexing.

Yet, she couldn't bring herself to scratch through the words because they brought her a measure of happiness that, after all the trials and tribulations suffered in the first book, they were fighting their way toward something more lasting, and she wasn't quite certain she had it within her to deny them a triumphant end.

She imagined if she confessed all that to Knightly he'd again laugh with abandon, would offer her no pity for her struggles. Although she wouldn't mind the laugh. She'd always loved the manner in which it boomed, uninhibited and carefree.

She also liked that she could discuss her writing with him, even if she didn't go into much detail. At times, she wished her name was on the cover, so she could speak to others about it. What a disaster that would be. Bremsford would see her skewered, the hateful little man.

"Prepare yourself," Knightly suddenly said. "Your suitor approaches."

Looking in the direction he indicated, she watched as Chidding trotted his dun-colored horse toward them. Once more, she and Knightly drew their own steeds to a halt waiting for the viscount's arrival. He was outfitted in all gray—dark gray trousers, coat, and hat, light gray shirt, waistcoat, and neckcloth. As he came to a stop before them, possessively closer to her than to Knightly, he gracefully removed his hat from his head. "Miss Leyland. Lord Knightly."

"Chidding," Knightly stated flatly.

Rather than reaching over and smacking him for greeting Lady Letitia with far more warmth, she smiled sweetly at the viscount. "My lord, what a pleasure to encounter you on this fine day. I hope you're well."

"I am, Miss Leyland, although somewhat taken by surprise at the sight of the two of you together."

She imagined he could excuse a dance, but the park? "It's just a friendly outing, mending fences as it were. I'm more convinced than ever that Knightly and I really didn't suit and together we'd have had a miserable existence."

Although she kept her gaze on Chidding, she could feel her former lover's glare boring into her. She tried not to appear too satisfied in getting a rise out of him.

She would have to commend him later for not responding with a cutting remark.

"Why don't you join us while we take in the scenery, Chidding?" he offered instead. "My horse gets antsy when he has to stand around too long."

The steed was presently standing nearly as still as a statue.

"Don't mind if I do," the viscount said.

Regina soon found herself between the two gents. They'd never both concurrently been in her presence for any length of time, so she'd had no chance to compare them. Knightly of the dark hair and skin bronzed by the hours he spent riding was devilishly handsome. Chidding's hair was a burnished red. His fair skin reflected a man who spent more time in his library than outdoors, quite possibly because the sun was likely to burn him to a crisp or perhaps he was simply more studious by nature. He possessed pleasing features, everything perfectly aligned and proportional. He was more slender, not quite as tall. She doubted he had the wherewithal to lift her into his arms, but then she was fully capable of standing on her own two feet. She'd once felt treasured when Knightly cradled her against his chest and carried her to bed. Now dependability, steadfastness, and the keeping of promises were worth more to her than gold.

"Splendid weather we're having today," Chidding stated.

And it was. Bright blue sky and billowing white clouds. A gentle light breeze that stirred feathers on hats but didn't threaten to yank them from their moorings. "It is indeed."

They journeyed several paces in silence.

"How is your mother?" she finally asked, remembering that his mother was alive, unlike Knightly's.

"Aging, you know. She has a difficult time remembering things of late. I'm rather certain she would like to have you for tea some afternoon."

"I'd enjoy that."

"Your own mother passed as I recall."

"A few years back now. But a reminder of loss never fails to bring a twinge of pain, does it?"

"I suppose not. No." He looked around her to Knightly before settling back into place. "I wonder if he is to be trusted? He won you over once. I can't believe he's not attempting to do so again."

"I was young and innocent then. Not so much now. I promise you, my lord, he has no sway over me. And my heart is quite closed to him."

His dark eyes reflected sadness and understanding. "Is it forever closed, do you think?"

Her smile was soft, and she hoped both inviting and reassuring. "No, my lord. I believe the right man holds the key to unlocking it again."

"Sometimes, Miss Leyland, I am dazzled by how lyrically you speak. I wonder if you've ever considered turning your talents toward writing a novel."

Suddenly she felt like the young girl who'd tumbled down a rabbit hole in the book she was reading to Arianna each night before bed, and she was having a difficult time drawing breath. It was an innocent statement, a form of flattery. Nonetheless because of Bremsford, she was suspicious of anyone striving to find her out and wary of his comment. "I wrote some articles for a lady's magazine while I was traveling through Europe, but I don't know that I have the patience or skill for penning an entire tome."

"I read those articles. My mother showed them to me. They were rather well done. You painted a portrait, so my mother was able to envision you on those journeys. She commented once that she felt like she was traveling along with you."

"That was very kind of her. And you, for telling me."

She was rather certain he was blushing.

He tipped his hat slightly. "Well, I shan't impose upon your time any longer."

"It was no imposition, my lord, but rather a joy. Thank you for gracing my afternoon."

Now he truly was blushing, pleasure more than embarrassment radiating from his eyes. "Good day, Miss Leyland."

"Good day, my lord."

"Knightly."

"Chidding."

The viscount loped away.

"He's smitten," Knightly said.

"It was rude of you to listen."

"I tried not to."

She scowled at him. "I doubt that very much."

"Does he possess that key to which you were referring?"

"That, my lord, is none of your concern. I believe I've had sufficient time in the park and enough of your company."

Before he could respond, knowing Millie would follow her, she nudged Queen into a gallop. Oh, the horse was quick to respond and smooth. Regina would like to have her in an open field. They would be as one. Damn, Knightly. He'd always known the gifts that would please her the most. The mare pleased Regina immensely. She was going to keep her.

CHAPTER 14

⌒⌒⌒⌒

I knew my giving in to temptation would be frowned
upon—or worse, would see me exiled from polite society.
The notion left me flummoxed because I truly could not
understand how something that felt so right could in fact
be so terribly wrong.
—Anonymous, *My Secret Desires, A Memoir*

June 22, 1875

REGINA was traveling to the theater in Chidding's
coach. Their first public outing together. He'd paid her
a visit the day before. They'd sipped tea in her drawing room.

"The weather has been quite pleasant of late,"
he'd said.

The state of the climate was his favorite topic, it
seemed. She couldn't recall ever discussing it with
Knightly, and then berated herself for the constant
comparison of the two men. They were nothing alike.
One was reliable, one was not.

So they'd nattered on about the weather for a while.

Then he'd surprised her with, "It's my understanding you like the theater."

She'd smiled warmly. "I do, indeed." As a young girl, she'd often stood backstage and observed her mother during rehearsals. The activity that went on behind the curtain—the workers arranging the sets, the seamstresses who provided the costumes, the actors waiting in the wings to make their appearance—had fascinated her far more than what occurred on the stage. But she didn't mention any of that to him because she didn't want to remind him that her mother had been scandalous and that she, herself, had begun life in an unspeakable manner.

"Would you honor me by accompanying me to the theater?"

Hence there she was, traveling in his gleaming carriage with its worn and frayed upholstered squabs. But she didn't mind that some upkeep was needed. His attention and desire to be with her were more important than any conveyance.

He'd coerced a widowed cousin, the Countess of Finsbury, to serve as chaperone. Sitting beside Regina, she used the waning light of sunset to read, of all things, *My Secret Desires*. If it wasn't upending her life, Regina might have been pleased that the lady seemed to be completely absorbed by the story. She suspected their present guardian wasn't going to be nearly as watchful as Mrs. Dorsett. She also suspected Chidding was too much of a gentleman to take advantage of the opportunity to do something he ought not.

"How long since you've been to the theater?" he asked now.

"Oh, years." Five to be precise.

"Your mother was an actress, I believe."

So much for not wanting to remind him of that bit of her history. "She was."

"You had no interest in following in her footsteps?"

"I hadn't her talent for pretending to be what I wasn't. Neither did I fancy being the object of a good deal of attention, which, of course, those upon a stage are. Every move watched. Every line heard. Every performance judged."

He studied her for a long moment, no doubt striving to determine if a hidden meaning resided in the depths of her words. "I prefer a quiet life," he finally said. "My estate provides that."

"I've never been to Cornwall."

"I think you'd like it there." His cheeks turned a brilliant red to match his hair, and he looked out the window, as if embarrassed by what he'd possibly revealed—he envisioned her there.

"I'm sure I would," she said softly.

He looked at her and smiled. She wondered if a time would come when he would be comfortable enough with her not to blush at every turn, although she found it quite endearing.

A short while later, with Lady Finsbury trailing, he escorted Regina into the theater, and she sensed his pride in doing so, in having her hand nestled within the crook of his elbow. That carried far more weight than anything else. He was glad of her company, found pleasure in having her decorate his arm.

He was well-liked, and they were greeted by several lords and ladies, even a few who had snubbed her in the past. He brought her respectability and in turn could bring it to her daughter. Soon, she would tell him about Arianna.

Before they were too involved, before turning away from her would cause her public humiliation. Before he would be forced to explain why he had lost interest. She prayed she'd not misjudged him, that he wasn't a rumormonger, that he would keep what she shared with him to himself and wouldn't be petty enough to want to hurt her daughter.

He leaned toward her. He was not a tall man, didn't tower over her as Knightly did, and she drew comfort from that. They were more equal. "I do hope you weren't offended by what my cousin is reading." His voice was low, laced with chagrin.

"Not at all. I know several ladies who have enjoyed reading it."

"Have you read it?"

It was one thing to lie to Knightly in order to exact revenge, but this man was quite possibly her future, and she certainly wasn't going to have him dictate her reading choices. "I have, yes. Despite its uproar, I found nothing in it offensive."

"Neither did I."

He could have knocked her over with a feather. "It didn't seem like the sort of book you'd read. I thought you like mysteries."

"They are my preferred reading." He leaned nearer, lowering his voice even more. "Quite a few gentlemen are reading it, hoping, I think, to discover that they are, in fact, the inspiration for Lord K."

She laughed lightly, delighted by his revelation and

teasing tone. She imagined they'd relish many joy-filled moments of sharing gossip. "I wasn't aware of that. Mostly I've only heard of their dislike for it."

"I've always found naysayers to be more boisterous, perhaps because they wish to drown out the truth." He glanced up. "Shall we make our way to our box?"

Our box. As though it was already theirs. As though they were together in a more permanent capacity than a single night at the theater entailed. "Yes, I think we should."

He glanced back over his shoulder. "Lady Finsbury, we're going up now."

Their chaperone had been carrying on a conversation with another lady and politely excused herself to follow them. As they made their way up the stairs, Regina wondered how Chidding might feel to know she was the author. Would he take pride in it since he'd enjoyed the book? Would he be horrified to learn he might have been reading about her escapades with another? That was far more likely. Unless she did claim it was all fiction, merely her fantasies, and happenstance that she'd referred to the gentleman in the book as Lord K. Because of course, at the time, Knightly had been foremost in her mind.

He had a right to know the funds he'd acquire through marriage could be stripped away. How had everything suddenly become so complicated? But it was all for pondering later, when she was abed, unable to sleep because of the trouble she—and her blasted half brother—had brought to her door. Penning the book had been cathartic. If only she'd burned it afterward. It had brought Knightly back into her life, endangered her ability to properly care for her daughter, and threatened her relationship with Chidding. A double-edged sword. More quadruple-edged because no matter how she turned it, she was in danger of being sliced by it.

She would never again seek revenge.

She forced the thoughts aside, intent on enjoying her evening. She did love the theater. The scent of it. Sawdust from sets created. Paint applied often to ensure nothing resembled the inside of Chidding's carriage unless it was supposed to. The sweat from too many bodies clustered together in the narrow seats where most people sat. The sound of her mother's voice reaching the rafters with what seemed to be so little effort. But she'd brought that voice up from her soul and projected it to the world. When she was not on the stage, she'd needed to rest it, so had never read a story to Regina. Instead, she'd had Regina, before she could read, recount tales she'd made up, and later, to read books to her. Perhaps Regina had found solace in writing articles during her travels and then a book later because creating stories from nothing, along with reading, encompassed some of her favorite memories of her mother.

This theater, in particular, was beautiful, with its scrolled woodwork and red carpeting. The huge crystal chandeliers created a sparkling sort of light. The first time Knightly had brought her here, she'd been awestruck because she'd never viewed the theater from this perspective. Her father had never invited her to join him in his box. A small part of her resented that oversight because she would have liked to have been curled on his lap while he pointed toward the stage. "There's your mother, the woman I love."

She wondered if he'd ever brought his family. If he'd sat beside his wife, striving not to give any indication he was watching his lover.

They reached the landing, and Chidding guided them into a corridor rather than turning for the next flight of stairs. Her heart gave a little lurch because she was familiar with this hallway. She'd walked it half a dozen times with Knightly. Could the man not leave her in peace for even a moment? Did everything have to always remind her of the dratted scoundrel? Until recently, she hadn't realized how she longed to be completely free of him. With no memories, no encounters, no sightings.

Then Chidding stopped beside drawn curtains, slipped a hand between the part, and drew the thick velvet aside.

Oh, God, she knew this box. Intimately. She knew it was mostly shadows and the casual grazing of a hand over her arm could not be seen. She knew the view she would have of the stage. How the actors' voices carried so clearly the performers could be standing right before her, on the same level.

Because people were striving to edge past them, to get to their own boxes, she stepped inside, grateful to see no other occupants. She hadn't wanted him here, hadn't wanted him interfering. Still, she couldn't stop herself from saying, "This is Knightly's box."

"It was," Chidding said. "He lost it to me in a card game. Shall we make ourselves comfortable?"

He indicated the two rows of tufted chairs. She

made her way to the front row, purposely sitting in a chair she'd never before occupied. He settled beside her. Lady Finsbury gave a little groan as she lowered herself into a chair behind them.

Regina shifted to face Chidding more squarely. As far as she knew he had no gambling debts. He was frugal, careful with what little money he had. "I didn't think you were one for making wagers."

"I'm not. But I do enjoy going to the club. I like the atmosphere of the Dragons' library, and it provides an opportunity to visit with the gentlemen I know, to keep up on matters of import, to discuss new ways to manage our estates. I'm not the only one to experience a decrease in the income they provide. But, as a general rule, the gaming doesn't appeal to me."

"Yet, you won the box."

"Odd thing that. After our encounter at the park, that evening I was at the club, in the library, when Knightly approached and invited me to a game in a private room. Only the two of us. I confessed to having no coins with which to wager, but he wasn't interested in coins. Rather he wanted my horse, of all things."

She couldn't imagine it. Knightly wasn't going to give up Shakespeare. What need of he for another horse? What game was he playing?

"Mentioned you fancied the theater," Chidding continued, "and was willing to put up this box. One hand. That's all we were dealt. And I won. So here we are."

Before she could respond, the lights dimmed, and the curtains were drawn aside.

"You are pleased to be here, aren't you?" he asked, and she heard the doubt in his voice.

She smiled reassuringly. "I do love the theater."

Turning her attention to the stage, she fought to concentrate on the performance rather than all the memories bombarding her. Sitting here with Knightly, her chaperone behind her. The way he managed to skim his finger secretively along her arm. His knee touching hers. Later, when Mrs. Dorsett had begun snoring, he'd pressed his mouth to Regina's ear and whispered, "I want you, Reggie."

With the urgency reflected in his voice, she'd been able to do little more than nod.

"After I return you home, sneak out of your residence. I'll be waiting for you at the end of the drive."

At the Wolfford ball, he'd kissed her as he'd promised, in the garden, and several times since. She'd known what he wanted, had known what would happen if she met him.

The first time she'd sat in this box had been her last night as a virgin.

CHAPTER 15

❦

May 1870

TREPIDATION and excitement coursed through Regina
as her maid prepared her for bed. As much as she
trusted Millie, she couldn't confess that as soon as the
residence grew quiet, she was going to slip out into
the night. Her plans were a secret, a delicious secret,
and no one else knowing added to the wonder of them.

Knightly wanted her; she wanted him. She rather
imagined her mother had felt the same about her earl.
What was a bit of misbehavior when the want was so
great it became a need, one that required an answer-
ing, a satisfaction?

Once she was beneath the covers, she said good
night to Millie and snuggled down as though preparing to sleep, while her maid closed the door in her
wake. Then Regina waited. Quiet as a mouse. Holding
her breath. Perfectly still. Listening. Until no sounds
of movement were to be heard.

Gingerly, determined the bed would not squeak,
she eased out from beneath the covers, her feet hitting
the floor, snatched up her night wrap, and slid it on.
Quickly she tugged on her slippers. Taking nothing

else, she crept out of the room and down the stairs. She crossed the entryway to the door. It had already been bolted for the night, but she would need it unbolted when she returned so she had no qualms about unlocking it now.

Her heart was thundering. Other than kissing Knightly, she'd never done anything so risqué before, anything that might upset her father if he was to learn of it. She'd always been such a good girl, hoping to retain his love for her. But she knew tonight she was going to be very, very bad. And she absolutely didn't care what it might cost her. Because she was in love. Madly, irrevocably, determinedly in love.

And she was loved in return. Unconditionally. He didn't care about her lack of pedigree. Within his eyes, she was perfection. She was not left to feel wanting.

Once outside, she dashed down the drive, her legs moving at a frantic pace before her courage deserted her. She wasn't very far from the residence, however, when Knightly was suddenly beside her taking her hand and slowing her movements.

"What's the rush, princess?" he asked.

Stopping, she wrapped her arms around his neck. "None, now I'm with you."

He laughed. A laugh that sang to her. "I thought maybe you were impatient for the journey we are going to make."

"I am." She pressed a kiss to his neck. "I want all of you. I want it so badly it frightens me."

"To be honest, how much I need you scares me a bit, too." He cradled her face between his hands. "You're everything to me, Regina."

With the moonlight shining down upon him, he dropped to a knee. With a gasp, she covered her mouth with one hand because he held on to the other. "Are you proposing *now*?"

"A preliminary proposal, to be followed by a more public one later, because I want you to know I intend to marry you, to make you my wife. Not because of any dowry. Because I don't need it. I want you purely for you. You complete me and make me a better person. Tonight, I want you giving to me freely without worry that I may be taking advantage. So, I ask of you now, with the moon and the stars and the heavens as witnesses, will you honor me by becoming my wife?"

The joy coursing through her knew no bounds. She thought she might actually explode with it. "Oh, yes, my lord. I want nothing more. I love you, Arthur."

He shot to his feet so swiftly she was surprised he didn't lose his balance, but then he was so perfectly aligned she didn't think he'd ever stumble or teeter. As his arms came around her and drew her close, she stepped onto his booted feet and wound her arms around his neck as he lowered his head and captured her mouth with a ferocity that made every other kiss he'd ever bestowed upon her seem tame in comparison—while she'd considered each of them to be wild.

But this was something more. A vow. A promise. She was his and he was hers. Forever, until the end of time, until the sun no longer rose in the east or set in the west. It was all-encompassing. He was pouring every ounce of his love for her into it, and she was gushing hers with equal fervor.

He broke free, cradled her face once more, and held her gaze. "My carriage awaits."

Taking her hand, he tugged her forward. Her foot landed on a pebble. "Ow!"

Stopping, he looked back at her. "What's wrong?"

"Just a small stone. Nothing to worry over."

"Are you wearing slippers?"

"Yes, I was too anxious to take the time to button up proper shoes."

"I won't stand for you getting hurt." He swept her up into his arms, and she laughed as she nestled against his chest. "I mean it, Reggie. With me, you'll never again know a moment of unhappiness."

"I love you, Arthur."

He carried her all the way to his carriage. Once they were inside, and it was rushing toward London, they were kissing again and the fire of desire licking at her made her wonder if she might lose her virginity in the vehicle. She wanted to tear off his clothes and hers. She wanted flesh against flesh and bodies entwined.

While her secret places might be untouched, her mind wasn't wholly innocent. Her mother had told her what transpired between a man and a woman. When her mother had passed, Regina had gone through her bedchamber, gone through her things, and she'd found a book with illustrations of nude people in various positions. Her mother had only shared the basics, but Regina had grown warm leafing through the pages and discovering all the various physical ways people could demonstrate their love. She wasn't afraid of what was going to happen tonight. Mum had assured she wouldn't be.

She was looking forward to exploring his body and her own sensuality.

Taking hold of her plait, he untied the ribbon, tucked it into his waistcoat pocket, unraveled what her maid had worked so diligently to create, and combed his fingers through the strands. "I wondered how long your hair was. It must go past your bum."

She feathered her fingers through his hair, brushed back the rebellious locks that always fell forward. "I want you. I want you as I've never wanted any man."

With a growl, he drew her wrap and gown aside, exposing the spot where her neck met her shoulder and pressed his mouth there. She felt the pull of her skin as he suckled, creating a line of want that traveled to that sensitive spot between her thighs, causing it to throb and liquid heat to pool. She moaned low. "I don't know if I can wait."

"You'll wait. It'll make it all the more pleasurable."

"Have you had a lot of women?"

"None like you. None I've wanted so desperately I thought I might perish if I couldn't have." He cupped her face, turned it toward him, and held her gaze. "I burn for you."

That was a perfect description of how she felt, that at any moment she might ignite. "I know I should be frightened, but I'm not because it's you."

He flashed a grin. "I'll make it good for you." He drew her up against his side. "We'll be there soon. For now we wait because I want your initiation into love-making done properly."

"What was your first time like?"

He chuckled low. "Incredibly quick."

"Will mine be as well?"

"No, we're going to travel at a leisurely pace to ensure you're ready for me." He brought her onto his lap and nuzzled her neck. "I'm going to suck on your breasts." He growled low, causing heat to swamp her. "I'm going to kiss my way down to the sweet valley between your thighs and feast there."

"Oh, God." She dropped her head back, lost in the images his words created. "Do it now."

"No. I want you completely naked, spread out before me so I can worship you as you deserve."

"You'll be naked, too."

"Absolutely." He moved a hand down and wrapped it around her calf. "Everywhere, flesh against flesh, fire against fire. The flames will consume us, and just when you think you will die, you'll soar into pleasure such as you've never known."

Reaching up, she loosened two buttons on her nightdress. "I'm hot now."

He lowered his mouth to the tiny V of flesh she'd revealed. "What you feel now is only a spark. I intend to turn you into a blaze and leave you naught but smoldering ashes."

As though the spark had struck him as well, he was kissing her hungrily, their tongues clashing. She held tightly on to his hair, ensuring he couldn't leave her, that his mouth remained on hers. This one was different from the others they'd shared. This one was a prelude to fulfillment. It was untamed, a wild and ferocious thing. He gripped her knee, and she suspected he held it with such purpose to prevent himself from traveling farther up her leg, because if he explored what he had yet to touch, he might not be able to stop himself from keeping his promise of ensuring she was ready for him. She could sense the tension in him, the tightness coiled in his muscles. Against her hip was pressed the burgeoning evidence of his desire. It emboldened her, gratified her, empowered her.

"I'm going to suck on your nipple, kiss my way down your torso, and lick your cock," she dared to whisper.

At her knee, his hand spasmed. His other hand knotted in her hair, pulling her head back so he could graze his mouth along her throat. "Christ, Reggie. You're going to have me spilling my seed before we even get to the residence."

She laughed lightly. "I don't think I've ever been wanted like this."

"I've wanted you like this since the first moment I set eyes on you."

"I feel like you're devouring me."

"Soon, love, soon now."

In spite of the fire growing hotter, they managed to limit their attentions to kissing. Deeply, greedily, all-consumingly. The first kiss he'd bestowed upon her—in the garden at the Wolfford ball—paled in comparison to what he was delivering now. It was a claiming, a vow. An admittance of an uncontrollable passion. She felt it from the tips of her toes to the crown of her head. Every inch of her was responding with need. She couldn't stop her hands from moving over him—his shoulders, his arms, his chest. She wanted all of him. She'd never experienced such a driving force within herself.

She knew at that moment she'd do anything to have him. All of him.

The carriage came to a stop, and they lurched apart. So involved in each other, they'd not even noticed it slowing. The door opened. He leapt out into the pale light provided by the gas lamps along the drive. He looked a mess. His neckcloth halfway undone, his shirt partly out of his trousers on one side. His hair askew. She'd done that to him. She'd mussed him and was going to do it again. After tonight, she was going to do it every chance she got.

He extended his hand toward her and assisted her in climbing out of the carriage. Her feet had scarcely hit the drive before she was back in his arms and being carried up the steps. The door opened. He barely greeted his butler before heading up the stairs.

She buried her face against Knightly's shirt, not certain if she wanted the servant to recognize her—because there was only one reason for her to be here this time of night. Although she supposed it was a bit late to worry over her reputation. The driver and footman knew who she was.

What did it matter anyway when he was going to marry her?

She'd been raised by a woman who didn't believe pleasure required marriage vows to be enjoyed. *When you love someone, Regina, it is natural to want to be joined with them. Never be ashamed of your body's response. It's a gift, really. Nature, perhaps, striving to make up for the pain we endure each month and during childbirth. Glory in it.*

With him, she would.

He swept into his bedchamber and kicked the door closed behind him. His goal was obvious, his long strides making short work of crossing the distance.

When he reached the bed, he slowly lowered her onto it as though he feared hurting or scaring her. But nothing he did would frighten her.

Kneeling, he removed one slipper, and then the other, setting both aside before pulling her to her feet. He eased off her night wrap and then concentrated on releasing the buttons on her nightdress from their mooring. She watched his blue eyes darken as the sliver of skin revealed began to widen. When the last button was free, his breathing became harsh as he slid his hands beneath the material and flattened his palms against her collarbones. His skin was like fire against hers. Lifting his gaze, he captured and held her own. His contained a need that nearly made her sink down onto the bed in a molten pool of desire. She'd never before seen such hunger, as though she was essential to his continuing to exist. She was both flattered and terrified she could be so important.

He didn't move and it suddenly occurred to her that he was waiting for permission, as though she hadn't signaled in the coach all of her was his for the taking. "Yes." Her voice was a rasp she'd not expected, as if the fire burning between them had scorched her throat.

His eyes darkened even more before he lowered them, slid his hands out over her shoulders and toward her arms, causing her nightdress to slither down her body. She was aware of his breath catching. "You're so beautiful."

"The way you watch me makes me feel so."

"Lie down. Spread your arms and legs wide."

She scrambled onto the bed, staring at the purple velvet canopy, doing as he asked. When she rolled her head to watch him, his clothing except for his trousers was gone, a heap on the floor, and he was sitting in a chair, tugging off his boots. He was gorgeous. His arms ropy, his torso defined muscle. Her mouth went dry at the sight.

When his feet were bare, he stood and unbuttoned his trousers. He glanced over at her, and again held still, his hands curled around the opening to his trousers, providing a barrier to what lay beyond.

"Yes," she said without hesitation.

His trousers came off in one fluid motion, and she shifted onto her side, taking in all his glory. The drawings in her mother's book paled in comparison to his magnificence as she took in the whole of him. She grinned. "You are . . . beautiful."

He laughed. "The way you watch me makes me feel so."

Then he prowled to the bed, climbed onto it, and took her into his arms, blanketing his body over hers as his mouth took complete possession of hers. He was right. There was something magical about all that lovely skin—his and hers—rubbing and sliding together. It was almost a melding, like they were exchanging bits of each other, and she knew she'd never again be the same, wouldn't be whole without him.

He cupped her breast, kneaded it, and swirled his thumb around her areola, causing her nipple to pucker and strain toward his touch. After removing his mouth from hers and lowering it to close around the turgid peak, he fulfilled his earlier vow. He suckled. She felt like she was composed of thousands of bits of string, and all were being tugged at once, straining and vibrating with pleasure. She brushed the strands from his brow and buried her fingers in his hair.

She loved the way his hard planes fit against her soft curves. They were perfect. She'd known they would be.

As he'd promised in the carriage, he kissed his way down to eventually lick the most private part of her, which she was discovering was also the most sensitive. She very nearly came up off the bed. Her gasp and cry caused him to laugh darkly. "Like that, princess?"

"Yes. Yes. Yes."

"And I've only just begun."

To drive her mad with desire, want, and need. With each stroke of his tongue, the pleasure ratcheted up and her body tightened a little more, in anticipation of what exactly she couldn't say. All she knew was she never wanted him to stop. She would gladly spend the rest of her years in his bed with her legs scandalously spread, creating a haven where he could feast to his heart's content—and hers. His fingers began working in tandem with his mouth, and the pleasure intensified until she was convinced she would die of it. But what a lovely way to go.

Suddenly she was screaming his name, begging him to stop, urging him to continue. A wave of ecstasy took her under and lifted her to the heavens, bowing her back. He drove himself up to her mouth, again took possession of it, capturing the last of her cries, holding her tightly as the cataclysm rocked her, and her body trembled from the force of it. She could taste herself on him and was overwhelmed by the wonder of all he'd done to her, all he'd given her.

He trailed his mouth to her ear. "I want to be inside you." His voice sounded strained, as tight as his muscles felt beneath her fingertips.

"Yes."

He rose up. "Stop me if it hurts."

Only she knew she wouldn't. She wanted him buried deeply inside her, wanted the joining her mother had told her about, the bond it formed, the connection it created. She wanted him. Needed him, all of him. To be hers, all hers.

He pushed in. Her body welcomed him. She ignored the discomfort, already sensing the additional pleasure awaiting her. More than physical, spiritual almost. This was the man with whom she was going to spend the remainder of her life, and they'd have so many more nights like this. His body pounding into hers. Her fingers tracing the outline of his muscles, digging into his buttocks, urging him on.

Looking down on her, he held her gaze as he rocked against her. Her body quickly adjusted, adapted to his rhythm, and the pleasure began undulating through her with his movements. She was crying out his name as he growled hers, his back arching, his jaw tightening, his eyes smoldering.

Breathing heavily, he collapsed on top of her. She closed her arms and legs around him, holding him tightly. She never wanted to let him go. She'd thought she couldn't love him any more than she already did, but he'd proven her wrong.

She loved him more than ever, this maker of promises, keeper of vows.

CHAPTER 16

⤸⤺

*"I want to kiss every inch of you." His voice was fraught
with need, a need I understood because if given the
chance, I would gladly kiss every single inch of him.*
—Anonymous, *My Secret Desires, A Memoir*

June 22, 1875

Bɣ the time the play came to its conclusion, Regina
was naught but a vessel of riotous emotions playing
havoc with her ability to think clearly. That she had
managed to remain and not run screaming from the
theater was a testament to her fortitude. Knightly—
the man had no need of other horseflesh, and he most
certainly had a knack for winning at cards—had
given this box to Chidding for only one reason: to torment *her*.

Every time Chidding brought her to the theater, she would be reminded of her time here with
Knightly. The secretive touches, smiles, whispers.
And the first time he'd taken her to his bed. Only after he'd returned her home had she realized he'd kept

the green velvet ribbon that had originally secured her plait. A memento. A gift from her.

If Chidding had wanted to surreptitiously graze a finger along her arm or intertwine his hand with hers, she'd offered him no opportunity, because she'd sat there with her hands clutched and her arms against her sides in an effort to prevent her from traveling the path of memories. But, of course, it had proved a futile endeavor. Her posture had stiffened all the more as she'd been bombarded with images of Knightly and all the things he'd done with her, to her, for her. The pleasure. Dear Lord. So much pleasure. Even when they weren't in bed.

The tour he'd given her of his home that night. The magnificent library, with all its books, the wonder of it—even before he'd lifted her onto the desk and taken her there, standing between her spread legs and pounding into her as her lungs filled with the fragrance of ancient tomes, bound in leather that eventually absorbed her cries.

As the stage curtains were now drawing to a close, following the motions of those observers seated around her, she stood and clapped and yelled, "Bravo!" No matter that she had no idea if the performers were deserving of the accolades.

"Shall we?" Chidding asked politely, studying her somewhat confusedly, and she wondered exactly what her face might be revealing. She was grateful she wore gloves, so he wasn't aware her palms had grown damp. She dearly hoped he couldn't feel the slight trembles going through her as she lightly placed her hand on his arm.

When they were in the carriage slowly wending its way through the crowded street, he said, "I suppose you knew the box was Knightly's because you attended the theater with him."

A lit lantern hung inside the vehicle, and his cousin had arranged herself so she could use its light to once again read. Regina was torn between elation that the countess was so enamored of the story and worried about the strain she was placing on her eyes. "I did, yes."

"I hadn't considered it might prove difficult for you to visit the . . . scene of the crime, as it were."

Oh, he was astute. Shy but astute, and a little funny referencing his preferred reading material. "It was unexpected, is all."

"You handle the unexpected admirably."

"I've had far too much experience with it."

She had his admiration but tonight had reminded her of the wonder of being loved. Only she hadn't been. She had to keep reminding herself of that. He wouldn't have left her if he'd loved her. Nevertheless, in that box with Knightly, she'd believed within the depths of her heart he had adored her, and she had marveled at the glorious sensation and acknowledgment.

By the time they arrived at her residence, all those turbulent emotions had settled into one, forming an uncomfortable knot in her stomach: anger. Fury, in fact.

Still, like her mother, she performed. With a smile, when Chidding handed her down from the carriage. A gentle touch on his arm when he escorted her to the door. When he lowered his head and kissed her, a quick brush of his lips over hers, she sighed.

"Good night, Miss Leyland," he said.

"Thank you for a lovely evening, Lord Chidding."

With a smile and a duck of his head, he shoved open her door. She stepped through and turned to bestow upon him her own smile before slowly closing the portal that provided a bridge between them.

When she spun around, the smile was gone, and rage was flashing. Her butler, patiently waiting for her wrap, took a step back as though she breathed fire. "Have my carriage readied."

She was surprised the heat in her order didn't burn him to a crisp. She didn't know what game Knightly was playing, but she was determined to find out.

WHEN SHE ARRIVED at Knightly's residence, the hour was such that decent folk were abed. His abode was dark except for pale light filtering out through an upstairs window—his bedchamber window. At the realization he might actually be entertaining a lady, a momentary pain struck in her gut, something rather similar to what she suspected one endured when being kicked by a recalcitrant horse. Standing in the exact spot where the footman had handed her down, she stared at the wavering light and imagined Knightly moving toward some long-limbed beauty as he'd once approached her: slowly and provocatively, taking her breath and her sense. Perhaps she should leave this confrontation for tomorrow.

But her fury at what he'd done was diabolically

beautiful and needed to be vented, before it cooled, so he'd fully understand she was no longer one to be trifled with.

Taking a deep, shuddering breath, she marched up the wide steps, fighting not to recall the many times she'd dashed up so anxious to be with him that she'd begun to think of time as a thief and had wanted as few moments as possible stolen from them.

After reaching the door, she grabbed the knocker and began pounding it and a fist against the wood with enough force and determination that if a cemetery was nearby, she'd wake the dead. At the very least, she'd awaken his servants, possibly his neighbors, and she didn't bloody well care.

She was beginning to fear the damage she might be doing to her hand when the door suddenly swung open and he stood there in all his mussed-up glory, in shirtsleeves only partially buttoned, trousers, bare feet, and his hair in need of a good brushing. His brow deeply furrowed, he took hold of her arm, pulled her into the entryway, and closed the door. "What the devil are you doing here? Is something amiss? Is it your daughter?"

His reference to Arianna and the true concern woven through his voice threw her off her game for a second or two before she was able to snatch back the vehemence this encounter required. "You bastard. You gave Chidding your box, forcing me to sit there with all the memories bombarding—"

A keening wail startled her, causing her to jerk her attention upward to where it seemed to be originating.

"Bloody hell. Wait here."

Then he was racing up the stairs while his paramour, no doubt, carried on like the hounds of hell were attacking her. Regina had no intention of waiting. She would confront him and the woman, ensure his lover understood exactly how dastardly he could be.

While his long legs allowed him to take the steps two at a time, she'd spent enough hours chasing after a rambunctious child that her stride might be shorter, but it was incredibly quick. She reached the top of the stairs, not far behind him, close enough to turn into the hallway and see him hurrying past his bedchamber.

She dashed after him, completely confounded when he shoved open a door at the end of the corridor. Why was his mistress so far away from his chamber? Did she reside here? Had he secretly married while she was away, and no one was aware? Had he been married all along?

By the time she rushed into the room, he was kneeling beside an older, white-haired woman who was cowering in the corner, clutching his shirt.

"I heard them knocking. They've come for me. They always come in the dead of night. Please, don't let them take me away. I can't go back. I'll die."

"It's all right, Mother. No one's come for you. I won't let anyone come for you. I promise. You're safe here."

"But I heard them. I heard them banging. They want in."

And he must have heard Regina's panting as she fought to catch her breath after the mad dash, or perhaps something else alerted him to her presence, because he twisted around slightly. "No, look. It's just a lady come to visit me." He leaned in slightly and lowered his voice, calm and reassuring with only the tiniest bit of humor, as though to share a secret. "I think she's rather cross with me and intends to take me to task."

Her brown eyes large and blinking, the woman looked past him to Regina and studied her, possibly trying to determine if she was real or a phantom. "Are you courting her?"

"No." He glanced over his shoulder at Regina and jerked his head to the side. "Would you pour her a brandy?"

Against the wall stood a small table with a single decanter and glass upon it. Striving to make sense of what she was witnessing, she did as he bade, her hand shaking slightly. She'd thought his mother was dead. He'd never mentioned her except for the once. What precisely had he told her then? She couldn't recall.

After carrying the snifter over, she carefully lowered herself to the floor, managing to keep her balance because of all the times she'd done so with Arianna. Taking the offering from her, he placed it against his mother's lips.

"Here, take a sip. It'll help to calm your nerves and allow you to sleep."

All the while, with distrust evident in her expression, the woman kept her gaze homed in on Regina. Finally she took control of the snifter from her son, sipped again, and released a slow breath, perhaps sending her fears on their way. "Are you going to introduce us?"

"Where are my manners?" he asked, as though they

were in a ballroom rather than a corner of a bedchamber where only a little while before he'd been striving to calm a terrified woman. "Allow me the honor of introducing Miss Regina Leyland, daughter of the Earl of Bremsford. My mother, Elizabeth Pennington, Duchess of Wyndstone."

Regina smiled softly. "I'm honored, Your Grace."

Her brow furrowed, she looked at her son. "Miss? Why is she *miss* if she's an earl's daughter?"

"Her mother was an actress, Bremsford's mistress."

"I think I remember hearing something about him and an actress . . . before . . . you know. She's very pretty." Shaking her head, she pressed her fingers to her mouth. "Forgive me, Miss Leyland. I'm talking about you as if you are not present and can't hear what I'm saying. You're very pretty."

"Thank you, Your Grace."

She shifted her attention to her son. "I'm so very tired."

"Come on, then, let's get you to bed. You should be able to sleep now."

Regina watched as he set the snifter on the bedside table and then helped his mother—so tenderly it made Regina's eyes sting—to her feet and into bed, pulled the covers over her, and lowered himself to press a kiss to her forehead. "You are safe, Mother. Here you are always safe. Have pleasant dreams."

Then he turned and offered his hand to Regina, drawing her up so she was standing beside him. Immediately he released his hold and indicated the doorway. "Shall we?"

"Good night, Your Grace," she said.

"Good night, Miss Leyland. I do hope you won't remain cross with my son for long. He's such a good boy." She closed her eyes.

Regina led the way into the corridor. Knightly drew the door closed behind them. She carried on and walked into his bedchamber.

"Would the drawing room not be a better place for you to vent your anger with me?" he asked.

With all the emotions bombarding her, she didn't know if any place in the entire world was well suited for finding the peace she sought. "I thought you might want to be near in case she calls out again."

He released a deep sigh. "Thoughtful of you, but she should sleep now that her fears have been put to rest. So you took issue with my losing my box to Chidding in a card game. Is that what brought you to my door?"

"You don't lose at cards."

"I lost to you a little over two weeks ago."

Truthfully, she no longer cared about the damned box. She had more pressing suspicions rampaging through her. "You told me your mother was dead."

"I believe I admitted to not knowing if she was alive."

"When did you learn she was?"

His intense gaze homed in on her, and she had the sense he was delving into her soul, or perhaps his own, striving to determine if she could be trusted, if he should reveal the answer. She wondered if he felt like he was standing at the edge of a precipice, and if he gave voice to the truth, he'd be flinging himself off it, not certain if she'd be there to catch him. *I will catch you.*

She didn't know what prompted that unspoken vow, but she knew the veracity of it. For some reason, what she'd witnessed tonight seemed incredibly important. Something he'd discovered—she knew not when but certainly not before they were to wed. She'd heard no rumors of him courting anyone. He didn't dance at balls. Mostly she saw him conversing with men, but seldom with women. A man who had once flirted with anyone wearing a skirt had become an enigma. Why?

Finally, he closed the door to his bedchamber before walking over to a table that housed far more decanters than the one in his mother's room. "Brandy?"

"No, thank you. All I desire is an answer to my question."

He poured scotch into a glass and tossed it back. Then he stood there still and quiet, staring at the pattern on the wallpaper. She watched the muscles of his throat work as he swallowed. Following another long sigh, he turned and captured her gaze. "The morning we were to wed."

CHAPTER 17

❧

June 1870

"I MUST say, m'lord, you're quite well turned out."

Studying his reflection in the cheval glass, Knight had to agree with his valet's assessment. His gray trousers and cravat complemented his dark blue jacket and waistcoat. His hair, for once, was actually behaving, not falling across his brow. Although it would later, when he took his wife to bed. Afterward, she'd brush it back and give him her smile filled with such love that it never failed to render him speechless and confirm he was the luckiest of men—to have acquired her unconditional devotion. After today, she would be his to have and to hold for eternity, because even death would be unable to dim his adoration for Regina.

A knock sounded. "Come."

His butler stepped into the chamber. "M'lord, His Grace seeks an audience in the library."

His father. The Duke of Wyndstone. Who was opposed to the marriage and had even told Knight he'd "not marry the chit." He wondered if his sire had changed his mind, was here to accompany him to the church, after declaring forcefully he wouldn't be in attendance because no ceremony would take place.

"As you know, Carter, the wedding breakfast will be held at my wife's residence. I have no idea when we might return here but do have a footman keeping watch for our arrival as I want all the servants lined up to greet my countess, their mistress."

"Yes, m'lord. Shall I inform His Grace you'll be joining him shortly?"

Knight walked over to a small desk, picked up the tiny leather box, and opened it. Inside was nestled the ring with its multitude of diamonds that he would be placing on the bride's finger. "He can cool his heels for a bit. I'm not quite ready."

"He doesn't seem to be in an accommodating mood, m'lord."

"Is he ever?" He glanced over at his servant, who seemed to be striving to arrive at a diplomatic response. "You don't have to answer that. It was rhetorical."

He slipped the leather box in his pocket to hand off to King, who would be serving as his best man. Bishop and Rook would be standing with him as groomsmen. He'd never expected to be the first of their group to marry, but then he'd never anticipated meeting anyone like Regina Leyland, who called to something deep inside his soul and made him want to share his life with her. Every aspect of it.

Making his way down the stairs, gray top hat in hand, he reflected on how Regina took pride in being with him, the uptilt of her chin, the security of her hand tucked within the crook of his elbow, the shine in her eyes—the *possessive* shine as if to say, *Yes, he is mine*. It was only fair, because he wanted to show her to all the world, the woman he loved without measure, the one who completed him, when he'd never before realized exactly why he was incomplete. He'd spent years searching for that sense of wholeness, thinking he'd find it if he could ever please his father. His coffers now exceeded the duke's, and he wasn't shy about flaunting his wealth, ensuring all aspects of his life were larger or grander than his sire's. His clothing, his residence, his yacht, his carriages, his horses. He was wholly independent of his sire. Yet it never seemed to be enough to bring his father even a scintilla of pride.

As he strode into the library, his gut clenched at the sight of his father standing by the window gazing out at what was heralded as one of the most beautiful gardens in England. He took a deep breath and prepared himself not to allow this man to ruin his good mood or dampen his spirits. He'd soon be with Regina and never again without her. "Good morning, Father."

The duke swung around, his jaw set so tightly it was a wonder words could escape from between his lips. "I forbid you to marry."

Something ominous was threaded through his tone, his demand. The short hairs on Knight's nape bristled, and every other aspect stilled. Most lords were relieved when their sons finally married, knowing an heir would soon be on the way and the line of succession secured. "I'm seven and twenty, past the age when you can send me to bed without my supper. I do as I please. It pleases me very much to take Regina to wife. Besides, I would think you would welcome the possibility of an heir."

"Not from you."

It wasn't the first time his father made him feel he fell far short of expectations. "If not me, then whom?"

"My younger brother."

"Uncle Walter?" He was the sort of gentleman who avoided anything more strenuous than the lifting of a glass of scotch. His entire life he'd received an allowance and earned his own coin only when he had luck playing the horses.

"Followed by his son," the duke continued.

A son who was lumbering along the same path as his father. Without imagination, goals, or ambitions. Knight shook his head. "I don't know why you'd prefer either of them."

"Because they carry the blood of my ancestors."

Knight was beginning to wonder if his father was going a bit mad as he aged. "As do I."

The duke strode over to the decanter table, poured himself two fingers of scotch, and downed it in one swallow, before turning, his features hard and implacable. "Every Pennington male has been fair of hair and brown-eyed."

Knight considered making his way to the table and pouring himself a scotch, but he didn't want Regina smelling liquor on his breath and thinking he'd needed to bolster his courage to wed her. What he required was an understanding of the gibberish his father was spouting. "Then I'm an exception."

"Because you're not of my blood."

It took everything within Knight not to bark out

his laughter and leave the room, but bloody hell. His father looked to be deadly serious. "My mother might disagree."

"When you were born with your dark hair and blue eyes, she told me dark hair existed in her family. But I never met any of her relations who were not blond. And your eyes, I thought, like Francis's, would eventually turn brown. But they never did. I finally confronted her, and she confessed to taking another to her bed. You are the result."

Knight felt as though fists had been pounded into him until he was black and blue, inside and out. How was it possible this information could be kept from him all these years? "You're mistaken, surely."

"I am not. You look nothing at all like me."

That much was true, and Knight had always found a bit of a relief in it. But at the moment his world was spinning out of control. Then his father—not his father—continued, his voice dripping with icy disdain.

"At the time, a divorce required an act of Parliament, and I had too much pride to announce I was a cuckold. I was listed as your father on the birth records. That made you legally mine. But I had my heir. Francis, healthy and strong. What need had I of you? You would be the spare in name only. I would tolerate you, but not her." He poured himself more scotch and downed it.

Knight decided the day of his wedding was not the best one on which to commit murder, but at that moment he loathed a man he had merely disliked before. "Did you kill my mother?"

A corner of the duke's mouth lifted into a sneer.

"That would have been a kindness. I needed her to suffer for what she did. I had her committed to a madhouse."

Balling his hands into fists, he took a step toward a bloke who deserved a good pummeling. "You bastard."

"You're the bastard, in actuality if not legally."

These revelations explained the smacks from his youth as well as his father's indifference to him. "But legally is what matters," Knight said with a bit of smugness. "I'm your heir apparent, and you can't do a damned thing to prevent me from inheriting your titles and entailed properties." Primogeniture, the law of the land, protected the heir from a wrathful father.

"I could take your life, but I decided to offer a bargain instead."

Knight didn't like the cold calculation reflected in those brown eyes. Or the hatred, the fury. "You have nothing I want."

"Not even your mother's freedom?"

"I'll find and set her free." Although he'd long ago hired investigators to uncover what had happened to her, they'd yet to meet with success, but now at least he knew they needed to concentrate on madhouses.

"You'll never learn where I secreted her away. Even if you do, she is my wife, and the law allows me to determine her fate. Until I say otherwise, she is insane."

He didn't know how much longer he could restrain himself before beating the loathsome creature before him to a bloody pulp. "You mentioned a bargain."

"Swear on your mother's life that you will never marry and thus have no legitimate firstborn son so that when you die someone with true Pennington blood will once again hold my titles and properties—do that, and I'll place my conniving wife in your care."

CHAPTER 18

◦◦◦◦◦

*As his mouth trailed along my throat, I wanted to
leave this place, this garden, to be lying with him in a
bed, where intimacy could be fully explored and know
no bounds.*
—Anonymous, *My Secret Desires, A Memoir*

June 22, 1875

SOMETIME during the telling of his tale, Knight and
Regina had made their way to the settee near the fireplace, sitting in opposite corners, but the smallness of
the furniture placed them within easy reach of each
other. Not that they were touching. They both seemed
to be tightly wound, like a mummy in a sarcophagus.
He felt much as he had that beastly morning, shocked
by what he'd learned, furious at what was being demanded of him, devastated with the knowledge of
how he would ruin her life if he defied the duke, how
he would ruin her life if he didn't. No matter which
path he took, she would suffer because of it. He would

suffer as well—continued to suffer because of the loss of her and the guilt.

Any semblance of control he maintained at the moment would shatter if she placed so much as the tip of her finger on him. He wanted to throw a vase against a wall, tear the room asunder as their lives had been. She'd deserved none of it.

Once he'd begun talking, she'd uttered not a sound, but he'd watched the horror flick over her features as his words were unveiled. He hated the truth of them, but more he hated what he'd not told her.

She studied him now as though he'd transformed into a creature she didn't recognize, but he also saw the sorrow and confusion. Finally with a long, slow breath, she settled back against the plush cushion no doubt striving to absorb the ramifications of all he'd shared. After a few minutes of silent reflection, she leaned forward, her brow deeply furrowed, and he wanted to reach out and press his fingers to the lines in order to erase them, and then have his mouth soothe where they had existed.

"Why didn't you tell me all this at the church?" she asked hesitantly.

"He'd sworn me to secrecy, laid out all the rules, creating an intricate web that allowed me no room to maneuver. I grappled to understand precisely who and what I was. I was burning with contempt for the man." He forced himself to hold her gaze. "And I was ashamed, Reggie."

"Of the circumstances of your birth?" Reaching out, she placed her hand over his where it rested on his thigh. It should have brought him comfort and a great deal of relief. Instead, it served only to make him feel all the worse. "You must have known that I, of all people, would have understood the turmoil battering about like a tempest within you. I'd been there for most of my life."

Desperately he wanted to look away, but she deserved to know the truth, to know everything, and in the end, he had little doubt she'd be grateful she wasn't his wife. "Not my birth, but my reaction to the bargain he proposed." After swallowing hard, he forced out the words that he'd never shared with a soul. "I told him to go rot in hell. I had an appointment to keep. I left for the church, determined to leave my mother to her fate. Because I wanted you more than I wanted to save her."

A long silence followed. Her thumb skimmed repeatedly over his knuckles. "But you didn't," she said quietly, "you didn't abandon her."

"But what sort of son—what sort of *man*—does it make me that I almost did? Selfish, cruel, undeserving of happiness. Disgusting."

"Arthur, your father"—she shook her head—"the duke was asking you to alter the plans you'd made for your life . . . and not only your life but mine. Under the circumstances, anyone would need a moment to consider and reflect. Besides, it's in your nature to run odds and analyze. You never make decisions on a whim. I suspect that's the reason he waited to bring all this to you on the morning you were to wed rather than when we made our betrothal announcement. If he'd given you time, you'd have undoubtedly found another solution, another way to save her and to have me."

"I don't know about that. There isn't a day that goes by when I don't consider what I might have done differently. The carriage ride to the church felt like the longest journey of my life." Years of lies and deceit had bombarded him. How could he inflict them on her? She had been his most precious truth. "I almost ordered my coachman to not stop, to carry on past St. George's . . . but I couldn't leave you to face the blasted *ton* alone. Still, I do regret how I handled matters. I thought you'd be spared the worst of it if they believed the decision was yours."

"They never find fault with one of their own. Especially when he charmed so many of them, as you did. Still do."

He couldn't smile at her teasing, not when the guilt still ate at him.

"Then I bungled things with you as well. It's possible I could have convinced him to let the marriage go ahead, if I swore that we'd have no children. But the only way to *guarantee* no offspring was to never make love to you. I couldn't deny you children and pleasure. If we didn't marry but stayed together by living in sin, we could have children, but they'd be bastards. Knowing the trials and tribulations you endured growing up, I refused to ask that of you. I determined, stupidly, it would be easier for you in the long run if I could make you hate me. So I lied. I wanted no other women. You must believe that."

"I do. Now. You were quite convincing before. My mother could have taken lessons in acting from you." She lifted her hand from his and cupped his cheek. "You did succeed quite magnificently in making me

despise you. So strongly. Frighteningly in fact. The
hatred was almost a physical presence, a burning that
fairly set me ablaze. However, in a strange way it was
a gift, really. It helped to mold the strength I needed
to carry on, the fortitude to face an uncertain future
with certainty."

Placing his hand over hers, he held it while turning
his head and pressing a kiss against the heart of her
palm. "I'm so sorry, Reggie. I should have found a
way to make it easier for you."

"Arthur, learning I couldn't have you as my husband never would have been easy. If not for the fury
and hatred, I would have felt despair and been overwhelmed with such sadness I might have never left
my bed. Instead, I was determined to prove I didn't
need you—didn't need any man. My father, in his
desperation to see me wed, had convinced me that
I did. *Society* had convinced me that I did. But I
don't."

But he knew her daughter was another matter.
The innocent always were. Now Regina was making
decisions to protect her child just as he'd made decisions to protect his mother. Her resolution would lead
her to marrying another, and he had to make peace
with it. "I need you to know that I loved you." *Love
you still. The woman you were then; the woman you
are now.*

Tears welled in her lovely brown eyes as she brushed
the strands of hair back from his brow. "Do you know
I love you all the more for the choice you made?"

"Ah, Christ." No matter the hardships it had
caused her, she understood the dilemma he'd faced

and didn't blame him for rescuing his mother rather than marrying her. "You make it so damned hard not to love you."

Then his mouth was on hers, and she opened herself up to him, welcoming him. It wasn't like before, beside the stream. Too much past had flavored that kiss. Now the burden he'd been carrying seemed lighter—although it would never leave him completely. She was still not his to have and to hold forever, but maybe for one more night. She wasn't yet betrothed to Chidding. Perhaps she never would be. She understood now that Knight couldn't marry her, so he wasn't offering her any sort of false hope. She knew the truth of the situation, and having told her, he felt somewhat untethered.

But also sorrowful, because as she ran her fingers through his hair, he was acutely reminded of what he'd given up, was giving up. A woman he thoroughly enjoyed being with. She'd held him enthralled from the moment he'd met her.

He loathed the duke for not revealing the truth sooner, before he fell in love with such a remarkable woman. But then he suspected the old man had waited until he'd known Knight would suffer greatly, to allow him to experience the joy and then to snatch it away. More devastating to have loved and lost, to have had a gauge for assessing the immeasurable pain. It had all been a game, a game the duke had judged he would eventually win, and the innocent, unsuspecting boy who had grown up in his household would pay a heavy price for not being of his blood. Punished for what had never been his fault, for something over which he'd had no control. Diabolical and cruel.

But Reggie's tongue tangling with his, her hands skimming over his shoulders were a salve, a balm to all the wounds he'd received that long-ago morning, wounds not yet properly healed. Because guilt and the injuries he'd inflicted on Regina had caused them to continually fester.

Reaching for her, without separating their mouths, he dragged her onto his lap so he could more easily access all he desired—all he would desire until he drew his last breath. She was all that was good, bold, and kind. Even her act of revenge had done no real damage to him, but it threatened her, and he would do whatever necessary to ensure she didn't suffer for it.

But for now, all he wanted was the pleasure. All he wanted was her back in his arms.

REGINA DIDN'T KNOW if it was all the reminiscing she'd done while in the theater box, or the fury that had been undulating through her during the journey here, or the anger she'd been able to only partially unleash upon her arrival, or finally knowing the full story behind his perceived betrayal, but all her senses were attuned. Want, need, and desire were rampaging through her. He had loved her. Loved her still. She loved him.

While her broken heart was no longer perfect, the shards put back into place but still revealing cracks, she felt more whole than she had in a good long while. Just as she'd needed the kiss by the stream, she needed what he was offering her now. One final coming together, one proper goodbye. She couldn't have him forever, but she could have him tonight. She would take it and allow it to wash away the last remnants of hurt that had lingered for far too long.

Sliding his mouth from hers, he journeyed along her throat. She dropped her head back to give him easier access to the sensitive skin.

"You still smell of gardenia," he purred.

She smiled. "You smell of sandalwood. I think you bathed before I arrived."

"Mmm." Placing his hand on the back of her head, he tipped it down until their eyes met. "I want to do more than kiss you."

"I want you to do more than kiss me."

With a moan, he pressed his face against her bosom and clutched her to him. "I've missed you more than you'll ever know, but after tonight . . . you may not need a man, but your life will be easier with a husband."

It wasn't a proposal. He wasn't going to marry her. It was a proclamation that he was giving her up. She still experienced the tiniest pinch of hurt, but she had a greater understanding of the sacrifice he was making. He could have asked her to be his mistress. She wasn't altogether certain she'd have said no. Instead, he was acknowledging how much legitimacy meant to her. As she'd told him, she wasn't her mother's daughter. She didn't want to follow that path of being *kept*, of being the reviled object of unkind gossip, of living with a questionable reputation. She wanted, needed, deserved the respectability that had been denied her all her life. She rested her cheek on the top of his head. "I know. But I think we need a proper goodbye, to put the past fully behind us, so we can both move forward with more clarity."

He chuckled low, darkly, seductively. "I was thinking more along the lines of an *improper* goodbye."

Her laugh was cut off as his mouth swooped in to cover hers. She'd always found such joy in his arms, such happiness in being with him, and of late, she'd been fighting all those feelings because she'd been justified in being cross with him. But the sensations had continued to hover at the edges of their time together, striving to break through the barriers she'd erected to protect herself from him. But the walls had tumbled when he'd gifted her with the knowledge that she'd been and was still truly loved.

She was aware of his hands busily undoing the fastenings on the back of her gown. Enough of his buttons had never been done up that she had only to tug on the cloth for him to cease his actions, reach back, draw his shirt over his head, and toss it aside. The man had always had the most exquisite chest, just a sprinkling of hair that arrowed down into his trousers, providing a path for her hands to follow.

She eased her gown off her shoulders until it pooled at her waist, teasing him with the sight of all that remained to be undone. But he merely studied her and trailed a finger slowly along the edge of her corset where it met the upper swells of her breasts.

"You're larger than you were before."

"A woman's body changes when she carries a child." *Your child.* But now was not the time for that revelation to be revealed. She didn't know if it ever would be.

The dimple formed. "I'm not complaining."

"You once said they were perfect."

"They're still perfect." He pressed a kiss to the valley where her breasts met. "*You're* still perfect. Let's get you out of all these silly womanly trappings."

Easing off his lap, she stood as he went to work releasing hooks, pulling ribbons and lacings, removing what he could, having her step out of what he couldn't until she was completely bare. Kneeling before her, he cradled her hips and kissed the shallow curve of her abdomen.

"Her father would find all the changes wrought by bringing his child into the world incredibly beautiful."

The reverence in his tone had tears forming in the corners of her eyes. She threaded her fingers through his hair. "I feared you might be disappointed with the changes."

Shaking his head, he looked up at her. "You're more stunning than ever."

Shoving himself to his feet, he lifted her into his arms and began striding toward the bed.

"Your trousers need to come off," she admonished.

"I always loved that you never pretended shyness."

"My mother was the mistress of a lord. When he visited, they spent a good bit of time in the bedchamber. As I got older, she wasn't secretive about what happened when that particular door was closed. For her, the art of lovemaking was never something to be ashamed of but to be celebrated. 'It's the natural course of life,' she told me. I'm grateful she was honest about it."

"As am I." He set her down gently on the mattress and went to work on the fastenings of his trousers.

With anticipation, she watched as he shed them and tossed them aside. He remained magnificent, a feast for the eyes. Sculpted muscles, taut flesh, and hard cock—for her. He climbed onto the bed and stretched out beside her. "Better?"

She smiled. "Much."

He began slowly, languorously trailing the blunt tip of his finger around her face. "How can you be more beautiful now?"

When the circle was complete, he cupped her chin and blanketed his mouth over hers . . . releasing a storm of desire, want, and need. They were intertwining themselves in such a manner as to make it impossible to know where one of them ended and the other began. It had always been thus with them, however, and she found comfort in the fact that even after all these years of being separated, it felt as if they'd made love only last night. They were so in tune. Hands moving frantically to caress what hadn't been touched in so long, to become reacquainted with a body that had changed during the intervening years. She was familiar with her transformations, many the result of having a child. But, somehow, she'd expected him to remain the same.

Yet, he seemed slightly broader, a little more muscular, more substantial, giving her more of him to love.

She trailed her fingers and mouth over him, relishing his doing the same with her. He'd always had wicked ways about him, gliding his hands softly along the inside of her thighs, but not going as far as the juncture where they met, not yet pressing the pad of his thumb against her womanly core that yearned—begged—for him to offer some surcease from all the craving.

Separating himself from her slightly, balanced on an elbow, he kneaded her breast, the heat in his gaze as he watched the movements setting her own skin afire. Their legs were entangled, his impressive cock pressing into her thigh. Sliding her hand from his firm buttocks, she folded her fingers around his hard length. Slamming his eyes closed, he growled low. While she knew more victories were to come, this small one still thrilled her, that she could have such power over him.

When he opened his eyes, the blue was darker, smoldering. Lowering his head, he took the peak of her nipple into his mouth and suckled. The sound that escaped her was a mixture of a groan and a squeal as he sent pleasure coursing through her with his ministrations.

Perhaps it was because she'd gone so long without any sort of release, or perhaps it was simply being with him again, but every inch of her throbbed, sending out joyous bursts of pleasure. She was back in his arms and didn't know where she'd find the strength to leave them. But then a good bit of her life had involved finding the strength to meet the challenges tossed her way.

However, moments like this, with him, were very much like being granted a reward for doing what one ought, even as what they were doing was precisely what one ought not.

When she was younger, she'd experienced a bit of a thrill at misbehaving, but now that she was older, she didn't feel she was misbehaving at all. Society's strictures were all nonsense. The release of her book had shown her that. Some people were appalled but still they read it. Hypocrites. Why should only the married be able to experience this wondrousness?

Her mother had known that, and while Regina couldn't condone her father's unfaithfulness to his wife, she did hold with her mother's belief that love was rare and should be treasured when found. What better way to treasure it than through the act of love?

And that's what this was, what it had always been with Knightly: an act of love.

For a while, her memories of the time spent with him had been tainted by her misperceptions of what had transpired between them, the reasons he'd not made her his wife. She'd believed he'd suddenly realized he couldn't marry someone beneath his station or that he'd planned all along to jilt her at the last moment. His attentions and declarations had all been a farce, a way to bed her and leave her. But now she knew the truth, and all the times they'd been together had returned to their proper hue, only brighter and more vivid, something to be recalled in later years with a smile.

At this moment, she was fully aware that the time for them to be together was ticking away. They weren't promising each other forever, but only now. Knowing the truth was liberating. No false hopes, no deceptive expectations. And in the reality, she found exaltation.

He kissed the underside of her breast, his breath wafting warm along her skin, heating her to her very core. Frantic with need, she tightened her grip on him, sliding her hand up, down, up, stopping to circle the pad of her thumb over the smooth dome, spreading the dew gathered there. Her reward was his low feral growl before he began moving along the length of her torso, taking his time to place a lingering kiss against each rib.

He slid farther down, and she lost her hold on his cock. Why did the man have to be so remarkably tall? But his wide shoulders were within reach, and she took advantage of their nearness to dig her fingers into them as he peppered kisses over her stomach.

Lifting his head, he gave her a heavy-lidded look that sent her heart galloping. Adjusting his position so he was no longer supported by one arm, he placed a hand on the inside of each thigh and spread her legs wide enough to accommodate his broad shoulders as he settled between her thighs. He'd been there before. She knew the glory that was coming, that he would deliver. Her breathing stilled, became a timid thing, in anticipation of the wickedness she welcomed.

He blew a breath over the springy curls between her thighs, and her own breath released on a sigh. He kissed the inside of one thigh and then the other. Another duo of kisses, a little higher up. Then once more farther down.

She squirmed as her body tried to move her heavenly area closer to his questing mouth. His dark chuckle rang out. He knew he was tormenting her. Damn him for enjoying her writhing and suffering.

"Do it," she ordered, breathless with need. "Feast upon me."

He lifted his head, his eyes a cauldron of desire. He held her gaze, his shoulders tense against her fingers. Seeing him positioned thus between her legs had flames of yearning crackling within her, burning at her very core. Her nerve endings were sparking, and the manner in which he studied her might have been the most erotic thing she'd ever seen.

Within his eyes were so many promises: of passion, of fire, of incredible pleasure.

Then he lowered his head to fulfill them.

The first stroke of his tongue had her gasping, spreading her legs farther apart, and lifting her hips to meet his luscious mouth and bask in his wicked ways. She couldn't hold still, undulating against him like some wild creature caught in a trap of its own making, with no avenue for escape. He gripped her hips, digging into her flesh, holding her captive while simultaneously setting her spirit free as he hungrily devoured.

A hard press. A quick, long stroke. A swirl of his tongue. A closing of his lips over that tiny bud aching with need. A suck that drew pleasure from every part of her as though all aspects of her were somehow connected with intertwining strings. She knew little about the inner makeup of the body—just a general knowledge of bone and muscle and tissue—but surely there existed a fine web of silken threads along which pleasure traveled, for how else could she experience such exquisite sensations everywhere when his attentions were devoted to only one aspect of her?

"Oh, Arthur!" It came out very nearly a squeal, a desperate beckoning for more as her skin tightened, very much like the tension ratcheting up as a catapult was being prepared to fling its arsenal over the castle wall.

He heeded her request, his ministrations increasing in fervor, until she was crying out as all the pent-up passion and desire shot through her and hurtled her into the abyss where pleasure in all its splendor reigned. Her fingers dug into his shoulders, her legs clamped around him, and her cries echoed about them as wave after wave of ecstasy coursed through her. When she was lethargic and spent, he moved up and thrust into her, reigniting her desire.

Braced on his arms, he hovered over her, gazing down on her, his hips pistoning like some great beast of a locomotive. He was so majestic with his hair flapping against his brow, dew gathering on his chest. As her thighs squeezed his hips, she stroked her hands over his shoulders, his arms, his back.

With his movements, slamming into her, almost as though to punish himself for all the years they'd been apart, he brought forth more pleasure within her. Perhaps because it had been so long for her as well. She didn't know if she'd ever be fully sated. Once more she was spiraling toward completion, his name echoing around her, a benediction.

Then he did what he'd never done before. As his body reached its crescendo, he withdrew, his seed— thick and hot—spilling against her thigh, his body jerking and trembling in the wake of its release.

She knew why he'd done it. When they'd come together five years earlier, he had planned to marry her and so it hadn't mattered if she got with child. They'd simply say the little one arrived early. But now it mattered. He wasn't going to marry her. She was going to marry another, and it would be wrong for her to be carrying a babe in her belly when she walked up the aisle to exchange her vows.

An overwhelming sense of loss battered her. Wrapping her arms around him, she clung to him as if by doing so, she might hold him forever.

Somewhere a clock chimed midnight, and she could have sworn that within its reverberations she heard *But you can't.*

IT HAD BEEN a good long while since Knight had felt such peace, although it was a bittersweet sensation because he was acutely aware a great deal of his contentment was the result of having Regina's warm body resting snugly against his own, her finger lazily drawing circles over his chest. And it was very likely this would be the last time she would ever visit his bedchamber. She was destined to be welcomed into another. But at the moment she was with him, and he wanted to make the most of it.

"You were cross when you arrived . . . about the theater box."

"You lost it to him on purpose," she said lethargically. "Why?"

"Because I knew he didn't have one and you enjoy the theater. I thought it would provide an opportunity for him to quicken his courtship. It never occurred to me it would come with memories you might not wish to visit."

She pressed a kiss to a rib. "I decided a nefarious reason was behind what you did. I should have known better." She shifted until she was able to flatten her hand on his chest and rest her chin on it. "I don't mind the memories now."

Giving her a soft smile, he combed his fingers through the silken strands of her hair. "He's a decent bloke. Chidding."

Her gaze wandered over his features, and he wondered if she was striving to memorize every line and arch of his face as he was hers. "He kissed me tonight."

No, the vixen had been watching him to gauge his reaction, and he suspected he'd had no success at disguising the flinch, as though his bare back had been flogged. He hadn't needed to know that tidbit, didn't want to consider the pleasures the man would have with her. Still, he couldn't stop himself from asking, "Did you enjoy it?"

Because he most certainly didn't want her to have a lifetime of unpleasantness. He wasn't that selfish of a bastard.

"It was rather chaste, as if he feared offending me. I have the impression he's not quite as passionate as you."

"Perhaps he's simply more gentlemanly, and the passion will come."

She brushed the hair back from his brow. "What

would your father—" She stopped, shook her head. "How do you refer to him now?"

"On occasion, *father*. It's the habit of a lifetime. More often by his title, when I can remember. Frequently *bastard*, even though he's not one and I am."

"Are you bothered that your true parents were in fact not married and, technically, you are a bastard?"

"Initially, I did struggle with the circumstances of . . . my birth. I wasn't who I'd always understood myself to be. I wasn't *his* son. My life—I—had been a lie. Who was I really? What was I really? But during my darkest moments I would think of you, and from you I learned legitimacy does not define a person. So I looked to my achievements as a way to measure myself as a man." He considered loving her and being loved *by* her his greatest success.

Her fingers lingered in his hair before trailing down to stroke his jaw. "I grew up knowing I wasn't legitimate. For you, the suddenness of it must have been a blow."

"The harder part was imagining Mother being unfaithful. She doesn't seem the sort."

"Do you have any idea who truly sired you?"

Slowly he shook his head.

"Have you asked your mother?"

"I haven't even told her that I know the truth of things, and I most certainly haven't revealed anything at all about the bargain. She wouldn't take it well, would feel guilty, and that rather defeats the purpose of my rescuing her. She went through twenty years of hell. I want whatever time remains to her to be carefree and without worry."

Her eyes were brown, fathomless depths into which he'd always fallen when given the chance to stare into them, as he was now. But after tonight there could be no more opportunities. He needed to attend to the task of prodding Chidding more quickly toward the altar and thwarting her brother's attempts to prove she was Anonymous.

"What do you think *the duke* would do now if you were to marry?"

"I vowed I would not."

Lifting herself up, she straddled him. "He is not an honorable man. Look what he did to your mother. What he did to you. He had years in which he could have told you the truth. He could have chosen to be gentle in the telling. He could have chosen to not let it matter. Instead at every turn he was deliberately cruel."

"His actions would not excuse my being dishonorable. I swore on my mother's life not to marry. In addition, he has demonstrated his cruelty knows no bounds. I can't discount the retribution he might decide to take. Who he would hurt. What sort of torment he might inflict on those I love."

"Why is his blood so damned important?"

"It has always been thus among royalty and the nobility."

"But we are comprised of more than red fluid. Other aspects of us are so much more important." Leaning down, she peppered kisses over his brow, his cheeks, his jaw. "Yet your determination to remain honorable and protect others are reasons I love you so."

And one of the reasons he would spend the remainder of his life with regret for the pain he'd inflicted upon her.

"It nearly killed me that day not to make you my wife." Was nearly killing him now to know he never could.

"If the Duke of Wyndstone were any sort of decent man, he'd be proud to call you son."

Although he'd never be proud to call the man father. He gave her a cocky grin. "I think you're somewhat biased."

"Doesn't mean I'm wrong."

He needed to get her home soon. But not right now. He needed her one more time.

Cradling her hips, he raised her up and brought her down, thrusting into her as he did so, as her velvet heat surrounded his cock. She rode him with fire and determination.

She'd never been shy but neither had she been this confident, this controlling.

Their need for each other was like a tempest—all fury and force and destruction. Tearing down walls that would need to be rebuilt, taking possession and tossing them about with persistence, encompassing them fully until nothing existed outside of them.

Only hunger, pleasure, and need existed. Only this small world of touches, kisses, and strokes. Squeezing, pinching, and soothing. No troubles, no worries. No nightmares. Only dreams. Splendor and richness.

Her cries urged him on, to pump faster, to delve deeper, harder. When she fell apart, his name woven through her screams echoing around him, he knew a glorious triumph. He very nearly spilled his seed into her, but at the last second, he withdrew, the grandeur of the moment dimming somewhat because he couldn't give her all of himself.

But he was grateful to have tonight, to have had the opportunity to give to her all that he could. One last time.

CHAPTER 19

*I could scarcely wait for the arrival of each ball. Within
the ballroom, we proved ourselves examples of perfect
decorum. But we always found an alcove, a conservatory,
a niche in the garden where we would not be discovered.
Where shadows and our passions reigned.*
—Anonymous, *My Secret Desires, A Memoir*

June 23, 1875

REGINA had arrived at his residence alone, save
for her coachman and footman, but she was returning to her estate in the wee hours tucked in against
Knightly's side, Shakespeare tethered to the back of
the conveyance.

Now that they were no longer in his bedchamber,
now that clothes were not littered about the floor but
were on bodies as they were meant to be, emotions
were playing havoc with her as she considered the
reality of their situation. She understood fully—and
even commended—the decision he'd made on the day
they were to wed, but that didn't mean she didn't still

feel its bite. Or that his unwillingness to break a vow for her—a vow made to an unscrupulous man—didn't create an agonizing ache in her chest.

"Should I offer to purchase the box back from Chidding?" he asked.

He probably should because she would continue to consider it *their* box—hers and Knightly's. She would no doubt always recall their time together within it. She should rid herself of everything that would conjure up memories of him. But then there was Ari, and she would remind Regina of him every day. "I don't think it's necessary. Unless you want it back."

"I no longer used it. It was simply languishing."

"Then best for it to remain with him. Actors don't like to be aware of empty seats."

He pressed a kiss to her temple. "Should I ask him if his intentions are honorable?"

She laughed lightly. "I'm quite capable of handling the matter myself. Besides, if his intentions weren't honorable, I don't believe he'd have provided us with a chaperone."

"Stupid man. If I could have had you to myself without one . . ."

"Don't you think all the sneaking around and forbidden aspect of our time together added to the allure?"

"You and you alone were the reason for the allure. Never doubt your appeal, Reggie."

"You said when I married, I'd never see you again." Recently she'd wanted his complete absence from her life more than anything. Now the thought made her melancholy. "Will that still hold true . . . after tonight?"

"More so. Can you not understand I can't be within sight of you without wanting you?"

"And when you are not within sight of me?"

"Then, too, but it's easier to control, not as painful. Your husband would probably appreciate not having me about as a reminder of your—our—past. It rather dominated the gossip rags before, and it's beginning to do so now. Which is all to the good because it'll speed up the tortoise."

"I don't blame him for being slow or cautious. I draw some comfort from his not rushing to get his hands on my coffers."

"Where will you live?"

"His estate, I assume. Once it's brought up to snuff. Have you ever been there?"

"Years ago. It'll suit you. Plenty of room for galloping. How is Queen, by the by?"

"Content in her new home." And another reminder of time spent with him that she wouldn't rid herself of. So many gifts he'd given her. Some she could hold in her hands; some she could hold only in her heart.

"I never thought to ask, but where was your daughter born?" His voice was a low murmur.

"Paris. In a little garret."

"Above the artist's studio?"

She detected the tiniest fissure of jealousy, and almost confessed all, but their parting was going to be hard enough as it was. The truth of her daughter would only serve to cause more pain for all of them because they couldn't be together. As long as he believed her lies about Ari's father and her birth month, she could spare him that misery at least, of enduring the agony of watching another raising his daughter. "Above a bakery actually. I awoke up mornings to the most wonderful aromas and started my day with fresh bread slathered in butter."

"I wish I'd been there with you."

She wished he'd been as well. "You'd feel differently after her crying kept you awake for most of the night. Although overall, she's been incredibly good and has brought me great joy."

"And she's going to be a writer like her mother."

She laughed lightly. "Not like me. She will tell her own tales in her own way."

"It's good you'll give her that freedom."

"My mother never expected me to follow in her footsteps onto the stage. Which is a good thing as I'd have been lousy at it."

"Oh, I don't know. That night at the Dragons, you almost had me convinced you weren't the author."

She smiled against his throat. He'd not bothered with neckcloth, waistcoat, or coat. Only shirtsleeves and trousers. Who was to see this time of night? "I hated you then."

The words came out without any rancor.

"As well you should have. I hated myself."

She heard in his tone that he still did, that he didn't quite forgive himself for the hurt he'd caused. She wished she had the power to absolve him of all guilt. "Does your mother often have episodes like the one I witnessed earlier?"

"She did at first, but it's been a long while. I think her fears were brought to the fore because of the loud knocking—I'm surprised the door didn't cave in. I didn't realize you had such a temper."

"It grows hotter as I age, I believe. Sometimes I don't care at all what people think of me, and other times I foolishly give a fig." Easing back slightly, she settled her palm against his strong jaw. So many things she wanted to say, so many she shouldn't because they would only serve to make the future harder to face.

In the end, she said nothing. Simply held him in place as she kissed him, not with the fervor of earlier, but with an emotion reserved for letting go. Or perhaps the sentiment more closely reflected a packing up of the past to store it away for later reflection, when she was silver-haired and wrinkled, surrounded by grandchildren. Some of whom might be his as well. Was it fair to deny him that joy? Or would the truth make his burden a heavier weight to bear?

She sensed in him a shadow, within which was the acknowledgment of the need to carry on in solitude. To spare him any further suffering, she held silent.

The horses had turned down the drive, the moments were slipping past and soon none at all would be left to share with him. Then how was she to go on? As he had taught her: with courage and boldness.

The carriage came to a stop. The kiss ended, but they held each other tightly.

The door clicked open. He made to move toward it, and she stayed him with a touch. "Don't come with me."

Because when her butler opened the door, she would pull Knightly in and take him up the stairs to her bed, to prolong the inevitable parting. He merely nodded, took her hand, and pressed a kiss to the back of it. "Thank you for tonight."

She forced a smile when she wanted to weep. "Thank you for . . . well, for almost everything."

Then, with the help of her footman, she was exiting the carriage. Without looking back, she dashed up the steps. The door opened and she hurried through it to the front drawing room. The draperies had been closed, but she peered through a slit where they met and watched as Knightly climbed out of the carriage and mounted Shakespeare. For the longest of moments man and beast simply waited there. Perhaps Knightly thought she'd give in and invite him to join her.

But she held strong.

Finally, he urged his horse into a gallop, and she sank into a nearby chair. Shakespeare, the bard, had it wrong. Parting was not such sweet sorrow. It was a hideous ache that left naught but mourning in its wake.

CHAPTER 20

⟡⟡⟡

Passion, I discovered, was not limited to hands and lips exploring. It could be a look across a crowded room. The reading of a poem. A smile. A laugh. A sigh. It could encompass a grand gesture or be as simple as a solitary word uttered at the right moment.
—Anonymous, *My Secret Desires, A Memoir*

June 29, 1875

Sitting on a bench that her mother had often shared with her father, Regina watched Arianna, her laughter echoing among the blossoms, scampering around the garden with Princess nipping at her heels. And of course, seeing her daughter with the dog reminded her of Knightly in this very garden, legs splayed as he sat at the tiny table. It had been a week since she'd seen him, a week of missing him more than she ever had before, which was utterly ridiculous. They had no future. He'd made his choice. And she'd made hers. Nothing was more important than ensuring her daughter had a life of acceptance that she herself had been denied.

"Madam, you have a visitor."

She lifted the card from the salver her butler presented to her. Her heart slammed against her ribs as she read the name embossed on it. "What the devil is he doing here?"

"I really can't say, ma'am," Shelby said, his tone flat.

"Of course you can't." How would he know the reason behind Bremsford calling? Naturally she was a sight, dressed in a simple, yet comfortable frock, with strands of her hair flying about her face because she'd been enjoying the warmth of the sun and the slight breeze cooling her. Coming to her feet, she began tucking the loose tresses back into place. "Tell him I'll join him shortly . . . and have tea brought in." Although she couldn't for the life of her imagine he was here for tea.

After leaving the nanny with instructions to keep a close watch on her daughter, she experienced a moment of panic in which she feared he was there to destroy her, had obtained the information for which he was willing to pay a thousand quid. She needed to gird herself. She hurried up the back stairs to her chambers, quickly washed her face, tidied her hair, and decided the frock would do. No need to take the time to slip into something nicer and remind him how well her father had provided for her.

A few minutes later, she strolled into the drawing room. Her guest was standing at the fireplace, his back to the door. "My lord."

The seventh Earl of Bremsford turned, and she was awash in memories of the sixth, her father, as a younger man, pretending to be a pony and giving her a ride on his back, lifting her onto his shoulders so she could pluck leaves from tree branches. For some reason, she'd always been more fascinated with leaves that were hard to reach than flowers that could be gathered with ease. But then far too many times she'd been accused of striving to grasp what was never within range.

"Miss Leyland." He gave a quick nod of his head that could almost have been a bow.

"Your presence is an unexpected"—she cut herself off because it most certainly wasn't a pleasure, which was how she would normally greet a guest whose arrival surprised her—"well, just . . . unexpected."

"I imagine *shocking* is probably the word for which you're searching." His lips didn't quite form a smile, but reflected the barest hint of his trying to make a joke at his own expense, and she wondered if he could be as fun-loving as her—their—father.

Hearing the slight rattling of china, she held still and studied him, aware of his scrutinizing her in return. She'd never been this close to him. It was uncanny, how very much he favored his father. Same jaw, nose, brow. His cheekbones were a tad sharper, perhaps inherited from his mother. He was a little more slender, but that might change as he aged.

The maid entered, set the tray on a table, and, following a shallow curtsy, quietly left.

"Would you care for some tea?" Regina asked, waving a hand toward the tray as though the man couldn't tell what had been delivered.

"No, thank you."

"Scotch?"

He glanced toward the sideboard, and she hoped he didn't realize it had originally been set up to accommodate their father. "No, thank you."

She indicated the nearest sitting area. "Would you at least like to make yourself comfortable?" As if either of them could be comfortable in this situation fraught with years of mistrust and curiosity.

Without a word, he settled into a large plush chair, the one in which her father had always sat. It was a little dizzying to see a man who looked so much like him perched so stiffly on the cushion. She couldn't imagine the current Bremsford ever lounging.

She wanted to sit in a chair on the far side of the room. Instead, she gathered up her pluck and took the nearer one facing him. For several minutes, they simply stared at each other, noting the similarities—brown eyes, blond hair—and differences. Noses, chins, lips.

If he had somehow managed to determine she was Anonymous, she didn't think he'd have waited to inform her that he was on the verge of taking everything from her. But despite her best efforts, she couldn't think of any other reason for him to be there. Finally, when her nerves were stretched to the point of snapping, she said, "I assume you've come with some purpose in mind. Don't suppose you'd be kind enough to share it."

"I've always heard you're quite . . . up-front about things. Neither bashful nor timid, I've been told." Slowly, he tapped the well-manicured fingers of his right hand on the arm of the chair. Did he find her boldness an afront? Was his wife a shy creature? He cleared his throat. "Father died disappointed that his *legitimate* family had never been welcoming of his *illegitimate* one."

She didn't know if, by pointing out the disparity of their places within Society and the law, he was merely obtuse, being deliberately rude, or truly striving to be kind.

"I've been reckoning with that of late," he continued, "and experienced tremendous guilt at harboring ill feelings toward you when the circumstances of your birth were not your fault."

She couldn't very well ask if that guilt had prompted him to place a bounty on the identity of Anonymous because if she wasn't the author, why would she care about his actions? However, she could be upset over something else he'd done without giving herself away. "Was it your guilt that urged you to demand of Lord Knightly that he confirm I was the author of *My Secret Desires*?"

His cheeks actually turned a mottled red. "When I saw the two of you riding together at the park, I feared he might have mentioned our encounter. He denied any association he or you might have had with the book, of course."

"He had no reason not to."

"I simply thought with all the conjecture that he was Lord K—"

"I doubt I am the only woman to have been in his life."

"True. Before you, there were any number from what I understand. He does seem to have a penchant for enjoying the ladies. And they him, if rumors are to be believed."

She couldn't help but wonder if that was another jab, an attempt to make her feel like she hadn't been special. But then Knightly had never asked any of the others to marry him. She also knew there had been very few since her. "Young swells will be young swells, I suppose."

"Quite. Hopefully you will not hold my inquisitiveness against me. I . . . well, as I said, my attitude toward you did not please Father while he was alive, and I wished to ensure your character before I"—he reached into his coat pocket, withdrew a cream-colored envelope, and held it out toward her— "extended an invitation to the ball my countess and I are hosting Tuesday next."

She stared at the square of vellum as though it was Cleopatra's asp on the verge of striking. "You're joking, surely."

He set the invitation on the table beside his chair. "I assure you I am not."

"Five years ago, I was to marry an earl who would one day become a duke. You didn't think my character good enough then?"

"My mother was alive then," he stated hotly. "I had to choose between which of my two parents I would keep happy."

She immediately felt contrition. "I'm so sorry. I didn't realize she'd passed."

"Three years ago."

While she'd been away. Her father hadn't mentioned his wife's passing, but then he rarely spoke of his other family—perhaps fearing she might feel diminished in some way. Most of what she knew of the life he'd lived beyond here she'd gathered from gossip. "It's hard to lose both parents, especially so closely together."

Still, she could hardly signify he was attempting a reconciliation at a ball, rather than with a quiet dinner or a tea in the garden or simply a series of visits. "Will your sisters accept my presence at your affair?"

"They will indeed. We've discussed it and they are amenable to the idea. Perhaps because our family is suddenly smaller, we've come to the realization the members of it are so very important. You will be treated as an honored guest, I assure you. Chidding will no doubt be pleased to have you there, and I have always rather liked the viscount. Knightly is sure to approve."

"You've invited him, in spite of your recent harsh words?"

"One does not snub a man who will, as you so succinctly put it, one day become a duke. We merely had a misunderstanding. I am not one to hold grudges."

She found that a trifle difficult to believe. "Share with me a memory."

"Pardon?" He'd sat up straighter, as though she'd suddenly aimed a pistol at him and he was preparing to bolt.

"You're asking me to put past snubbing aside, and yet I'm not getting a sense of true remorse or even a real desire to know me. If we are to build a bridge, we must at least gather some materials. A memory would be a start, something involving . . . Father, perhaps."

He looked like he very much wished he'd accepted her earlier offer of scotch, although the way his gaze wandered around the room, she suspected he wished he'd drunk an entire bottle. Finally, his attention landed back on her, while his fingers began their tapping again. "We have a pond on our estate, almost a lake really. We would clamber into a small boat, only he and I, and he'd paddle out to its center. I don't recall how old I was when we started doing it. I can't remember a time when we didn't. When I was four, he finally allowed me to hold a pole by myself. I snagged a catch. Blasted fish pulled me right into the water. I was terrified, thought surely I was going to drown. Father grabbed me by the scruff of my shirt and dragged me out of the abyss. Then he held me tightly. I could feel him shaking." He cleared his throat. "It's the only memory I have . . . where his actions indicated that he might actually treasure me."

She had never doubted her father's love, was struggling with the fact this man had. She wanted to know so much more about what their relationship had entailed. Had her father been strict with him? Or had he spoiled and indulged his son as he had her?

"Your memory," he suddenly snapped gruffly.

Emotions, it seemed, weren't something with which he was comfortable. Or perhaps he was perturbed that she was asking him to earn her presence at his ball. Still, she smiled warmly. "You were in a play at school, had the role of Hamlet. It was written up in the school newspaper and you were showered with acclaim for your performance. 'That's your brother,' he said. He was quite proud."

His brow furrowed. "He mentioned me?"

"On the rare occasion."

"He never mentioned you. We knew about you, of course, gossip and conjecture being what they are, but he never spoke about you . . . after his initial admittance of your existence."

The words had come out crisply, like bullets fired by a militia, and she decided he was finding it truly difficult to be here, to offer an olive branch. But she decided he was at least trying, and she dearly wanted to reassure him that they could at least be friends, of a sort.

"I doubt any of you ever asked about me or were comfortable with my existence. Mother and I knew our place in his life. We didn't mind him talking about you. It gave us a glimpse into a larger part of his world that otherwise would have been kept secret from us. I know what I am, my lord. I don't fool myself into believing I am otherwise. I shall consider your invitation."

He stared at her in bewilderment as though he'd come upon a unicorn. Quite suddenly, he lunged to his feet. "Very good. I fear, Miss Leyland, my sisters and I may have done you a disservice all these years."

She rose. "Society likes to keep us in boxes. I'm glad you're striving to break free of yours."

"I'll see myself out. Good day."

It wasn't until she heard the closing of the door that she walked over, picked up the envelope, slipped a fingernail beneath the wax, and pried it loose in order to pull free the invitation.

Lord and Lady Bremsford request the honor of your presence . . .

Her mother had never been allowed to step foot in that residence. She wondered if she dared.

KNIGHTLY HAD RETURNED late from his club to find a missive from Regina: *If you would be so kind as to visit this evening, I require your opinion on a matter.*

As his carriage carried him toward her residence, he speculated on any number of matters that might require his opinion.

Am I more attractive naked or in clothing?

Either way I can scarce take my eyes off you.

Do you prefer me in green or red?

In nothing at all.

Do you prefer my moans or my sighs?

I adore them both.

Would you rather have me in bed or against a wall?

I want only to have you.

With the last, he released a frustrated sigh. He couldn't have her, not for any length of time, anyway, not as his wife, not if he was going to honor the vow he'd made. Five years ago, the cost had seemed absurdly high, and he'd refused to ask her to pay the price which he must, but now that he was spending time with her again, the temptation to break the vow was as strong as the temptation to ask her to sacrifice marriage and the legitimacy of her children for him.

Yet, he knew he wouldn't do it, couldn't bring himself to do it. She'd grown up without it, suffered because of it. She deserved to have children not labeled as bastards. That she'd already given birth to one tormented him, and he would do all in his power to ensure Arianna didn't endure heartache as her mother had. He'd already established a trust for the girl that would provide her with a substantial yearly income. And it contained no daft clauses about bad behavior. When she was grown, the young lady could ride a horse through the London streets without wearing a stitch of clothing, and still, she'd receive her funds.

He wasn't quite certain when he was going to tell Regina about what he'd done. After she was married, he supposed. Or maybe he'd simply have his solicitor inform her. An anonymous benefactor. He wanted neither Regina nor her daughter feeling any obligation toward him. He couldn't help but reflect that too much of their lives involved being anonymous.

The carriage drew to a halt. He opened the door and leapt out without waiting on a footman. Light spilled through the windows of the front drawing room, a welcome beacon as he sprinted up the steps and knocked on the door.

She opened it, her hair slightly askew, and he longed to release the strands from their confining hairpins. "I didn't think you were coming."

He couldn't blame her for worrying. After all, once before he hadn't come to her rescue. "I was at the club. I only just got your message. Is there trouble?"

"I don't think so. Please come in." She turned away and headed into the drawing room, leaving him to shut the door and follow.

It was nearing eleven, the house was quiet, the servants no doubt retired for the night. Her daughter was probably nestled in her cradle. No, she was too old for a cradle now. How had she looked shortly after she was born with her mother fussing over her? He hated the sights he'd been denied, and he could envision the joy it would bring the duke to know precisely what Knight was suffering.

He ambled into the drawing room, crossing the threshold just as she turned away from the decanter table, a tumbler of what was most likely scotch in one hand, a snifter of brandy in the other.

"Let's sit over there." She indicated the small settee situated in front of some bookshelves. Having sat upon it numerous times, he knew it placed her within easy reach.

"Not by the fire?" Sitting opposite each other seemed a safer way to go if they were to avoid temptation, although perhaps he was merely being idiotically optimistic because he couldn't envision that being at opposite ends of Britain was far enough away from her to make him not want her.

She carried on to the settee. "No. Bremsford sat there earlier, and I'm not certain I'll ever be quite comfortable in that space again."

His gut clutched almost painfully because he'd not been here to provide a buffer between her and the man. "Bremsford. What the devil was he doing here?"

"Inviting me to his ball, if you can believe it." Elegantly, she lowered herself onto the cushions and held the glass toward him.

Taking her offering, he settled beside her, giving his knee the freedom to touch hers. If she noticed, she didn't react. Simply took a sip of her brandy, closed her eyes, and sighed heavily before concentrating on him. He wondered if they'd married five years earlier, if by now, they'd have grown bored with each other, if he'd no longer relish the sight of her. But he couldn't imagine that what he'd felt for her then would not have merely deepened. "Why would he invite you to his ball?" he finally asked, deciding they needed to get to the matter at hand.

As she was a writer, her telling wasn't particularly concise, but remarkably detailed, including facial expressions, tones, and the emotions that had been roiling through her. Thus, he was able to envision it all as clearly as if he'd been there, observing the encounter. When finished, she shook her head. "He seemed sincere. However, it struck me as a rather grand start to the forging of a relationship. Although perhaps having so many people around would lessen the awkwardness. It's not like we'd be confined to each other's company the entire time."

He was having a difficult time reconciling the man who'd approached him at the Dragons with the one who'd been in her parlor that afternoon. "Do you *want* to have a relationship with him?"

Cupping her snifter in both hands, she rubbed its bowl as though it was Aladdin's lamp, and he wondered what she might wish for if a genie appeared. "When I was younger, I would write stories in which my father's other children and I were fast friends and went on adventures together. Invariably one of them would save me from some disaster or I would rescue them from danger. I longed to have friends other than my dolls. It breaks my heart that presently Arianna's friends are all made of porcelain or cloth. Bremsford and his sisters have children. Would they welcome Ari? Would they be there for her? Would it be easier for Chidding to ask for my hand if he knew he wouldn't make an enemy in the process?"

Her eyes held his, and he wanted desperately to give her the right answer.

"What if his quest to find Anonymous wasn't truly about me," she continued, "but simply his desire to confront someone who wrote something he believes to be subversive? Maybe he doesn't even know about the clause in the trusts. Perhaps it's all simply coincidence, and it's my own duplicitousness that's causing me not to trust him."

She wanted family, and the hope that she was on the verge of acquiring it was reflected within the brown depths of her eyes. To belong. To no longer live on the outskirts of Society, just as she'd lived on the outskirts of London. She wanted to be in the center, and he wished to God he could give her that. "As the heir apparent, he was bound to have been kept apprised of everything, if not by your father, then by the solicitor upon the earl's passing. I find it inconceivable Bremsford isn't aware of the details of both trusts."

"I would be unwise to attend, then . . . to accept what he said as truth."

After setting his glass aside, he rested an arm along the back of the settee and traced his fingers along her cheek. "I know what it is to lose family . . . and the miracle of discovering not all family is lost to you. If you want him and his sisters in your life, I suggest you venture into this possible quagmire cautiously. At the ball, if matters don't go as you'd hoped, you can always leave. I'll be there to keep a watch over things." He hadn't planned to attend, but nothing would keep him away now. He would greet his host with a glare that promised retribution if he created any sort of stir that caused her the least bit of harm or sadness. "Or I could meet with him before the . . . when is the blasted ball?"

"It's Tuesday next."

"I could speak with him, and then provide you with a more knowledgeable opinion."

"If you wouldn't mind."

You're asking me for something of little consequence and not at all burdensome when I would willingly die for you. But he kept that declaration off his tongue because he suspected she'd prefer he break his vow for her. If she wanted him. Her feelings for him had no doubt changed, and while she'd admitted to understanding why he'd not carried through on his promise to her, it had to hurt that he was holding firm on the vow he'd made to the duke. She'd no doubt be happier with Chidding. They had no past that would ever raise its ugly head to create distrust or misgivings. "I'll tend to it on the morrow."

She released a long, slow, deep breath and seemed to melt into relaxation before his eyes. Obviously, it had been weighing on her. Desire for acceptance against fear of public rejection. He resented being part of a society that could make anyone feel small or inconsequential, hated even more anything he might have done that had added to her feelings of lacking in self-worth. "Could be he simply finally came to his senses and realized what a treasure you are."

She laughed at that, her cheeks turning pink. "I'm rather certain that's *exactly* what it was." Her smile diminished slightly. "That he wasn't involved in my life, that he didn't visit here, never bothered me—or so I thought. After he left today, I experienced a measure of gratitude that we might establish a rapport and I'd have a stronger, more immediate connection to Father. We could trade memories. My father led a life I knew very little about, so in a way, I never completely comprehended the whole of him. I have one photograph of him and Mother, taken when they enjoyed a trip to the seaside. I imagine his son has a dozen paintings depicting our father throughout various stages of his life. To be honest, I'm a bit terrified of what I might discover in his residence. Yet I refuse to be cowed."

The bravery of this woman humbled him. From the start she'd done things she'd rather not in an attempt to please her father. Alone, she'd brought a daughter into the world. Now she would marry to ensure that her daughter was never found lacking and would one day marry well. He wondered if a need to continue to please her father might also be driving her toward accepting Bremsford's invitation.

"It's your fault, you know," she said so softly, so wistfully he almost didn't hear her, but still his entire body tightened to such a degree that he thought if a feather landed on him, he might shatter.

"Oh?" was all he could manage in response, hating the notion of facing his culpability for any of her unhappiness.

"All those years ago, you made me feel accepted. It was a novel sensation. I never take it for granted. If I can win over my father's son and his other daughters, I suppose I feel I'd never be found lacking by anyone ever again."

He shifted until he could take her lovely face between his hands. "You are not lacking in any regard. You don't require their acceptance or approval to have any worth. You're more valuable than the whole lot of them because there is no pretense to you. You are good, kind, and generous in all regards. Good Lord, you even forgave me." *When I still can't forgive myself.*

"I don't know if I'm all that good. I sent you a missive because I knew if I went to your residence, I wouldn't be able to behave. I thought here, within my dominion, I could resist temptation. I was wrong."

SHE WAS SO wrong. And a bit disconcerted by the dawning realization she'd invited him here not truly for his opinion regarding Bremsford's visit, but because she'd missed him and hadn't wanted their last parting to be the final one. Because she'd wanted one more memory of him here, within her bed.

She had no resistance to him. As their mouths locked, she was gratified he had none to her. A storm raged within each of them, threatening—no, promising—to carry them out to a sea of pleasure.

He was reaching for her lacings and she for his buttons when sense finally took hold of her again.

"No," she commanded, staying both their actions. He immediately went still, his breathing already harsh and heavy with the power unleashed. "Not here. My bedchamber."

"Thank God, I thought you were going to send me on my way."

She knew her smile reflected wickedness. "Not until I've had *my way* with you."

Their journey to her bedchamber was not a quick dash, because they continually stopped to ensure the fire didn't ebb. A short kiss. A long one. Her back pressed against a wall as he devoured her mouth while flattening his body against hers, rubbing the bulge in his trousers against her mound, driving her to madness. Breathing became laborious as sensations flowed through her.

How she wanted him naked.

When they finally made it to her chamber, closing the door in their wake, she was surprised to discover their clothing wasn't scorched. She felt as though every inch of her was alight.

In a matter of minutes, their attire was cast aside, and they were tumbling onto the bed with a laugh, a murmur, and then a groan as hands and mouths touched where they wanted, intimately. Heated glances, hot tongues, determined fingers.

Like an untamed creature, she writhed beneath him, begging, demanding he fulfill the promise ignited with every stroke, every squeeze, every lick. Oh, the wondrous sensations this man brought to life with his tongue. She was rather certain the things he did were illegal. For surely if Society objected to her book, it had to object to this sort of wanton, all-encompassing gratification.

Then he was driving into her, filling her, and she was digging her fingers into his backside, pushing him, lifting her hips so he went even deeper. His feral growl reverberated throughout his entire body, was absorbed by hers, heightening her pleasure.

They moved in tandem with a wildness that had them both crying out as they reached the pinnacle of ecstasy, and they returned to reality in a gloriously sated heap.

SOMETHING WOKE HIM. Had the warm body at his back stirred or had it been the slender thigh nestled between both of his and pressing gently against his bollocks? Maybe it had been a change in the tempo of Regina's warm breath wafting over his shoulder as she slept.

He'd drifted off holding her, but now she held him. He could hear her breathing, short little pants that didn't match the slow rhythm of her breath teasing his flesh. Something was amiss.

Opening his eyes, he found himself staring into blue.

"Bloody hell!" He shot up in bed, slammed the back of his skull against the headboard, and struggled to bring the sheet up higher, but it was caught beneath the woman. At least it was pooled at his hips, hiding most of his nakedness. His breaths came in harsh, heaving gasps while Regina roused and looked over his side.

"Ari, what are you doing here?" she asked sleepily, but with the slightest measure of alarm.

"The monster came."

"Oh, darling, I told you there are no monsters." She tossed back the sheet—he slapped a hand down to tuck the linen in against his arse even though it was turned away from the child—and climbed out of bed.

"What are you doing?" he asked.

Strutting about naked, she went to a chair and grabbed her night wrap.

"You can't just—" He waved a hand toward him, her, the girl.

She smiled placidly, indulgently. "She doesn't understand"—she imitated his motions—"she's four."

After donning her wrap and securing it into place by knotting the sash, she walked over and lifted her daughter onto her hip.

"I want to sleep with you," Arianna said.

"Not tonight, darling." She looked at Knight. "I might be a while. It takes some time to settle her down after a nightmare. Don't leave."

"I won't."

He watched as she carried her daughter through the door that was presently standing ajar. Arianna opening it must have been what awakened him.

After releasing a quick breath, he scrambled out of bed, snatched up his trousers, and pulled them on. Grabbing his shirt, he worked his head through the opening, his arms through the sleeves as he tore across the chamber into the hallway, and down it until he reached the room from which light spilled forth. He came to a halt in the doorway, drinking in the sight of Regina putting her daughter to bed as she'd no doubt done a thousand times or more. Once the child was snuggled beneath the covers, resting on her side, her hand tucked beneath her cheek, Regina sat on the edge of the bed, rubbed her back, and began to sing a lullaby.

His chest ached to such a degree he was surprised his heart retained the ability to beat. Never in his life had he ever wanted to lay claim to something more: mother and daughter, to make them his, and hold them close for all eternity. To protect them, nurture them.

Arianna said something he couldn't hear. Her mother had gone silent at the first word, then she glanced over her shoulder. "Would you care to join us?"

Did the sun rise in the east and set in the west?

The child was very nearly swallowed in that bed. He sat at the foot of it, where there was an abundance of room because her legs didn't stretch that far. Her blue eyes were focused on him, wide and unblinking. He couldn't carry a tune in order to sing her a lullaby. What comfort could he bring her? "Do you know what a knight is?"

"You," she whispered.

"That's right. I'm Knight. And a knight slays monsters."

"What's *slays*?"

"*Slays* means to make them go away forever." He leaned forward slightly. "They can't even get into dreams any longer."

"Will you make mine go away?"

"I already have. I'm going to have a chat with Princess before I leave, so she'll keep guard from now on and there will be no more monsters." The smile she gave him wrapped tightly around his heart.

"I love you," she whispered drowsily.

Even though she said that to everyone and it probably meant nothing at all, before he knew this child, he'd only ever said it to one person in his life—Regina—and it did mean something when he gave voice to the sentiment. "I love you, too."

He caught a glimpse of Regina wiping a tear from the corner of her eye before rubbing her daughter's back. "Sleep now, Ari."

The lass closed her eyes, Regina began softly singing again, and Knight wanted to stay there forever.

CHAPTER 21

❦

The dreams that filled my sleep had become the same as those that filled my waking hours. Moments spent with Lord K and his incredibly wicked mouth.
—Anonymous, *My Secret Desires, A Memoir*

June 30, 1875

"KNIGHTLY, this is a surprise. Come to threaten me, have you?"

Standing in the center of the drawing room, Knight had been impatiently waiting as the butler fetched Bremsford. A couple of minutes into his wait, he'd almost gone searching for the damned lord. "Do you need threatening?"

Bremsford laughed, but it was tinged with a bit of unease. "I should hope not. You made your point clear enough the last time we met. Although you are *not* her husband, it seems you are the champion of my father's daughter."

It was a subtle dig, but Knight said nothing because he was deserving of it. "You invited her to your ball."

The earl's eyes widened slightly. "She told you, did she?"

"Not too long ago, you had naught but contempt for her. Why the sudden change of heart?" He agreed with Regina that mentioning the bounty would only serve to make the earl suspicious of their interest in it. He also believed if anything had come of the earl's quest to uncover Anonymous, they would have heard the news by now. Bremsford had never struck him as someone who could hold a secret.

"I have always admired Chidding. He informed me a few days ago that he intends to ask for . . . my"—he cleared this throat—"Miss Leyland's hand."

Knight experienced a sense of loss that nearly overpowered him. Even as he understood the reason the viscount was giving her attention and knew where that attention was headed, hearing the confirmation was like being stupid enough to enter a boxing ring with Bishop and being delivered a blow that dropped him to his knees. His friend had a punch that could easily fell a man—had on more than one occasion.

"In addition, my good wife has not been overly pleased," Bremsford continued, "that I will not allow us to attend any ball to which my father's . . . unlawful . . . offspring has been invited. She's unhappy and I can't have that. Besides, I certainly have no intention of snubbing Chidding's wife. He may be merely a viscount, but he is well respected among the peers. Hence, I thought to test the waters of acceptance."

His reasons certainly sounded logical, even if he did struggle with finding the appropriate identifier for Regina. Knight doubted the man would ever refer to her as *sister*. "You could have invited her to dinner."

"It would have made for a more awkward . . . encounter. One can't politely escape the table or conversation. Striving to make small talk during seven courses can upset digestion and create dire consequences I wished to avoid. At a ball, our opportunities to get to know one another would be like parrying during a fencing match. We come together, do our little maneuvering, and part. We take our time getting to know each other instead of striving to bombard years of avoidance into hours of acquaintance."

He had no corresponding argument for that rationale, and it very much mirrored what Regina had assumed. It would be much more relaxing than striving not to be seen lacking for a long period of time while all eyes would no doubt be upon her.

"Look, Knightly, I don't know why you care or what this has to do with you, but I wish her no ill will. My mother is no longer with us, so she can't be hurt by the chit's presence. My father's dying wish was that I be more accepting of his by-blow. I'm not saying it'll be easy, but I'm willing to give it a go. If I discover I can't be magnanimous regarding her presence in my residence, I can always retire to the cardroom. I'm trying, man. I can do no more than that."

For Regina's sake, Knight wanted the words to be true. He wanted her embraced by family. He wanted her to have the support some families provided. He

wanted less strife in her life and more joy. He nodded. "Right, Bremsford. I wish you success with this
endeavor." He walked toward the door, but stopped by
the earl. "However, my earlier warning remains in effect. Hurt her, and you will be destroyed."

CHAPTER 22

*I desired not only his touch, but his words. They were
not those of a poet, but of an inquisitive man. We spoke
of significant things. He sought my opinion on matters of
import. With obvious admiration, he listened to my views.
Never before had I felt so visible, so substantial. Never
had I been held in such esteem. I found it all to be the most
powerful of aphrodisiacs.*
—Anonymous, *My Secret Desires, A Memoir*

July 6, 1875

Excitement warred with trepidation as the carriage
hurtled toward her destination. Knightly believed the
earl's son to be sincere, but he did admit to having a
tiny fissure of doubt. After all these years, why now?

Not that she blamed him for his reservations. She'd
experienced similar qualms, bouncing between accepting the invitation and tossing it into the fire. But in
the end the desire to know her father's other children
was greater than her fear of being made a fool.

Knightly had offered to accompany her, but it was

enough to know he'd be there. She had decided her best course was to accept the offer Chidding had made during the last ball they'd attended. The viscount was courting her after all. Whereas Knightly was looking out for her from a distance and making love to her—it seemed if they were in a residence that contained a bed, they would soon make their way to it—but was remaining true to the vow he'd made to never marry.

Lady Finsbury was once more serving as chaperone and using the waning sunlight to read. *My Secret Desires.* Regina had mixed feelings about it. She knew not everyone read as rapidly as she did. Still, it had been some nights since their trek to the theater. She should hold her tongue, but instead she heard herself saying, "I take it that the book cannot hold your interest."

The widow glanced over at her. "Pardon?"

She nodded toward the tome. "You were reading it when we went to the theater. It must be dreadfully dull if you've not read it since."

Lady Finsbury laughed. "Oh, this is my third reading. I keep hoping the ending will change, you see. Of course, it can't because books don't work that way, but I continue to search for a hint that Lord K does indeed come back to her. They belong together. The emotion between them . . . well, it brings me to tears. I'm not one to cry easily, am I, Chidding?"

Sitting across from them, he grinned affectionally. "You are not."

"I do hope the author will write a sequel in which they obtain the happiness together they deserve."

"You think she deserves a man who left her?"

"I am convinced he had a good reason for doing so. We just don't yet know what it is. It's obvious he loves her. Which is the reason there absolutely must be another book."

"Do you hold with the notion that man is Lord Knightly?" Chidding asked.

"A very close resemblance, to be sure. But then this is all fiction, I'm rather certain. However, if I were to write a book, I'd use him for inspiration. Handsome with a bit of devilishness to him. However any of the Chessmen would suffice, would they not? Charming, the lot of them, and yet each demonstrates a hint of wickedness. I've written to the publisher, insisting he tell the author to write more books. And that he work up the courage to publish them."

Regina couldn't help but smile at the woman's passion. She liked Lady Finsbury and wished with everything within her that she'd feel the same about the earl's sisters. Surely blood created a commonality, a recognition of similarities in traits, like calling to like.

The carriage slowed as it turned into the drive and entered the queue. Regina was sitting on the side that offered the best view of the massive manor house, and she peered out the window as the building came into view.

"Have you been here before?" Chidding asked.

"No." Feeling somewhat guilty at spying in her youth, she looked at him and admitted, "Mother and I walked by a few times, but I've never been this close to it and certainly not inside. I assume you have."

"Several times. It's quite grand."

Suddenly she realized she'd never been to *his* London residence. "Is yours similar?"

"Not nearly as posh. A bit run-down to be honest."

"That will no doubt change once you marry."

"No doubt." Now he was the one to gaze out the window, and she suspected it didn't sit well with him to be dependent on his bride's dowry, but it was the way for most of the aristocracy. Some were even turning to American heiresses to fill their coffers.

"Needs must," she said quietly, and was rather certain within his eyes she saw gratitude at her understanding of the reality of the situation. Just as he was using her, so she would be using him. Needs must, indeed. If only life were like a work of fiction, in which one could take chances, do as one wished, and consequences suffered were not nearly as dire as those that permeated real life. Even death was not permanent in a story. The reader need only turn back to the first page, and all was once again well before trouble and strife visited.

After a series of starts and stops, during which she'd begun to feel somewhat nauseous, no doubt a result of her nervousness beginning to sharpen with the realization of the approaching nearness of the evening upon which she was about to embark, the carriage arrived at a spot where footmen waited. One opened the door, lowered the steps, and helped her out, followed by Lady Finsbury, and then Chidding.

The viscount offered his arm, and she placed her hand in the crook of his elbow, praying he couldn't detect her slight quivering. He lowered his head slightly. "Chin up. It won't be as bad as all that."

She offered him a reassuring smile while wondering how he might react if she confessed she would be following her mother's advice and imagining everyone naked. Even as the image took shape, she inwardly shook it off. That had been her mother's method, not hers, and she most certainly didn't want to envision Bremsford sans clothing. Her mother's suggestion might work for strangers but not for those one knew. Best to simply storm into the breach, determined to secure victory.

Quite a number of people—chatting, laughing, smiling, completely at ease—were making their way inside. When she crossed the threshold, she felt like she'd stepped into another world. Certainly, Knightly's residence was as grand, if not grander, than this one, but her father had grown up within these walls, had raised his family here, at least during a few months each year.

Chidding escorted her into the parlor where he relinquished his hat and walking stick. The weather was warm, and she'd not bothered with a wrap, not that she'd have retained the wherewithal to hand it off because her attention had been captured by a portrait hanging over the mantel. In oils, her father stood behind a woman—his countess, no doubt—sitting on a settee, his hand resting on her shoulder, a young girl on either side of her. Next to her father stood a lad she'd wager had seen at least a dozen years. It was the whole of his legitimate family.

He'd never had a portrait painted of himself with Regina and her mother.

Unexpectedly, she feared he'd been ashamed of

them, hadn't wanted to reveal them to an artist. His secret family, the one not to be shared with others. A ludicrous notion when he'd given her a ball and sought to find her a husband. Yet now that the doubts had taken root, they haunted her. Had she and her mother been undeserving of the coins required to create such a lasting treasure? Had he worried that perhaps they were only a temporary fixture in his life? Had he expected to grow bored with the actress?

The room had faded away, leaving only her, this portrait, and her thoughts. But her surroundings began to return to her, and she became aware of Chidding near at hand.

"Are you all right?" he asked softly.

She nodded. "I knew—hoped—there would be portraits of him here. I just . . . I suppose I didn't expect to see him with his family." Appearing content, happy even, and proud. "Nor do I recall with such clarity him looking so young. I remember him more as white-haired, even though I was born somewhere between the birth of his son and his eldest daughter." *She* was the eldest daughter. The other was the next daughter. Following her was another.

"I always saw my father as somewhat larger than life," Chidding said kindly. "When I look at his portraits now, he seems unremarkable."

She couldn't be certain she knew the man in this portrait at all. "I can't imagine your father appearing unremarkable if he favored you."

There was his blush again, making her feel somewhat protective of him. "That's kind of you to say. Shall we make our way to the ballroom?"

She glanced around. "We seem to have lost your cousin."

"I'm certain Lady Finsbury has gone on in order to secure a chair advantageous to the lighting so she may continue with her reading."

He tucked her hand back into the crook of his elbow, and she wondered if a time would come when he considered her too brash for his tastes. She could envision him more easily with someone quieter, shyer, who didn't set about attempting to pen a description of how glorious it was to be kissed by a man who was lost to an animalistic frenzy because he was so mad to have the taste of her.

Gracefully, he skirted them around those entering the drawing room and led her down a hallway that spilled into a grand room with stairs branching out in a circular triumph on either side. The ceiling was painted with cherubs flying among clouds and goddesses in long white shifts lounging about beneath trees. A huge chandelier had already been lit in preparation of the arriving darkness that would soon be upon them. She imagined her father strutting through this room toward another hallway entrance beneath the alcove formed where the stairs came together. The walls were littered with huge portraits. Some so large they had to be the precise proportions of their subjects.

She'd seen such in other residences, but these were her relations. She carried the blood of some of these men and some of these women. For the first time, she had an inkling of understanding why the Duke of Wyndstone was appalled at the thought of handing his title over to someone not of his blood. The travesty of it.

As they began to ascend the stairs, she slowed her movements, taking time to study each portrait that was at eye level. Chidding didn't rush her, but stood at her back, shielding her from those who wanted to pass. The steps were wide enough that people could easily slip past them.

On each frame was mounted a small golden plate engraved with the full name and an identifier of those in the portrait. *The fifth earl and his countess. The fourth earl. Second countess of the third earl.* They were all so regal, but haughty. Not a smile among them.

"My mother would have made a wonderful countess."

"Of course." Chidding's voice was low as though he understood this was all a moment of discovery for her. "She was an actress and acting is an enormous part of being an aristocrat."

She wondered how much of his treatment of her was a performance, and then chastised herself for the thought.

A gaggle of people edged by them, and when they were no longer in earshot, he lowered his head slightly. "Just because we're here, doesn't mean we have to go into the ballroom. We can leave."

"I have been dragging my feet, haven't I? It's just that it's all so overwhelming. There's so much history here, and it's my history. And I've never quite had it before." She tucked her hand back into the crook of his elbow. "I'm ready to attend the ball, my lord."

"Very well, Miss Leyland. Let's make a night of it, then, shall we?"

As they carried on, she caught only glimpses of

the other portraits because her attention was more drawn to the man beside her. Would he extend his instinct toward kindness to her daughter? She rather thought he would. She decided, like that long-ago rose that Knightly had given her mother, Chidding's kindness might be the best part of him, and perhaps it was all that mattered.

"His lordship, Viscount Chidding, and Miss Regina Leyland!"

Standing at the top of the stairs, her hand tucked within the crook of Chidding's elbow, she took a deep breath. His other hand came to rest on top of hers reassuringly. She glanced up, and he smiled warmly.

"I always find it unnerving to be announced," he said. "Much more pleasant not to stand up here alone. Shall we?"

It was possible she might in fact, eventually, fall in love with this man. Most certainly she would always appreciate him. "Most assuredly, my lord."

As they began their descent, he said, "Bremsford's not a bad fellow, you know."

Not the highest of praises, but she knew he was striving to lessen her anxiousness. The not-a-bad-fellow was studying her intently, his features set in a mask that reflected none of his thoughts. She wondered if he'd hoped she wouldn't make an appearance, so he could have claimed to have reached out to her and been rebuffed. She was still wary of his reasons for offering the olive branch.

Certainly, with her father's passing, she'd found

herself reflecting on choices made. She could only surmise her . . . brother had done the same.

At his side, his wife was much easier to read. Avid curiosity widened her eyes, and her mouth curled up slightly at the corners, a hostess who was welcoming a guest. It was that smile that caused some of the tension to ease from around Regina's taut nerves.

"Chidding," Bremsford said succinctly, and she was left with the impression that he wasn't quite pleased the viscount had arrived with her.

"Lord Bremsford." Chidding's tone was cordial but supported with a bit of steel and perhaps a tad of warning.

Her father's son turned to her. "Miss Leyland, we're remarkably grateful you could join us this evening."

"I very much appreciate the invitation."

"Allow me the honor of introducing my wife, Lady Bremsford."

Even though she was technically family, it seemed, for tonight at least, everything was to remain formal. Elegantly, Regina lowered herself into a deep curtsy. "Lady Bremsford, it is indeed an honor to make your acquaintance at long last."

She recognized she was being a bit taciturn, perhaps even ungracious with the mention of time, but Bremsford had been married a decade now, wed at twenty-five. Of course, she'd not been invited to the wedding or the breakfast that followed, but the intricate details had been given a good bit of ink in the newspapers.

"My dear Miss Leyland, it is such a pleasure to welcome you into our home." She stopped short of saying it was a pleasure to welcome Regina into their family, but Regina couldn't hold that against the lady, because, after all, Regina remained the product of the woman's unfaithful father-in-law. The earl and his countess had three children, and Regina wondered if Arianna might be given the opportunity to play with her cousins.

"The residence, what I've seen of it, is magnificent."

"I can take no credit there. Most of the decorating was done by my predecessors, and my dear husband is very much in favor of honoring tradition and leaving everything as it is."

She'd never envisioned anyone referring to Bremsford as *dear* anything. But she was encouraged because surely if this woman found him so, perhaps in time, Regina might come to like him as well and would find herself referring to him as her *dear brother*. Even if presently, when she glanced over at him it was to find him scrutinizing her as though he expected her to steal the silver.

She suspected it was going to take some time for them to become comfortable with each other.

Averting his gaze, he lifted a hand, palm outward, and quickly turned it inward, as though seeking to capture an errant wisp of air. Two couples began walking toward them. Regina recognized the woman, Lady Warburton, who'd been glaring when she'd beaten her at the Twin Dragons. She'd been dreading the encounter, but now the woman was watching her with curiosity and interest rather than animosity. Much as she imagined she studied a new animal exhibit at the zoological gardens.

"My sisters and their husbands," Bremsford said curtly, his tone indicating he, too, had been dreading this moment. "Lord and Lady Barrington. Lord and Lady Warburton."

Regina curtsied. "My lords. Lady Barrington, I am honored to make your acquaintance."

"It has been a long while in coming," she said, studying Regina's features, no doubt searching for evidence of her father within the lines and curves.

Regina gave her attention to the other sister. "Lady Warburton, I must apologize. We've been in each other's company before, at a table at the Twin Dragons. I didn't realize precisely who you were. I do hope you didn't feel I was snubbing you by not acknowledging our . . . relationship."

The woman blinked her large brown eyes. "No, I . . . I may have been a bit . . . rude, to be honest. But you have a knack for winning."

"And my wife one for losing," Lord Warburton muttered, not quite beneath his breath.

She rolled her eyes. "He doesn't approve of my gambling."

"I could offer you some tips so your pin money will go further."

Her half sister widened her eyes. "Would you indeed?"

"I'd be delighted to do so, Lady Warburton."

"Splendid. I'd not really expected"—she shook her head—"I'm not certain what I'd really expected from this encounter. You're quite nice, Miss Leyland. I can see why Lord Chidding favors you."

Regina didn't need to look to know that at her side,

he was blushing. "Please, you have my permission to call me Regina."

"How very kind. You may call me Josephine. And this is Clara. We are, after all, related, in a manner."

"I need to return to greeting my guests," Bremsford said gruffly. "If you'll excuse me . . ." He escorted his countess back to the foot of the stairs and signaled to the majordomo.

"Bremmie's not quite comfortable with this arrangement of having you in the residence," Clara said. "He and Mother were quite close."

Bremmie? Regina almost laughed at that. Had her father been addressed as such as well? She couldn't imagine it. "I was quite taken aback to receive the invitation to be honest."

"We've gone far too long pretending you didn't exist—as a kindness to Mother, I suppose. But it was hardly kind to you."

"I do understand. It can't have been easy . . . for any of you."

Clara offered her first smile and Regina could see her father in it. "I rather think I'm going to like you, Regina. And I'm quite looking forward to putting all this awkwardness behind us."

"And to learning how to win at cards," Josephine said with a sly smile.

Regina thought she could come to cherish her sisters very much.

KNIGHT HAD TAKEN up his position against a wall near the front of the ballroom where Bremsford and his countess were greeting their arriving guests. Hence, he saw Regina the moment she stepped through that yawning doorway on Chidding's arm. As he'd no doubt see her doing a thousand times in the future, if he continued to attend balls. But what was the point of putting himself through the torment of watching her with another man when he, himself, was never going to marry?

Other than stunningly beautiful, as was her natural state, she looked at ease, content, and Chidding certainly appeared solicitous toward her. And proud when her name quickly followed his as their arrival was announced to the chamber already teeming with guests. Quite a few directed their attention toward the stairs as the name of the former earl's mistress's daughter echoed between the walls, and he suspected gossips had already ensured everyone knew Bremsford had graciously invited his father's by-blow to the ball, and each wanted to witness this momentous occasion when the earl welcomed this woman born of sin.

It took everything within Knight to remain where he was and not stride forward to greet her when her slippered feet took that last step, but she'd chosen her protector for the night, and he'd known she'd made the only choice she could. While they were painting a reconciliation for the *ton*, nothing could come of it. Her future was with Chidding.

Suddenly his flute of champagne was being gently tugged from his grip. He looked over at Rook.

"If the tightness of your jaw is any indication, you're likely to snap the stem of this glassware," his friend said. "Bremsford wouldn't have invited her if he intended to be rude to her."

"Now that the moment is here, he may be having second thoughts."

She stood before her father's son and his wife and curtsied, so elegantly and gracefully. She should have the opportunity to curtsy before the Queen. But that honor would be forever denied her because of the circumstances of her birth.

He was in a position to see Bremsford's face, and the man actually looked pleased that she'd come, exhibited a flash of triumph, perhaps because his negotiations had resulted in a truce, and he was honoring his father's dying wish.

"Bremsford and his wife seem gracious enough," Rook said.

"I'm still struggling to fathom his sudden change of heart."

"They're orphans now. You don't always realize the mooring your parents provided until it's gone. Perhaps he's grown more appreciative of even the slightest of familial ties. Your defense of her at the club could have caused him to evaluate his stance where she was concerned." While Rook had not been there to witness it, Knight had told him about it.

Bremsford lifted a hand, palm out, and turned it. A signal. Knight's gut tightened until he saw the earl's two sisters and their husbands striding over. Amid a lot of curtsying and bowing, introductions were apparently being made, the earl ignoring the people queuing up in the doorway. Knight suspected Bremsford had informed his majordomo that upon Miss Leyland's arrival, he was to dispense with any further announcements until he'd properly welcomed her.

"Is she going to marry Chidding?" Rook asked.

"I imagine so."

"He's a decent enough bloke, but can you live with that?"

He'd have to. "Why would I care?"

"Christ, Knight, the depth of your feelings for her is clear to anyone with eyes. I daresay you love her more now than you did when you proposed."

It was the way of love to evolve and change, because people evolved and changed. Love, he was discovering, was an odd thing, a beast that continued to grow. "What know you of love?"

"That it will never have its way with me. I think you suffer enough for the both of us."

Yet, in spite of the suffering, he was grateful to have loved her and to have been loved by her. He would undoubtedly still love her when he was on his deathbed, while she would eventually come to love the good man who was presently watching her and gently urging her away from the intimate group. The next guest's name rang through the room, competing with the music that was playing.

"If you'll excuse me—"

He'd taken only one step when Rook said laconically, "I'll probably dance with her later."

Knight swung around, and Rook lifted the flute he'd taken from him earlier and downed its contents before winking. "Just so you know."

"I'm sure she'll enjoy it." He wouldn't, however, but with Bremsford's acknowledgment of her, those who'd feared offending him might be worried they would if they didn't dance with Regina. Her dance card could very well be filled. He wanted that acceptance for her, to experience the full approval of the *ton*.

The couple had nearly reached the area where a throng mingled when he caught up with them. He bowed. "Miss Leyland." Took her gloved hand, pressed a kiss to her gloved knuckles. Reluctantly released his hold. "Lord Chidding."

"My lord."

He gave his attention back to Regina. "All went well, I take it."

"They were most welcoming. I was worried for nothing. They want us to be family."

"I'm glad." He turned his attention to Chidding. "Would you mind if I took . . . your lady on a turn about the floor?"

"Not at all." He touched her arm where it was bare. "I'll fetch you a champagne while you're occupied, shall I?"

She smiled warmly at him. "That would be lovely."

As Chidding turned away to find her some refreshment, Knight escorted her onto the dance floor, grateful the tune that had only just begun to play was suited to a waltz. "Chidding seems more at ease tonight than he was at the park."

"We've spoken more this evening about matters other than the weather than we have in the past." Inscrutably, she held his gaze, and he had the unsettling warning he wasn't going to like the words following that statement and that quite possibly this would be their final waltz. His hands tightened their hold as though needing to secure a last bit of memory. "I'm going to tell him. When he returns me home. About Ari. And the other. Regarding my tenuous hold on my trusts."

Which might mean revealing she was Anonymous. The danger it might put her in to be fully destroyed if Chidding wasn't willing to hold her secret. Her acceptance by Society was fragile. Her financial situation should she be discovered untenable. "Is it really necessary to mention the second?"

"He's courting me for the income I can provide. Before he asks for my hand, he needs to know it can go away on a whim."

"Is he close to asking do you think?" Bremsford had indicated he was.

"He's making it quite clear he has an interest."

"I assume you'll say yes."

He detected the slightest welling of tears before she blinked them back. "I will not have my daughter raised on the outskirts of town like a leper. Coming here tonight was like a slap in the face, that I'd not expected. My mother was never allowed entry into this residence. Nor was I while my father was alive. I was kept away from his deathbed. To be honest, I didn't even know he'd died until I read about it in the *Times*. Chidding might not have sired her, but I think he can be a good father to her, a father in all ways that matter. Although I'll be better able to judge once I view his reaction to the truth."

Something she'd judged Ari's sire couldn't be. A good father. "I complicated your life five years ago."

"I'm not angry about it any longer, Arthur. The memories of that time are no longer bitter, but once again sweet. Maybe you were correct about my true reasons for penning the tome, to bring you back into my life. To help me resolve my feelings, to prepare me for accepting another."

In your place went unsaid, but he heard it all the same. "I wish you naught but happiness."

"We shall see how Chidding reacts to my news."

"Unless he's a fool, none of it will make any difference at all." He knew they were coming to the end of this tune. Perhaps she did as well. Because they spoke no more but merely watched each other intensely as though to ensure that during all the previous staring not a single iota of their features had been overlooked by the other. He would never again hold her, touch her, or be this near to her. His chest felt so tight he was amazed his ribs didn't simply shatter with the force of it. He inhaled deeply in order to take in her gardenia fragrance one last time. They smiled at each other, but it wasn't one of joy, rather one of knowing, of acknowledging the final farewell.

When the dance came to its end and they stilled, he held her gaze while lifting her hand to his lips. "Be happy, Reggie."

Then he escorted her off the dance floor and into another man's keeping.

WHEN SHE'D FIRST arrived, been greeted by her half brother, introduced to her half sisters, Regina had experienced a sense of rejoicing at finally being admitted into this inner circle of family. She'd wanted to shout, "Look, Mother, here am I at last, where you and I should have been all along. Accepted and welcomed."

When she danced with Chidding, after finishing off the flute of champagne he'd brought her, she extended the acceptance to him, no longer comparing him to Knightly. Without words, she and her former lover had bid each other adieu. It had most assuredly hurt, but pain was often necessary in order to move on. She thought she'd done it when she went to Europe, but she'd only delayed the true parting. Tonight, she felt completely unencumbered by their past. He'd been her first love. Now she could ensure Chidding became her last.

It hadn't been difficult to dance with each of the Chessmen, even knowing that Knightly had probably put them up to it in order to ensure she wasn't viewed as a pariah tonight. Bremsford hadn't asked for a dance, and she was actually glad of it because she didn't think either of them was ready for such proximity, an actual coming into physical contact, and their choice would be to either stare at each other or strive to make conversation. Perhaps in time, because they were certain to encounter each other more in the future. Surely his edict that he wouldn't attend any ball to which she'd been invited no longer applied.

When they were more than an hour in, after just finishing her second dance with Chidding, she waited on the dance floor with him for the next waltz to start because he'd claimed it as well. He'd informed her that he intended to be scandalously bold this evening and dance with her four times rather than the acceptable two. Tongues would be wagging come morning. But rather than begin another tune, the orchestra remained quiet.

Guests were no longer being announced. Bremsford and his wife had been making the rounds, and danced a couple of times. Now from the top of the stairs, he called for silence with a booming voice she suspected could be heard out on the terrace. He'd inherited that thunderous sound from their father, and she wished he was with them at this moment to see all his children gathered in one room. What joy it might have brought him.

"Ladies and gentlemen, my dear countess and I are honored to have your presence here this evening. We also have an esteemed and revered guest to whom it is my intense pleasure to introduce you."

In spite of the massive throng, somehow his gaze landed on her, and her breath caught. He was going to point her out to the crowd, publicly acknowledge her as his sister. Reaching out blindly, she grabbed Chidding's hand. It was an odd time to notice it was smaller than Knightly's. She chided herself. No comparisons. The time for comparing was well past. His grip was still reassuring and firm.

"Ladies and gentlemen"—he waved a hand over the sea of people as if to part it in order to reveal his find—"I present to you . . . Anonymous."

Horrified, she was aware of icy tingles skittering along her spine and a chill sweeping through her. The bastard. With every word he'd uttered, he'd been setting a trap, and she, so desperate for acceptance, had fallen into it.

"Miss—"

"I am Anonymous!" suddenly rang out with an explosive boom that made Bremsford's voice seem like the squeak of a mouse.

The earl couldn't have looked more shocked if he'd just been told his head was to be placed on the block and the executioner was whetting his axe. Knightly was slowly and methodically prowling his way up those stairs, a feral predator on the hunt who would show no mercy to his prey. Regina was left with the impression he was striving to determine how many limbs he could tear from Bremsford before he would be stopped.

"You—you—you can't be," her father's son stuttered. "You're Lord K."

"I can be both, man. Why would I not, while penning a novel, base the main gentleman of the tale after myself? And it is fiction, of course. My fantasies that I could so seduce a woman as to put her under my spell that she would do anything I asked of her. Isn't it the dream of every man in attendance here tonight . . . to be so adored?"

He'd nearly reached Bremsford. The earl backed up and slammed against the wall, apparently forgetting it was there. "Why not publish it with your name on it?"

"The intrigue."

"It's not you." His voice wasn't quite so loud or quite so sure. "It's *her*. It's—"

"Watch what you say, Bremsford, or you'll find you can't say anything at all with a broken jaw. I've warned you before of what would happen if you spread lies."

The earl blanched, his skin taking on a sickly hue, suggesting he might bring up his accounts at any moment. Regina was confident he had no proof to substantiate what he'd been on the verge of announcing. Otherwise, he'd have tossed it in Knightly's face.

It was a bluff. But once he'd have named her, the damage would have been done. Lies took on a life of their own, were often impossible to stop. Without proof, she didn't think he could have regained the trusts, although maybe he could have convinced the trustees she was no longer deserving of the benefits they provided. She was fairly certain he could have sown enough doubts, so she'd no longer be welcomed in any grand parlors. So Chidding wouldn't marry her. He was striving to take everything away from her.

Knightly was saying something to Bremsford that caused the earl to flinch and grow deathly pale.

Then Knightly turned to the crowd with a confident, dashing smile and a spread of his arms that encompassed the entire chamber. "I'm more than happy to sign your books."

CHAPTER 23

～～～

Desire, I was discovering, was a ravenous thing. Each
meeting with Lord K would only serve to quell its appetite
for a short while, and when it reawakened, it was with a
hunger that far exceeded what it had been before.
—Anonymous, *My Secret Desires, A Memoir*

July 6, 1875

AFTER Bremsford's failed unveiling, Regina had no
wish to stay at that horrid affair. It appeared the jovial
mood of the evening had turned sour for everyone,
because people began rapidly dispersing, hasty exits
being made. Bremsford had disappeared, no doubt
having slunk out rather than face his guests after his
confrontation with Knightly. How could her father
have raised such an atrocious and odious son?

As Chidding's carriage journeyed back to her residence, she regretted not being able to find a moment
with Knightly to express her gratitude for serving
as her champion. But he had been swallowed by the
crowd, and it was no doubt for the best that they'd not

spoken. She'd felt enough eyes upon her before his surprising announcement to know nearly everyone thought Bremsford was going to declare her as Anonymous. His gaze had been focused on her and when his waving hand had come to a halt it was directed at her. She was surprised he hadn't sent a lightning bolt from his fingertips to brand her. The scapegrace.

"I was certainly surprised by Knightly's proclamation," Lady Finsbury said smartly, after a while, disturbing the quiet that somehow seemed astonishingly thick. "Bremsford was obviously taken aback as well. To be honest, I can't envision Knightly as the author. Based on the emotions brought forth and revealed in the story, I assumed the writer was a woman. Men are not quite so open with their feelings. At least my dear departed husband wasn't. With his hesitancy to utter the word *love*, I rather thought he considered it blasphemous."

Except for the rumbling of the wheels, the squeaking of the springs, and the thundering of the horses' hooves, silence reigned for a few minutes. Regina wasn't sure she had the wherewithal to effectively carry on any sort of conversation without revealing the truth of the matter.

"What think you, Miss Leyland?" Lady Finsbury suddenly blurted. "I daresay you know the man better than most. Do you think Lord Knightly capable of pouring his heart out on paper?"

Pouring out his heart, yes, but not with pen on paper. With deeds and actions. "I think each of us has a secret place within us into which no one else can ever venture, no matter how well they know us."

"You see, something as lyrical as all that. I could envision you writing the book more than he."

"I can't imagine, cousin, he'd have any reason to lie," Chidding said, nearly sharply, as though he wished to bring an abrupt end to the topic at hand.

"I can imagine a good many reasons," Lady Finsbury murmured, before opening the book that had been responsible for the ruination of the night and leaning toward the swinging lantern so she could again read what she'd already read.

Regina had never been more grateful to arrive at her residence than she was when the carriage finally came to a stop.

"I'm going to see Miss Leyland safely inside," Chidding said. "I may be a few minutes, cousin."

"Take your time," she responded distractedly.

As she and Chidding were going up the steps, Regina said, "She is not the most diligent of chaperones, is she?"

"Would you want her to be?"

"No, as a matter of fact, I've always thought it a frightfully ridiculous custom. All it does is teach young women how to climb out of windows and down trees."

He laughed lightly. "I suspected as much."

After the butler had opened the door to them, Chidding said, "May I have a quick word in your drawing room?"

She noticed the slightest tinge of pink along the curves of his cheeks and was struck by the possibility he had something incredibly serious to discuss—or ask of her. But then she also had something serious to tell him. "By all means."

Desperate for a brandy, she led the way, but turned slightly to face him after crossing the threshold. "Would you care for scotch or brandy?"

"No, thank you."

"I hope you don't mind if I indulge. It's been a rather tumultuous night." It had begun with trepidation, become glorious, and ended with devastation on so many levels she didn't know if she'd ever be able to count or sort them all.

Once she had her snifter in hand and had taken a sip, relishing the burning sensation that finally restored warmth to her chest, she indicated the sitting area near the fire because she couldn't have him on the settee she'd shared with Knightly. She sat in the chair in which her father's son had once placed his backside. Tomorrow, she would have it tossed out, possibly burned, and replaced. While she still had the means to purchase new furnishings. In spite of Knightly's declaration, she couldn't be certain her trusts were safe or that Bremsford wouldn't devise another scheme for striving to take them from her.

She indicated the chair opposite her. Instead, Chidding walked to the fireplace, rested his forearm on the mantel, and studied her. Perhaps she should go first, tell him—

"I was watching you when Lord Knightly claimed to be Anonymous. Originally you were quite shocked, and then relief washed over your features like a cascading waterfall. More than relief really. Gratitude, as though you'd been slated for execution and granted a reprieve. You're Anonymous."

She held his gaze. She saw no censure there or

doubt. Just a steadfast reckoning. No matter how he had looked at her, however, she would have answered the same. "Yes."

"And Knightly knows that."

"Yes, because he is Lord K. While I took liberties and embellished the tale, still truth resides in the story."

"Bremsford was going to announce you as the author. It's the reason he invited you and the reason Knightly spoke up."

"Yes." She was beginning to hate that word, so small to encompass so much. "I don't know if you'll believe me, but I was going to tell you the truth of it this evening after we returned here. Because I needed you to be aware . . . I realize your interest in me is more financial in nature. However, my residence and income can go away in the blink of an eye if Bremsford can prove I am Anonymous. He is willing to pay for proof."

"I'm aware of his hunt but why would it affect your income?"

She explained the clauses to him.

"The law is written so it is the distribution of indecent material that is illegal," he said when she was finished.

"I imagine he will argue if I had not created it, it would not be available to be distributed. Therefore, I am at fault, the instigator behind the unlawful actions of others."

"I think he would also have to prove it is indecent. My cousin loves the book, and I found nothing objectionable in it."

"Is it a chance you're willing to take? That everything will not be stripped away from me, from us?"

"I am. We might not even need it."

She gave him a questioning look.

He looked at the ceiling before bringing his gaze back to her. "The evening Knightly invited me to play the private game with him, he offered me some investment advice, a couple of businesses that show great promise. It may be a year or so before I receive any reward, but the man knows investing. And he guaranteed it. I only have to pay back the loan he gave me if his recommendations come to fruition."

She felt the prick of tears because, naturally, Knightly would do what he could to mitigate Bremsford's interference in her happiness.

Chidding crossed over to her and went down on one knee. Her heart gave a hard lurch. "I adore you, Miss Leyland. While I know what you will have with me cannot even begin to compare with what you had with another, I promise to ensure you have no regrets."

Her eyes burned as tears welled. She cupped his face between her hands, needing him to know the truth of what she was going to say. "I think, my dear Lord Chidding, you underestimate your worth. You deserve a woman who will give you the best part of herself, her devotion and her heart. And I am so sorry to say, that is not me."

"You still love him."

"Damn it, but I do."

WITHIN HIS LIBRARY, still quaking with rage, his entire body tense with fury, Knight tossed back two fingers of scotch and cursed himself soundly for not trusting his instincts. He'd felt in his gut that Bremsford was up to no good. He should have pushed harder the afternoon he'd gone to ask him about his sudden change of heart. But Regina had held out such hope for being welcomed into the family that he'd wanted it for her as well and allowed himself to be swindled into putting his suspicions aside and believing she would at last have the familial associations for which she yearned.

He knew how important legitimate family was to her. It was one of the reasons he'd let her go.

After confronting Bremsford and turning to the crowd, he'd briefly caught sight of Regina, her features portraying a vortex of emotions—anger, hurt, disbelief, relief—just before Chidding ushered her from the ballroom. Knight had wanted to speak with her, but it would be best if they avoided each other in the future to prevent giving anyone reason to suspect he'd not spoken true, to avert throwing any suspicion at all upon her as being the actual author.

Hearing the library door open, he cursed soundly again and tossed back more scotch.

"You're not usually one for slamming doors," his mother said calmly, like the first breath of spring heralding in new life while he was a tempest in danger of destroying all in its wake.

Upon entering the residence, he'd slammed shut the front door and for good measure he'd done the same with the door to this chamber. A rational person would have heeded the warnings his actions prefaced—*here be dragons; enter at your own risk*. "I'm sorry to have disturbed your slumber. I shall remain quieter."

"I'd not yet drifted off. Pour me a brandy, will you?"

"I'm not fit company tonight, Mother."

The woman, who was slowly learning not to cower within this residence, walked over. While he ignored her, he could still feel her looking up at him, studying him. "That is when one is usually most in need of company, Arthur."

"Not tonight." He tightened his jaw. "But you should know, as it will no doubt be reported in the newspapers tomorrow, that at this evening's ball, I declared myself to be Anonymous."

"But you're not."

Her declaration, filled with such unbridled conviction, almost had him turning toward her, but he didn't want her to see the truth reflected in his eyes or features. Nor was he going to reveal the identity of Anonymous. He would not risk ruining Regina's life yet again. Not when she was so close to having all she longed for with Chidding.

Out of the corner of his eye, he watched as she poured a splash of brandy into a snifter before reaching for the scotch and filling his glass to its rim. He almost smiled at that but wasn't certain he'd ever find it within himself to smile in the future.

His mother picked up her snifter. "Join me by the fire."

Inwardly, he cursed yet again, this time a string of coarse epithets a gentleman should never use. He considered, instead, heading out the door leading onto the terrace and from there disappearing into the shadows of the garden where his mother would never find him—remembering a time when he was five and had done just that. But she *had* found him then, and he suspected she would tonight as well. While they had barely a dozen years of memories, the seven before she was taken from him and the five since she'd been returned, some innate instinct existed between them, bound them together. Picking up his glass, he strode over to the chair opposite hers, lowered himself into it, and took a large swallow of the scotch, relishing the burn.

"Anonymous is the woman who was here the other night," his mother said. "Miss Leyland."

Bollocks. How had she figured it out? But where was the harm in admitting it? She made no morning calls, and no one called on her. She'd made no contact with any friends she may have had before. He wondered if she was embarrassed to admit she'd been locked away. Still, he couldn't give voice to the confirmation, but it must have been visible in his features because she nodded. "And you love her."

"Why would you think that?"

She gave him a small, indulgent smile. "Although it has been some years, I do remember what yearning looks like." She studied the flames licking at the logs. "Your father stole twenty years from me, twenty years of watching you grow up, seeing you at school, helping to shape you into the man you would become. He stole from me the few years remaining to Francis. Perhaps if I'd been there, the accident wouldn't have happened."

"You can't blame yourself for Francis's death."

"I don't. If anything, I blame my husband because how are we to know what actions taken lead to specific outcomes." Her eyes came back to rest on him.

"How many years with Miss Leyland did he steal from you?"

After a quick shake of his head, he took another long swallow of the scotch.

"Was she the price for my freedom?"

"Mother—"

"Was she?"

She was usually not so assertive. She'd picked a hell of a night to be so, to begin overcoming her fears. He was not going to burden her with guilt for the duke's actions. "We did not suit. She is soon to marry another. With him, she will have the happiness she deserves that I couldn't have given her."

She took a slow sip of her brandy, closing her eyes as though relishing the flavor. But when she opened them, they contained the faraway look he remembered from his boyhood when she'd seemed to have traveled elsewhere in her mind. Then she shook it off, but he noted a lingering remnant, of a memory perhaps. "He told you of my wickedness, I presume. And that you are not of his loins. Perhaps he even forbade you to marry. He was always so deuced proud of his bloodline. Do you hate me for it?"

"No." The word came out quickly and unfettered, filled with conviction. "Nor were you wicked. He was not an easy man to have as a father. I cannot imagine he was any easier as a husband. I very much doubt yours was a love match."

"But that does not justify infidelity, does it? I took vows, didn't I? I had intended to uphold them, to be a good and proper wife. I was seventeen when we married. Three years later, I still had yet to conceive, to provide him with his heir. He became increasingly unkind, abusive really." She waved a hand. "Not with his fists, but with words. Oh, they could hurt, agonizingly so. His anger was driven by his frustrations, I supposed."

"That does not excuse his behavior toward you."

She shook her head. "No, I quite agree. Still, I was so terribly young and feeling . . . insufficient. My friends were having children. Why not I? One winter night, he was particularly horrible, said some horrendous things, and stormed out. Went to the nearby village to visit his mistress—made no bones about telling me where he was going. I was overwhelmed with such despair. In spite of the cold, I began wandering through the garden. A full moon lit my way. I came across a solitary white rose in bloom, among the brambles and thorns. I fell to my knees and wept. That was how he found me."

She looked back toward the flames, and Knight shifted slightly to the edge of the chair, placing his elbows on his thighs. "The duke?"

His mother slid her attention back to him and smiled softly. "No, the gardener. He was kind and warm. He took me to his cottage and made me feel like the rose. Something so pretty that could exist among such ugliness. It was only ever the one night. He quickly found employment elsewhere—horrified by what had transpired between us, I think, or fearful the duke might discover our . . . duplicity. Soon after, I realized I was with child. Convinced myself it was the duke's and merely coincidence that . . ." Her voice trailed off.

"Francis had blond hair and brown eyes—like the duke."

She nodded, arched a brow, and lifted a shoulder. "And like the gardener. After Francis was born, three years passed, and I again didn't conceive. Do you know your father boasted that his mistresses were wise enough to take precautions and never burden him with any bastards? I began to suspect that wasn't the case at all. That perhaps he couldn't sire children. That the failure of which he accused me rested instead with him. Oh, but he wanted his spare. Life became quite miserable again, because I wasn't carrying out my duties." Her lips formed a gentle smile of reminiscence. "Then I met John. And he gave me you."

He was struck with a sense of wonder at her radiant expression that encompassed all the love she held for not only him but the man who'd sired him. He felt the tiniest of pinpricks behind his eyes, feared he might be on the verge of weeping, no doubt a result of all the various emotions that had been bombarding him throughout the evening. "Who was he?"

His voice was rough, scratchy, and raw. Until that moment he hadn't realized how desperately he wanted to know who had sired him.

"He was a tenant farmer on the ducal estate. I would deliver baskets of goods at Christmas. That was how we first met. I began taking Francis on picnics near the fields where John toiled. He was tall and broad of shoulder. Dark hair and the bluest eyes. Sometimes, if I searched long enough, I could find a swath of the blue of his eyes in the sky. You look very much like him, and when you came to get me, at first, I thought you were him. He was so very kind. He had a beautiful smile, and the most wonderful laugh. And he could make me laugh. I loved him, Arthur, and he loved me. I've no doubt of that. But what we had was illicit. The guilt gnawed at us. One day, he simply left. Without saying goodbye. However, he did hold you once. You were only a couple of months old. Of course, I claimed you were the duke's child, but I think he knew the truth of it. I believe that made it difficult for him to stay. But not a single day goes by that I don't think of him. I miss him, but I wish him well and hope he found love elsewhere."

Knight was having a difficult time absorbing it all, particularly the irony that even the heir his father had loved so well had probably not carried his blood. But he also felt like a great burden had been lifted. "I was born of love, then."

"You were, yes."

"Bishop's wife is an inquiry agent. I could ask her to find him if you like."

She shook her head. "After all these years, I'd rather just hold on to the memories. And I've created a story for him in which he's acquired great happiness. But if you want to know him . . ."

"I prefer your memories of him, I think."

"What of your memories of Miss Leyland, Arthur? Are you going to be content to live the remainder of your life with only those?"

KNIGHT WAS STILL awake at the crack of dawn to snatch the newspaper from his butler's hands the moment it arrived.

"But, m'lord, I've not even ironed it yet," the servant called after him as Knight headed to his library.

Standing at his desk, he started at the back because gossip was usually nearer the end than the beginning, and he knew someone in attendance at a ball was always willing to blather the latest rumors making the rounds to reporters on the hunt for scandalous happenings at aristocratic affairs. It was one of the reasons some lords found themselves at the altar—their compromising transgressions discovered and announced in print the following morning. But scanning the headings, he found no reference at all to the identity of Anonymous. Nothing to suggest the author had been revealed at the Bremsford ball.

Surely, he'd been convincing enough. Lady Finsbury had even asked him to sign her damned book.

He turned to the next to last page, which would have been the second page he'd encountered if he'd gone in the proper order, and there it was: *I Am Anonymous.*

Only it wasn't describing the shock and uproar his announcement had caused. As he quickly scoured the length of the column, he didn't find any mention of himself, because it wasn't a piece written by an enterprising gossipmongering reporter. It was a letter. Penned by the scandalous author herself.

Dear gentle reader,

I am Anonymous, the author of My Secret Desires.

I spent a large portion of my life hidden away, and so it was I preferred anonymity to

acclaim. But the need for some to uncover my
identity is distracting, taking attention away
from the story's purpose, which is to entertain
and perhaps in a small way to reassure those
who have known the intoxicating power of love
that they are not alone if unable to resist the
temptations it offers. Passion is a fundamental
necessity of our existence, for without it, how
would we endure the daily trials and tribula-
tions we face?

A second story is in the works with a much
happier ending. I hope you will join me on that
journey.

Yours most sincerely,
Miss Regina Leyland

Bracing his arms on the desk, he slammed his
eyes shut and bowed his head. Why had she done
it? Why had she not accepted the protection he'd offered? They certainly weren't going to arrest *him* for
indecency. If he was no longer welcomed among the
aristocracy, what did he care? Besides, he deserved
paying that price. If not for him, she'd have never
written the story.

"I am my mother's daughter after all," a soft voice
murmured, and yet it carried the weight of conviction
straight to his soul.

Jerking up his head, he drank in the sight of her,
still in the gown she'd worn to the ball. Her hair was
no longer tightly bound but looked in danger of spilling from its pins. She couldn't have gone to sleep. In-

stead, she must have written the letter after returning from the ball and afterward journeyed through London to deliver it to the newspapers of consequence.

Although he hadn't slept, either, and could well imagine what a sight he made. During the wee hours, he'd discarded his coat, waistcoat, and neckcloth. Buttons were undone, sleeves rolled up. Perhaps he was delirious from lack of sleep, and she was a figment of his imagination. If he moved from where he was rooted, took her in his arms, she might disappear like a wisp of smoke. He looked down at the newsprint, back up at her. "Why did you do it?"

With her brow slightly pleated, she strolled forward and flattened her palms on his desk. "Because I'm weary of all the secrets and the strangling hold they have over me. The constant worry of discovery. All my life, I wanted to be accepted for who I was. Last night, I thought at long last that was happening . . . with Bremsford. But walking through his residence, seeing the evidence of my father with his other family, I began to doubt that even he had ever truly accepted me. He would have been appalled by the book. You claimed to have written it. I realized I've never had to pretend with you or prove my worth. With you, I was always free to be me, without fear of judgment or having to consider my words."

The weight of all she'd shared, in particular the last bit, should have made him feel like he'd been standing beneath a bricklayer's scaffold and a ton of bricks had fallen upon him. Instead, he took his first deep breath in what must have been weeks—no, months. No, years. Perhaps ever. Because he experienced the same when he was with her. He wasn't a son who couldn't meet his father's expectations. He wasn't, as he'd discovered only a few years earlier, a bastard who had no right to become duke. With her, he'd never been a title to be acquired or the possessor of so many coins that at least one if not two future generations would have no financial worries.

"As I said upon first entering, I am my mother's daughter. I'll be your mistress if you'll have me."

Unflinchingly she held his gaze, daring him to accept this aspect of her as well and to not find fault with it. Without the benefit of marriage, she would continue to lie with him. She would bring other bastard children—his bastard children—into the world and protect them as best she could.

"I'm not asking that you provide for me. Actually, I'm going to provide for myself. I spoke with my publisher in the dead of night—he wasn't too happy about being roused from his bed, but he deserved to know who I was and what I'd done regarding the letter I'd delivered to several newspapers—and he's agreed to begin printing more books today, with my name on them." As it should have been from the beginning. "He's very interested in volume two, assures me he'll fight the courts on any indecency charges if it comes to that. He reckons I can earn a fairly decent income, nothing like Dickens, of course, but I can live modestly."

"What of Chidding?"

"Funny thing, that. I understand he's on the verge of having a modest income as well, thanks to some investment advice you gave him."

"I wanted to ensure you gained a husband who wanted you for more than coin."

"He did ask for my hand last night but giving it wouldn't have been fair to either of us. He is deserving of a woman who loves him. And I am madly in love with someone else."

He was barely aware of getting to her, wasn't quite certain if he'd leapt over the desk or gone around it, but suddenly between his hands he was cradling her beautiful face with its slightly red and swollen eyes from lack of sleep. "I don't want you for my mistress. I want you as my wife. I want to be there every time you put our daughter to bed."

Her deep brown eyes flared. Her brow furrowed as she studied him, and he knew she was striving to determine if he merely accepted her daughter as he might his own or—

"You know the truth of her, then," she whispered. "That there was no Spanish matador, no Italian sculptor, no Parisian artist, no German clockmaker. There's only ever been you."

He wanted to crush her to him and take her luscious mouth and show her that there had only ever been her, but more needed to be said. "It's easy to lie about the month in which she was born. It's not so easy to ask me to look into her eyes and not see my own."

"Hence you've known from the beginning, but you didn't let on."

"It seemed important to you that I not know."

"And when you told her you loved her?"

"I meant it. I fell in love with her the moment I met her, much as I did her mother. I set up a trust for her.

She'll never do without. I set up one for you as well that would go into effect if ever you lost what your father gave to you. I didn't think you'd accept it otherwise. However, you won't need it if you'll have me as your husband."

She looked at him with amazement and awe, her eyes filled with light, her smile soft with wonder. "What of the vow you made to the duke?"

"I made a vow to you first—I never should have turned my back on it. I'm sure the duke will issue threats, but I'll handle him. I'll hire guards to ensure my mother, you, and all I hold dear are protected from any vengeance he might seek. I recently read that passion is a fundamental necessity of our existence. Without it, how would we endure? Without you in my life, all I've done for five long interminable years is endure. Without joy. Without hope. Without a heart. Just a shell of a man. I love you, Reggie. I won't give you up easily. Not again. You once accepted my offer of marriage. May I hold you to it now?"

Her smile rivaled the brilliance of the sun. "I suppose I am not my mother's daughter after all. I find marriage to be a much more agreeable state than mistress."

He thought a moment like this required, deserved, tenderness, but to know the dream they'd once held would become reality overpowered him and destroyed any resistance he might have had. He unleashed the passion she'd referred to in her letter and claimed her mouth as he intended to claim every aspect of her—with all that he was and would ever be.

With her, nothing seemed impossible, and everything seemed perfectly right, even the breaking of a vow.

He lifted her into his arms, relishing the feel of her snuggling against his chest, her arms looping around his shoulders, her face pressed into the curve of his neck as she delivered kisses against his skin.

"I'll obtain a special license," he vowed as he started up the stairs. "Unless you want to wait, have a large wedding."

She nipped at his jaw. "We've waited long enough. I want to be married as soon as possible."

"Then you shall be."

He would make her his, to have and to hold forever. Five years had taught him the torment of not having her in his life. While he didn't regret the price he'd paid to gain his mother her freedom, speaking with her last night, the honesty of her words, had convinced him the duke was not a man to whom he needed to honor any vows made. He would give Regina the legitimacy and the family she wanted. She would never doubt that with him she was valued for herself. She would never question his love for her, not again.

He strode into his bedchamber, kicked the door shut behind him, and hoped his mother would have the good sense to ignore that particular slam. Then he was divesting Regina of her clothing and his own. They tumbled onto the bed in a frenzy of want and desire. And hunger.

Ah, Christ, the hunger. Open mouths crashing together, tongues tangling, exploring. Every aspect seemed new and yet somehow familiar. He remembered how he'd gone to her the night before they were to wed because he'd thought making love to her after they were married would be different, more proper, more tame, and he'd wanted one more night of sin, of debauchery with her. What a fool he'd been. Their circumstances were never going to reduce their need or their passion. He suspected what they felt for each other would only increase with the years. He'd never tire of having her. He'd always want her one more time.

God, he'd probably be on his deathbed and think, *Just once more.*

And this beautiful, courageous woman would no doubt accommodate him. Although if she merely held his hand, he would be content. Strange, how the slightest touch from her had always been so incredibly fulfilling as though he'd somehow won, when he hadn't even realized he'd been engaged in a contest or game.

He stroked his hand slowly over her body, one that had changed to accommodate her bringing his child into the world. It would no doubt change with the birth of more of his children. He would give her as many as she wanted. He would give her everything that was within his power to give her. While he knew she didn't doubt his love, still he would spend the remainder of his life proving the depth of it to her. What he felt for her was a gift, to himself. It warmed him, gave him purpose. Joy and happiness.

She was his now, for eternity.

They were on their sides, facing each other. She swung a leg over his hip, stroked her mound against his cock, and he was aware of how hot and wet she was. Groaning low, he flattened a hand against her bottom and pressed her up against him as he trailed his mouth along her silken throat. "You make me mad with wanting, woman. You always have."

She laughed as she nipped the tender skin at his collarbone and then soothed the pinch with her tongue. "Only fair. You turned me into a wanton, you know."

"Not so wanton if there was no matador or artist—"

Her hand covered his mouth and she shifted slightly to capture and hold his gaze. "I made you think there were others because I wanted only to hurt you. Let's not dwell on the little hurts we inflicted."

"The big and little ones made us who we are now, Reggie. I love you more deeply today than I did before. I appreciate you more. Want you more. Perhaps I needed to go through a bit of fire to be forged into the man who deserves you. I'll never take you or having you for granted."

Tears welled in her eyes. "Oh, Arthur. It might be careless of me to say it, but once again, I would do anything Lord K asked of me."

"Then spread your legs, sweetheart, as I'm in the mood to feast."

REGINA THOUGHT SHE would never, ever grow tired of looking down to see Knightly's dark head between her parted thighs or feeling his tongue stroking so intimately. To have her fingers buried in the thick strands of his hair and to have them tightening their hold on him as the pleasure began rippling through her.

She briefly wondered if she should be a little more

risqué in what she revealed in the second volume—
and then decided she'd not dare. Besides, moments
like this were only for them. When they were both
free of all familial and societal restraints and could be
true to themselves, true to each other.

No judgment at all. Whatever one of them needed,
the other would provide.

As her thighs trembled and her breath came in harsh
pants, he increased the frenzy of his ministrations. He
knew her so well, read her so easily. The sensations
built until she was crying out his name, arching her
back, her body spasming as she came apart with the
force of what he'd done to her. How could she ever be
this liberated with anyone else? Or this vulnerable?

But when he lifted his head and his heavy-lidded
smoldering gaze captured hers, she nearly came again.

Then he was prowling up her body, leaving a trail
of kisses in his wake. Reaching down, she wrapped
a hand around his cock, lifted her hips, and guided
him home.

As she took him to the hilt, his eyes darkened, and he
groaned low and deep. He began pumping his hips in
a frantic rhythm, lowering his head to take her mouth,
his tongue mimicking the actions of his lower body.
He was raised up, supporting himself on his arms. She
wound her arms around him and pressed him down
until he was flattened against her, his chest caressing
her breasts.

It was heavenly to have all of him moving in tandem against her. And to know she did in fact have all
of him, body, heart, and soul.

She was aware of his muscles tensing, his entire

body beginning to go rigid. She dug her fingers into his buttocks. "Don't leave me."

He stilled, lifted himself slightly, and studied her. "I'll never leave you again."

When he spilled his seed into her, when that muscle in his jaw ticked, she kissed it before clutching him close, relishing that he was once again all hers.

KNIGHT AWOKE TO find himself still holding Regina, her finger drawing lazy circles on his chest. They'd both drifted off to sleep for a time. The momentous night had certainly taken a toll on them. Turning his head slightly, he pressed a kiss to her head. "When did you know you were with child?"

"I began to suspect about a month after we were to wed. I imagine it happened the last night we were together."

With a groan, he slammed his eyes closed. "Why didn't you send word to me?"

She sighed. "I thought you didn't want me. Why would you want our child?"

"You had to have known I'd have provided for you."

"I did. Or at least I assumed you would. But it wasn't what I wanted. I had no desire to be like my mother." She laughed lightly. "At least not until this morning. I never understood why she would settle for being only a piece of his life."

"Even if we weren't to marry, Reggie, if you were my mistress, you'd be the whole of mine." He shifted until he could face her and cradle her cheek. "I love you so very much."

"I love you, too, Arthur."

He lowered his mouth to hers, the kiss one of gentleness and surrender. And victory.

He wasn't the only one who had needed to go through a bit of fire to be forged into someone who could face life's challenges without ever considering backing down. She'd been so sheltered, waiting for someone to free her from the tower. But in the early hours of that morning, she'd discovered she possessed the means to free herself.

And she'd known that in the doing, if she'd begun to fall, he'd catch her.

Just as she'd always be there to catch him, if needed.

With the years and maturity, they'd become more equal, better suited to each other.

Pressing her body up against his, running the sole of her foot along his leg, she embraced him more securely and deepened the kiss. He responded with a satisfied growl, a squeezing of her bottom, and a rolling over, so she was straddling him.

Rising up, holding his gaze, she took him into her body once more and set the tempo. A leisurely meandering, a saga that seemed to encompass the whole of their story. When they finally, sated and lethargic, collapsed together, she wondered if they might simply spend the remainder of their lives in bed.

But when their bodies had cooled and their breathing had slowed, he pulled her in tightly against his side and said, his voice low and with purpose, "I need to get you home, and then I need to let the duke know that in this contest of wills, he has lost."

CHAPTER 24

꧁ ❧ ꧂

My body burned with need. I could scarcely sleep for the
wanting. I longed for the feel of his flesh against mine and
the entwining of our bodies until we were very nearly one.
—Anonymous, *My Secret Desires, A Memoir*

July 7, 1875

REGINA was once again in the garden, watching
Arianna play, when Shelby approached, silver salver
in hand. Only this time, two calling cards rested on
it. They belonged to her father's two other daughters.
While she was tempted not to be at home to them
because she was fairly certain they'd been allies in
Bremsford's attempt to reveal her identify and dis-
credit her, she couldn't bring herself to be quite that
rude. Might as well let them vent their spleens now
rather than at an affair she might attend with her soon-
to-be-husband.

He'd brought her home only a few hours earlier.
Then he'd left with the promise to return as soon as

he'd finished with the unpleasant task of confronting the duke.

With a sigh, knowing her guests were waiting, she rose. "Have tea brought to the parlor."

As she walked, she tucked in strands of her hair that had come loose. As she had with their brother, she considered changing into a more elegant frock but in the end decided to greet them as she was, without artifice or pretense. They were family after all. Of a sort.

Vanity did get the better of her, however, and she stopped to study her reflection in a mirror over a table in the hallway. As a result of the outdoor air, her cheeks were a rosy hue. Her skin and eyes were aglow, wrought by happiness and having spent a good part of the morning making love and being made love to. She wouldn't allow them to dim her joy. They could have their say and then take their leave.

Shoring up her resolve with a deep breath, she strode into the drawing room to find them providing a united front, their backs to her, standing near enough to each other she doubted a shadow could pass between them. Muttering something, they were staring at the landscape above the fireplace. She refused to acknowledge the bite of hurt the image caused or how she'd longed for a sibling with whom to share her troubles. "Ladies."

In unison, they spun around, and while she knew she should curtsy—they were actual ladies after all—she was too shocked to do much of anything except stare at what they were each holding: her book.

"You naughty girl," Lady Barrington—Clara— said, "not to tell us you were the author."

"We were hoping you might sign our books," Lady Warburton—Josephine—said.

Confused, she shook her head. "That's the reason you're here?"

"Not entirely," Clara said kindly. "When we saw your letter in the newspaper this morning, we realized it was your name our brother intended to announce last night."

"We deduced he'd invited you to the ball for the sole purpose of doing so," Josephine added. "He wasn't truly attempting a reconciliation as he'd informed us. He was using us as . . . props. As a bit of stage scenery in order to lure you into complacency until he was ready to make his proclamation to all and sundry."

"You truly didn't realize what he was about?"

They shook their heads, their faces reflecting embarrassment and sorrow.

"You must believe us," Clara urged. "We didn't know about his plans, and now that we do, well, we don't approve of them in the least."

"This morning, we didn't half give him a piece of our minds," Josephine said, "venting our immense displeasure with him. It was a cruel thing to attempt to assert. If you'd wanted people to know who you were, you'd have put your name on the book. For some reason, you wanted anonymity, and he should have left you to it. It's so unlike him to be . . . duplicitous. It took us until this afternoon to work up our courage to visit you. Surely, you must think the worst of us."

"I . . . I'm not certain what to think, honestly. I try not to judge." But she had earlier, assuming they were in on his cruel prank. She gestured toward a small sitting area. "Please sit."

The sisters settled on the settee, and Regina took the chair opposite them. Before another word could be uttered, a maid appeared with a tea tray and placed it on the low table nearest to Regina, who set about preparing tea for her guests. When they all had a cup and saucer in hand, they took a moment to sip and enjoy. Some of the tension drained from Regina's body. "I think your brother was searching for a way to have my trusts converted back to the earldom."

"He confessed as much," Clara said.

"We gave him what for," Josephine added. "Father arranged those trusts to see to your care. Bremmie should leave them be."

She smiled. "I'm so glad you came to explain things."

"Well, we"—Clara looked over at Josephine who nodded—"we found you to be rather pleasant and enjoyed the small bit of conversation we had."

Regina couldn't help it. She arched a brow. "You really do want to learn how to win at cards, don't you?"

The woman blushed. "No! I mean, well yes, but that has no bearing on our being here."

"I'm teasing."

"Oh! Jolly good. I see. Yes, that was rather funny."

Although she didn't sound like she'd truly thought it was. Perhaps Regina should wait and get to know them a little better, to understand their sense of humor, before trying to tease. But she did feel a need to be honest with them. "I always wanted sisters."

"Hopefully you will find us to be quite adequate."

She suspected she'd find them more so, especially when they became exceedingly comfortable with each other.

"It was terribly sweet of Lord Knightly to claim to be Anonymous," Josephine said slyly. "He is Lord K, is he not?"

How did she respond to that? "Lord K represents my memories of Lord Knightly. There is some truth to him and some fantasy."

"But mostly truth?"

She smiled warmly. "Yes, mostly truth."

"And in the book you're writing, the one you mentioned in your letter, he does return to his lady, doesn't he?"

"Yes," she assured her sister. "*The* gentleman does return."

STEPPING OUT OF his carriage a few days later, Knight stared up at the manor house in which he'd grown up. The ducal seat in Yorkshire. It had been years since he'd been here. Not since he'd left Oxford. By then he'd been able to afford his own accommodations, and as he and the duke had constantly been at odds, he'd worked to put himself into a position that he was never beholden to the man.

As a result, the sight of the now decrepit building came as a shock. It was rather like the ugliness of the duke's soul taking physical form. How had it come to this?

The front lawn was naught but weeds and brambles, the setting of a Grimms' fairy tale in which witches and ogres dwelled. He wasn't certain he wanted to see the gardens at the back in which his mother had taken such joy. He suspected no gardener tended these grounds any longer. Based on the grime visible on the windows, he doubted any servants were about.

As he cautiously made his way over broken pavestones, not wanting to turn an ankle, he had a moment of wondering if he might find the skeleton of the duke inside. He couldn't recall the last time he'd heard of a sighting of the man, wasn't even certain if he was fulfilling his duties in the House of Lords. He did know he wasn't in London, because he'd gone to the duke's residence in Mayfair, only to discover it locked. He still had his key, so he'd let himself in and had been greeted by a house shrouded in white sheets and dust. Little remained of the furniture. He'd been unable to venture a guess as to how long since anyone had walked the hallways.

Therefore, he'd come here as it seemed the logical place to find the man who had raised him.

At the top of the steps, he found that door locked as well, but again he had a key and made quick use of it. The hinges creaked as he shoved open the portal, and he remembered a time when he and Francis had been able to sneak out without getting caught because everything was kept well-oiled. Perhaps if it hadn't been so, they'd have not managed to creep out unnoticed in order to go for that fateful midnight ride.

He stepped into the once-grand entryway. No shrouds over anything, but the dust was thick and lacy spiderwebs decorated the elaborate molding and the giant crystal chandeliers. Gingerly, he made his way from room to room, horrified by the lack of care that greeted him. Surely the man he'd once called father was not in residence. He had to be at the earl's estate. A rat squeaked and raced by. How could anyone live here?

He considered going up the stairs and checking in the master's bedchamber first but decided to carry on to the library. The duke had always dominated that chamber. It was where he read, went over his accounts, met with anyone of import, and delivered a slap to his mother's second son. At the reminder, Knight felt a stinging in his cheek, a phantom sensation to be sure. He would never lay a hand on any of his own children.

Although it was late afternoon, a few hours yet before the sun bid its farewell, still the shadows encroached within this domicile as though they were permanent residents, free of the sun's power to chase them away. Strange odors wafted in and out. Dampness, the leavings of creatures. He suspected rodents might not be the only inhabitants.

The door to the library was yawning open, no liveried footmen standing guard as in the past. But then he'd yet to see anything that was as it had been in the past.

He strode into the chamber and staggered to a stop at the sight that greeted him. Everything within this room was as run-down as the rest of the residence, empty shelves where books had once lived. The man sitting in the faded brown velveteen chair near the fireplace was not yet a skeleton but wasn't far from being so. Skin and bones. He'd once dressed immaculately. Now his clothing hung off him.

"What the devil are you doing barging in here?"

the duke rasped as though he'd not uttered a word in years.

"What's happened to the estate?"

He licked his lips, picked up a glass of amber liquid, and swallowed some of the contents. "Poverty. The estates no longer provide an income—at least not one that covers the cost of maintaining them properly."

"Hence you gave up? You wouldn't even try to salvage this place? What of your pride? This is the legacy you will leave to your bloodline?"

He cackled. "It is the legacy I leave to you."

Another attempt to punish him, but in this one the duke would find no satisfaction.

"It is not." Knight advanced until he stood before a man he'd once longed to please, to have him bestow upon Knight some semblance of approval. Now the rotter could go to hell for all he cared, and he suspected he was well on his way to an eternity of fire and brimstone. "You have forbidden me to marry, to have legitimate children, an heir to pass this onto. Why would I pour any of my hard-earned coins into this property?"

"Your pride will have the better of you. You'll invest in it."

Knight glanced around before leveling his gaze on the duke. "Not unless I wed and have the potential for an heir. In which case I'll return both estates to their former glory."

"You can afford all that will be required to do so?"

"Ten times over."

The old man looked at the empty hearth, filled with ash, the remains of his life. "No."

"So be it. This then remains the legacy to *your* bloodline. It will crumble around you and those who carry the blood of your ancestors will know you were not a fitting guardian of what was left by those who came before you. I am also your legacy, however. Because of your hatred of me, I am the remarkably successful man I am today. I wanted to exceed your expectations, make you proud, make myself worthy—not realizing it was an impossible feat. But I no longer seek to impress you and am happier for it."

The duke glared at him.

"Five years ago, I broke a promise I made to a woman in order to make a promise to you. In a few days' time, I will break the vow I made to you in order to honor the one I made to her. We will have children. One of those may be a son."

The duke tried to stand but fell back against the chair. "I will see him destroyed. He cannot have this. You made a vow to me."

"I made one to her first. You can threaten me all you want, but you'll not lay a hand on any of my children."

"You vowed on your mother's life. I'll take her from you."

"You'll never touch her again."

"She is my wife still. Legally my property. I'll have her committed as I did before."

"I've hired men to guard her. You or any minions you send will not get within ten feet of her. She'll not be dragged away again. But if you make any attempt to steal her away, I shall have my solicitor begin divorce proceedings on her behalf. As you are well aware, the law regarding divorce has changed. It's a matter now handled in the courts. You've been unfaithful. I'm sure you've had mistresses. You've been cruel, sending a sane woman to a madhouse. You abandoned her. During the past five years, you've provided not a farthing for her care. I need secure proof for only two of my assertions to see her free of you. I will win."

The duke was practically frothing at the mouth, his fury so great. But Knight wasn't yet finished with him.

"I will hire men to spy on you, to keep watch. If there is so much as a hint that you intend to harm anyone whom I hold dear, I shall have *you* committed, and you shall live out your remaining days as you condemned my mother to live out hers. But if you leave us in peace, I will restore the estates, claiming it as your work, not mine. The magnificence of your estates will be credited to you, so those who come after will herald your greatness, even if they don't carry your blood. Otherwise, it will all remain in shambles, and that, too, will be credited to you." When the duke died, Knight would restore everything for his son, if he had one, but he, himself, would take the credit and ensure the records indicated each of the duke's failures.

"I'll go to Parliament and have you declared illegitimate. You'll not inherit a damn thing."

"Then do so, Your Grace. I never wanted the titles or the properties. However, enjoy and take pride in how you will be remembered: cuckolded, impoverished, an embarrassment to the titles. The choice is yours."

He turned on his heel.

"I curse you!"

Knight slowly pivoted back around. "Lucifer fell from heaven into hell, and it's where I've spent the past five years. Now I am going to rise from hell back into heaven. Curse me all you want." He grinned. "But I shall live my remaining years with an angel at my side while you are left with nothing and no one."

FAR TOO OFTEN, Regina found herself staring out windows, opening the front door and looking out it as though doing so would broaden her view, give it more depth, allow her to see farther into the distance. She paced the drive. She took Queen on numerous rides to the gate and back.

It wasn't that she didn't trust Knightly to be a formidable match to the duke. It was simply she knew Wyndstone to be vile, unscrupulous, petty, vindictive, hateful . . . so many hideous words could be applied to him. While Knightly was all that was decent, noble, and virtuous.

Could good truly defeat evil?

In books, yes, but in real life?

She'd hardly slept a wink since he'd left to confront his fath— the duke. Too many days had passed; she'd been without him too long. Although she knew he had miles to travel to reach Yorkshire and to return to her, still her nerves were stretched taut and fraying. She should have gone with him, for moral support if nothing else. If the duke insisted Knightly honor the vow—he would find a way around it. Before the duke had ambushed him on the morning they were to wed.

Now Knightly had the time to gather up the arsenal he needed to assure victory. They would be together regardless, one way or another, within the law or outside of it.

It was late afternoon, and she was pacing with worry in the front drawing room when she heard the rumble of coach wheels and pounding of horses' hooves. Running to the front door, she threw it open and dashed down the steps. The vehicle had slowed but not yet come to a complete halt when Knightly was leaping from it—gracefully, boldly, and with such surety.

His expression took her breath because it spoke volumes. Triumph, love, gladness. And happiness. Utter happiness. A grin so wide that had it been night, it would have illuminated the residence.

He swept her up into his arms, spun her around, and then took her mouth as he lowered her feet back to the ground, even if it felt a bit unsteady beneath her, as though she rested on clouds.

She wondered briefly if they'd married five years ago if she would appreciate as much what she now held. It had been so easy then to fall in love, to imagine a future together. But what she felt for him now was so much deeper and richer. More substantial. She'd never take for granted any moment spent with him, would never expect glorious times together to be their due.

She also knew what they had would last a lifetime because their love had been tested and forged by the fires of obstacles not of their making, but they'd survived and come out stronger, their love tempered into an unbreakable bond. No matter what challenges life threw at them in the future, they would win. They would always win.

When he pulled back, he took her face between his palms and the depth of love reflected in his eyes made her chest ache even as it felt like it was expanding in order to absorb all his adoration and admiration. "Lord, but I missed you," he said.

"All went well, then?"

He grinned, that solitary dimple winking at her. "He'll not be bothering us."

"I want to know all the details."

"I'll share them later. For now, I think we should tell our daughter the news."

Our daughter. She loved how easily those two words rolled off his tongue. They had decided to wait until he'd sorted matters with the duke before informing Arianna that they were going to become a family.

KNIGHT KNEW HE would never grow tired of having Regina's hand nestled in his, of walking so closely together that her bosom periodically brushed against his arm, as they made their way into the garden where their daughter frolicked with the pup.

Nor would he grow tired of the way Ari's face lit up once she spied him or the manner in which she ran to him, slammed into his leg, wrapped her arms around it to catch her balance, and looked at him with such happiness. "The monsters haven't come back."

"Hopefully they never will." After releasing his hold on Regina, he untangled the child from about him and knelt before her. "But if they do, I'll be here to protect you. I'm going to live with you and your mother now."

"Because you're a knight?"

"Because I'm your father." He'd not expected how voicing those words to this sprite would cause an agonizing ache in his chest because he'd not said them sooner. What he felt for this child was overwhelming in its complexity and purity. He'd die for her, just as he would for her mother.

Three tiny pleats appeared between her brow. She looked up at Regina and back at him. "I know. Princess told me."

She could have knocked him on his arse by giving him a light push with one of her tiny fingers. "Princess told you?"

She nodded again. "She tells me lots of things."

Regina lowered herself to the ground. "Arianna, do you even know what a father is?"

She shook her head.

Regina ruffled her fingers through the lass's curls. "You'll learn."

Then his daughter, his beautiful, wonderful daughter, lurched forward and wound her arms around his neck. "I love you," she announced enthusiastically.

"I love you, too, moppet."

Breaking free, with a laugh, she raced off. Knight pushed himself to his feet, then helped Regina to hers. "She doesn't really understand, does she?" he asked.

She snuggled against him, and he dropped his arm around her shoulders, bringing her in close. "I'm afraid I sheltered her, not wanting her to realize what she didn't have. I never explained to much degree family or parents. I referred to my father as her grand-father, of course, but I suspect she was too young to truly comprehend her lack of a papa."

He pressed a kiss to the top of her head. "For the best. Hopefully a time will come when she won't even remember a point in her life when I wasn't there."

"There never was really."

He looked down at her, knowing he would never take for granted the love he saw reflected for him in her brown eyes as she studied him.

"I named her Arianna because it was the closest I could come to naming her after her father: Arthur."

"I'd have thought, during *that* time, any reminders of me would have been the very last thing you'd have wanted."

"When she was born, and I first held her, I momen-tarily lost my head and forgave you all your sins. She was the greatest of gifts, Arthur."

He shifted until facing her fully, pulling her near until they were aligned, pressing close. "I'm going to give you so many more gifts, Reggie. I'm going to give you everything you've always wanted: legitimacy, ac-ceptance, more children."

She ran her fingers up into his hair. "All I've ever wanted is you."

EPILOGUE

*Two weeks after Lord K asked for my hand, we were
married in a small ceremony, with only our beloved
daughter, his mother, his firmest friends along with their
wives, and my sisters in attendance. That night, our
wedding night, was the most glorious and splendid night
I've ever known, filled with the rapture of our love.*
—Regina Pennington, *My Secret Desires, Vol. II*

June 1877

KNIGHT stood at the window in the library, knowing
he needed to finish going over the reports provided by
his two estate managers, man of affairs, and solicitor, but as usual he preferred to watch his family. His
daughter was growing in leaps and bounds, his wife
was more beautiful, and his mother—visiting for the
afternoon—was more relaxed and happier.

He'd taken up residence within the manor Regina's
father had provided for her. In the end, her brother
had given up his quest to have her trusts dissolved and

everything handed over to him. Regina's letter appearing in the newspapers had taken the wind from his sails, especially when it became abundantly clear that more people cherished the book than found fault with it. The second volume had been released to even greater acclaim.

His London residence was where his mother lived. Without him there, she had regained her confidence and begun managing the household. She'd even had a few ladies over for tea.

"Your Grace?"

He still flinched at the address. The previous duke had passed only a few months earlier, and Knight wasn't yet comfortable with his elevated status, and most of his peers had learned not to address him by his new title. He wanted as little about him as possible to be associated with Wyndstone. He turned to face the butler. "What is it, Shelby?"

"Mr. John Gurney has come to call, sir. I've shown him to the front drawing room as you requested."

He'd been expecting the man's arrival, had corresponded with him a few times. It was beneficial to have a firm friend whose wife had the ability to find lost things. Neither of whom pried or questioned his request. "Thank you, Shelby. Give me fifteen minutes and then inform my mother to meet me in the drawing room, but don't tell her about our guest."

"As you wish, sir."

Knight took one last look out the window at the idyllic scene playing out before him and hoped he wasn't on the verge of making a horrendous mistake.

But when he strode into the drawing room, he had an inkling of why Arianna hadn't seemed at all surprised when he'd announced he was her father. Even if she hadn't comprehended exactly what a father's role was, she'd known they belonged together.

Presently he could be staring at his own reflection within a cheval glass or a clear stream. Or a reflection of what he might look like in another quarter of a century. The man's dark hair was streaked with silver, his neatly trimmed beard all silver. His eyes were a startling blue, shining with a generosity and benevolence of spirit. Knight couldn't imagine the man ever taking the flat of his palm to his son's cheek—at least not without a damned good reason. He rather thought that even without their similarities in appearance, had he passed this gent on the street, he'd have immediately felt a connection to him, would have recognized blood calling to blood, like to like.

For several minutes they simply looked at each other, took each other in. Finally, his guest inclined his head in a shallow nod of acquiescence. "Your Grace."

"Arthur or Knight will suffice. I've not yet grown accustomed to being duke." Wasn't certain he ever would. "May I offer you a libation?"

His father, his true father, shook his head. "No, thank you. Your mother . . . is she well?"

"Quite. I am given to understand you showed her a kindness . . . when she most needed it."

"It was indeed my honor and privilege to have known her . . . as a friend."

Knight was striving to determine how much to divulge, how much the man might wish to know, how much he'd rather leave to the past. During their correspondence, Knight hadn't admitted to knowing the man was his father, nor had Gurney acknowledged being so. He suspected in their own way they were each striving to protect a woman they loved.

Light footsteps echoed faintly. Then his mother was entering the room. "Arthur, Shelby informed me you wish to—oh, my word. John?"

Knight had turned and stepped aside in time to witness his mother's features softening with delighted surprise.

"Hello, Lizzie."

In a million years, he'd have never imagined his mother, Elizabeth, being addressed so informally, but she suddenly looked like a young girl, blushing with pleasure. He thought if the duke hadn't died, he might have gone to the estate to strangle him at that moment.

"In all these years, you haven't changed one iota," she said.

He grinned warmly. "My barber might disagree."

"The silver gives you a very distinguished air. I rather like it." She cast a brief glance Knight's way. "It seems my son has been . . . getting up to some mischief. Knowing how he can be rather demanding, I do hope he didn't force you to come."

"On the contrary, I was pleased to receive the invitation and to have the opportunity to see how you've fared."

"Well, do sit. I want to hear about all you've been up to these many years. I want to know everything about your family."

"I have no family."

"You never married?"

Slowly he shook his head. "My heart remained engaged elsewhere."

This time when his mother looked at Knight, tears were welling in her eyes. He walked over to her, bussed a kiss across her cheek, and said in a low voice near her ear, "He has a family here if it's what the two of you want."

He stepped away from her. "I'll leave you to discuss matters in privacy. It was an honor to meet you, sir. For the happiness you gave my mother, I shall always be in your debt."

Striding from the room, he was rather certain that on this day, the size of his family was going to grow by one.

SITTING ON THE bench, Regina observed Arianna playing in the garden under Princess's watchful eye. The spaniel had turned out to be a rather good guardian, and at six, their daughter had recently declared she was too old for a nanny. They'd also begun celebrating her birthday on the true date and month of her birth. The twentieth of March. She was too young to truly note the difference.

Hearing the soft footfalls, Regina glanced over and watched her husband approach, his strides long and leisurely, his features calm and serene, a small smile playing over his lips. Strange that he was older now but appeared younger. She'd noticed the transformation after they were married. He was no longer battling demons—whether in the form of guilt or the duke. He was at peace with the decisions he'd made.

She couldn't bring herself to address him by his recently acquired title. He was still her Knightly, her Knight, her Arthur. He'd begun making all the repairs needed on the estates, but she didn't know if they'd ever make their home there. But then, *he* was home, more than any physical dwelling.

He was also a master tactician when it came to investments. He'd been correct about the ones he'd recommended to Lord Chidding380. Apparently, they'd paid off handsomely and the viscount had visited a few days earlier to pay back the money Knightly had loaned him. He'd also shared with Regina that he'd been courting someone and would soon be asking for her hand, once he brought his estate up to snuff. He'd blushed when he'd admitted to loving the young lady. Regina had kissed him on his reddened cheek and wished him all the happiness in the world.

Now Knightly dropped down beside her, took her hand, lifted it to his mouth, and pressed a kiss to the heart of her palm before closing her fingers over it, so she could hold the gift he'd bestowed.

"How did the reunion go?" she asked.

"Well, I think."

She wasn't surprised. Bishop's wife had thoroughly investigated the man after locating him working as an estate manager in Shropshire, and all of Knightly's concerns regarding the gent's character had been put to rest before he'd ever made contact with Mr. Gurney.

"I believe they still have feelings for each other. He

calls her Lizzie. When he did, it knocked thirty years off her. I don't know if I've seen her so happy."

"Do you think he recognized you as his son?"

He nodded. "We didn't openly acknowledge it, but I think we will in time. Both of us are aware that whatever our relationship is to become will depend upon Mother and what she wants. They're talking now, but before he leaves, I'd like to introduce him to the rest of my family." He held her gaze. "With your permission, of course. He won't hurt Ari or you. Of that, I'm certain. He's a good man, Reggie."

"I look forward to making his acquaintance."

He lowered his gaze to her lap where a sheaf of paper was resting. "What have you there?"

She extended it toward him. "Ari has written another story." She'd mastered all her letters and was constantly applying ink to paper.

After slipping on his spectacles, he began reading it. "Mmm," he murmured. "She apparently wants a cat now. This tale is her least creative, nothing but a girl playing with her cat."

"Will she get a cat?" She didn't know why she bothered to ask. He denied their daughter nothing.

"I suppose she will." Placing a hand against Regina's swollen abdomen, he bent over and pressed a kiss there. "Unless you can convince her to be content with a brother or sister."

She didn't want to admit she was hoping for a girl, a sister for Arianna. She'd grown close to her own two sisters. They often had tea together, and she enjoyed their company. They all wished they'd not wasted so many years estranged.

Because Knightly had loved his brother so, she did hope to provide him with a son someday and to have the opportunity to witness a loving relationship between a brother and a sister. She was fairly certain Knightly would ensure his son would respect all females and treat them kindly.

Arching her spine, she released a long sigh. "I'd best get back to my writing."

The Lord's Mistress, the story of an actress who fell in love with an earl, was due to her publisher next week. She intended to give the fictitious couple the wedding and truly happy ending her parents had never acquired in real life.

Knightly closed his hand around the nape of her neck. "Would you like me to rub your back before you settle down to work at your desk?"

She smiled. "You know what will happen if you rub my back. Our clothing will disappear, and we'll end up in bed."

His grin was devilishly seductive. "Why do you think I'm offering?"

She arched a brow. "Perhaps we should wait until your mother and her guest leave?"

"Fair point. But where's the harm in a little sampling?"

Then his mouth was on hers, somehow taking possession and surrendering at the same time. She'd never grow tired of the way he worshipped her. How close they'd come to never having this joy, each other, for the remainder of their lives.

When she'd written the first volume of *My Secret Desires*, she'd believed she was exorcising him from her life. How lucky she was to have misjudged the power of the written word, not to have realized the book would deliver the love of her life back to her. That at long last, they, too, would acquire their happily-ever-after.

AUTHOR'S NOTE

$\mathcal{P}$UBLISHED anonymously in 1888, *My Secret Life* was supposedly the memoir of a young man's sexual exploits, although the actual author, eventually known only as Walter, has never been identified. The book was categorized as indecent and banned. Publishers in Britain and the US were arrested for publishing it. My discovery of this book planted the seed for Regina writing her sexual memoirs.

Regarding the situation in which Knight found himself—

Per British law, a person who is first in line for inheriting a title cannot be denied his birthright. Before the Peerage Act was passed in 1963, a peer could not renounce his title. If my understanding of these laws is correct, then Knight and his father had no choice except to battle against each other for what they each held dear.

I hope you've enjoyed Knight and Regina's story. I always envisioned him as being his queen's champion, her knight in shining armor.

Next up, the last Chessman gains his queen.

Want more of The Chessmen: Masters of Seduction?
Don't miss the first book in the series

The Counterfeit
Scoundrel

Available now!

READ MORE BY LORRAINE HEATH

THE CHESSMEN: MASTERS OF SEDUCTION SERIES

THE COUNTERFEIT SCOUNDREL

THE NOTORIOUS LORD KNIGHTLY

——— ONCE UPON A DUKEDOM SERIES ———

SCOUNDREL OF MY HEART

THE DUCHESS HUNT

THE RETURN OF THE DUKE

——— SINS FOR ALL SEASONS ———

BEYOND SCANDAL AND DESIRE

WHEN A DUKE LOVES A WOMAN

THE SCOUNDREL IN HER BED

THE DUCHESS IN HIS BED

THE EARL TAKES A FANCY

BEAUTY TEMPTS THE BEAST

——— THE TEXAS TRILOGY ———

TEXAS GLORY

TEXAS SPLENDOR

TEXAS DESTINY